Bob Dylan

TARANTULA

狼蛛

[美] 鲍勃·迪伦 著　罗池 译

GUANGXI NORMAL UNIVERSITY PRESS
广西师范大学出版社
·桂林·

狼蛛
LANG ZHU

图书在版编目（CIP）数据

狼蛛 : 汉英对照 / （美）鲍勃 · 迪伦著 ; 罗池译. —桂林 : 广西师范大学出版社，2020.8
书名原文：Tanrantula
ISBN 978-7-5598-2528-5

Ⅰ. ①狼… Ⅱ. ①鲍…②罗… Ⅲ. ①散文诗－诗集－美国－现代－汉、英 Ⅳ. ①I712.25

中国版本图书馆 CIP 数据核字（2020）第 068772 号

广西师范大学出版社出版发行
（广西桂林市五里店路 9 号　邮政编码：541004
网址：http://www.bbtpress.com）
出版人：黄轩庄
全国新华书店经销
广西广大印务有限责任公司印刷
（桂林市临桂区秧塘工业园西城大道北侧广西师范大学出版社集团有限公司创意产业园内　邮政编码：541199）
开本：889 mm × 1 194 mm　1/32
印张：16.75　　字数：303 千字
2020 年 8 月第 1 版　　2020 年 8 月第 1 次印刷
定价：108.00 元

目 录

译后记

附录

狼蛛出没

（1971 年版前言）[1]

1966 年秋，我们原计划出版鲍勃·迪伦的“第一本书”。别家出版社都很羡慕。“你们做这本肯定大卖。”他们说，尽管他们并不清楚“这本”到底是什么，只知道它的作者是鲍勃·迪伦。一个大红大紫的名字。“而且呀，你看约翰·列侬的书[2]都卖了多少。这本怕要翻番——也许还不止。”这种话不必细究了。

鲍勃偶尔会光临我们的办公室。对于那时候的他来说冒着大太阳出一趟远门相当不易，而且还要去到我们位于第 12 大街和第 5 大道路口的旧写字楼，那幢神奇的建筑铺着大理石阶梯，厚重的墙壁上挂满了名家的画像和照片，比如 W. B. 叶芝。我们也出过叶芝的第一本书，以及他的全部著作。

有一天当鲍勃出现的时候，我们坐在大橡木案台后边的接待员小姐便有了主张，她不计较他的打扮，但要打电话上楼请示一下合不合适放这个人进来。这在当时有点搞笑，因为极少还有什么地方能让他感到自己是不受欢迎的人。只要他一进门，大家就看过来然后窃窃私语然后退到一旁。他们觉得压迫他会有失体面。他们也不知道该跟他说些什么才好。

我们谈了他的书，他对它的期望以及他对装帧的想法。还有他对书名的想法。我们只知道它是“一个进行中的项目”，一个年轻音乐人的第一本书。这位一夜成名的腼腆男孩，他有时也写诗，而且他对我们很多人有某种神奇的影响。

我们不是很确定怎样才能搞好这本书——先别提钱。我们不知道鲍勃会走到哪一步。我们只知道一家好出版社能给作者提供一个超越自我的机会。如罗伯特·洛厄尔[3]所言，“向着剃刀的锋口上自由驰骋”，我们觉得鲍勃就在做这样的事。

我们为这本书做了一个我们喜欢的设计。鲍勃也喜欢,然后我们就定了。我们还整了些印有鲍勃头像和“狼蛛”一词的纪念章和购物袋。我们想吸引所有的人都来关注该书即将出版这件事。我们想把《生活》《展望》《纽约时报》《时代周刊》和《新闻周刊》以及所有的媒体都拉过来炒一炒鲍勃。我们给他送去一份校样以便他能好好看上最后一遍，然后我们就可以付印、装订，然后喂饱那些涌来的订单。

那年六月，鲍勃暂时放下他正剪着的影片[4]。我们谈了一会儿这本书还有拉莫[5]和兰波等等，鲍勃承诺在两周内最后“再改改”。但没过几天鲍勃就不干了。一场摩托车事故[6]迫使他停工。

这本书也可以就那个样子付诸出版。但我们不能那样做。鲍勃也不想那样。但现在他也不打算“再改改”。所以就那样留着了。

时间匆匆，转眼到了年底。有些人愤怒了。那本所谓的书在哪儿呢？他承诺过。麦克米伦出版社承诺过。他们甚至还整了一堆纪念章和购物袋，有些存货被人从仓库里顺出来卖钱，因为上面印有鲍勃的头像，也许头像总比书要好些。

还有几份校样已经在不同的人手中流传，让他们得以先睹为快。这些预览校样有各种版本。有些是散页，有些用螺旋装订。

时间又匆匆。还是有很多人在谈论这本书，在纳闷它到底什么时候才出来。但它出不来了，除非鲍勃想要它出来。他不想。

时间匆匆又匆匆，让那些人越来越好奇、越来越愤怒。这是他的作品又怎样，他们说。他有他的想法又怎样，他们说。他到底有什么权利。于是他们就想办法搞到了一两本校样，然后他们就拿这些版本开印了。结果卖得比纪念章还要好。

有些报纸看到有盗版流出就决定刊载这本书的节选，还有长篇评论以及种种揣测和非难。鲍勃不喜欢这种方式，我们也不喜欢。我们知道一个艺术家有权利对他的作品的去向做出他自己的决断。一个出版社应当保护这种权利，而不是放弃。人人都应该知道。你不能偷拿不属于你的东西，真正属于我们的唯一事物就是我们的作品。

诗人和作家向我们讲述他们的感受而我们由此听到我们自己的感受。他们为无法表达的东西找到表达的方式。他们有时说真话，他们有时撒谎，都是为了让我们的心灵免于破碎。

鲍勃一直都敢为人先，他的创作方式常叫人难以理解。但他那时在《狼蛛》里写的很多东西现在看来已经不那么难以理解了。人们在改变，他们的感受力在改变。但《狼蛛》却没有更改。鲍勃想让它出版，于是现在就到了出版它的时候。这是鲍勃·迪伦的第一本书。按照他二十三岁时写下它的方式——就是这个样子——现在你懂了。

出版人

注 释

1 本书根据西蒙与舒斯特公司（Simon & Schuster）2004 年版翻译，所附原文及页编码亦据此本。

2 当时约翰·列侬已经出了两本实验文集小册子：《亲笔作》（*In His Own Write*，1964）、《死扳牙佬》（*A Spaniard in the Works*，1965）。前者第一印在美国和英国就卖了 14 万册。

3 罗伯特·洛厄尔（Robert Lowell，1917—1977），美国著名诗人。

4 迪伦自己动手剪辑他的1966年环球巡演的纪录片，名为《吃掉纪录》（*Eat the Document*），未正式发行。

5 让-菲利普·拉莫（Jean-Philippe Rameau，1683—1764），法国音乐家。

6 1966年7月29日，迪伦驾驶一辆500cc摩托车在纽约住所附近翻车，他借此无限期取消了很多合同，淡出公共场合长达7年多。

Guns, the Falcon's Mouthbook & Gashcat Unpunished

1 aretha/ crystal jukebox queen of hymn & him diffused in drunk transfusion wound would heed sweet soundwave crippled & cry salute to oh great particular el dorado reel & ye battered personal god but she cannot she the leader of whom when ye follow, she cannot she has no back she cannot...beneath black flowery railroad fans & fig leaf shades & dogs of all nite joes, grow like arches & cures the harmonica battalions of bitter cowards, bones & bygones while what steadier louder the moans & arms of funeral landlord with one passionate kiss rehearse from dusk & climbing into the bushes with some favorite enemy ripping the postage stamps & crazy mailmen & waving all rank & familiar ambition than that itself, is needed to know that mother is not a lady...aretha with no goals, eternally single & one step soft of heaven/ let it be understood that she owns this melody along with her emotional diplomats & her earth & her musical secrets

the censor in a twelve wheel drive semi
stopping in for donuts & pinching the
waitress/ he likes his women raw & with

老枪，猎鹰之口书[1]&逍遥法外的狗男女

阿瑞莎[2]／水晶点唱机的圣歌&生哥儿女王[3]弥漫于迷醉输灌中萦绕应要听取深情声波之残跛&山呼赞颂哦举世无双的金城旋舞[4]&你们被痛扁的人格神啊但她做不到她哪是你们要追随的领袖[5]，她做不到她使不上劲儿她做不到……漆黑繁花铁道的那些扇面之下[6]&无花果叶遮蔽处[7]&所有夜猫子的犬只，耸如拱门&疗救那些尖酸懦夫、骸骨&往故的口琴大军而更持久更响亮的是殡仪店主的呜咽&怀抱再加上一个从傍晚开始排演的热烈亲吻&攀进树丛跟某个冤家对头撕碎张张邮票[8]&抓狂的邮递员&挥别所有地位&大过头的惯常野心，须知母亲并非淑女……阿瑞莎没有目标，永远单身&一步轻轻登天／让人们明白她拥有这旋律乃至她的情绪外交使团[9]&她的土地&她的音乐奥秘

审查官开十二轮驱动半挂拖卡
进店来吃甜甜圈&掐一把
服务员／他喜欢女人生鲜&淌满

2 syrup/ he has his mind set on becoming
a famous soldier

manuscript nitemare of cut throat high & low & behold
the prophesying blind allegiance to law fox, monthly
cupid & the intoxicating ghosts of dogma...nay & may
the boatmen in bathrobes be banished forever & anointed
into the shelves of alive hell, the unimaginative sleep,
repetition without change & fat sheriffs who watch for
doom in the mattress...hallaluyah & bossman of the
hobos cometh & ordaining the spiritual gypsy davy camp
now being infiltrated by foreign dictator, the pink FBI &
the interrogating unknown failures of peacetime as holy
& silver & blessed with the texture of kaleidoscope &
the sandal girl...to dream of dancing pillhead virgins &
wandering apollo at the pipe organ/ unscientific ramblers
& the pretty things lucky & lifting their lips & handing
down looks & regards from the shoulders of adam & eve's
minstrel peekaboo...passing on the chance to bludgeon the
tough spirits & the deed holders into fishlike buffoons &
yanking ye erratic purpose...surrendering to persuasion,
the crime against people, that be ranked alongside murder
& while doctors, teachers, bankers & sewer cleaners fight
for their rights, they must now be horribly generous...
& into the march now where tab hunter leads with his
thunderbird/ pearl bailey stomps him against a buick &
3 where poverty, a perfection of neptune's unused clients,
plays hide & seek & escaping into the who goes there? &
now's not the time to act silly, so wear your big boots &
jump on the garbage clowns, the hourly rate & the enema

蜜汁／他已下定决心要成为
一个著名的士兵

手稿夜魇中割喉竞争起起＆落落＆眼看那说预言的盲者[10]效忠司法之狐，丘比特月刊＆那些醉人的教义之灵……不行＆但愿那些穿浴服的船夫被永久放逐＆受膏后进入活地狱的暗礁，那毫无想象的沉眠，一成不变的重复＆在床垫上守候大审判的肥胖县警们……哈拉路亚＆游民大佬驾到＆敕命那属灵的吉卜赛人戴维营地[11]现在已渗入了外国独裁者，粉红 FBI ＆那些在讯问中的和平时期未知失败一如神圣＆白银＆蒙福于万花筒结构＆凉鞋姑娘[12]……梦中那些麻药上头的舞蹈处女[13]＆弹管风琴的浪游阿波罗／不科学的漫谈家＆那些幸运的漂亮尤物＆嘟着嘴唇＆传递着目光＆注视在亚当＆夏娃巡回戏班的肩膀上躲猫猫……传承着一个机会去把那些强悍的精神＆地契持有者痛殴成死鱼样的丑角＆猛拽起你们反复无常的决心……屈从于游说，是反人类罪，与谋杀同级＆而那些医生、教师、银行家＆下水道清洁工都为他们的权益而战，他们现在肯定慷慨得要命……＆现在进入游行在这里泰伯亨特[14]开着他的雷鸟[15]领头／珀尔贝莉[16]把他狠狠踹上一辆别克＆在这里贫穷，一个典型的海神潜在客户，它玩起捉迷＆藏＆逃进了那边是谁？[17]＆现在不是扮傻的时候，穿上你的大头靴＆扑向那些垃圾小丑，计时付费＆灌肠男＆在这里新科参议员＆小妖

men & where junior senators & goblins rip off tops of
question marks & their wives make pies & go now & throw
some pies in the face & ride the blinds & into aretha's
religious thighs & movement find ye your nymph of no
conscience & bombing out your young sensitive dignity
just to see once & for all if there are holes & music in the
universe & watch her tame the sea horse/ aretha, pegged
by choir boys & other pearls of mamas as too gloomy a
much of witchy & dont you know no happy songs

the lawyer leading a pig on a leash
stopping in for tea & eating the censor's
donut by mistake/ he likes to lie about
his age & takes his paranoia seriously

the hospitable grave being advertised & given away in whims
& journals the housewife sits on. finding herself financed,
ruptured but never censored in & also never flushing herself/
she denies her corpse the courage to crawl–close his own
door, the ability to die of bank robbery & now catches the
4 heels of old stars making scary movies on her dirt & her face
& not everybody can dig her now. she is private property...
bazookas in the nest & weapons of ice & of weatherproof
flinch & they twitter, make scars & kill babies among lady
shame good looks & her constant foe, tom sawyer of the
breakfast cereal causing all females paying no attention to
this toilet massacre to be hereafter called LONZO & must
walk the streets of life forever with lazy people having
nothing to do but fight over women...everybody knows

们扒掉一个个问号的顶部＆他们的老婆做馅饼＆快走吧＆给那脸上摔几块馅饼＆搭上盲车[18]＆进入阿瑞莎的虔诚大腿＆运动让你们找到那不知善恶的水仙女[19]＆轰开你们年轻敏感的尊严只为一了＆百了地看看是否会有洞洞＆宇宙中的音乐＆只为观赏她驯服海马[20]／阿瑞莎，被唱诗班男童＆妈妈们的其他珍珠宝贝认定太阴郁一身巫里巫气[21]＆你懂不懂没有快乐的歌

律师用皮带牵着一头猪
进店来喝茶＆吃了审查官的
甜甜圈绝非故意／他喜欢谎报
年纪＆对他的妄想症却十分认真

宾至如归的墓地也登广告＆发传单在奇想＆报刊上有一位主妇坐在那儿[22]。发现她本人被资助过，决裂过但从未被审查过＆而且也从未冲洗她自己／她否认她的尸体有勇气去爬行[23]——关上他本人的门，再无能耐去死于银行抢劫＆现在抓着老明星们的脚踵去拍恐怖片吧讲讲她的污秽＆她的脸蛋＆现在不是人人都看得上她了。她是私有财产……火箭筒归巢＆武器结冰＆防雨布畏缩＆它们叽叽喳喳，制造创伤＆杀死婴儿就当着淑女的羞于直视＆她的永世仇敌，早餐麦片粥之汤姆索亚导致所有女性都不予关注这场史称**朗索**[24]的卫生间大屠杀＆必须行走在生活的街道永远跟懒汉们一起无所事事除非为女

by now that wars are caused by money & greed & charity
organizations/ the housewife is not here. she is running
for congress

the senator dressed like an austrian
sheep. stopping in for coffee & insulting
the lawyer/ he is on a prune diet &
secretly wishes he was bing crosby
but would settle for being a close
relative of edgar bergen

passing the sugar to iron man of the bottles who arrives
with the grin & a heatlamp & he's pushing "who dunnit"
buttons this year & he is a love monger at first sight...
you have seen him sprout up from a dumb hill bully into a
bunch of backslap & he's wise & he speaks to everyone as if
they just answered the door/ he dont like people that say he
comes from the monkeys but nevertheless he is dull & he is
destroyingly boring...while Allah the cook scrapes hunger
from his floor & pounding it into the floating dishes with
roaring & the rest of the meatheads praising each other's
power & argue over acne & recite calendars & pointing to
each other's garments & liquid & disperse into segments &
die crazy deaths & bellowing farce mortal farm vomit & why
for Jesus Christ be Just another meathead? when all the tontos
& heyboy lose their legs trying to frug while kemosabe & mr
palladin spend their off hours remaining separate but equal
& anyway why not wait for laughter to straighten the works
out meantime & WOWEE smash & the rage of it all when

人打架……现在人人都知道了战争起于金钱&贪婪&慈善组织/那主妇不在这里。她正奔向国会

参议员穿得像一只奥地利
绵羊。进店来喝咖啡&侮辱
律师/他正在节食&
暗暗许愿他能成为宾克罗斯比[25]
若能做埃德加伯根[26]的至亲
也可以接受

把糖递给瓶瓶罐罐的钢铁侠吧，他来时带着满脸笑容&一盏热力灯&他是今年按下“谁干的”[27]电钮的人&他乍一看就是个爱情贩子……你已经见到他从笨嘴笨舌的山地佬变成呼朋唤友的老油子&他很精明&他对每个人说话好像他们刚来应门似的/他不喜欢别人说他是从猴山下来的尽管他还是那样的没劲&他真无聊死人了……而安拉大厨从他的地板上铲起饥饿&把它掼进那些呼啸的浮空菜碟[28]&剩下的蠢蛋们互相赞美对方的大能&争论痤疮&背诵月份牌&互相指点对方的衣着&液体&消散为碎片&死得癫狂&咆哮闹剧凡人农场呕吐&为什么耶稣基督即是下一个蠢蛋？当所有的汤桶&嘿小子[29]练扭摆舞折断了双腿而基莫沙比&帕拉丁先生[30]在闲暇时间保持虽隔离但平等[31]&再说了何不趁这时候等着哈哈一笑就把事情办好&**哇呀呀**一炮走红&风靡一时而前情

former lover cowboy hanging upside down & Suzy Q. the angel putting new dime into this adoption machine as out squirts a symbol squawking & freezing & crashing into the bowels of some hideous soap box & it's a rumble & iron man picking up his "who dunnit" buttons & giving them away free & trying to make friends & even tho youre belonging to no political party, youre now prepared, prepared to remember something about something

the chief of police holding a bazooka
with his name engraved on it. coming in
drunk & putting the barrel into the face
of the lawyer's pig. once a wife beater,
6 he became a professional boxer & received
a club foot/ he would literally like to
become an executioner. what he doesnt know
is that the lawyer's pig has made friends
with the senator

gambler's passion & his slave, the sparrow & he's ranting from a box of black platform & mesmerizing this ball of daredevils to stay in the morning & dont bust from the factories/ everyone expecting to be born with whom they love & theyre not & theyve been let down, theyve been lied to & now the organizers must bring the oxen in & dragging leaflets & gangrene enthusiasm, ratfinks & suicide tanks from the pay phones to the housing developments & it usually starts to rain for a while...little boys cannot go out & play & new men in

人牛仔却翻转倒挂&天使苏西 Q.[32] 把新崭崭的角子投进这台收养机器叫它喷出一个符号呱呱叫&冰冰冻&咔咔撞进某个丑恶肥皂箱[33] 的肠肚&一片轰隆&钢铁侠捡起他那些“谁干的”电钮&把它们免费派送&努力结交朋友&即便你不属于任何政治派别，你已经做好准备，准备牢记有关某事的某事

警察头子扛着一杆火箭筒
上面刻有他的名字。来时已经
大醉&把炮管捅进律师的
那头猪的脸上。曾经打老婆，
后成为职业拳击手&获得
内翻足／他真真切切地希望
成为一名行刑官。但他不知道
的是律师的那头猪结交
了参议员

赌徒的激情&他的奴隶，麻雀&他正在一个黑色厚底鞋纸箱上慷慨陈词&催眠着死大胆们一直跳舞到天亮&不要从工厂爆出去／人人都期望跟他们生来就跟所爱的人在一起&他们没有&他们被辜负了，他们被哄骗了&现在组织者们必须牵阉牛进圈&拖出传单&坏疽性狂热病，线人&自杀坦克从投币电话到住宅开发区&通常会先下一场雨……小崽子们就没法外出&玩耍&新来人开

bulldozers come in every hour delivering groceries & care
packages being sent from las vegas...& nephews of the
coffee bean expert & other favorite sons graduating with a
pompadour & cum laude–praise be & a wailing farewell to
releasing the hermit & beautifully ugly & fingering eternity
come down & save your lambs & butchers & strike the
roses with its rightful patsy odor...& grampa scarecrow's
got the tiny little wren & see for yourself while saving him
too/ look down oh great Romantic. you who can predict
from every position, you who know that everybody's not
7 a Job or a Nero nor a J.C. Penney...look down & seize
your gambler's passion, make high wire experts into
heroes, presidents into con men. turn the eventual...but
the hermits being not talking & lower class or insane or in
prison...& they dont work in the factories anyway

the good samaritan coming in with the
words "round & round we go" tattooed on
his cheek/ he tells the senator to stop
insulting the lawyer/ he would like to
be an entertainer & brags that he is
one of the best strangers around, the pig
jumps on him & starts eating his
face

illiterate coins of two head wrestling with window washer who's been reincarnated from a garden hoe & after once being pushed around happily & casually hitting a rock

着推土机每小时递送吃食杂货&拉斯维加斯寄出的爱心包裹……&咖啡豆行家的侄甥&其他宠儿们毕业时顶着大奔头[34]&优等生——值得嘉许&一声哭丧送别来解脱那隐修士&美丽的丑陋&弹弄着永世降临&拯救你的羊羔&屠夫&劈打玫瑰以其恰当的帕琪[35]风味……&爷爷的稻草人已经搞到了微微小的雏鸟儿&你亲眼看看吧同时也要拯救他/俯视哦伟大的浪漫家。你能从一切位置作出预言，你深知任何人都不是约伯不是尼禄也不是杰西潘尼[36]……俯视&攥住你的赌徒激情，让走钢丝行家们成为英雄[37]，总裁们成为骗子。改变结局吧……但隐修士们并不说话&低等阶级或神经病或囚犯……&反正他们也不在工厂里干活

大善人[38]进来时有一句
话“我们转&转”文在
腮帮上/他叫参议员停止
侮辱律师/他希望
成为一个艺人&吹嘘他是
这一带最佳门外汉之一，那头
猪扑上他&开始吃他的
脸

两面头像的文盲硬币们在和擦窗工摔角[39]他是从一把园锄化身而来&自从有一次被推着快乐地转悠&时不时地

once in a while is now bitter hung up on finding some inferior. he bites into the window ledge & by singing "what'll we do with the baby–o" to thirsty peasant girls wanting a drink from his pail, he is thinking he is some kind of success but he's getting his kicks telling one of the two headed coins that tom Jefferson used to use him around the
8 house when the bad stuff was growing…the lawrence welk people inside the window, theyre running the city planning division & they hibernate & feeding their summers by conversing with poor people's shadows & other ambulance drivers, & they dont even notice this window washer while the families who tell of the boogey men & theyre precious & there's pictures of them playing golf & getting blacker & they wear oil in the window washer's union hall & these people consider themselves gourmets for not attending charlie starkweather's funeral ye gads the champagne being appropriate pagan & the buffalo, tho the restaurant owners are vague about it, is fast disappearing into violence/ soon there will be but one side of the coin & mohammed wherever he comes from, cursing & window washers falling & then no one will have any money…broad save the clean, the minorities & liberace's countryside.

the truck driver coming in with a carpet
sweeper under his eyes/ everybody says
"hi joe" & he says "joe the fellow that
owns this place. i'm just a scientist. i
aint got no name" the truck driver hates
anybody that carries a tennis racket/ he

偶然撞上一块石头现在就苦苦沉溺于寻找某种劣等货。他咬紧窗台&唱着“我们要怎样对付小宝宝”[40]给那些来他的桶里讨口水喝的饥渴的乡下姑娘们，他还以为他取得了某种成就其实不过是他乐滋滋地告诉双头硬币之一说等到脏东西长起来之后汤姆杰斐逊就经常用他擦洗房子……劳伦斯韦尔克[41]的朋友们都在窗户里边，他们掌管着城市规划署&他们冬眠&通过跟穷苦人的影子&其他救护车司机交谈来喂养他们的夏季，&在谈论夜魔怪的时候那些家人根本没注意这个擦窗工&他们是宝贝疙瘩&还有很多他们打高尔夫球的照片&越来越黑了&他们在擦窗工联盟的大会厅穿着油布&这些人把自己当成美食家因为没有出席查理斯塔克韦瑟[42]的葬礼天哪呀香槟酒正般配异教徒&野牛，即使餐厅老板都对此含糊其词，但它正在暴力中迅速消逝[43]／很快那里就只会剩下硬币的一个面&穆罕默德无论他来自哪里，诅咒&擦窗工坠落&然后没有谁还能剩点钱……大大节省清洗[44]、少数派&利伯拉切[45]的田园。

卡车司机来时在眼皮底下
有台扫毯机／人人都说
“嗨老大”&他说“老大那家伙他
拥有这块地盘。我只是科学家。我
可默默无名”卡车司机讨厌
一切拿网球拍子的人／他

drinks all the senator's coffee & proceeds
to put him in a headlock

9 first you snap your hair down & try to tie up the kicking
voices on a table & then the sales department people with
names like Gus & Peg & Judy the Wrench & Nadine with
worms in her fruit & Bernice Bearface blowing her brains
on Butch & theyre all enthused over locker rooms &
vegetables & Muggs he goes to sleep on your neck talking
shop & divorces & headline causes & if you cant say get
off my neck, you just answer him & wink & wait for some
morbid reply & the liberty bell ringing when you dont dare
ask yourself how do you feel for God's sake & what's one
more face? & the difference between a lifetime of goons
& holes, company pigs & beggars & cancer critics learning
yoga with raving petty gangsters in one act plays with
V–eight engines all being tossed in the river & combined
in a stolen mirror...compared to the big day when you
discover lord byron shooting craps in the morgue with his
pants off & he's eating a picture of jean paul belmondo &
he offers you a piece of green lightbulb & you realize that
nobody's told you about This & that life is not so simple
after all...in fact that it's no more than something to read
& light cigarettes with...Lem the Clam tho, he really
gives a damn if dale really does get nailed slamming down
the scotch & then going outside with Maurice, who aint
the Peoria Kid & dont look the same as they do in Des
Moines, Iowa & good old debbie, she comes along & both
her & dale, they start shacking up in the newspapers &
10 jesus who can blame 'em? & Amen & oh lordy, & how the

喝光了参议员的咖啡&继而
给他吃了个勒脖摔

首先你剪掉你的头发&使劲把那些瞎蹦乱跳的声音捆在桌面上&然后营业部的人比如古斯&佩格[46]&扳手朱迪&在果果里长了虫虫的娜迪妮[47]&跟榜爷爆浆浆的熊脸伯妮斯&他们都痴迷着更衣室&蔬菜&马格斯他要睡在你的颈脖上聊逛街&离婚&头条新闻&如果你说不出从我脖子上下来，那你就回应他&打眼色&等待某种病态的答复&自由钟敲响在你没胆量问自己到底是什么感觉的时候看在上帝的分上&再多一张脸又如何？&同样一生有千差万别，打手&肉洞，公司猪猡&乞丐&练瑜伽的癌症批评家跟狂热的小匪徒们在独幕剧中跟V8引擎[48]一起全都被抛进河里&结合在一面偷来的镜中……相较于那个大日子里你发现拜伦勋爵在停尸房[49]掷骰子的时候他没穿底裤&他在吃一张让保罗贝尔蒙多[50]的照片&他请你吃一块绿色灯泡&你意识到从未有人跟你说过这个&毕竟生活没那么简单……实际上它也不过是用来看书&点烟的东西……但是铁钳莱姆，他确实很闹心黛尔是不是真的被逮到砸了威士忌&然后就跟莫里斯出去了，他可不是皮奥里亚小毛孩[51]&不要以为还跟他们在艾奥瓦的得梅因[52]一模一样&好心的老黛比，她一路行来&包括她&黛尔两人[53]，她们开始在报纸堆里鬼混&耶稣啊谁又能指责她们？&阿门&天啊，&怎么大游行都不

parades dont need your money baby...it's the confetti &
one george washington & Nadine who comes running &
says where's Gus? & she's salty about the bread he's been
making off her worms while dollars becoming pieces of
paper...but people kill for paper & anyway you cant buy
a thrill with a dollar as long as pricetags, the end of the
means & only as big as your fist & they dangle from a pot
of golden rainbow...which attacks & which covers the
saddles of noseless poets & wonder blazing & somewhere
over the rainbow & blinding my married lover into the
ovation maniacs/ cremating innocent child into scrapheap
for vicious controversy & screwball & who's to tell charlie
to stop & not come back for garbage men aren't serious
& they gonna get murdered tomorrow & next march 7th
by the same kids & their fathers & their uncles & all the
rest of these people that would make leadbelly a pet...
they will always kill garbage men & wiping the smells but
this rainbow, she goes off behind a pillar & sometimes a
tornado destroys the drugstores & floods bring polio &
leaving Gus & Peg twisted in the volleyball net & Butch
hiding in madison square garden...Bearface dead from
a flying piece of grass! I.Q.–somewhere in the sixties &
twentieth century & so sing aretha...sing mainstream
into orbit! sing the cowbells home! sing misty...sing for
the barber & when youre found guilty of not owning
a cavalry & not helping the dancer with laryngitis...
11 misleading valentino's pirates to the indians or perhaps
not lending a hand to the deaf pacifist in his sailor jail...
it then must be time for you to rest & learn new songs...
forgiving nothing for you have done nothing & make love

需要你的钱呢宝贝……都是花纸头&一个乔治华盛顿[54]&娜迪妮跑了过来&说古斯在哪儿呢？&她给面包撒盐而他偷走了她的虫虫这时美元正变成一张张纸片……但人还要为了纸片操刀子&总之你没法用一美元买来一丝激动即便这样标价[55]，力有穷尽&就跟你的拳头一样大&他们在一大罐金光彩虹里悬荡……攻击着&掩护着那些没鼻子诗人的马鞍[56]&奇光熠熠&在彩虹之上的某处[57]&蒙着我的已婚情人的眼走进那些狂热拥趸/把纯真的儿童焚化成废料场以供凶残的论战&死变态&他要去告诉查理[58]该停手了&别再回来因为那些垃圾人不是认真的&他们明天就会被谋杀&明年3月7日[59]又有同样的小毛孩&他们的父亲&他们的叔伯&其余的这些人都把铅肚皮[60]当成玩物……他们会不断地杀死垃圾佬&抹掉臭迹除了这道彩虹，她藏在一根柱子后面&有时龙卷风会摧毁一片药房&洪水冲来脊髓灰质炎[61]&把古斯&佩格缠在排球网上&榜爷躲在麦迪逊广场花园[62]……熊脸死于一根横飞的草叶！I.Q.——在20世纪&60年代的某处&于是唱着阿瑞莎……唱着主流上了轨道！唱着牛铃回家去！唱着迷雾[63]……唱给理发师[64]&当你被控有罪只因为不曾拥有一个骑兵&不曾帮助那个患喉炎的舞者……误导瓦伦蒂诺[65]的海盗们去找印第安人或者也可能是因为没向那个身陷水手牢狱的耳聋和平主义者伸出援手……以后肯定有的是时间给你休息&学唱新歌[66]……什么都不宽恕因为你什么都没干过&跟那高贵的女清洁

to the noble scrubwoman

what a drag it gets to be. writing
for this chosen few. writing for any–
one cpt you. you, daisy mae, who are
not even of the masses…funny thing,
tho, is that youre not even dead yet…
i will nail my words to this paper,
an fly them on to you. an forget about
them…thank you for the time.
youre kind.
  love an kisses
  your double
  Silly Eyes (in airplane trouble)

工做爱

真是一篇生拉硬拽。只写
给这特定的几位。写给任何
人除了你。你呀，黛西梅[67]，是
不属于大众的……但，真好笑，
你也还不是死人呀……
我要把我的话在这纸上钉牢，
然后把它们飞给你。然后忘掉
它们……多谢你花时间阅读。
你是好心的。

爱着吻着
你的替身
傻眼儿（于班机故障中）

注　释

1　口书（Mouthbook），或戏拟纹章描述，如美国国徽上白头海雕衔着“合众为一”（E Pluribus Unum）卷轴，或指《狼蛛》这本书是一种需要念诵吟唱的口头文学。另参见《旧约·以西结书》2-3，神将写满哀号、叹息、悲痛的书卷赐给先知，吩咐他吃下这书卷，吃后口中觉得甜如蜜；然后神差遣他去对以色列人讲说神的话语，而不是往哪说话深奥、言语难懂的民那里去。《新约·启示录》10，在末日时，那踏海踏地的天使手持着展开的小书卷，神叫先知取来将它吃尽了，口中甜如蜜，肚子却发苦，但因此便可指着多民多国、多方多王再说预言。

2　阿瑞莎（aretha），本书的女主角之一。或出自美国黑人女歌手阿瑞莎·富兰克林（Aretha Franklin，1942—2018），少女时代演唱福音歌曲成名，20 世纪 60 年代初与迪伦同为哥伦比亚唱片公司制作人约翰·哈蒙德（John Hammond，1910—1987）旗下的签约歌手。

3　圣歌&生哥儿女王（queen of hymm & him），在美国音乐史上，盲诗人、作曲家芬妮·克罗斯比（Fanny Crosby，1820—1915）曾被誉为“圣歌女王”；拥有“点唱机之王”绰号的是黑人歌手路易斯·乔丹（Louis Jordan，1908—1975），又被称为“摇滚乐的祖父”；阿瑞莎·富兰克林在 1967 年离开哥伦比亚改签亚特兰大之后大获成功，也被誉为“灵歌女王”，而当时迪伦的《狼蛛》已完稿。

4　金城（El Dorado），传说中印加帝国的黄金宝藏；旋舞（reel），可能指某种致幻剂效果，开头的这一句就充满了迷幻回旋的音韵。

5　参见迪伦歌曲《地下乡愁蓝调》（“Subterranean Homesick Blues”，1965）：“初哥要当心 / 到处都是各种人渣 / 在剧院周围晃荡 / 姑娘在漩涡旁 / 寻找新的凯子 / 不要追随领袖 / 要看好停车表……”

6　参见美国诗人埃兹拉·庞德的短诗《在地铁站》（“In a Station of the Metro”，1913）：“这些面孔在人潮中的显露；/ 湿黑的枝条上的花瓣。”

7　参见《旧约·创世记》3:7，夏娃和亚当偷食了伊甸园的禁果，“他们二人的眼睛就明亮了，才知道自己是赤身露体，便拿无花果树的叶子，为自己编作裙子”。本书凡涉《圣经》处均引自和合本。

8　参见迪伦歌曲《墓碑蓝调》（“Tombstone Blues”，1965）：“他四处漂泊 / 用无与伦比的集邮册赢得朋友 / 并感化了他的叔叔。”

9　参见迪伦歌曲《像一块滚石》（“Like a Rolling Stone”，1965）：“你从前常骑着镀铬的骏马和你的外交官出游。”

10　说预言的盲者（the prophesying blind），或指如古希腊的荷马一般的盲歌手、诗人。另，美国民谣史上有多位盲人歌手，如瞎子柠檬·杰弗逊（Blind Lemon Jefferson，1893—1929）、瞎子布莱克（Blind Blake，1896—1934）、瞎子威利·麦克泰尔（Blind Willie McTell，1898—1959）等，他们对迪伦都有影响。另，迪伦本人初出道时曾用“盲童咕噜儿”（Blind Boy Grunt）等化名在多处兼职。

11 吉卜赛人戴维（Gypsy Davy），原型出自18世纪苏格兰传统民谣，大意讲一个贵妇迷上了流浪吉卜赛人戴维的歌声和魔咒，后来抛弃富裕生活与之私奔。美国民谣歌手伍迪·格思里（Woody Guthrie，1912—1967）的同名歌曲（1944）中提到私奔的贵妇在营火旁聆听戴维弹琴歌唱，迪伦歌曲《墓碑蓝调》中有：“吉卜赛人戴维用喷火枪烧毁营地 / 他的忠奴佩德罗跟随他。”诗中此处可能指戴维受命去处置营地案件。另有戴维营（Camp David），美国总统休假地，总统罗斯福曾命名该地为“香格里拉”。

12 凉鞋姑娘（the sandal girl），参见迪伦歌曲《地下乡愁蓝调》：“（年轻人要循规蹈矩）不要穿凉鞋 / 尽量避免丑闻 / 不要当流民 / 你最好只吃口香糖……”

13 麻药上头的舞蹈处女（dancing pinhead virgins），参见西班牙诗人加西亚·洛尔卡短诗《吉他之谜》（“Adivinanza de la Guitarra”，1921）：“在圆圆的十字路口 / 六位少女 / 舞蹈。/ 三个是肉身，/ 三个为白银。”另参见中世纪欧洲经院哲学的经典辩题：一个针尖上头可以有多少个天使跳舞？

14 泰伯·亨特（Tab Hunter，1931—2018），美国影星、歌手。

15 雷鸟（thunderbird），美国福特公司的高级跑车品牌。

16 珀尔·贝莉（Pearl Bailey，1918—1990），美国黑人戏剧演员、歌手，名字 Pearl 意即珍珠。

17 参见迪伦歌曲《荒凉路》（“Desolation Row”，1965）：“赞美尼禄的海神 / 泰坦尼克拂晓时扬帆 / 人人都在大吼：/‘你站在哪一边？’”

18 搭盲车（ride the blinds），指在列车末尾的行包车厢里蹭免费车，或胡乱扒上一趟不知目的的货车去流浪。参见瞎子威利歌曲《旅行蓝调》（“Traveling Blues”，1929）：“司机先生 / 让可怜人搭

个盲车吧 / 他说我无所谓呀哥们 / 但你知道这火车不是我的。”

19　不知善恶的水仙女（nymph of no conscience），在古希腊神话中，河神阿尔斐俄斯爱上了海仙女阿瑞图莎（Arethusa，音近“阿瑞莎”），穷追不舍，满世界奔跑，最后他们合为同一道水流。

20　参见英国诗人勃朗宁诗作《我的最后一位公爵夫人》（“My Last Duchess”，1842），美人虽美但不驯，被杀害后成为某人独占的艺术品，就连海神，纵使能驯服海马，也被铸成了一尊珍奇的铜像。

21　一身巫里巫气（a much of witchy），戏拟美国诗人 E. E. 卡明斯（E. E. Cummings）长诗《成人童谣》（*Adult Nursery Rhymes*）中的谐音名句：“如果呼呼风许许多地揭露夏天谎言的真相”（what if a much of a which of the wind gives the truth to summer's lie）。

22　参见迪伦歌曲《发自别克 6 型》（“From a Buick 6”，1965）：“我搞上这个墓地女人，你知道她给我带孩子……我需要一个推土机妈妈阻挡死人 / 我需要一个自卸车妈妈清空我的头脑。”

23　参见莎士比亚戏剧《李尔王》第一幕第一场：“无牵无累地爬向死亡。”

24　朗索（LONZO），可能出自美国乡村音乐组合朗索和奥斯卡（Lonzo & Oscar）。

25　宾·克罗斯比（Bing Crosby，1903—1977），美国歌手、电影演员，歌声甜美，曾雄踞美国排行榜 24 年。实际或指美国幽默主持人诺姆·克罗斯比（Norm Crosby，1927— ）。

26　埃德加·伯根（Edgar Bergen，1903—1978），美国口技大师、喜剧家、电台主持人，所谓“至亲”可能指伯根的一个木偶人，他用腹语术借木偶人说笑话。

27　谁干的（who dunnit），常指侦探小说中的俗套情节。

28　浮空菜碟（floating dishes），大概指魔毯、飞碟之类，后文还有“浮驳船”“飞天盘”等称谓。另参见迪伦歌曲《铃鼓先生》（“Mr. Tambourine Man”，1965）：“带我去远行吧，乘上你的飞旋魔法船……"

29 "汤桶"（Tonto），印第安语意为野小子，西班牙语意为傻瓜，是美国老牌西部剧《孤胆奇侠》（*Lone Ranger*）系列中男主角的印第安裔跟班。"嘿小子"（Hey Boy）是美国西部剧《枪战英豪》（*Have Gun–Will Travel*）系列中男主角的跟班、华裔门童金章（音）的绰号。另参见迪伦歌曲《鲍勃·迪伦蓝调》（"Bob Dylan's Blues"，1963）："啊，孤胆奇侠和汤桶 / 他们正沿路策马赶来。"

30 "基莫沙比"（Kemosabe），出自印第安语，可能意为偷窥者、好伙伴、模范童军，是《孤胆奇侠》中"汤桶"给男主角、蒙面警长约翰·里德起的外号。"帕拉丁先生"（Mr. Paladin），是《枪战英豪》中门童"嘿小子"对男主角、阔绰的私家侦探怀尔·帕拉丁（化名）的称呼。

31 美国一方面实行种族隔离政策，另一方面又宣称在法律面前人人平等（separate but equal）。

32 苏西Q(Suzy Q),同名摇滚歌曲于1957年由戴尔·霍金斯(Dale Hawkins，1936—2010）演唱成名。

33 肥皂箱（soap box），常指街头政治讲演。

34 大奔头（pompadour），原指女式的高卷发髻，当时也指猫王等早期摇滚歌星的发型。

35 帕奇（Patsy），常指爱尔兰佬、乡巴佬、凯子，又音近"馅饼"（pasty）。美国滑稽戏中常用来调侃背黑锅的蠢货，如有人问：谁干的？众人答：帕奇·玻利瓦尔。刺杀J. F. 肯尼迪的奥斯瓦尔德（Lee Harvey Oswald，1939—1963）否认指控时辩称："他们就因为我在苏联住过便抓了我，我只是个帕奇。"也可能指英年早逝的美国女歌手帕琪·克莱因（Patsy Cline，1932—1963），她的成名作有一首名为《穷人的玫瑰或富人的黄金》（"A Poor Man's Roses or a Rich Man's Gold"，1957），歌词大意：我今天必须决定是要穷人的玫瑰还是要富人的黄金，一个富可敌国但冷冰冰，也许可以用爱来温暖，另一个是穷光蛋但我们接吻时颤栗，如登天堂，永世难忘，今夜他把玫瑰献给我，对我来说它比黄金意味更多。

36 杰西潘尼(J. C. Penney),美国大型连锁商场,创始人潘尼(James Cash Penney, 1875—1971)是勤劳肯干、白手起家的创富神话。

37 迪伦常说,走钢丝艺人才是真正的艺术家。

38 大善人(the good samaritan),参见迪伦歌曲《荒凉路》:“大善人正在打扮 / 他在为秀场做准备 / 他要参加今晚的嘉年华会。”

39 “和擦窗工摔角”(wrestling with window washer),原文戏拟绕口令“我们在看擦窗工用温水擦洗华盛顿的窗户”(we were watching window washers wash Washington's windows with warm washing water),故后文提到杰斐逊等。

40 《我们要怎样对付小宝宝》(“What'll We Do with the Baby-O”)是一首美国传统民谣,大意讲年轻父母虐待婴儿的笑话;另有流行歌曲《宝贝噢》(“Baby-O”),1962 年由迪安·马丁(Dean Martin, 1917—1995)唱红。

41 劳伦斯·韦尔克(Lawrence Welk, 1903—1992),美国歌手、音乐人,长期主持老派演艺节目《韦尔克秀场》,因片头有开酒瓶声被称为“香槟音乐”,节目中捧红的艺人称为“音乐家庭”。

42 查尔斯·斯塔克韦瑟(Charles Starkweather, 1938—1959),美国系列杀人犯,后来的电影《天生杀人狂》(*Natural Born Killers*, 1994)的原型。

43 19 世纪末,美国政府为压制印第安人的生存环境对野牛进行灭绝性捕杀。

44 “大大节省清洗”(broad save the clean),原文戏拟英国国歌《天佑女王》(God save the Queen)。

45 利伯拉切(Liberace, 1919—1987),美国钢琴家、秀场名流。又,音近“自由主义者”(liberal)。

46 古斯·乔达诺(Gus Giordano, 1923—2008)和他的妻子佩格(Peg Giordano, 1928—1993)创办了有名的爵士舞学校。

47 娜迪妮(Nadine),参见查克·贝里(Chuck Berry, 1926—2017)歌曲《娜迪妮》(“Nadine”, 1963)。

48　1955 年推出的雪佛兰小 V8 引擎在飙车族中大受欢迎。

49　停尸房（morgue），也常指存放无用旧报刊档案的资料室。

50　让 - 保罗 · 贝尔蒙多（Jean-Paul Belmondo，1933— ），当时最红的法国影星，“新浪潮”电影代表人物之一。

51　皮奥里亚（Peoria），美国中西部城市，常被视为美国内地主流大众的代表城市，据说，如果一出滑稽戏能在皮奥里亚唱红，那在全美国都吃得开。

52　得梅因（Des Moines），美国中西部城市，艾奥瓦州首府，法语本义为修道士。

53　美国女影星、歌手黛尔 · 埃文斯（Dale Evans，1912—2001），著有回忆录《最亲爱的黛比》（*Dearest Debbie*，1965）纪念她早夭的养女。另有美国女影星、歌手黛比 · 雷诺兹（Debbie Reynolds，1932—2016），1964 年主演了热门电影《永不沉没的布朗太太》（*The Unsinkable Molly Brown*）。黛尔的丈夫和黛比的前夫都是著名歌手。

54　指华盛顿头像的钞票。

55　参见迪伦歌曲《要花一大笔才笑，要搭一火车才哭》（“It Takes a Lot to Laugh, It Takes a Train to Cry”，1965）：“我搭上了一趟邮政列车，宝贝 / 但买不来一丝激动……”

56　没鼻子（noseless），没有嗅觉，没有洞察力，没有好奇心；马鞍（saddles）谐音“忧伤”（sadness）。

57　《彩虹之上》（“Over the Rainbow”），美国经典老歌，1939 年由朱迪·加兰（Judy Garland，1922—1969）在影片《绿野仙踪》（*The Wizard of Oz*）中唱红，阿瑞莎 · 富兰克林也唱过。

58　查理（charlie），指美国少年杀人狂查尔斯 · 斯塔克韦瑟，绰号“查理”，他原是垃圾场的清洁工。

59　明年 3 月 7 日（next march 7th），或指 1965 年 3 月 7 日美国亚拉巴马州民权运动示威遭到军警镇压的“血腥星期天”事件。

60　铅肚皮（Leadbelly，1889—1949），美国黑人民谣歌手、蓝调先驱，他曾两次因谋杀入狱又因献歌获减刑释放。

61 脊髓灰质炎（polio），迪伦的父亲在其 6 岁时感染脊髓灰质炎，另外，美国最著名的成年人感染病例是富兰克林·罗斯福。

62 麦迪逊广场花园（Madison Square Garden），纽约的一座体育馆、大型活动场地。

63 《迷雾》（“Misty”，1954），爵士乐老歌。阿瑞莎·富兰克林也唱过。

64 理发师（barber），可能指塞缪尔·巴伯（Samuel Barber，1910—1981），美国古典音乐作曲家，他和伴侣梅诺蒂（Gian Carlo Menotti，1911—2007）联袂创作了多部歌剧。

65 瓦伦蒂诺（valentino），可能指鲁道夫·瓦伦蒂诺（Rudolph Valentino，1895—1926），美国默片时代电影明星、探戈舞者，有“拉丁情圣”之誉，死于腹膜炎。参见迪伦歌曲《别了，安吉丽娜》（“Farewell Angelina”，1965）：“看斗鸡眼海盗们坐在高处晒太阳 / 用短筒霰弹枪射击铁皮罐……金刚和小精灵们 / 在屋顶上跳 / 瓦伦蒂诺式探戈 / 此时装殓师的双手 / 合上死者的眼睛 / 不叨扰任何人。”

66 新歌（new songs），参见《新约·启示录》5:9，“他们唱新歌说：‘你配拿书卷，/ 配揭开七印，/ 因为你曾被杀，/ 用自己的血从各族、各方、各民、各国中买了人来，/ 叫他们归于神’”。

67 黛西梅（Daisy Mae），美国老牌连环画、电影《小阿伯纳》（*Li'l Abner*）中漂亮的女主角。

Having a Weird Drink with the Long Tall Stranger

12 back betty, black bready blam de lam! bloody had a baby blam de lam! hire the handicapped blam de lam! put him on the wheel blam de lam! burn him in the coffee blam de lam! cut him with a fish knife blam de lam! send him off to college & pet him with a drumstick blam de lam! boil him in the cookbook blam de lam! fix him up an elephant blam de lam! sell him to the doctors blam de lam...back betty, big bready blam de lam! betty had a milkman, blam de lam! sent him to the chain gang blam de lam! fixed him up a navel, blam de lam (hold that tit while i git it. Hold it right there while i hit it...blam!) fed him lotza girdles, raised him in pneumonia...black bloody, itty bitty, blam de lam! said he had a lampchop, blam de lam! had him in a stocking, stuck artichokes in his ears, planted him in green beans & stuck him on a compass blam de lam! last time i seed him, blam de lam! he was standing in a window, blam de lam! hundred floors up, blam de lam! with his prayers & his pigfoot, blam de lam! black betty, black betty blam de lam! betty had a loser blam de lam, i spied him on the ocean with a long string of muslims– blam de lam! all going quack quack...blam de lam! all going quack quack. blam!

跟陌生的瘦高个喝一杯怪怪酒

嘿嘿黑贝蒂[1]，黑黑面包皮砰砰嘣！真够力生个小弟弟砰砰嘣！雇来个残障砰砰嘣！挂他在轮盘上砰砰嘣！烧他在咖啡里砰砰嘣！砍他用鱼刀砰砰嘣！送他去上大学&疼他用鼓槌砰砰嘣！煮他在菜谱里砰砰嘣！给他吃一头大象砰砰嘣！卖他给医生砰砰嘣……嘿嘿黑贝蒂，大大面包皮砰砰嘣！贝蒂得了个挤奶工，砰砰嘣！送他去苦力营砰砰嘣！给他长一个肚脐，砰砰嘣（抓住那奶头在我挤它的时候。牢牢抓住它在我抽它的时候……砰！）喂他吃一大堆束腰，养育他在肺痨……黑黑真够力，小不点儿屁屁，砰砰嘣！说他得了个痒排妞[2]，砰砰嘣！装他在袜子里，塞蓟菜进他的耳朵里，栽他在豆角地里&塞他到罗盘上砰砰嘣！我上次栽种他，砰砰嘣！他站在窗户里，砰砰嘣！一百层楼高，砰砰嘣！带着他的祈祷团&他的蹄子，砰砰嘣！黑贝蒂，黑贝蒂砰砰嘣！贝蒂得了个输家砰砰嘣，我望见他在大海上跟一长串的穆斯林——砰砰嘣！全体叫呱呱[3]……砰砰嘣！全体叫呱呱。砰！

13 sorry to say, but i'm going
to have to return your ring.
it's nothing personal, excpt
that i cant do a thing with
my finger & it's already
beginning to smell like an
eyeball! you know, like i like
to look weird, but nevertheless,
when i play my banjo on stage, i
have to wear a glove. needless
to say, it has started to affect
my playing. please believe me.
it has nothing whatsoever to
do with my love for you…
in fact, sending the ring back
should make my love for you
grow all the more profound…

say hi to your doctor
love,
Toby Celery

很抱歉这么说，但我还是
必须把戒指退还给你。
这无关个人感情，只是
我无法让我的手指
做任何事&它早已经
开始臭得像一颗
眼球！你懂的，就像我喜欢
一副怪样，尽管如此，
在台上弹班卓琴的时候，我
还是要戴上手套。不用说，
它已经影响了
我的演奏。请相信我。
无论什么事情都不能
干扰我对你的爱……
实际上，把戒指寄回去
也是表明我对你的爱
已变得更加深厚……

向你的医生问好

爱你，

<u>托比芹菜</u>

注　释

1　以下一段戏拟美国黑人传统民谣《黑贝蒂》（“Black Betty”），1939 年由铅肚皮演唱成名，原歌无器乐，边唱边拍击打节奏。另，迪伦的妈妈也叫贝蒂（Beatrice “Beatty” Stone），下文一些描写与迪伦家事有关。

2　痒排妞（lampchop），戏拟美国木偶戏艺人莎莉·刘易斯（Shari Lewis，1933—1998）的袜子玩偶搭档羊排妞（Lamb Chop）。

3　全体叫呱呱（all going quack quack），出自铅肚皮演唱的另一首美国黑人传统民谣《灰鹅》（“Grey Goose”）：“（有一只煮不熟、咬不动的灰鹅）我上次见到他，/ 啊，他正飞越大洋，/ 带着一长串的小毛鹅，/ 他们全体叫呱呱、叫呱呱。”

(*Pointless Like a Witch*)

14 trip into the light here abraham...what about this boss of yours? & dont tell me that you just do what youre told! i might not be hip to your sign language but i come in peace. i seek knowledge. in exchange for some information, i will give you my fats domino records, some his an hers towel & your own private press secretary... come on. fall down here. my mind is blank. i've no hostility. my eyes are two used car lots. i will offer you a cup of urn cleaner–we can learn from each other/ just dont try & touch my kid

got too drunk last nite. musta drunk
too much. woke up this morning with
my mind on freedom & my head feeling
like the inside of a prune...am
planning to lecture today on police
brutality. come if you can get away.
see you when you arrive. write me
when youre coming

（像女巫一样不着边际）

行到亮光里来亚伯拉罕[1]……你的这位老板怎么样？&别跟我说你只是按吩咐做事！我也许不会对你的手势语叫好但我为和平而来[2]。我寻求知识。为交换情报，我可以给你我收藏的胖子多米诺[3]唱片，他和她用过的毛巾&做你的私人新闻秘书……来嘛。快跪下。我的心思一片空空。我没有敌意。我的眼睛是两个旧车场。我愿为你奉上一杯洗缸水——我们可以互相学习／但不要试探&骚扰我的孩子

昨晚喝多了。肯定是喝得
太多了。今早醒来时
我的心思自由自在&我的脑袋觉得
像一颗梅干的内核……我正
计划今天对警察暴力发表
演说。乞请拨冗光临。
到时候见。来之前
通知我

your friend,

homer the slut

你的朋友，

荡妇荷马

注　释

1　参见迪伦歌曲《重访61号国道》（"Highway 61 Revisted"，1965）："上帝对亚伯拉罕说：'宰一个儿子给我'……"另，迪伦的爸爸也叫亚伯拉罕（Abram Zimmerman）。

2 "我为和平而来"（I come in peace），流行科幻中的套话。另参见《新约·马太福音》10:34中耶稣说："我来并不是叫地上太平，乃是叫地上动刀兵。"

3　胖子多米诺（Fats Domino，1928—2017），美国钢琴家、歌手，对摇滚乐发展深有影响。

Ballad in Plain Be Flat

the feet were stuck between the petticoat & tom dick & harry rode by & they all screamed...her lips was so small & she had trenchmouth & when i saw what i had done, i guard my face/ the time is handled by some crazy cheerleader snob & sticking her tongue out, dropping a purple tostle cap, she mingles with a bus, caresses a bloody crucifix & is praying for her purse to be stolen up gunpowder alley! her name, Delia, she envies the block of chain & kingdom where the khaki thermometer kid, obviously a front man & getting a commission growling "she'll drown you! split your eyes! put your mind where your mouth is! see it explode! just 65 & she dont mind dying!" is bending over for scraps of food, fighting an epileptic fit & trying to keep dry in a typical cincinnati weather...Claudette, the sandman's pupil, wounded in her fifth year in the business & she's only 15 & go ahead ask her what she thinks of married men & governors & shriner conventions go ahead ask her & Delia, who's called Debra when she walks around in her nurse uniform, she casts off pure light in the cellar & has principles/ ask her for a paper favor & she gives you a geranium poem...chicago? the hogbutcher! meatpacker! whatever! who cares? it's

朴素降B调谣曲[1]

两脚被卡在衬裙中间&汤姆迪克&哈利[2]骑马路过&他们都大叫起来……她的嘴唇那么小&她得了战壕口炎&当我看到我干下的事情，我护住自己的脸／时间掌控于某个疯狂啦啦队长势利鬼&探着她的舌头，耷着紫色毛线帽，她和一辆班车交融，爱抚一具血腥十字架&正为她在火药巷被人偷去的钱包祈祷！她的名字，迪莉娅[3]，她羡慕那一串链动滑轮&王国那里有个卡其色温度计小毛孩，明显是个主唱&领了一个任务去叫嚷“她会淹死你！撕开你的眼睛！把你的头脑塞进你的嘴巴！看它爆炸！就在65年&她可不在乎死！”正埋头于残羹冷炙，抵抗一阵癫痫发作&努力在典型的辛辛那提气候[4]中保持干燥……克劳黛[5]，梦仙弟子，在她从业的第五年负了伤&她年仅15岁&上前去问她怎么看那些已婚男士&州长&慈坛社[6]会员们上前去问她&迪莉娅，她穿着护士制服到处走走的时候人称黛布拉[7]，她向地窖里投下纯洁的光&她有原则／问她要一纸恩惠&她给你一首天竺葵的诗[8]……芝加哥？杀猪佬！肉贩子！[9]随便！

also like cleveland! like cincinnati! i gave my love a cherry.
16 sure you did. did she tell you how it tasted? what? you also
gave her a chicken? fool! no wonder you want to start a
revolution

look. i don't care what your daddy
says. j. edgar hoover is just not that
good a guy. like he must have infor–
mation on every person inside the
white house that if the public knew
about, could destroy those people/
if any of the knowledge that he's
got ever got out, are you kidding,
the whole country would probably
quit their jobs & revolt. he aint never
gonna lose his job. he will resign with
honor. you just wait & see…cant you figure
out all this commie business for yourself?
you know, like how long can car thieves
terrify the nation? gotta go. there's a
fire engine chasing me. see you when i get
my degree. i'm going crazy without you.
cant see enough movies

your crippled lover,
benjamin turtle

谁在乎呢？而且就像在克利夫兰！像在辛辛那提！我送给爱人一颗樱桃[10]。你确实送了。她有没有告诉你味道怎么样？什么？你还给她送了只鸡？蠢货！难怪你要发动一场革命

瞧。我不才管你的老爹爹
说什么。J. 埃德加胡佛[11]可不是
个好相与的。像他肯定会有
白宫里面每一个人的情
报如果叫公众知道了，
就可以毁掉那些人/
如果他掌握的那些内容哪怕
泄漏一点，别开玩笑了，
整个国家可能都要
辞掉工作&造反。他可从来不
会丢掉工作。他会带着荣誉
辞职。你就等&看吧……你能不能
自己想想这一大套共党勾当？
你懂的，就像要多长时间偷车贼[12]
才能恐吓全国人？我得走了。有一辆
救火车在追我。等我拿到学位时
再见吧。没有你在身旁我都要疯了。
电影总是看不够

你的跛脚爱人，
本雅明海龟

注　释

1　标题参见迪伦歌曲《朴素D调谣曲》（"Ballad in Plain D"，1964）。

2　汤姆迪克 & 哈利（tom dick & harry），相当于张三李四王老五的意思，用法最早可溯至17世纪神学家约翰·欧文，后有一部1941年的同名电影，1948年音乐剧《凯特亲亲我》（*Kiss Me, Kate*）中的选段也以此命名。达尔文在其著作《贝格尔号航海记》中也曾以这三个名字命名加拉帕戈斯群岛龟。

3　迪莉娅（Delia），可能指迪莉娅·格林（Delia Green，1886—1900），一个在圣诞节因口角被男友枪杀的14岁美国黑人女孩，有多首民谣唱到这个悲剧，如瞎子威利·麦克泰尔的《迪莉娅》（1928），迪伦曾翻唱过这首歌。

4　美国辛辛那提市位于温带大陆性湿润气候和副热带湿润气候的交界地带，四季降水较均匀，年均降雨量约1000毫米。

5　克劳黛（Claudette），可能出自美国乡村摇滚乐队艾佛利兄弟（The Everly Brothers）演唱的热门歌曲《克劳黛》（1958）；也可能指美国女子流行乐四重唱组合"科尔德兹"（The Chordettes，1946—1963），代表作有《梦仙》（"Mr. Sandman"，1954）。

6　慈坛社（Shriner），美国共济会慈善组织。

7　黛布拉（Debra），可能指黛布拉·佩姬（Debra Paget，1933— ），美国女演员，在电影《温柔地爱我》（*Love Me Tender*，1956）中扮演猫王的爱人。另，《旧约·士师记》4–5中有一位女先知名叫底波拉（Deborah），并记载了她创作的最早的歌诗。

8　一首天竺葵的诗（a geranium poem），或出自T. S. 艾略特（T. S. Eliot）的诗作《风夜狂想曲》（"Rhapsody on a Windy Night"，1911）："好似个疯子，摇撼一株死了的天竺葵。"另，迪伦在歌曲《满眼忧伤的低地女士》（"Sad-Eyed Lady of the Lowlands"，1966）中亦有："排队等待天竺葵那一吻。"

9　芝加哥曾经是美国最大的肉类市场。美国著名诗人、民谣学家卡尔·桑德堡（Carl Sandburg）的诗作《芝加哥》（“Chicago”，1914）第一行说到芝加哥是“全世界的猪肉商”。当时的芝加哥市长戴利（Richard J. Daley，1902—1976）也出身屠宰场工人家庭，是反对民权运动的强势人物。

10　《我送给爱人一颗樱桃》（“I Gave My Love a Cherry”），英格兰传统童谣。

11　约翰·埃德加·胡佛（J. Edgar Hoover，1895—1972），把持美国联邦调查局长达48年，建立密档，左右政局，连美国总统都要让他三分。

12　偷车贼（car thieves），参见艾伦·金斯堡诗《美国》（“America”，1956）：“俄国要把我们活活吃掉。俄国迷恋强大动力。她要把我们的车都从车库里偷走。”另，参见迪伦歌曲《答案在风中吹响》（“Blowing in the Wind”，1963）中，“需要多少……才能……”的句式。

On Busting the Sound Barrier

17 the neon dobro's F hole twang & climax from disappointing lyrics of upstreet outlaw mattress while pawing visiting trophies & prop up drifter with the bag on head in bed with next of kin to the naked shade– a tattletale heart & wolf of silver drizzle inevitable threatening a womb with the opening of rusty puddle, bottomless, a rude awakening & gone frozen with dreams of birthday fog/ in a boxspring of sadly without candle sitting & depending on a blemished guide, you do not feel so gross important/ success, her nostrils whimper. the elder fables & slain kings & inhale manners of furious proportion, exhale them against a glassy mud...to dread misery of watery bandwagons, grotesque & vomiting into the flowers of additional help to future treason & telling horrid stories of yesterday's influence/ may these voices join with agony & the bells & melt their thousand sonnets now...while the moth ball woman, white, so sweet, shrinks on her radiator, far away & watches in with her telescope/ you will sit sick with coldness & in an unenchanted closet...being relieved only by your dark jamaican friend–you will draw a mouth on the lightbulb so it can laugh more freely

冲破声障

霓虹多布罗[1]F孔的轰鸣&高潮来自正挠摸参观纪念品的街头不法床垫的扫兴歌词&用脑袋上的包袱把漂泊者在床头托起紧紧偎依那赤裸阴影——多嘴的心[2]&银雨之狼必不可免的威胁一个子宫以其入口处锈蚀水洼，深不见底，一个猛然醒悟&已冰封于生日迷雾的梦寐／在悲哀的弹簧床上没有蜡烛落座&靠着一本污损的指南，你并不觉得有那么巨大的重要性／成功，她的鼻孔抽抽着。那些故老相传&弑杀君王&暴戾部分的吸入方式，又把它们哈在一面光亮如镜的淤泥……对水汪汪的乐队花车的骇人惨状，稀奇怪诞&在对未来背叛施予额外帮助的花丛里呕吐&讲述昨日影响的惊悚故事／但愿这些话音交织着苦痛&钟铃&立刻融入它们的千篇十四行诗……这时有一个卫生球女人，白绒绒的，那么可爱，蜷缩在她的散热器旁，远远地&用她的望远镜观察／而你会冷冰冰地恹坐着&在一间失去魔法的衣橱里……只有你的牙买加黑朋友才能给你抚慰——你会在灯泡上画一张嘴巴那样它就可以笑得更加自由

18 forget about where youre bound.
youre bound for a three octave
fantastic hexagram. you'll see
it. don't worry. you are Not bound
to pick wildwood flowers…like
i said, youre bound for a three
octave titanic tantagram
your little squirrel,
Pety, the Wheatstraw

忘掉你所受的绑缚吧。
你要绑定一把三个八度[3]
奇妙的六芒星。你会看到
它。别担心。你并不是绑死了
要去林里采野花……就像
我说的，你要绑定一把三个
八度的泰坦尼克七巧板

你的小松鼠，
麦秆子皮蒂[4]

注　释

1　多布罗（Dobro），美国乐器品牌，也泛指加装金属共鸣器的丽声吉他、横板钢吉他。

2　多嘴的心（a tattletale heart），出自爱伦·坡短篇小说《泄露真相的心》（*The Tell-Tale Heart*，1843）。

3　可能指一把乐器有三个八度音阶，如口琴。

4　皮蒂麦秆子（Peetie Wheatstraw，1902—1941），美国黑人民谣歌手，在其著名照片上他手持一把丽声吉他。

Thermometer Dropping

the original undertaker, Jane, with bangs, & her hysterical
bodyguard, Coo, who comes from Jersey & always carries
his lunch/ they screech around the corner & tie the
old buick into a lamppost/ along came three bachelors
sprinkling the sidewalk with fish/ they spot the mess.
first bachelor, Constantine, he winks at second bachelor,
Luther, who immediately takes off his shoes & hangs them
around his neck. George Custer IV, third bachelor, weary
19 from trying to chew up a stork, takes out his harmonica &
hands it to first bachelor, Constantine, who after twisting
it into form of a fork, reaches into shoulder holster of the
bodyguard, removes a sickle, & replaces it with this out of
shape musical instrument...Luther begins to whistle "Comin
thru the Rye" George IV gives out with a wee chuckle...
all three continue down the avenue & dump the leftover
fish into the unemployment office. all except of course for
a few trout, which they give to the lady at the lost & found/
accident is reported at 3 P.M. it is ten below zero

do people tell you to your
face youve changed? do you

温度计下落

治丧业先驱，珍妮，剪刘海，&她的歇斯底里保镖，古古，来自泽西&总是带着他的午餐／他们在角落里尖叫不休&把旧别克车绑上电线杆／一路走来三个单身汉在人行道抛洒着鱼儿／他们找到了食堂。第一个单身汉，君士坦丁，眨巴着眼瞧向第二个单身汉，路德，而他立刻脱掉鞋子&把它们挂在脖子上。乔治卡斯特四世[1]，第三个单身汉，费劲地嚼着一只鹳鸟已疲惫不堪，掏出他的口琴&把它递给第一个单身汉，君士坦丁，而他将它拗成了一个叉状，然后插入保镖的挂肩枪套，取出镰刀，&用这把走形走样的乐器将它替换……路德开始吹起《走出麦田》[2]乔治四世[3]发出一声微微窃笑……三个人都继续走下大街&一路把剩下的鱼抛进失业办公室。当然除了几条鳟鱼，他们交给失物&招领处的女士／事故于下午3点报道，气温零下十度[4]

有没有人当面告诉你
你已经变了？你有没有

feel offended? are you seeking
companionship? are you plump?
4 ft. 5? if you fit & are
a full blooded alcoholic
catholic, please call
UH2–6969

ask for Oompa

觉得被冒犯？你是不是在寻找
伙伴？你发福了吧？
1 米 35 ？如果你符合 & 是
一个纯血的酒精中毒
天主教徒，请拨打
UH2—6969

洽询欧帕[5]

注　释

1　乔治·卡斯特四世（George Custer IV），可能指在小大角战役中被印第安人屠没的美国名将乔治·阿姆斯特朗·卡斯特（George Armstrong Custer，1839—1876）的玄孙辈后裔，具体不详，如卡斯特三世在越战时任空军上校，曾获多枚勋章。另也可能指英王乔治四世，见下文。

2　《走出麦田》（“Comin thru the Rye”），出自《走出麦田》（“Comin' thro' the Rye”，1782），苏格兰诗人彭斯根据传统民谣改编的歌词，大意：珍妮的身体汗淋淋，湿透了衬裙，从麦田里来，如果一个身体遇见一个身体，从麦田里来，如果一个身体亲吻一个身体，那是很自然的，每个姑娘都有情郎，但当我从麦田出来，人人都笑我。塞林格小说《麦田守望者》（*The Catcher in the Rye*，1951）的书名亦出于此，当年有多位歌手改编过这首歌。

3　乔治四世（George IV，1762—1830），与诗人彭斯同时期的英国国王，以风流、奢靡著称，不问政事，虽在任内赢得了拿破仑战争，又因试图与王后离婚引发争议。

4　气温零下十度（ten below zero），出自波波·詹金斯（Bobo Jenkins）同名蓝调（1957）。零下 10 华氏度相当于零下 23 摄氏度。参见迪伦歌曲《匪徒蓝调》（“Outlaw Blues”，1965）：“跌跌撞撞走进一个可笑的潟湖是不是很惨？ / 尤其是在气温零下九度 / 下午三点钟的时候。”

5　欧帕（Oompa），英国儿童文学家罗尔德·达尔（Roald Dahl，1916—1990）小说《查理和巧克力工厂》（*Charlie and the Chocolate Factory*，1964）中的爱唱歌、爱开玩笑的矮精工人。

Prelude to the Flatpick

mama/ tho i make no attempt to disqualify the somber moody you. mama with the woeful shepherd on your shoulder. the twenty cent diamond on your finger. i play no more with my soul like a tinker toy/ i now have the eyes of a camel & sleep on a hook...to glorify your trials would be most easy but you are not the queen–the sound is queen/ you are the princess...& i have been your honeyed ground. you have been my guest & i shall not smite you

> "are there any questions?" the
> instructor asks. a blond haired
> little boy in the first row
> raises his hands an asks
> "how far to mexico?"

poor optical muse known as uncle & carrying a chunk of wind & trees from the meadow & the kind of uncle that says "holy moly" in a mild whisper meeting the farmer who say "here. have some hunger for you." & lay some good fine

拨弦序曲

妈妈／我从没想过抛弃那个郁郁寡欢的你。妈妈你的肩上驮着忧伤的牧羊人[1]。你的指上戴着两毛钱的钻戒。我不会再耍弄我的灵魂像个万能工匠[2]／我现在有一双骆驼的眼睛[3]&在吊钩上睡觉……颂赞你所受的考验是最容易的但你不是女王——声音才是女王／你是公主……&我已成为你的流着蜜的土地。你已成为我的宾客&我必不会伤害你

“还有问题吗？”那
讲师问道。有个金发的
小男孩从第一排
举起手来问道
“去墨西哥有多远？”

老眼昏花的可怜缪斯被称为伯伯&从牧场携来大片大片的风&树林&这一类伯伯会悄悄声地对农民说“天娘呀”而那农民会说“来吧。请你吃饥饿。”&在他那令人作

work in his nauseous lap/ chamber of commerce tries to tell
poor muse that minnesota fats was from Kansas & not so
21 fat, just notoriously heavy but theyre putting up supermarket
across the meadow & that should take care of the farmer

“does anybody wanna be anything
out of the ordinary?” asks the
instructor. the smartest kid
in class, who comes to school
drunk, raises his hand & says
“yes, sir. i’d like to be a
dollar sir”

the dada weatherman comes out of the library after being beaten up by a bunch of hoods inside/ he opens up the mailbox, climbs in & goes to sleep/ the hoods come out/ tho they don’t know it, theyve been infiltrated by a bunch of religious fanatics...the whole group looks around for some easy prey...& settle for some out of work movie usher, who is wearing a blanket & a pilot’s cap/ it is one second to fourth of july & he does not fight back/ the dada weatherman gets mailed to Monaco. grace kelly has another kid & all the hoods turn into drunken business men

“who can tell me the name of
the third president of the
22 united states?” a girl with

呕的膝头摆上些精致的作品／工商会试图告诉可怜缪斯，明尼苏达胖子[4]来自堪萨斯&没那么胖，就是重得臭名远扬但他们正在牧场那边建超市&就能关照农民了

“有谁想要做个不同
寻常的东西吗？”讲师
问道。班上有个最聪明的
小孩醉醺醺地来上学，
他举起手&说
“有，老师，我就想做一
块钱，老师”

达达主义气象员[5]离开图书馆之前还在里边被一帮流氓痛殴／他打开邮件箱，爬进去&睡觉／那些流氓也出来了／但他们不知道这事，他们已经被一帮虔诚的狂信徒渗透了……全伙出动到处找肥羊……&先搞搞某个下了班的电影院引座员，他裹着毛毯&一顶飞行帽／还差一秒钟就到七月四日[6]&他没有反抗／达达主义气象员收到寄往摩纳哥的邮件。格蕾丝凯利[7]又得了一个小孩&所有流氓都转身一变成了喝醉酒的生意人

“谁能告诉我美国
第三任总统的
名字？”一个后襟上

her back full of ink raises
her hand & says "ernest tubb"

more blue pills father & gobble the little quaint pills/ these gushing swans, rituals & chickens in your sleep– theyve been given the ok & the mad search warrant yes & you, the famous Viking, snatching the time bomb from Sophia's filter tip, down some jack daniels & get out there to meet James Cagney...a swinging armadillo for your friend, your faithful mob & mona lisa behind you... God ma, the swains are baking him & how i wish i could ease him & honor him with peace thru his veins. make him calm. almighty & slay the horrible hippopotamus of his nitemare...but i can take no martyr's name nor sleep myself in any gust of dungeon & am sick with cavity... ludicrous, the dead angel, monopolizing my vocal cords, gatherin her parent sheep onward & homeward into obituary. she's hostile. she's ancient...aretha–golden sweet/ whose nakedness is a piercing thing–she's like a vine/ your lucky tongue shall not decay me

"is there anyone in class who
can tell me the exact hour his
or her father isn't home?" asks
23 the instructor. everybody
suddenly drops their pencils
& runs out the door–all except

沾满墨水的姑娘举起
手来&说“欧内斯特塔布”[8]

再吃点蓝药丸[9]爸爸&吞下一把古怪小药丸/这些呱呱不绝的天鹅，仪式&你睡梦中的鸡群——他们已经获得同意&癫狂搜查证是的&你，一个著名的维京人[10]，从索菲亚的过滤嘴夺取定时炸弹，喝下杰克丹尼&从那里去会见詹姆斯卡格尼[11]……对你的朋友、你的忠实暴徒&你身后的蒙娜丽莎[12]而言是一只摇摇摆摆的犰狳……上帝老妈呀，乡民们在炙烤他&我多么希望我能让他好过点&荣耀他让和平流过他的血管。让他安宁。大能者&杀戮他梦魇中那些丑恶的河马……但我既不能得知烈士的姓名也不能在地牢的寒风里叫自己入睡&我害怕洞穴……滑稽啊，死亡天使[13]，垄断了我的声带，收拢她父母的绵羊往前&往家去到讣告之中。她是怀恨的。她是远古的……阿瑞莎——金醇美妙/她的赤裸是穿透性的东西——她就像一条藤蔓/你幸运的巧舌不会令我腐坏

“有没有哪位同学
能说出他或她的父亲
不在家的准确时间？”讲师
问道。所有人都
突然间放下了铅笔
&跑出门外——当然

of course the boy in the last
row wearing glasses & who's
carrying an apple

juicy roses to coughing hands assembling & pluck national anthems! all hail! the football field ablaze with doves & alleyways where hitchhikers wandering & setting fire to their pockets resounding with the nuns & tramps & discarding the weedy Syrian, surfs of halfreason, the jack & jills & wax Michael from the church acre, who cry in their prime & gag of their twins...empty ships on the desert & traffic cops on the broomstick & weeping & hanging onto a goofy sledgehammer & all the trombones coming apart, the xylophones cracking & flute players losing their intimates...as the whole band groaning throwing away measures & heartbeats while it pays to know who your friends are but it also pays to know you aint got any friends...like it pays to know what your friends aint got–it's friendlier to got what you pay for

down with you sam. down with your
answers too. hitler did not change
24 history. hitler WAS history/ sure
you can teach people to be beautiful,
but dont you know that there's a
greater force than you that teaches
them to be gullible–yeah it's called

除了那个最后排的
戴眼镜的男生＆他正
拿着一个苹果

水灵灵的玫瑰在咳喘两手里聚合＆奏国歌！高呼万岁！足球场上群鸽熊熊奋飞＆街巷里搭便车的人们左右徘徊＆放火点燃他们的衣兜回应那些修女＆踏步声＆丢弃瘦弱的叙利亚人，半智半昏的浪花，杰克＆吉尔们[14]＆教堂墓地里来的蜡像米迦勒，哭嚎在他们的青春年华＆他们的双生子笑料……荒漠上的那些空船＆骑扫帚的交通警＆泪淋淋＆高挂在一把傻乎乎的大磅锤上＆所有的长号都破碎，木琴分崩离析＆长笛手失去了他们的知交……当整支乐队呻吟着抛开节拍＆心跳这时就要知道你的朋友是谁但同时也要知道你没有找到任何朋友……正如还要知道你的朋友们需要什么——如果你的付出有所回报那就更友好了

滚吧你山姆。也滚吧你的
那些答案[15]。希特勒没有改变
历史。希特勒[16]**就是**历史／确实
你可以教育人变得更美好，
但你知道吗还有一种
比你更强大的力量会教育
他们愚蠢可欺——啊这就叫

the problem force/ they assign every–
body problems/ your problem is that you
wanna better word for world…
you cannot kill what lives an expct no–
body to take notice. history is alive/
it breathes/ now cut out that jive/
go count your fish. gotta go. someone's
coming to tame my shrew. hope they re–
moved your lung successfully. say hi
to your sister

love,
Wimp, Your
Friendly Pirate

问题之力／他们给每一个
人分配问题／你的问题是你
要为世界找个更好的词……
你不能杀死生命同时又期望没
有人会发现。历史是活的／
它在呼吸／那就别扯淡／
去数数你的鱼吧。要走了。有人
要来驯服我的悍妇[17]。但愿他们成功摘
除了你的肺。代问
你的姐妹好

爱你，
窝囊废，你的
友善的海盗

注　释

1　耶稣用过牧羊人的比喻，后人也常用牧羊人比喻耶稣。

2　万能工匠（Tinkertoy），美国益智拼接积木，类似乐高。

3　骆驼有三层眼皮，可防风沙。诗人狄兰·托马斯（Dylan Thomas，1914—1953）所著诗作《像暮光中的祭坛那样》（"Altarwise by Owl-Light"）中有"我的骆驼的眼睛会像针一样穿过那寿衣"（My camel's eyes will needle through the shroud）。

4　"明尼苏达胖子"（Minnesota Fats），美国热门电影《江湖浪子》（*The Hustler*，1961）中一个桌球赌神的绰号。迪伦本人生于明尼苏达州，初出道时有点小胖，曾吹嘘来自堪萨斯或其他民谣发达

地区。

5　达达主义气象员（the dada weatherman），参见迪伦歌曲《地下乡愁蓝调》："你不需要气象员 / 也知道风往哪个方向吹。"

6　7月4日是美国的国庆节。

7　格蕾丝·凯利（Grace Kelly，1929—1982），美国影星，曾出演希区柯克电影《后窗》、《电话情杀案》，1954年凭《乡下姑娘》（*The Country Girl*）获得奥斯卡奖、金球奖，1956年嫁给摩洛哥亲王，随后息影，并多次拒绝了希区柯克等大导演的新片邀请，1965年2月生第三个小孩。

8　欧内斯特·塔布（Ernest Tubb，1914—1984），美国乡村音乐歌手，被誉为"得克萨斯行吟诗人"。美国第三任总统应该是托马斯·杰斐逊。

9　蓝药丸（blue pills），可能指汞丸（pilulae hydrargyri），旧时用于梅毒、肺结核、便秘、寄生虫、止痛等。林肯曾长期服用汞丸治疗便秘或抑郁症。

10　据说维京人早在一千年前就曾来到现在的美国。

11　詹姆斯·卡格尼（James Cagney，1899—1986），美国男影星，以在影片《人民公敌》（*The Public Enemy*，1931）中扮演私酒巨头而成名，同时也是美国主流政治的积极参与者。参见迪伦歌曲《乔伊》（"Joey"，1976）。

12　你身后的蒙娜丽莎（mona lisa behind you），参见迪伦歌曲《约翰娜幻象》（"Visions of Johnna"，1966）："在美术馆里，'无限'正接受审判 / 和声嗡嗡：所谓救赎肯定就是这下场 / 但蒙娜丽莎肯定懂得公路蓝调 / 从她微笑的样子就看得出来……"

13　死亡天使（the dead angel），参见迪伦歌曲《满眼忧伤的低地女士》。

14　杰克和吉尔（Jack and Jill），出自英语传统童谣，小男孩和小女孩总做幼稚的傻事，比如两人上山提水然后扑通滚下来。

15　迪伦在1965年的一个访谈中就学校教育问题说：像华盛顿是

第一任总统这样的知识毫无用处，根本不是答案，也不是问题，你最好先读我的书，里面说到这个，提到“答案”这样的词。

16　参见迪伦歌曲《说唱约翰·伯奇偏执狂蓝调》（“Talkin' John Birch Paranoid Blues”，1962）。

17　驯服我的悍妇(tame my shrew)，出自莎士比亚喜剧《驯悍记》。

Maria on a Floating Barge

in a sunburned land winter sleeps with a snowy head at the west of the bed/ Madonna. Mary of the Temple. Jane Russell. Angelina the Whore. all these women, their tears could make oceans/ in a deserted refrigerator carton, little boys on ash wednesday make ready for war & for genius...whereas the weary archaic gypsy–yawning–warbles a belch & tracking the cats & withstanding a ratsized cockroach she hardly appears & looks down upon her sensual arena

dear fang, how goes it old buddy?
long time. no see. guess what? was
gonna vote for goldwater cause you
know, he was the underdog but then
i found out about this jenkins thing,
& i figger it aint much, but it's
the only thing he does have going
for him so i'm changing my vote to
johnson. did you get the clothes i

浮驳船上的玛丽亚

在灼日炎炎的土地里熟睡的冬季把积雪脑袋枕向床铺西头／圣母。神殿的玛丽。珍妮拉塞尔[1]。妓女安吉丽娜。这些娘儿们，她们的眼泪能流成大洋／一个废弃的冰柜纸箱里，小男孩们在圣灰星期三为战争＆为天才做好了准备……然而那疲惫的远古吉卜赛人——打着哈欠——打个颤音饱嗝＆追踪群猫＆抵挡一只大如硕鼠的蟑螂时她几乎不露面＆俯视着她的官能竞技场

亲爱的芳，老伙计过得怎样？
好久。不见。你猜怎么着？本来
准备投票给戈德华特[2]因为你
懂的，他已经是条落水狗[3]不过呢
我发现了这个詹金斯[4]玩意儿，
＆我寻思它根本没啥的，但却是
他唯一能搞到手来支持自己的
东西所以我就改了主意投给
约翰逊。你有没有收到我

sent you? the shirt used to belong
to sammy snead so better take good care
of it

see you
Mouse

寄给你的衣服？那件衬衫原属于
萨米斯尼德[5]所以最好对它精心
打理

下次见
<u>老鼠</u>

注　释

1　珍妮·拉塞尔（Jane Russell，1921—2011），美国女影星、歌手和性感偶像，演艺界的政治保守派，好莱坞基督教社团发起人。

2　巴里·戈德华特（Barry Goldwater，1909—1998），美国保守派领袖，1964年代表共和党竞选美国总统，大败给J.F.肯尼迪的继任者林登·约翰逊（Lyndon Johnson，1908—1973）。参见迪伦歌曲《我将自由自在第10号》（"I Shall Be Free No. 10"，1964）："我是自由派，在某种程度上 / 我希望人人都自由自在 / 但如果你认为我会让巴里·戈德华特 / 搬到我家隔壁，娶我的女儿 / 你肯定是认为我发疯了！"

3　"落水狗"（underdog），一般指落败者、受压迫者。在电视动画片《超级落水狗》中，小狗擦鞋仔遇到危难时会冲进电话亭，吃下一颗超能丸，变身为Underdog（超人［Superman］的戏拟），拯救他心爱的姑娘。

4　沃特·詹金斯（Walter Jenkins，1918—1985），林登·约翰逊的首席顾问，在1964年总统选举之前不久发生性丑闻，共和党藉此大肆炒作，但对选情影响甚微。另，"詹金斯"（up Jenkins）也指一种互相猜硬币、输家付账的酒桌游戏，在台底下进行。詹金斯这个姓氏的本义指约翰的儿子（John's son），亦即约翰逊（Johnson）。

5　萨姆·斯尼德（Sam Snead，1912—2002），美国著名高尔夫球手，50多岁仍活跃于赛场。

Sand in the Mouth of the Movie Star

26 a strange man we're calling Simply That wakes up to find "what" scribbled in his garden. he washes himself with scrambled egg, puts his glasses in his pants & pulls up his trousers. there's a census taker knocking on his door & hi orders for the day are nailed up on his mailbox reading that the route on junky monday is therefore as follows: two pints of soft liberty. a book of zulu sayings. citizen kane translated into dirty french. an orange t.v. studio. three bibles each autographed by the hillbilly singer who can sing salty dog the fastest. the back page of a 1941 daily worker. a salty dog. any daughter of any district judge. a tablespoon of coke & sugar heated to 300 degrees. jack london's left ear. seven pieces of deadly passport. a corn on the cob. five wooden pillows. one boy scout resembling charlie chan & a stolen titerope walker/ "what" is in my garden, he says over the phone to his friend, wally the fireman/ wally replies "i dont know. i really couldnt say. i'm not there" the man says "what do you mean, you dont know! what is written in my garden" wally says "what?" the man says "that's right"...wally replies that he is on his way down a pole & asks the man if he sees any relationship between doris day & tarzan? the man says "no,

电影明星嘴里的沙子[1]

有个古怪人我们叫他就那谁一觉醒来就发现他的花园里乱画了个“什么”。他用炒蛋擦身，把眼镜塞进裤衩&提起长裤。人口普查员来敲他的门&他今天的单子都已经钉在他的邮箱上可以读到垃圾星期一的安排如下：两品脱的软自由。一册祖鲁格言集。公民凯恩[2]的下流法语译本。一个橘子电视演播室。三本圣经上面均有那个唱咸水狗[3]最顺溜的山地民谣歌手签名。一张 1941 年工人日报[4]的末版。一只咸水狗。某个地区法官的某个女儿。一大勺加热到 300 度的可卡因&蔗糖。杰克伦敦的左耳[5]。七本要命的护照。一根玉米棒。五条木枕头[6]。一个酷似陈查理[7]的童子军&一个偷偷摸摸的走钢丝艺人／“什么”就在我的花园里，他打电话告诉他的朋友，火夫沃利[8]／沃利回道“我不知道。我真的没法说。我不在那儿”那人说“你是什么意思，你不知道！什么写在我的花园里”沃利说“什么？”那人说“没错呀”……沃利回复说他正一路从电线杆过来&问那人是否看出多丽丝黛[9]&人猿泰山之间有什么关系？那人说“看不出，

but i have some james baldwin & hemingway books" "not
good enough" says wally, who again asks "what about a
27 shrimp & an american flag? do you see any relationship
between those two things?" the man says, "no, but i see
bergman movies & i like stravinsky quite a lot" wally
tries again & says "could you tell me in a million words
what the bill of rights has to do with a feather?" the man
thinks for a minute & says "no i cant do that but i'm a
great fan of henry miller" wally slams the phone & the
man, Simply That, he gets back into bed & begins reading
"The Meaning of an Orange" in german...but by nitefall,
he is bored. puts the book down & goes to shave while
looking into a picture of thomas edison/ he decided over
a bowl of milk to go out & have a good time & he opens
the door & who's standing there but the census taker "i'm
just a friend of the person who lives here" he says & goes
back in the house & out the back door & down the street
& into a bar with a moose head...the bartender gives him
a double brandy, punches him in the groin & pushes him
into a phone booth–obviously the man's crime is that he
sees nothing resembling anything–he wipes the blood
away from his groin with a hankie & decides to wait for a
call/ "what" is still written in his garden. the clinics are
integrated. the sun is still yellow. some people would say
it's chicken...wally's going down a pole, the census taker
arrives to make a phone call & phone booths dont have
back doors/ junky monday driving, going down a one way
street & turning into a friday the 13th...Ah wilderness!
darkness! & Simply That

但我有几本詹姆斯鲍德温[10] &海明威的书”“还不够好”沃利说，然后又问“那么一只虾&一面美国旗呢？你看得出这两样东西之间有什么关系吗？”那人说，“看不出，但我看伯格曼的电影&我实在非常喜欢斯特拉文斯基”沃利不依不饶&说“你能不能用一百万个词告诉我人权法案跟一根羽毛究竟有何关系？”那人想了一分钟&说“不我做不到但我是亨利米勒[11]的铁杆书迷”沃利摔了电话&那人，就是就那谁，回到了床上&开始读《一只橘子的意义》[12]德文版……但到傍晚，他腻烦了。放下书&去刮胡子同时打量着一幅托马斯爱迪生的肖像／他喝了一碗牛奶就决定出门&好好乐一下&他打开房门&谁站在那儿呢除了人口普查员“我只是这家住户的一个朋友”他说&退回屋里&从后门出去&来到街上&走进一家挂着驼鹿头的酒吧……酒保给他一杯双份白兰地，胖揍他的裆部&把他推进电话亭——显然那人的罪行是他看不出任何东西与其他东西有相似之处——他用手帕擦干净他裆部的血迹&决定等一个来电／“什么”仍写在他的花园里。诊所都是综合性的。太阳仍是蛋黄。有些人会说是鸡肉[13]……沃利正从电线杆过来，人口普查员已经到了要打个电话&电话亭没有后门／垃圾星期一的飞车，驶过单行道&转进一个黑色星期五……啊旷野！黑暗！&就那谁

28 went five hours without a drink
of water. figger i'm ready for
the desert. wanna come? I'll
take along my dog. he's always
good for a laugh. pick yuh up
at seven

faithfully,
Pig

走了五个小时没喝一口
水。想来我已准备好
进入沙漠。要来吗？我会
带上我的狗。他总是
最有笑料。七点钟
接你

忠实的，
<u>猪猪</u>

注　释

1　标题参见英谚“ashes in mouth”，一嘴灰，无法下咽，令人极度失望，出自《曼德维尔游记》（*The Travels of Sir John Mandeville*，1883），说死海之滨结着诱人的水果，但一吃到嘴里就灰飞烟灭。1962 年 10 月 22 日，美国总统 J. F. 肯尼迪就古巴导弹危机发表谈话时说：“我们不会贸然地或无谓地轻启全球核子大战，那样即便拿到胜利的果实也会变成我们嘴里的灰，但如果必须面对，我们也不会畏畏缩缩。”

2　《公民凯恩》（*Citizen Kane*），1941 年的美国热门电影。

3　咸水狗（salty dog），一般指常年跑船的老水手，又指最受宠的狗、老友、放荡的情人、咸湿佬等。《咸水狗蓝调》（“Salty Dog Blues”）亦是一首美国传统民谣，歌词大意：亲爱的我根本不想做你的男人，让我做你的咸水狗吧，咸水狗，咸水狗。许多老歌手都唱过这首歌，其中与迪伦早期风格最接近的可能是密西西比的约翰·赫特（Mississippi John Hurt，1892—1966）1963 年版。

4　《工人日报》（*Daily Worker*，1921—1958），美国共产党在纽约发行的机关报。伍迪·格思里作为美共同路人，曾在该报开设随笔专栏。

5 杰克·伦敦长篇小说《海狼》（*The Sea-Wolf*，1904）中，海狼拉森患有严重的头疼病，后来右耳聋了，只有左耳能听见，他塞上左耳就表示拒绝交流。

6 木枕头，一般被认为是东方式睡具。

7 陈查理（Charlie Chan），美国通俗小说家比格斯（Earl Derr Biggers，1884—1933）在其系列作品中虚构的一个夏威夷华人警探，他聪明、勇敢、友善、忠于职守，是早期流行文化中少有的亚裔正面形象，有大量影视改编、衍生版本。

8 火夫沃利·西姆（Wallie Sims, the fireman），美国西部剧《卡西·琼斯》（*Casey Jones*，1957—1958）中炮弹特快列车的司炉；另也可能指美国喜剧明星考克斯（Wally Cox，1924—1973），动画片《超级落水狗》的配音者，马龙·白兰度的老友。

9 多丽丝·黛（Doris Day，1922—2019），美国歌手、影星，塑造了清纯甜美的主流形象，没参演过“人猿泰山”系列，但她是积极的动物保护主义者，也许因此跟人猿有“关系”。

10 詹姆斯·鲍德温（James Baldwin，1924—1987），美国黑人作家、民权运动家。

11 亨利·米勒（Henry Miller，1891—1980），美国作家，作品曾因犯猥亵长期被禁，当时在进步人士的共同努力下逐渐解除。

12 《一只橘子的意义》（“The Meaning of an Orange”），参见迪伦《重访61国道》唱片文案（1965）：“奶油法官正在写一本关于梨子的真实意义的书，去年。他写过一本讲南北战争名犬的，现在他有假牙、没孩子……”

13 参见迪伦歌曲《墓碑蓝调》：“太阳不是蛋黄，是鸡肉。”或可理解为：“太阳不是懦弱，它就是个脓包。”

Roping Off the Madman's Corner

green maggie of profanity slapstick & her cast of seven
coats shining & fighting the milkmaids & high whining
barndoor slam–heavens! & righteous 38–20 slightly built
on the ball & chain &leashing the lawyer's pigeon while
the rock n roll lead guitar player does his mother's violets &
his thing in the middle of the bailiff's workbench & green
maggie pushing you into hotrod driver's eyes & he's lisping
& he has no money to pay for his language & maggie's not
green & not funny & life gets unbearable but the orator is
29 not the reporter & hanging around at the press room &
shelling out to the day crew & merchants of venice & why
be bothered with other people's set ups? it only leads to
torture/ why it's incredible! the world is mad with justice

dear mayor wagner. has anybody
ever told you, you look like
james arness? i am writing to
say that you are my son's idol.
could you please send your
schedule & repertoire to him, with

圈禁疯人角

猥亵闹剧的绿玛吉[1]&她的七套华丽戏服的班底&力抗那些挤奶妹&高声哀鸣的谷仓门轰隆关上——天堂！&正直的38-20勉强建立在铁球&锁链&皮绳拴紧那律师的白鸽而摇滚乐主音吉他手伺弄他母亲的紫罗兰&他的活计正摆在法警的工作台中央&绿玛吉把你推进改装车司机的眼里&他结结巴巴&他没有钱去支付他的语言&玛吉不是绿的&不是好笑的&生活已难以承受但演说家不是记者&在新闻处瞎转悠&收买日班职员&威尼斯商人们&为什么要烦恼其他人的安排？这只会带来折磨/这真是难以置信！世界就是为公义而疯狂的

亲爱的瓦格纳市长[2]。有没有人
跟你说过，你长得很像
詹姆斯阿内斯[3]？我要写信
告诉你，你是我儿子的偶像。
不知你能否给他寄上你的
播出时间表&总剧目，还有

an autographed picture, at your
earliest convenience. he would
appreciate it kindly as that's
all he does is play your records
& defend you to his friends.
i do hope it's you that's reading
this & not some secretary
thank you
wishfully
Willy Purple

一张签名照，如果方便
还请尽早办理。他会
由衷感激你的因为
他整天都在放你的唱片
&跟他的朋友们为你辩护。
我真希望是你本人在看
这封信&而不是某个秘书

谢谢你
盼复
<u>威利紫色</u>

注 释

1 猥亵闹剧的绿玛吉（green maggie of profanity），参见迪伦歌曲《地下乡愁蓝调》。

2 小罗伯特·瓦格纳（Robert F. Wagner Jr.，1910—1991），1954—1965 年连任三届纽约市市长。

3 詹姆斯·阿内斯（James Arness，1923—2011），美国影星，以扮演西部片英雄马特·狄龙（Matt Dillon）而闻名，是少年迪伦的偶像，也可能是他艺名的由来。

Saying Hello to Unpublished Maria

you taste like candy TUS HUESOS VIBRAN yowee & i'm here because i'm starving & swallowing your tricks into my stomach ERES COMO MAGIA like the greasy hotel owner & it's not your father i'm hungry for! but i will bring a box for him to play with. i am not a cannibal! dig yourself! i am not a sky diver/ i carry no sticks of dynamite...you say NO SERE TU NOVIA & i am not a pilgrim neither TU CAMPESINA & you dont see ME crying over that i cant be sad & wonderful & yippee TU FORMA EXTRANA your horseness amazes me/ i will stand–oh honorable–on the window of your countess even tho i am not a window shade & bang SOLO SOY UN GUITARRISTA all i do is drink & eat. all i have is yours

i'm telling you, the next time you
threaten to commit suicide in front
of me, i'm just gonna haul off an blow
your brains out y'hear! y'read me?
i'm so sick of having you bring me

向未曾发表的玛丽亚问好

你的滋味就像糖果**你的骨骼震颤**[1]哇哟哟&我来这里是因为我饿坏了&把你的诡计吞进我的肚子**你如施魔法**就像油滑的旅店老板&我所饥渴的不是你老爸！但是我会带一个盒子给他玩玩。我不是食人族！搞懂你自己吧！我不是空中飞人／我也没扛着一捆炸药……你说**我才不当你的新娘**&我不是一个朝圣者也不是**你的农妇**&你看不到**我**在痛哭我不能悲伤&妙极了&好耶**你的奇形怪状**你的似马性让我惊奇[2]／我会——荣幸之至——站在伯爵夫人您的窗前尽管我不是一块窗帘&砰砰**我只是一个吉他手**我所做的一切就是吃吃&喝喝。我所有的一切都是你的

我要告诉你，下一次你
再当着我的面威胁要
自杀，我就狠狠一拳砸
烂你的脑袋你听好！懂了没？
我真受够了总是被你搞得

down that i'd just as soon tie you
up & ship you off to red china.
another thing! you better take
good care of my mother. if i
31 hear that youre taking out your
misery on her, i'm coming to see
what i can do about things once &
for all...why dont you learn to
dance instead of looking for new
friends? dont you know that all
the friends have been taken

yours,
Hector Schmector

心烦意乱我恨不得把你
绑起来&送你到红色中国去。
另一件事！你最好对我的
妈妈好一点。如果让我
知道你又搬出你那套
凄惨给她，那我就要看看
我到底能做点什么来个一了&
百了……为什么你不去学
跳舞呢而不是总想去找新的
朋友？你知不知道所有
的朋友都被人占了

你的，

赫克托耳施梅克托[3]

注　释

1　一个电台音效师曾告诉迪伦：骨头碎裂的声音就是嚼碎一颗薄荷糖。本段黑体字部分原文均为西班牙语。

2　参见迪伦歌曲《铃鼓先生》："我的疲倦让我惊奇"（my weariness amazes me）。

3　赫克托耳·施梅克托（Hector Schmector），这个名字也可理解为：盛气凌人的美食家。

Forty Links of Chain (A Poem)

fox eyes from abilene–garbage poet from the
greyhound circuit & who has a feeling for the most lost
pieces of frost & boast of glass jaw & grampa
playing tiddlywinks & finks in the sinks & the barf &
gook in the book
of his cook, the ma & he's back in town
screwing around
with his hairlip down...he needs a dime &
32 writing rhyme You
dont have to guess...you know
the rest/ watch his nose! you can see where he goes
by offering to pay his dues–fox eyes, he's
got lotza blues–Tiny the chick with the wet newspaper,
she used to bring french fries to the mechanics &
whose right arm once went deaf & dumb
(it can happen to some)
she sees fox eyes come

锁链四十环[1]（诗一首）

狐狸眼来自阿比林[2]——垃圾诗人来自
灵猩赛场[3]&他善于感受那些最为落失的
弗罗斯特篇什[4]&脆口薄牙[5]的牛皮故事&老
　　爷子
玩儿弹片片[6]&阴沟沟里爬爬虫&他的菜谱
那本书上的呕吐&
黏着物，老妈呀&他一回到城
就四处鬼混
拱起他那兔毛唇……他要一个角子&
写押韵的词妳
根本不用猜……剩下的事
你都明白／瞧他那鼻头！你能看透他往哪里走
他的路费都是你交——狐狸眼，他已经
学会许多蓝调——小小妞泰妮捧着湿报纸，
她以前常带炸薯条给机修工们&
他的右臂曾经变得聋&哑
(有些人会那么倒霉)
她看到狐狸眼正从

climbing out of the stop sign & he's got a hangover
on top of it & she say "oh great grooby fox eyes. lead
me to the
garbage" & he take her by the
lilywhitecottonpickin
hand & she say "yeah man i be a yellow monkey
oowee! "
& he say "jus you folly me baby snooks! jus you folly
me & you feel fine!" & she say "giddy up & hi ho
silver &
i feel irish!" & both go off & get a bus schedule & she
saying all the time "steady big fella! steady!" while
on
the other side of the street this mailman who looks
like
shirley temple & who's carrying a lollypop stops &
looks at a cloud & just then the sky, he gets kinda
pissed
& decides to throw his weight around a little &
bloop a
33 tulip falls dead–the mailman starts talking to a
parking
meter & fox eyes, he say "it sure wasn't like this in
abilene" & it's a hurricane & a bus reading baltimore
leaves them in a total mess–she falls on her knees &

停车牌爬出来&他那一头的宿醉
都高到了杆顶子上&她说“哦帅呆了狐狸眼。
　　快带我去
垃圾堆吧”&他握着她那只
百合一样白烂棉花[7]的
手[8]&她说“嘿哥们我要做个黄皮猴子哇
　　呀呀！”
&他说“你就糊弄我吧史努克宝贝[9]！你就
　　糊弄
我吧&你觉得爽就好！”&她说“急啊&
　　嗨唷
银光[10]&
我觉个爱尔兰佬！”[11]&两人都走开&去看班
　　车时刻表&她
说个不停“稳住稳住大家伙！稳住了！”这时
在街道的另一边有个邮递员[12]样子好像
秀兰邓波儿&拿根棒棒糖[13]站在那儿&
看一朵云&正好在天上，他有点窝火
&决定要施展一下他的能力&崩飞一棵
郁金香叫它倒地身亡——邮递员开始讲话给
　　停车
表&狐狸眼，他说“在阿比林肯定不会弄成
这样”&飓风来袭&从雷丁[14]到巴尔的摩的
　　班车
把他们抛在满地狼藉中——她跪下膝盖&

she say “i’m filthy” & fox eyes he say “go back to
florida baby there aint nothing here a city grill like
you can do” & the chick she does a handstand & she say
“i’m canadian!” & he say “get outa here & go to florida!”
& she starts reciting fox eyes poems about salvation & the loony bin, strikes in the coloring book factory & christmas
when they wrapped him in a shirt & he say “WHOA! GET OUTA
HERE! I STEAL YO MONEY OWEE JESUS GRILL’ YOU SOME SLUMP!”
& she moans & groans & she say “oh i really do love life &
love love & love living & he say “grooby! wail! wail!” &
she say “dont you understand” & she starts making this terrible
scene right there in the middle of the street...Tiny–i met Tiny
later at an outrageous party–she was sitting under a clock & i say
34 “you need an umbrella, friend” & she say “oh no! not another one!”
& she’s got a new boyfriend now & he looks like machine gun kelly...

她说“我脏死了”&狐狸眼他说“快回
佛罗里达去吧宝贝这儿没有什么事情是你这
　　种城里姑狼
能做的”&小小妞她做了个手倒立&她说
“我是加拿大人！”&他说“快离开这儿吧&
　　去佛罗里达！”
&她开始朗诵狐狸眼的诗，关于拯救&
疯人院，彩色印书厂的罢工&圣诞节
那天他们给他裹上一件衬衣&他说“**停！快
　　离开**
**这儿！我偷了你的钱了哇呀耶稣啊烤得你垂
　　头丧气！**”
&她呜咽着&呻吟着&她说“啊我真的热爱
　　生活&
爱爱着&爱活着”&他说“帅呆了！嚎！嚎
　　啊！&
她说“你懂不懂呀”&她开始搞起这番可怕
景象就在大街的中央……泰妮——我后来见过
　　泰妮
在一场光怪陆离的舞会——她正坐在大钟下
　　面&我说
“你需要雨伞，朋友”&她说“哦不用！已经
　　有一把了！”
&她已经找了新的男友[15]&他长得好像机枪
　　凯利[16]……

fox eyes–he lost all his money in a furnace–when last heard from
was riding fast freight out of salinas in a pile of lettuce &
still trying to collect unemployment...me? i made a special trip
downtown to get some graveyard figures–but it wasnt raining &
there were no buses going to baltimore/ just a broken jawed parking meter,
a water logged pen & a bunch of old shirley temple pictures
with her neck in a noose was all that i could find

look. idont care if you are
a merchant marine. the next time
you start telling me i dont
walk right, i'm gonna get some
surfer to slap your face. i think
youre being very paranoid about
the whole thing...see you at the
wedding

stompingly yours
Lazy Henry

狐狸眼——他在火炉里烧掉了全部积蓄——最近的消息
是坐着货运快车跟大堆莴苣一起离开萨利纳斯[17] &
仍试图领取失业金……至于我？我专门跑了一趟
市中心去找些墓地的雕像——但没有下雨&
也没有开往巴尔的摩的班车／只有一部牙崩嘴裂的停车表，
一支漏水钢笔&一沓老照片上秀兰邓波儿
把她的脖子套进绞索，我只得到这些

瞧。我不在乎你是不是
一个商船水手。下次
你再敢对我说我没有
走正道，我就去找几个
冲浪的人来抽你的脸。我觉得
你对所有的事情都太
疑神疑鬼了……婚礼上
见吧

你捶胸顿足的
懒汉亨利

注　释

1　标题出自美国黑人传统民谣、最早的蓝调之一《乔·特纳》（“Joe Turner”）：“人们告诉我乔·特纳来了又走了，天哪，他抓走了我的男人，他来时带着四十环的锁链。”

2　美国有两个阿比林（Abilene），均为内地农牧业中心，其中堪萨斯州的阿比林位于美国正中央，是西部片的一个经典地名，也是艾森豪威尔的故乡。

3　灵猩（greyhound），有名的猎犬、赛犬品种，也是美国最大的长途班车公司名（灰狗巴士），这里的赛狗场（circuit）也可指汽车站，或诗歌圈。参见艾伦·金斯堡诗《在汽车站的行包房》（“In the Baggage Room at Greyhound”，1956）。

4　美国诗人罗伯特·弗罗斯特有句名言：诗歌是在翻译中丢失的东西，也是在阐释中丢失的东西，一首小诗只意味着它所说的东西而且它说的就是它意味的，一点不少也一点不多。

5　脆口薄牙（glass jaw），指嘴鼻流血、不堪一击的拳手。

6　弹片片（tiddlywinks），一种桌面竞技游戏，用一个圆拨子把几十枚彩色小圆片一个个弹跳起来掉进杯子里。

7　烂棉花（cotton pickin），本义摘棉花，1940 年代转指南方黑人笨拙，引申为詈骂或叹词。

8　出自传统民谣《百合一样白的手》（“The Lily-White Hand”）。

9　史努克宝贝（Baby Snooks），美国同名广播剧（1944—1951）中的淘气女孩，常年由芳妮·布利斯（Fanny Brice，1891—1951）穿娃娃装扮童腔演出。根据芳妮·布利斯生平改编的音乐剧《滑稽女郎》（*Funny Girl*）是 1964 年的百老汇热门剧目。

10　“嗨唷银光”（Hi-Yo, Silver!），出自美国著名西部剧《孤胆奇侠》中蒙面警长召唤他的宝马“银光”时的招牌吆喝，而警长的印第安伙伴“汤桶”驱马时用蹩脚英语吆喝“驾！”，每集开头、结尾他们都会大喊一声飞驰而过。

11 “爱尔兰”（Irish），指被激怒、瞎扯淡等，参见美国爱尔兰裔歌手、笑星丹尼斯·戴（Dennis Day，1916—1988）的老歌《克兰西给他吃砰砰》（“Clancy Lowered the Boom”，1947），歌词大意：克兰西总是和和气气，但谁要是把他的爱尔兰脾气惹急，克兰西就给他吃砰砰，一顿精彩的暴打，砰砰砰。

12 《史努克宝贝》系列剧中有一个爱发梦的邮递员叮当杰瑞，总以为自己的身份是列车长、马戏团老板等等。

13 秀兰·邓波儿有一首热门歌曲《乘着棒棒糖飞船》（“On the Good Ship Lollipop”，1934）。

14 雷丁（Reading），美国宾夕法尼亚州城市，距巴尔的摩约150公里。

15 参见迪伦歌曲《豹纹药盒帽》（“Leopard-Skin Pill-Box Hat”，1966）：“啊，我看见你找了新的男朋友／你知道，我以前从没见过他／啊，我看见他／跟你做爱／你忘了关上车库的门／也许你以为他爱你是为了钱／但我知道他爱你的真正原因……”

16 机枪凯利（Machine Gun Kelly，1895—1954），美国绑匪，有根据其生平改编的同名电影（1958）。

17 萨利纳斯（Salinas），美国加利福尼亚州城市，果蔬业发达，曾号称“莴苣之乡”。

Mouthful of Loving Choke

crow jane from the wedding into the beast nest where
wild man peter the greek & ambassador frenchy do
primitive worship with hustling john from coney
striking a pose & dancing the pink velvet–all dramatics
& curiously belonging to the armenian hunchback
resembling arthur murray who's very turned off & gets
syphilis & crow jane, she gets the chilly blues watching
but she speaks like a champion & she dont kid around
"what you gonna do? i mean besides now's time for the
good men promenade a party?" some plaintive woos
in the twilight & throats ripping & laughing & fool's
terror snapping like a tail & taking it in the ribs & bop
music where south walls quivering & colliding bosoms
& weigh the likes of maid marian's bandits & i repeat:
two face minny, the army derelict/ christine, who's hung
up on your forehead/ steve canyon jones who looks like
mae west in a closet/ screwy herman x, who looks like
a closet/ jake the brown, who look like a forehead...
dino, the limping bartender, who steps in between Man
Mountain Sinatra who looks like the boy next door &
Gorging George, who has no last name...all these & their
agents & "how come you so smart crow jane?" & she

满口子深情的窒息[1]

乌鸦珍妮[2]从婚礼进入兽巢只见希腊野人彼得&法国大使正跟来自科尼[3]的大忽悠约翰搞原始崇拜他们在粉红丝绒上扭捏作态&跳舞——各种装腔作势&但古怪的是竟配上了一个酷似阿瑟默里[4]的亚美尼亚驼子那人很不得劲&有梅毒&乌鸦珍妮，她有冷漠蓝调观察力但她说话像个斗士&她不乱开玩笑"你要去干嘛？我是说除了现在正是好男人去舞会上晃悠的时候[5]之外？"昏光里有凄怨的求爱&撕裂的嗓门&笑声&傻瓜的惊恐像一条尾巴那样崩断&把它收进肋骨&波普乐[6]在南墙颤着&撞着胸乳&称量玛丽安姑娘[7]手下的绿林好汉们&我来数一遍：双面明尼，军队弃儿／克莉丝汀，她迷上了你的前额／史蒂夫坎庸[8]琼斯那模样好像衣橱里的梅韦斯特[9]／老怪赫尔曼 x，像个衣橱／棕种人杰克，像个额头……迪诺，那个瘸腿酒保，行走在人山辛纳屈[10]之间像邻居家的男孩&大嚼子乔治[11]，他没有姓氏……所有这些&他们的经纪人&"你怎么那么聪明呢乌鸦珍妮？"&她答道"你说话怎么那么种族歧视呢？&不要叫我乌

say back "how come you wanna talk so colored? & dont call me no crow jane!" & superfreak pushing & shoving amazing–totally amazing–" & i think i'm gonna do april or so is a cruel month & how you like your blue eyed boy
36 NOW mr octopus?" when the four star colonels come in & everybody says yankee doodle & plastered & some western union boy rides thru on a unicycle yelling "God save the secrets!" but is just coming on–he's mad & he's a horseshoe wizard–nobody cares tho & he's looking for the action & nobody cares about that either & he yells "help!" & two face minny, screaming, swinging from a chandelier & goes to bless him "you cant make nobody understand you too smart to think you know anything! not even john henry did that" crow jane jingle girl & she's a phantom & mouth like an oven & she dances on a cake of islam & "dont tell someone what you know they already know. that makes them think that you just like them & you aint!"...but then you take gwendeline, the different story & rides with lawrence of arabia & plays with her mercury–mumbling crummy world & "oh, the sadness!"...she gets some horny foreigners' attention but mainly all the cool people continue drawing noses on robert frost books "why be crazy on purpose?" say two face minny who's now on top the western union boy & steve canyon jones going off in the corner & crying "we aint never gonna get no messages that way!"...crow jane, she got this talent for robbing hardware stores & always being someplace at the wrong time but saying the right things "dont do your ideas–everybody's got those–let the ideas do you & talk with melody & money tempts ideas & it cant get close to melody & take all the money you

鸦珍妮！”&超变态挤挤&搡搡，神了——简直神了——“&我觉得我该去搞四月什么的是个残忍的月份[12] &**现在**你觉得你的蓝眼睛男孩怎样章鱼先生？[13]”当四星上校们进来&所有人齐喊扬基嘟嘟[14] &晕晕乎乎&有个西联[15]小子蹬着独轮车叫嚷而过“上帝保存机密！”[16]但接下来的是——他疯了&他是一个马蹄铁法师[17]——但没人在乎&他在寻找行动&这也没人在乎&他大呼“救命！”&双面明尼，在大吊灯上尖叫着，摇摆着&过来祝福他“你不能让所有的人都无法理解你太聪明过头了竟以为你无所不知！连约翰亨利[18]都不会这样做”乌鸦珍妮叮当姑娘&她是一个幽灵&嘴巴像烤炉&她在一块清真蛋糕上跳舞&“不要跟别人说你也知道他们早已知道的事。这会让他们觉得你不过和他们一样&你不是！”……但你却选了格温德琳，另一种故事&和阿拉伯的劳伦斯[19]一同驰骋&和她的墨丘利[20]一起玩耍——喃喃着破落世界&“哦，忧愁！”[21]……她引起一些外国猥亵佬的注意但主要是所有的冷静人士都继续在罗伯特弗罗斯特的书上画鼻子[22]“为什么要故意装疯？”比如双面明尼现在已领先西联小子&史蒂夫坎庸琼斯躲进角落&哭着“我们从来不会收到这样的消息！”……乌鸦珍妮，她获得了这项打劫五金店的天赋&总是在错误的时间出现在某些地方但会说着正确的话“不要再搞你那些观念——人人都有观念——让观念搞你吧&用旋律说话&金钱诱出观念&它不可能靠近旋律&你把所有能

can get but dont hurt nobody" crow jane, she got class
37 "& above all else, be all else!" oh the nites with broken arcs, the backs of greensleeves & bruised film–homely & absurd with rhythm & it gets to you after a while...a glass sidewalk meeting the cracker boy's soul & trees like fire hydrants standing in the path of the wooden horse & help mama! help those that cannot understand not to understand...the cracker boy wears spiked shoes but his hands are bare/ peter & frenchy still dancing the cocktail tango–the hunchback being carried out...honeymoon locked into footsteps of the riderless stallion/ rome falling with driving wishy washy half note–crawl with the blues feeling...& the going daylight. crow jane say come, hang out her limelight...there are green bullets in my throat/ i walk sloppily on the sun feeling them turn into yellow keys–i touch jane on the inside & i swallow

dear tom
have i ever told you that i
think your name ought to be
bill. it doesn't really matter
of course, but you know, i like
to be comfortable around people.
how is margy? or martha? or
whatever the hell her name is?
listen: when you arrive & you
hear somebody yelling "willy" it'll

捞到的钱都捞走但别伤害任何人”乌鸦珍妮，她上档次了“&总而言之，言而总之！”哦那些夜里拱门残破，绿袖子的后背[23]&疮痍影片——庸常&荒谬带着韵律&过不久它就找上你……有一条玻璃人行道遇见爆米花男孩[24]的灵魂&树林像消防栓矗在木头马的小路上&救命妈妈！救救那些无法理解的人不要去理解……爆米花男孩穿着钉鞋但他两手空空／彼得&法国佬仍在跳鸡尾探戈[25]——驼子被抬出去……蜜月深锁在闲荒种马的脚步里／罗马随着软巴巴的二分音符崩溃——带着蓝调感爬动……&流逝的日光。乌鸦珍妮说来吧，伸出她的聚光灯……我的喉咙里有几颗绿子弹／我懒洋洋地走在太阳上感觉它们变成黄色的钥匙——我弄着珍妮的深处&我吞下

亲爱的汤姆
我有没有跟你说过我
认为你的名字应该叫做
比尔。这当然没什么
要紧的，但你知道，我喜欢
让身边的人舒舒坦坦的。
叫玛吉怎样？或玛莎？或
随便她什么鬼名字？
记得：等你到站了&你
会听见有人喊“威利”那就是

38 be me that's who…so c'mon. there'll
be a car & a party waiting. it'll
be very easy to single me out, so
dont say you didnt know i was there
gratefully
truman peyote

我这个正主了……那就来吧。会有
一辆车&一场晚会等着你。你会
非常容易认出我的，所以
就不要说你不知道我在那里

感激不尽
杜鲁门佩奥特[26]

注　释

1　窒息（choke），如令人窒息的热吻，大概出自“一大口可乐”（coke）。

2　乌鸦珍妮（Crow Jane），出自美国密西西比三角蓝调歌手蹦蹦詹姆斯（Skip James，1902—1969）的同名老歌，大意：乌鸦珍妮，不要把头抬高，不然你会死的，你知道我恳求过她，不要把头抬得太高，不然会死的。“吉姆乌鸦”（Jim Crow）指黑人男性，“珍妮乌鸦”（Jane Crow）指黑人女性，美国黑人民权、女权运动家葆丽·默里（Pauli Murray，1910—1985）控诉种族和性别的双重歧视，1964 年发表题为《吉姆乌鸦和珍妮乌鸦》的演讲，次年发表论文《乌鸦珍妮和法律：性别歧视与民权法案》。另参见迪伦歌曲《黑乌鸦蓝调》（“Black Crow Blues”，1964）。

3　科尼岛（Coney Island），纽约著名海滨度假区。

4　阿瑟·默里（Arthur Murray，1895—1991），美国交际舞导师，以办班和销售函授教材大获成功。

5　出自英文打字机常用指法练习句：现在正是所有正派人来支援党的时候（Now is the time for all good men to come to the aid of the party）。

6　波普乐（bop music），二战后兴起的现代爵士乐风格，快速、复杂，注重即兴以及与蓝调的结合，对“垮掉派”文学深有启发。

7　玛丽安姑娘（Maid Marian），英格兰传说中侠盗罗宾汉的爱人。

8　史蒂夫·坎庸（Steve Canyon），美国同名漫画中一个美军飞行员，反映冷战时期的主流意识形态。

9　梅·韦斯特（Mae West，1893—1980），美国女影星、歌手、性感偶像；二战美军飞行员喜欢把他们的救生衣或降落伞称为“梅韦斯特”，因为显得胸大。参见后文“梅韦斯特跺脚舞”。

10　“人山”迪安（Man Mountain Dean，1891—1953），美国搏击明星，体重140公斤。弗兰克·辛纳屈（Frank Sinatra，1915—1998），美国最著名的男歌手、演员之一，1965年是他的声名巅峰时期。迪伦在谈到翻唱辛纳屈老歌时曾说：他是一座高山，你必须要攀登，即便你已在途中。

11　“娇子”乔治（Gorgeous George，1915—1963），美国搏击明星，迪伦曾见过他，并得到他的鼓励。娇子乔治原姓瓦格纳（Wagner）。

12　出自T. S. 艾略特长诗《荒原》（*The Waste Land*，1922）第一句：“四月是最残忍的月份。”

13　出自美国诗人E. E. 卡明斯诗《野牛比尔》（*Buffalo Bill's*，1920）：“耶稣啊他曾是个大帅哥，我想知道的是你觉得你的蓝眼睛男孩怎样，死神先生。”另参见迪伦歌曲《暴雨将至》（“A Hard Rain's A-Gonna Fall”，1963）：“哦，你到哪里去了，我的蓝眼睛男孩？ / 哦，你到哪里去了，我亲爱的年轻人？”

14　扬基嘟嘟（“Yankee Doodle”），美国最有名的传统民谣之一，常用作军歌，歌词大意：扬基嘟嘟进城去，骑着一头小马驹，小帽帽上插根鸡毛，他就觉得很时髦；我和老爸进军营，看见人挤人像一堆布丁。

15　西联（Western Union），美国金融和电讯公司，是当时美国最主要的电汇机构。

16　上帝保佑汇兑通信秘密。

17 美国牛仔相信马蹄铁有避凶趋吉的作用；掷马蹄铁是西部传统比赛。

18 约翰·亨利（John Henry），美国传统民谣中的一个钢铁般强悍的筑路工人，他抡锤叮当，比汽锤还能干。铅肚皮、伍迪·格思里、皮特·西格（Pete Seeger）等很多老歌手都唱过。

19 阿拉伯的劳伦斯（lawrence of arabia），出自1963年的美国热门电影《阿拉伯的劳伦斯》（*Lawrence of Arabia*），主人公T. E. 劳伦斯死于摩托车事故。

20 墨丘利（Mercury），福特汽车公司1938年推出的中档车品牌“水星”。

21 “哦，忧愁！”（“oh, sadness!”），可能出自法国当代小说家萨冈（Francoise Sagan，1935—2004）的成名作《你好，忧愁》（*Bonjour Tristesse*，1954）。

22 鼻子（noses），可能指倒问号（¿），或谐音笔记（notes）。那些人在老派诗集上找灵感。

23 《绿袖子》（“Greensleeves”），英格兰传统民谣。“绿背”（greenback）指美钞。

24 爆米花男孩（the cracker boy），美国畅销零食“杰克爆米花”（Cracker Jack）的品牌形象是一个穿水兵服的小男孩。

25 鸡尾探戈（cocktail tango），在法语中，“tango”意为橘红色，又指啤酒加石榴汁的鸡尾酒。

26 佩奥特（peyote），一种具有致幻作用的墨西哥仙人球，及人工合成迷幻药麦司卡林，垮掉派作家多曾尝试。文中戏指美国当代小说家杜鲁门·卡波特（Truman Capote，1924—1984），他曾鄙视凯鲁亚克的作品：“这哪叫写作，不过是打字而已。”

The Horse Race

"...always trying, always gaining"
—lyndon johnson

yes & so anyway on the seventh day, He created pogo,
bat masterson, & a rose colored diving board for His
cronies/ the sky already strung up shivered like the top
of a tent. "what's all this commotion" he said to his main
man, Gonzalas, who without batting an eyelash picked up
a rake & began flogging a cloud...seeing that Gonzalas
39 had the wrong idea, He told him to lay down the rake
& go build an ark/ when Gonzalas reaches twenty-five
he starts wondering when his parents will kick off. it's
nothing personal, it's just that he needs some money & is
beginning to resent the fact that he hasnt been laid yet/
"why did you not create an eighth day?" ask Gonzalas'
chauffeur to his Sausage Maker on the steps of the
boom boom parlor/ while handing in his perfume/ the
sky, changing into a sexy spaghetti odor, continues to
tremble-Gonzalas, meanwhile, sports a cane & tries to
hide his korean accent/ edgar allan poe steps out from
behind a burning bush...He sees edgar. He looks down

赛马会

"……尝试不断，收获不断"

——林登约翰逊[1]

没错&总之就在第七日，他创造了庞哥[2]、巴特马斯特森[3]&一块玫瑰色的跳水板给他的老友们／天空早就搭好了，颤巍巍地像一顶帐篷布。"搞什么乱七八糟的"他对他的男主冈萨拉斯说，而他一根睫毛都没眨就抓起耙子&开始抨击一朵云……看到冈萨拉斯起了坏念头，他就吩咐他放下耙子&去建一条方舟／等冈萨拉斯长到二十五岁他就动心思去琢磨他的父母要什么时候才翘辫子。这无关个人感情，只是他缺点钱而已&正开始厌恶一个事实，就是他还没睡过女人／"为什么你不造一个第八日呢？"在啪啪店的台阶上冈萨拉斯的司机问他的熏肠造主／同时递交他的香水／天空，正变成一种性感的意大利面条味儿，但仍颤颤不止——与此同时，冈萨拉斯甩弄着手杖[4]&试图隐藏他的朝鲜口音／埃德加爱伦坡从一个燃烧的树丛后面走出来[5]……他看见埃德加。

& says "it's not your time yet" & strikes him dead...
Gonzalas enters/ places fifth in the second

how come youre so afraid of
things that dont make any
sense to you? do people pass
you up on the street all the
time? do cars pass you up on
the highway? how come youre
so afraid of things that dont
make any sense to you? do you
water your raisins daily? do
you have any raisins? is there
anything that does make sense
to you? are you afraid of twelve
button suits? how come youre
so afraid to stop talking?
your valve cleaner
Tubba

他俯视下来＆说“还没轮到你呢”＆将他击毙……冈萨拉斯入围了＆在第二轮名列第五

你怎么会那么害怕
那些对你根本毫无
意义的东西？不是总有
人在大街上跟你擦肩
而过吗？不是总有汽车
在公路上跟你擦肩而
过吗？你怎么会那么
害怕那些对你根本
毫无意义的东西？你会
每天给葡萄干浇水吗？你
有葡萄干吗？那里
真有什么东西对你有
意义吗？你会害怕十二颗
纽扣的套装吗？你怎么
那么害怕停止说话？

你的阀门清洗剂
土霸

注释

1 林登·约翰逊（Lyndon B. Johnson，1908—1973），时任美国总统，肯尼迪的继任者，引语出自 1965 年 1 月 20 日总统就职演讲。

2 庞哥（Pogo），美国同名漫画中一只可爱又睿智的卡通负鼠，自由主义者。

3 巴特 · 马斯特森（Bat Masterson，1853—1921），美国西部传奇人物，同名电视连续剧曾热播。

4 手杖（cane），原文谐音 Cain（该隐）。参见迪伦歌曲《海蒂·卡罗尔的孤独死亡》（"The Lonesome Death of Hattie Carroll"，1963）："威廉 · 赞津格杀死了可怜的海蒂 · 卡罗尔 / 用他戴钻戒的手上滴溜转的手杖。"

5 参见《旧约 · 出埃及记》3:2，上帝的使者在燃烧的荆棘中向摩西显现。

Pocketful of Scoundrel

in a hilarious grave of fruit hides the wee gunfighter–a warm bottle of roominghouse juice in the rim of his sheepskin/ lord thomas of the nightingales, bird of youth, rasputin the clod, galileo the regular guy & max, the novice chess player/ the battles inside their souls & gloves being as dead as their legends but only more work for the living jesters–victims of assassination & dying comes easy...on the other side of the tombstone, the amateur villain sleeps with his tongue out & his head inside the pillow case/ nothing makes him seem different/ he goes unnoticed anyway.

41 dear Sabu
it's my chick! she tells me that
she takes long walks in the woods.
the funny thing about it is that
i followed her one nite, & she's
telling me the truth. i try to
get her interested in things

满袋子恶棍

一个欢欢闹闹的水果坟墓里藏着小小神枪手——在他的绵羊皮圆圈里有一瓶暖暖的寄宿店果汁／夜莺、青春鸟的托马斯老爷[1]，土包子拉斯普京[2]，规矩人伽利略＆马克斯[3]，象棋新手／他们的灵魂＆手套深处的战役已经死得跟他们的传奇一样只不过提供更多工作给活着的小丑——刺杀受害人＆死得顺顺当当……墓碑的另一面，业余反派耷拉着舌头沉睡＆他的脑袋埋在枕套里边／没有什么能让他与众不同／总之他就是没人搭理。

亲爱的萨布[4]
说说我那小妞！她告诉我
她在树林里走了很远。
但有趣的事情是
我跟了她一夜，＆她
对我说的是真话。我努力
想找她感兴趣的话题
比如枪械和足球，但她

like guns an football, but all
she does is close her eyes &
say “i dont believe this is happening”
last nite she tried to hang herself...
i immediately thought of having her
committed, but goddamn she’s my chick,
& everybody’d just look at me funny
for living with a crazy woman.
perhaps if i bought her her own car,
it would help/ can you fix it?
thanx for listening
All Petered Out

只是那样闭上眼睛&
说“我不相信这在发生”
昨晚她还试图上吊呢……
我立马就想把她给
绑了，但该死的她是我的妞，
&人人都等着看我傻乎乎
去跟一个疯婆子生活。
也许我给她买一辆她自己的车，
会有帮助／你能搞定吗？

多谢垂听
精疲力竭者

注　释

1　托马斯老爷（lord thomas），指美国剧作家田纳西·威廉斯，原名托马斯·拉尼尔·威廉斯三世，著有《与夜莺无关》（*Not about Nightingales*，1938）、《青春鸟》（*Sweet Bird of Youth*，1959）。另，托马斯老爷也见于传统民谣。

2　土包子拉斯普京（rasputin the clod），指格里高利·拉斯普京（Grigori Rasputin，1869—1916），农民出身的俄国巫医，极得沙皇宠幸，生活糜烂，后被刺杀。迪伦歌曲《我要做你的爱人》（“I Wanna Be Your Lover”，1965）中有：朱迪的眼里中了子弹，拉斯普京身份尊贵，他摸过她的后脑勺然后他死了。迪伦还曾戏称他最喜欢的表演艺术家第一位就是拉斯普京。

3　马克斯·尤韦（Max Euwe，1901—1981），荷兰国际象棋大师，写过很多棋书。

4　可能指萨布·达斯塔吉尔（Sabu Dastagir，1924—1963），美国印度裔演员。

Mr. Useless Says Good–bye to Labor & Cuts a Record

42 Phombus Pucker. with his big fat grin. his hole in the head. his matter of fact knowledge of zen firecrackers. his little white lies. his visions of sugar plums. his dishwater hands/ Phombus Tucker. with his bulldog wit. his theories on atomic nipples. his beard & his backache/ Bombus Thucker. with his soft boiled stovepipe. his aloneness & aloofness. his hatred for crap/ Longus Bucker. with his numbers & decimals. with his own special originality... spent hours & hours carving his name in the sand. when all of a sudden, a wave's commotion washed him & his name right into the ocean (ho ho ho)

look, you know i dont wanna
come on ungrateful, but that
warren report, you know as well
as me, just didn't make it. you know.
like they might as well have
asked some banana salesman from

没用先生对劳动说再见＆去录唱片

冯伯斯大褶子。咧着他的大肥脸。他脑袋上的洞。他对于禅宗爆竹的就事论事的知识。他那些善意的小谎话。他的糖球幻象[1]。他的洗碗水一样的手／冯伯斯打褶子。端着他的斗牛狗才学。他的原子奶头理论。他的胡须＆他的腰疼病／嗡伯斯耷茬子。戴着他的软趴趴烟囱帽。他的孤单＆孤高。他对放狗屁的憎恨／朗格斯尥蹶子。算着他的整数＆小数。他本人特有的创造性……费了好久＆好久时间在沙滩上刻他的名字。突然，一个浪头的震荡把他＆他的名字冲到了海里（嘀嘀嘀）[2]

你知道，我并不想
忘恩负义，但是
华伦报告[3]，你我都
知道，根本瞎扯。你知道。
比如他们有可能去
找某个来自得梅因的香蕉

des moines, who was up in toronto
on the big day, if he saw anyone
around looking suspicious/ or better
43 yet, they just coulda come & asked me
what i saw/ the doctors say i gotta tumor
coming up tho, so i got more important things
to do than to be bothered with straightening
out this whole mess...while youre down
there, see if you can get me murph the
surf's autograph

bye for now
your lightingman
Sledge

推销员，他事发当日
正在多伦多，问他有没有看见
周围有可疑的人／或者还要
更离谱，他们可能跑来＆问我
看到了什么／医生都说我很快就
要长肿瘤，所以我要找更重要的事情
来做而不是老发愁怎样理顺
这一堆乱麻……等你到了
那边，看你能不能给我搞到冲浪
墨菲[4]的自传

先到这里
你的灯光师
雪橇

注　释

1　糖球幻象（visions of sugar plums），出自美国传统赞美诗《圣诞节前的夜晚》（“The Night Before Christmas”，1823）：“孩子们暖暖地蜷缩在被窝里，／糖球的幻象在他们头脑中舞蹈。”

2　“嗬嗬嗬”（ho ho ho），圣诞老人的标志性笑声。

3　《华伦报告》（The Warren Commission Report），1964年9月发布的J. F. 肯尼迪刺杀案调查报告，认定只是精神病人个人作案，没有政治阴谋。

4　冲浪墨菲（Murph the Surf，1938— ），美国罪犯，曾获得过冲浪冠军，1964年10月因盗窃纽约自然史博物馆珍贵宝石被捕。参见迪伦《统统带回家》（“Bringing It All Back Home”，1965）唱片文案。

Advice to Tiger's Brother

you are in the rainstorm now where your cousins seek
raw glory near the bridge & the lumberjacks tell you of
exploring the red sea...you fill your hat with rum & heave
it into the face of hailstone & not expect anything new to
be born...dogs wag their tails good–bye to you & robin
hood watches you from a stained glass window...the
opera singers will sing of YOUR forest & YOUR cities
44 & you shall stand alone but not make ceremony...an old
wrinkled prospector will appear & he will NOT say to
you "dont be possessive! dont wish to be remembered!"
he will just be looking for his geiger counter & his name
wont be Moses & dont count yourself lucky for not
interfering–it is petty...do not count yourself lucky

hi. just a note to say that ever
since the robbery, things've
kinda quiet down. altho theo's
kidnappers havent returned him
yet, dad got promoted to den
mother, so things are not all

给老虎兄弟的忠告

此刻你身处暴风骤雨而你的老表们在大桥附近寻找质朴的荣光＆伐木工[1]跟你讲红海勘探……你用帽子盛满朗姆酒＆把它砸到冰雹的脸上＆不期待有什么新东西会诞生……狗狗们摇着尾巴向你告别＆罗宾汉[2]在一扇彩画玻璃窗后面观察你……歌剧团会唱起**你的**森林＆**你的**城镇＆你将孤身一人但没举行仪式……一个满脸皱纹的老探矿员会出现＆他**不会**对你说“不要总想独占！不要指望被记住！”他将只会去找他的盖革计数器＆他的名字不会是摩西＆不要以为你能置身事外就是幸运儿——这不值一提……不要以为你是幸运儿

嘿。写封短信告诉你
自从劫案之后，事情都
基本平息了。尽管那些绑匪
目前还没有把西奥送回来，
老爸已经升级为童子军小队
老妈子，所以事情也不是完全

going downhill/ mom joined the
future fathers of alaska. really
likes it/ you oughta see little
dumbbell. he's nearly two now.
talks like a fish & is already
starting to look like a cigar/
see you on your birthday

big brother
Dunk

p.s. adolph got you a trick piece of puke which
you put on the table & just watch the
girls throw up

都走下坡路／妈妈加入
阿拉斯加未来之父。真的
很喜欢／你应该见见小
哑铃。他现在快两岁了。
说起话来像条鱼&早就
开始长得像根雪茄了／
你生日的时候再见

大兄弟

邓克

又及，阿道夫给你一块恶搞呕吐物
你拿去往桌上一摆&就看着那些
姑娘作呕吧

注　释

1　伐木工（the lumberjacks），参见迪伦歌曲《瘦人歌》（"Ballad of a Thin Man"，1965）："在伐木工当中你也有很多熟人／如果有谁攻击你的想象力／他们会告诉你实情／但没人会尊敬你／其实他们只等着你开一张支票……"

2　罗宾汉（robin hood），参见迪伦歌曲《荒凉路》。

On Watching the Riot from a Filthy Cell or (The Jailhouse Has No Kitchen)

45 standing on a bullet holed volkswagen, a bearded
leprechaun & he's wearing a topless mafia cape–holding
up some burning green stamps & he speaks out to the
automobile graveyard "four score & seven beers ago" &
then he say "etcetera" but his voice is drowned out by
mickey mantle hitting a grand slam...the mayor of the
city, with alka seltzer, climbs down from a limousine
& asks "who the hell is that leppo?" when a thousand
angry tourists trample over him all donning baseball
gloves & here comes the squad/ "just who the hell are
you?" speaks a garbage disposal "i'm cole younger. gave
my horse to the pony express. other'n that, i'm just like
you" a rousing cheer & the ball crashes thru the fire box
"i work for the city. before i swat you you'd best tell me
your occupation" "i'm an actor. tomorrow & tomorrow &
tomorrow lights this petty grace from blow to blow like
a poor stagehand pounding fury signifying nothing. oh
romeo, romeo, wherefor fart thou? pretty good huh?" "i
work for the city, i'll trample you with my horse" "wanna
hear some oedipus?" but beneath the underground, Blind
46 Andy Lemon & his friend, Lip, sing rabbit foot blues in
spurs & light pullover design by Chung of paris–theyre

从一间肮脏囚室观察暴乱或（监狱里没有厨房）

被子弹洞穿的大众汽车上，站着一个大胡子矮精&他披着一件无兜帽的黑手党斗篷——捧着几张燃烧的绿票[1]&他对汽车墓场开口说“四廿&七啤前”[2]&接着他又说“诸如此类”但他的话音被米奇曼托[3]打出的大满贯淹没……市长大人，带着去痛泡腾片，从豪华轿车爬下来&问“妈的那矮子是谁？”这时一千个愤怒的旅游者把他踩倒在地全都戴着棒球手套&警队驾到／“妈的你又是谁？”一个垃圾处理机说“我是科尔扬格[4]。刚送我的马儿去驿站。此外，我也和你一样”一阵热烈欢呼&球砸穿了炉膛“我为城市效力。在我拍死你之前，你最好告诉我你的职业”“我是一个演员。明天&明天&明天照亮这小小优雅一下又一下就像一个蹩脚的后台助手捶打暴怒却毫无意义。[5]啊罗密欧，罗密欧，为河洗泥？[6]很不错吧？”“我为城市效力，我要用我的马把你踩倒在地”“想听听俄狄浦斯吗？”但在地底之下，瞎子安迪柠檬[7]&他的朋友，利普，唱着兔脚蓝调[8]穿着马刺&巴黎钟氏设计的轻套衫——他

standing in a fish bowl & everybody's throwing marbles at them...outside, however, after the tear gas disappears, we find that the leprechaun's got his hand in a bandage & his beard's gone & the mayor, we find out, is home making urgent phone calls to cardinal spellman/ it has been a long time nite & everybody has had lots of contact...i am ready for the cradle. the desert is full of cattle

sorry for not writing sooner. had
to have some teeth pulled. finally
read the great glaspy. helluva book
just a helluva one. that cat sure
tells it like it is. not much happening
around here. Chucky tried to get the
donkey to jump a fence. you can guess
what happened there. sis got married
to a real dog. i punched him out
right away. that's all for now
see yuh on thanxgiving
Corky

们站在一个鱼缸里&人人都朝他们扔弹珠……不过在外面，催泪瓦斯消散之后，我们发现矮精已经搞得他的手缠了绷带&他的胡子掉光了&我们还发现市长正在家里打紧急电话给施佩尔曼枢机[9]／那是漫长的一夜&人人都发生了很多接触……我已经准备好进摇篮了。沙漠里牛羊成群。

抱歉没及时回信。我
必须去拔掉几颗牙。终于
读到了不起的格拉斯皮[10]。了不起的书
就是了不起的。那家伙肯定能
说得恰如其分。我们这儿
没什么大事。查奇硬是要弄那
头驴去跳篱笆。你猜得出
后来发生了什么。小妹嫁给了
一条真正的狗。我当场把它
打杀出去。就那么多了

感恩节见
柯基

注　释

1　绿票（Green Stamps），购物积分券，常被当作消费主义的讽刺。

2　“四廿&七啤前”（four score & seven beers ago），戏拟林肯《葛

底斯堡战役演讲》（“Gettysburg Address”，1863）的开头“四廿又七年前的今日”（Four score and seven years ago），指1776年发表《合众国独立宣言》。

3　米奇·曼托（Mickey Mantle，1931—1995），美国棒球明星，一直在纽约扬基队效力。

4　科尔·扬格（Cole Younger，1844—1916），美国西部土匪头子，在密苏里、肯塔基等地洗劫银行、驿站、火车，1876被明尼苏达民团俘获，出狱后写回忆录为自己辩白。《大盗扬格》（“Bandit Cole Younger”）是美国早期蓝调名曲。

5　参见莎士比亚《麦克白》第五幕第五场：“明日明日又明日，蹑着小小的步伐一天又一天，直到那记录时间的最后一个音节；我们所有的昨日已照亮了傻瓜们走向死亡埋葬的去路。熄吧，熄吧，短暂的烛光！人生不过是一个会走动的影子，一个蹩脚的演员他在舞台上指手划脚片刻，就再无声息；它是一个愚人所讲的故事，充满喧嚣和暴怒却毫无意义。”

6　参见莎士比亚戏剧《罗密欧与朱丽叶》第二幕第二场：“啊，罗密欧，罗密欧！为何是你呀罗密欧？”

7　瞎子安迪柠檬（Blind Andy Lemon），混合了两个美国民谣歌手的名字，瞎子安迪（Andrew Jenkins，1885—1957）和瞎子柠檬。

8　《兔脚蓝调》（“Rabbit Foot Blues”，1926）是美国早期民谣歌手瞎子柠檬的代表作之一。美国风俗相信兔脚能带来好运。

9　弗朗西斯·施佩尔曼（Francis Joseph Spellman，1889—1967），天主教纽约大主教，越南战争鼓吹者。

10　了不起的格拉斯皮（the great glaspy），戏拟美国著名作家菲茨杰拉德的《了不起的盖茨比》（*The Great Gatsby*，1925）。

Hopeless & Maria Nowhere

47 raggity ann daughter of brazos & teeth in the necklace–ornery in the flesh & the border with the big laugh of bullfight ghost & LIBERACION & she, with the leather mother thief & peeking DOS PASOS MAS ee & crazy ALLA LUEGO UN RAYO & insane DE SOL & taking the brothers to bed & to boredom–heat in every corner like the silent parrot by SALA UN DIA & mad like a hatter & the pig barker–maria ESTAS DESNUDA she digs holes on my eyes the size of the moon while her father, he keeps the hill warm & uncritical from deacons & the youngster missionaries–maria sleep lightly PERO TE QUITARAS cursing blond dynamite & TUS ROPAS...there is a hatchet in maria's makeup & the spike driver moans, they sound on her sink like the fornicating rattlesnake–friendly on her nature & MARIA PORQUE LLORAS? & i give you my twelve midnights & kick you with leapyear & protect you from the crooked words & loyalty to the power works & these little frogs with notebooks...maria PORQUE TU RIES? freedom! she's the yardbird, the constant & the old lady is made of marias & dogs yelping & RECUERDOS oh how the furious yesterday, pyria SON HECHOS laying bang DE

绝望&玛丽亚不知所终[1]

碎布头安妮[2]，布拉索斯[3]的女儿&项链上的牙齿——骨子里的乖戾&与斗牛幽灵的哈哈大笑相邻&**解放**[4]&她，跟皮衣妈妈小偷&窥看**两步之外**嗯&疯了**随即强光一闪**&癫了**太阳**&带兄弟们上床铺&去无聊——每个角落里的热就像沉默鹦鹉被**你腌制一日**&疯得像个帽匠[5]&剥猪佬——玛丽亚**你赤身裸体**她在我眼睛上的挖洞洞有月亮那么大然而她的父亲，他维持山岗温暖&让执事长&青年宣教团无可指摘——玛丽亚浅睡**但你会脱下**咒骂金发绝代男&**你的衣服**……玛丽亚的化妆包里有一把手斧&打钉锤凄吟[6]，在她的水槽上它们的声音像通奸的响尾蛇——善待她的天性&**玛丽亚你为什么哭了**？我要给你我的十二个午夜&用闰年踢踢你[7]&保护你免遭恶语&忠于那大能的运作&这些小青蛙都有笔记本……玛丽亚**你为什么笑了**？自由！她是囚鸟，是恒量&那老太太是玛丽亚们构成的&狗子们狂吠&**那些回忆**哦多么狂乱的昨日，火爆**已变成**打滚砰砰**久远的**及傻孩子西蒙[8]**虚无**到现在仍是个有

ARCAICOS with simple simon NADAS is still right now
the poison nothing & maria, me & you, we make up three
TE QUIERO do not churchize my nakedness–i am naked
48 for you…maria, she says i'm a foreigner. she picks on me.
she pours salt on my love

ok. so i shoot dope once in a
while. big deal. what's it got
to do with you? i'm telling you
mervin, if you dont lay off me,
i'm gonna rip you off some more
where that scar is, y'hear? like
i'm getting mad. next time you
call me that name in a public
cafeteria, i'm just gonna haul
off & kick you so you'll feel
it. like i aint even gonna get
angry. i'm just gonna let one
fly. fix you good

better watch it
The Law

毒的无&玛丽亚、我&你，我们合为三个**我爱你**不要把我的赤裸奉入教堂——我为你而裸……玛丽亚，她说我是一个外人。她总找我的茬。她在我的爱情上倒盐

就这样，我时不时地要来
一针。不得了呀。但这和你
有什么关系？我跟你说
默温，要是你还不肯放过，
我也会狠揭你的疮疤
叫你体无完肤，听懂没？像
我疯了一样。下次你再
在公共食堂那样乱喊
我的名字，我就把你拖
出来&胖揍一顿那时你就有
体会了。好像我从来不会
发怒一样。我只是当你个屁
给放了。该好好修理你

小心点吧
<u>执法者</u>

注　释

1　标题出自1957年改编的百老汇音乐剧《西区故事》（*West*

Side Story）中，女主角玛利亚与男主角的一首合唱《某处》（“Somewhere”）。

2　碎布头安妮（Raggedy Ann），美国童书作家约翰尼·格鲁勒（Johnny Gruelle，1880—1938）创造的布娃娃女孩形象。迪伦曾在其自传《编年史》中这样形容琼·贝兹：“她看上去有点邪气……她不是那种‘碎布头安妮’玩具娃娃。”

3　布拉索斯（Brazos），美国得克萨斯州的一条主要河流，西班牙语意为“双臂”。

4　本章黑体字部分原文均为西班牙语。

5　疯得像个帽匠（mad like a hatter），英谚，就是很疯狂的意思。

6　打钉锤凄吟（the spike driver moans），出自美国民谣歌手戴夫·范容克（Dave Van Ronk，1936—2002）歌曲《打钉锤的凄吟》（“Spike Driver's Moan”）。

7　英国传统，在闰年或2月29日的时候女子可向男子求婚。

8　《傻孩子西蒙》（“Simple Simon”），英国传统童谣。

A Confederate Poke into King Arthur's Oakie

49 "...later i left the Casino
with one hundred & seventy
gulden in my pocket. it's
the absolute truth!"
–fyodor dostoevsky

son of the vampire with his arm around betsy ross–
he & his society friends: Rain Man. Burt the Medicine.
President Plump. the Flower Lady & Baboon Boy...they
all said "happy new year, elmer & how's your wife, cecile?"
& that got them into the party free...once into the party,
Burt just stood around with a toothpick in the back of his
neck watching for the doctor & tho the card game was
something else in itself, Flower Lady lost her shirt & went
to the bushes–who should come by but the little old wine
maker trying to be helpful–"get out of the picture" said
Flower Lady "you werent at the party!"...the little old wine
maker immediately took off his head & his belt & who do
you think it turned out to be but fabian–"i dont care how
many tricks you can do, just get outa here!"...just then, this
50 cable car on its way to washington came rumbling down

一个邦联佬儿混进亚瑟王的俄基舞[1]

“……然后我装着
一百&七十金盾
在兜里离开了大赌场。
千真万确！”[2]

——费奥多尔陀思妥耶夫斯基

吸血鬼之子一手搂着贝吉罗斯[3]——他&他的教友们[4]：雨人[5]。巫医伯特。胖墩总统。百花夫人[6]&狒狒小子……他们都说“新年快乐，埃尔默&你妻子莎西尔好吗？”&然后他们免费蹭进了舞会……刚进舞会，伯特就站在旁边用一根牙签插在他的后脖上观察着博士&尽管牌局根本不一样，百花夫人还是输掉了她的衬衫&钻进树丛——有谁会路过呢除了那酿酒的小老头想来帮个忙——“快走开”百花夫人说“这儿不是舞会！”……酿酒的小老头立刻卸下他的脑袋&他的腰带&你觉得最后会证明是谁呢除了法比安[7]——“我不管你还有多少花招，给我快滚开！”……当时，这辆缆车正一路咣当

the hill carrying crossword puzzles for everybody–Rain Man yelled "watch out Flower Lady, there's an elephant coming!" but by this time she was singing auld lang syne with Baboon Boy, who'd snuck up, stuck a lead weight life jacket around fabian & threw him in the swimming pool–the Plump himself tried to give a warning but he was so drunk that he fell in a barrel & a tractor being driven by some dogs ran him over & dumped him into a garage... the world didnt stop for a second–it just blew up/ alfred hitchcock made the whole thing into a mystery & huntley & brinkley never slept for a week...the american flag turned green & andy clyde kept pestering about a back paycheck–every gymnasium in the world was picketed... son of the vampire, who got a divorce from betsy ross & now is with little red riding hood made it into january first carrying some empty stomachs–he & red, they got a job hiding door knobs & got paid good wages & like all people who decide not to go to any more parties, they put their money where their mouth is...& begin to eat it

translate this fact for me, dr.
blorgus: the fact is this: we
must be willing to die for
freedom (end of fact) now what
i wanna know about the fact is this: could
51 hitler have said it? de gaulle? pinocchio?
lincoln? agnes moorehead? goldwater?
bluebeard?

下山往华盛顿给每个人运送纵横字谜——雨人喊“当心啊百花夫人，有一头大象过来了！”但这时候她正在跟狒狒小子唱友谊地久天长，后者已偷偷地在法比安身上绑了一件铅坠救生衣&把他扔进游泳池——胖墩本人也想发出警告但他喝得烂醉自己都掉进桶子里了&一辆狗拉牵引车从他身上碾过&把他甩进修车厂……世界不会停止一秒——它只是爆掉/阿尔弗雷德希区柯克把整件事拍成推理片&亨特利&布林克利[8]一个星期都没合眼……美国旗变绿了&安迪克莱德[9]总在为拖欠薪酬苦恼——世界上的每个健身房都有纠察队……吸血鬼之子，已经跟贝吉罗斯离婚&现在和小红帽把它做成一月一日载着些饿肚皮——他&红，他们找了个藏门把手的活儿&拿了高薪&跟所有已经决定不再参加任何舞会的人们一样，他们把他们的钱放进嘴巴的位置……&开始吃它

请帮我翻译这个事实，钹锣鼓
博士：事实如下：我们
必须心甘情愿地为了自由
去死（事实完毕）然后我
想知道的事实是这个：是不是
希特勒曾说过这话？戴高乐？匹诺曹？
林肯？阿格妮丝穆尔黑德[10]？戈德华特？蓝胡子[11]？

the pirate? robert e. lee? eisenhower?
groucho smith? teddy kennedy? general franco?
custer? is it possible that jose melis
could have said it? perhaps donald o'connor?
i happen to be a library janitor, so could
you please clarify things a little for
me. thank you...by the way, if you do not
have a reply to me by this coming tuesday,
i will take it for granted that all these
forementioned people are all really the
same person...see you later. have to take
down a picture of lady godiva as the
mental students are touring here in an
hour...

considerately yours,
Popeye Squirm

海盗？罗伯特e. 李[12]？艾森豪威尔？
格鲁乔斯密[13]？泰迪肯尼迪[14]？佛朗哥将军？
卡斯特[15]？有没有可能是何塞梅里斯[16]
曾经说过？或者是唐纳德奥康纳[17]？
我恰巧是图书馆的门房，所以想
请您给我稍微解释一下这些
事。谢谢……另，如果您不能
在这个星期二给我回信，
那我就当上述这些人
实际上全部都是
同一个人……下次见。我得去
把戈黛娃夫人[18]的画像拆下来因为那些
神经学生一个小时内就要来这儿
参观……

你体贴的
大力水手老拧巴

注　释

1　标题可能出自马克·吐温的滑稽幻想小说《一个扬基佬在亚瑟王朝廷》(*A Connecticut Yankee in King Arthur's Court*，1889)。俄基舞 (Oakie)，出自杰克·格思里 (Jack Guthrie，1915—1948) 的老歌《俄基布吉舞》("Oakie Boogie"，1947)，大意：我介绍一种最新的舞步，俄基布吉，你要越跳越快不能停，这就是俄克拉荷马舞步，每个人都要跳到疯了。杰克是伍迪·格思里早逝的堂弟，格思里家是俄克拉荷马人。南北战争时期的俄克拉荷马不属于南方邦联；大萧条时期俄克拉荷马州外出逃荒、打工的流动雇农被称为俄基佬(Okie)。另，杰克·奥基（Jack Oakie，1903—1978)，美国影星，曾在卓别林的《大独裁者》(1940）中扮演拿破仑 / 墨索里尼，迪伦很喜欢这部电影。

2　引自费奥多尔·陀思妥耶夫斯基半自传小说《赌徒》(1866)结尾处，大意讲：赌徒打算重新做人，但又回忆起七个月前自己押上最后一块钱然后大赢一把的刺激经历，暗示今晚再赌一把，重新做人的事明天再说了。

3　贝吉·罗斯夫人（Betsy Ross，1752—1836）受乔治·华盛顿委托缝制了第一面美国国旗。另参见迪伦歌曲《说唱约翰·伯奇偏执狂蓝调》。

4　教友们（society friends)，戏用贵格会的别名“教友派”(Society of Friends)。

5　雨人（Rain Man)，参见迪伦歌曲《我要做你的爱人》。

6　百花夫人(the Flower Lady)，参见迪伦歌曲《准女王简》(“Queen Jane Approximately”，1965)。

7　法比安（Fabiano Forte，1943—　)，当时走红的美国偶像派歌手。另，费边社（Fabian Society)，英国社会民主主义团体，主张渐进改良，代表了英国工党（当时的执政党）的意识形态。

8　亨特利（Chet Huntley，1911—1974）和布林克利（David Brinkley，1920—2003）两人联袂主持了当时广受欢迎的电视新闻。

9　安迪·克莱德（Andy Clyde，1892—1967)，英国电影演员。

10　阿格妮丝·穆尔黑德（Agnes Moorehead，1900—1974)，美国影星。

11　蓝胡子（Bluebeard，Barbe bleue)，法国民间故事中残忍杀害六个妻子的大财主。

12　罗伯特·李（Robert E. Lee，1807—1870)，美国内战时期的

南军元帅。

13 格鲁乔斯密（groucho smith），可能指格鲁乔·马克斯（Groucho Marx，1890—1977），美国笑星，“马克斯兄弟”成员。

14 泰迪肯尼迪（teddy kennedy），指特德·肯尼迪（Ted Kennedy，1932—2009），约翰·肯尼迪总统的幼弟、参议员。

15 卡斯特（custer），指乔治·卡斯特（George Armstrong Custer，1839—1876），美军名将，在与印第安人的战斗中全军覆没。

16 何塞·梅里斯（José Melis，1920—2005），美国古巴裔音乐人。

17 唐纳德·奥康纳（Donald O'Connor，1925—2003），美国歌舞片演员。

18 戈黛娃夫人（Lady Godiva），英国传说中为了让市民们能减免重税而情愿裸体骑马游街的善良贵妇。

Guitars Kissing & the Contemporary Fix

52 along black winds & white fridays, they wash out water & shriek of jungle & lenny immune to the mathematics, he, the greasy quack–the vagabond god...he plants flowers in their saddle bags & speaks of Jesus brave & graduating–tragedy, the broken pride, shallow & no deeper than comedy–bites his path, his noise, his shadow...resign from mind the heart of light & approve the doom, the bending & the farce of happy ending...those that would gas the memory & shut out the might of right, the sight of those defending & offending the blossom girls of the dark, pregnant, permanent & pale outlaw...fair gloria the bowlegged singer, the sign painter's bastard–joanne, raped by the town historian & silver dolly, devirginated at 12, by her father, a miner–maybelle with a chopped up arm from an uncle–doublejointed barbara, who grinds a compact into the face of a druggist & maureen, the jealous lover... none of them raking leaves–ratting on friends who are telephone operators or paying for the like of an e.e. cummings...none of them falling for the "purr lost soul" talk of the hillbilly brawny gospel singer & lenny as the pilgrim angel–the crime but that he reigns in highway christ clothes, boots & a swagger...the lone shark wolf

吉他之吻&当代困境

沿着那些黑风&白色星期五，他们冲洗水分&丛林的尖叫&伦尼[1]对数学免疫，他，这油滑的江湖医生——流浪的神……他在他们的驮囊里种花&谈论耶稣无畏&逐步——悲剧，破碎的骄傲，浅薄&不比喜剧深刻——啃吃他的道路，他的噪声，他的影子……放弃理智那光明的心&赞成厄运、屈服&结局美满的滑稽戏……那些会毒害记忆&遮挡正义的威能，那些防卫&侵犯的景象，黑暗中的如花少女们，妊娠，永生&白皙的歹徒……美美格洛丽娅罗圈腿歌手，广告牌画匠的私生子——琼安妮，被城镇历史学家奸污&银铃多莉，12岁失贞，被她爸，一个矿工——梅贝尔[2]带着叔叔的一条被砍下来的胳膊——柔骨芭芭拉，她在一个药剂师的脸上碾碎了粉盒&莫琳，妒忌的情人……她们没有谁去耙落叶——出卖那些做话务员的朋友或者为诸如e.e.卡明斯[3]之类买单……她们没有谁会为“可怜游魂”把那魁梧山地福音歌手&伦尼当成朝圣天使来谈论就倾倒——他的罪行不过是在主政时身穿公路基督的衣服、靴子[4]&到处显

in a world where piemen castrate the dogs & cities for Du
Pont, cat magazines & hiding in machines they chew gum,
53 their seeds, their portraits...lenny leaves the woodchuck,
the veteran of foreign war to his plymouth 6, his murder
page–the Arms Bros chair & to his kidnapper & the radio
siren/ the communists would call him lazy & the veteran
calls him a bum & yo ho ho & a bottle of rum but he's nice
to priests & dont tangle with the mayor's daughter'n law...
he wears silk & bows to yoyos, barbells & the strangers–he
steals bow ties & heading for the north & waves to soldiers
with amputated hands who picked up broken ashtray
pieces & staying clear of muffled & exploding roosters, he
pets ornaments & twin pipes/ there is a rhapsody to his
toughness & he sure is warm & worthlessly wild

the deer thru the woods quite out of it
all shall never be the slave but the target
for military & freedom's legs having no
substitute for death when sunday professor & the
children come out, say "watch it, you bound to
stumble now!" & the lady in waiting just collapsing
& asked if that's a threat or perhaps a friendly
warming & the innocent coon being scraped on the
table–liberty, an orphan sonnet, unwritten &
having no eyes & needs, no defense & getting
some glass in the veins–the conspiracy to kill

摆……在孤鲨狼的世界里馅饼店为杜邦、猫猫杂志阉割狗&城市&他们藏在机器里嚼口香糖，他们的种子、他们的肖像……伦尼离开土拨鼠，海外战争老兵去找他的普利茅斯6型，他的谋杀跟班——阿姆斯兄弟靠椅&去找他的绑匪&电台警报/共产党人会叫他懒鬼&老兵叫他废物&哟嘀嘀&来瓶朗姆酒[5]但他对牧师很好&不要跟市长的儿媳有什么纠葛……他穿丝袍&俯首于悠悠球、杠铃&陌生人——他偷了领结&一头往北去&挥别那些用残肢捡拾破碎烟灰缸的士兵们&避开那些蒙头&爆炸的公鸡，他抚弄饰带&双排气管/有一部狂文写到他的刚强&他确实是温暖&混乱的荒蛮

小鹿穿过树林离开了很远
决不会成为奴隶只会做军队的
靶子&自由的腿脚没有什么
替代死亡等到星期天教授&那些
孩子们出来，说“当心，你肯定要
绊一跤！”&女侍臣立马就倒了
&被问是不是一个威胁抑或是友善的
温暖[6]&那纯真的浣熊被按在桌上
刮擦——自由，一首零散的十四行诗，未写就&
没有长眼睛&需求，没有防卫&静脉里
流进一些玻璃——那阴谋企图杀死

the free & romantic to custom operating regularly on schedule & attacking now the once that run
54 with no sidecar...go ahead, shoot! all you need is a license & a weak heart

thru the braided hair & loafing beer can beach of wood-brains of the roadhouse & panel trucks filled with cucumber funk, jim beam sweating & lords & ladies in the rear view mirror–humanity in the gang bang mood & yodeling swimmers–the kinks from strike town & itty bitty pretty one lapping up the crankcase rotgut & lenny laughing in a fake sombrero & the jugglers trying to smother the queers & the girls from big city & panoramic way, you found lenny, the dog catcher killer & motorcycle saint–you either love him or hate him–attracting the filthy mamas, Tom the Wretched, Mike the Bull & Hazel, the pornographic back slapper...lenny can take the bad out of you & leave you all good & he can take the good out of you & leave you all bad/ if you think youre smart & know things, lenny plays with your head & he contradicts everything youve been taught about people/ he is not in the history books & he either makes you glad to be you or he makes you hate to be you...you know he's some kind of robber yet you trust him & you cannot ignore him

...the lion's den then, & anchors away & you remember the table–the hopped up table of worldly wiggies & unpatriotics & the slut madonna with her squatter's rights

自由&浪漫让习俗按计划稳步
运行&现在立刻发动攻击
无须挎斗车……前进，开枪！你需要的只是
一张执照&一颗软弱的心

穿过编结的长发&浪荡林际的啤酒罐沙滩——旅店的头头儿们&那些充斥黄瓜味儿、金宾酒臭汗的面包车&后视镜中的老爷&夫人们——群交状态下的人性&唱约德尔的游泳者们[7]——那些来自罢工小镇的变态佬&小不点美人儿狂饮曲轴箱猫尿&伦尼在冒牌阔沿帽后面大笑&那些变戏法的人试图闷死酷儿们&大城市来的姑娘们&全景式地，你发现了伦尼，捕狗队杀手[8]&摩托圣徒——你要么爱他要么恨他——吸引着那些下流婆娘，可怜虫汤姆，壮牛迈克&黑兹尔[9]，一个卖屁股的荡货……伦尼可以祛除你身上的邪气&让你正气满满&他可以祛除你身上的正气&让你邪气满满／如果你觉得自己聪明&知道事情，伦尼就跟你的脑瓜玩耍&他违背了你曾受教的有关为人的一切／他不在历史书上&他要么让你享受你的天性要么就让你憎恨你的天性……你知道他算是某种强盗但你信任他&你无法忽视他

……然后到狮子坑[10]，&起锚[11]&你想到那台桌——满桌子闹翻了天的那些世俗狂汉&不爱国者&享有占住权益的荡妇圣母&个个都性感&指摘偷车贼&某个结结巴

55 & everybody sexy & picking on the car thieves & some bumbling sacred cow telling how he marched right in & trimmed this chicken just like that but when peter pan of the throttle bums gets up to go someplace, it's growling & wondering & sentimental because you know he never does–while gloria talks of the fish in her finger with her hair dyed pink & speaking of tomorrow, calling it sunday & the engine slams & really slams into first gear–& it sounds like john lee hooker coming & oh Lordy louder like a train...the punchdrunk sailor with a scar below his nose suddenly slaps & kicks little sally & makes her let go of the bottoms of his dungarees & you Know he knows something's happening & it aint the ordinary kind of sound that you can see so clearly & carrrrashhhhh & a technicolor passion of berserk & napoleonic & suicide & lenny vanishes in the daytime & a bridge girder all lonesome & gone & the trumpets play what theyve always been taught to play in time of emergency–Babylon's sweetheart & the redblooded boy oozing all over & shock, the defunct rockabilly in a blindfold–dissolve into the motherland for touch & kneeling to instinct, gypsies & into the most northernmost forest he can find

...a roaring free for all is witnessed later between as
follows: rabbit seller, who, because he lives in a room
where the rain continues to fall thru the chimney, always
has a chronic cough & is constantly in an al capone type
56 mood–call him White Man/ the ex faggot g.i., who now
transports dummies from macy's to yankee stadium &
whose ears always bleed in heavy weather–call him Black
Man/ the hatcheck girl with a glass eye, whose father

巴的神牛讲起他怎样勇往直前&给这只鸡仔修剪修剪就像那样子但是当掐脖流浪汉们的彼得潘收拾整齐要去某个地方的时候，它在低吼&惊诧&感伤因为你知道他从没做过——这时格洛丽娅谈到她手指上的鱼[12]她的头发染成粉红&说到明天，称之为星期天&引擎猛撞&真的猛撞进一档——&那声音像约翰李胡克[13]来了&哦老天爷老大声了像一趟火车……那个在鼻子下面有个伤疤的晕菜水手突然掌掴&脚踹小莎莉[14]&叫她松开他工装裤的裆部&你知道他知道有些事情在发生[15]&它不是那种司空见惯的声音让你看得清清楚楚&车嗡冲哧呜撞啊&一部彩色的狂暴者受难记&拿破仑式的&自杀&伦尼在大白天消失&一座大桥孤零零的桁梁&远去&小号吹响它们一直被教导要在危急时刻吹响的曲调——巴比伦的心上人&热血男儿浑身泄漏&震撼，已故山地摇滚[16]蒙着眼罩——触动间便融入祖国&膜拜本能，吉卜赛&融入他所能找到的最北方的森林

……一场闹腾的大混战后来证明有如下参与者：兔子贩，他住在一个不断从烟囱里漏雨下来的房间，所以患上慢性咳嗽&经常有一种阿尔卡彭[17]类型的心态——称他为白人／前基佬大兵，他知道怎样把假人从梅西百货运到扬基体育场&他的耳朵在恶劣天气总是流血——称他为黑人／镶了颗玻璃眼的衣帽间小妞，她爸爸曾教她怎样像P.T.巴纳姆[18]那样走路&现在她

taught her how to walk exactly like P.T. Barnum &
now she discovers it means nothing–call her Audience/
the candle stick maker, with a mouthful of plastic &
his pockets full of used matches–call him Reward/ the
bathing beauty who wear a turban full of meatballs–call
her Success/ the tug of war rope & a holy bell–boom &
the pumphouse guardian stepping out of his coocoo &
saying "words are objects! sight is ego! did any of you
freaks ever know a lenny? i can remember his last
name..." & then some vigilante, he say "get back in your
clock! you ever heard of lions one, christians nothing?"
& after sending hitler out to murder the poor guardian,
he jumps back into the christians & clocks & all types
of mink, milk & vitamin C–grannies in titepants &
barechested undertakers goosing preachers wearing egg
cartons & U.N. generals in bathrobes & their feet stuck
in bongo drums & three million jealous teachers in used
roy acuff strings all flunking little de gaulles & prison
choruses bursting & singing hallaluyah...everybody even
Good St. Doc & the bird scientist sucking scruples &
nipples & trying to hide their shit...everybody saying
"disaster!" & pointing & examining hanging clowns
& making reports & going "gah gah" at dead pontiacs
& babies in Lorca graves...the tax collector stealing
57 everybody's useless sacrifice & H.G. Wells unheeded...
Lulu the Smith having a heart attack at the birth of a
black angel & john brown, Luke the snob & Achilles all
reaching for the Flying Saucer...one day, the day of the
Tambourines, the astronaut, Micky McMicky, will remove
a thumb from his mouth–say "go to hell" while lenny i'm
sure is already in a resentful heaven

发现这毫无意义——称她为观众／烛台匠，一嘴的塑料&他的口袋装满用过的火柴——称他为奖金／入浴美人裹着一条挂满肉丸子的头巾——称她为成功／拉拔河的绳索&一个圣钟——轰隆&水泵房看守走出他的咕咕鸟&说“语词即对象[19]！视野即自我！你们这帮怪胎有谁认识伦尼的吗？我只记得他的姓……”&这时有个治安队的过来，他说“回你的时钟去！你可听说过狮子一顶一，基督徒算球？”&把希特勒派去谋杀那可怜的看守之后，他又跳回基督徒&时钟&各式各样的貂皮、牛奶&维生素C——那些包臀裤老太太&裸胸殡葬师戳着挂鸡蛋盒纸板的布道家屁股&披浴袍的联合国将军们&他们的大脚卡在小手鼓里&三百万妒忌的教师在二手罗伊阿卡夫[20]琴弦中叫小戴高乐们全都挂科&监狱合唱团轰响&高唱哈拉路亚……所有人甚至包括好心的圣医者[21]&鸟类科学家小口啜着微滴&奶头&试图隐藏他们的狗屎……所有人都说着“有祸了！”&指点着&审查着吊挂小丑们&写着报告&对洛尔卡墓中那些死去的庞蒂亚克[22]&婴儿们大叫“嘎嘎”……税吏偷窃所有人的无用祭牲&H.G.威尔斯[23]没人注意……铁匠家的露露在黑天使诞生时犯了心脏病&约翰布朗[24]，势利鬼路加&阿喀琉斯全都抵达那个飞天盘……有一天，铃鼓之日[25]，宇航员米奇麦克米奇会从他嘴里抽出大拇指——说“见鬼去吧”至于伦尼我敢肯定早已经上了愤懑的天堂

dear dropout magazine,

gentlemen:

i understand that you are currently
putting a book together about
blacklisted or blackheaded artists or something.
if it is the former, then i shall have to
recommend that you place jerry lee lewis first
an foremost. if it is the latter, then i shall
have to recommend that you contact the
american
medical society to discover the exact worth of
such an undertaking

in all respects, i remain
a rabble rouser from the mountains
Zeke the Cork

亲爱的辍学杂志，
先生们：
我明白你们目前正在
拼凑一本书来搜罗
那些上了黑名单或长了黑头粉刺的艺术家
之类。
若是前者，那我就必须
推荐你们把杰瑞李刘易斯[26]放在第一位
打头。若是后者，那我就
必须推荐你们联系美国
医学会以便认识这种工作的
真正价值

在各个方面，我仍是
一个来自山区的暴民煽动家
<u>瓶塞子泽克</u>

注 释

1 伦尼（lenny），可能指伦尼·布鲁斯（Lenny Bruce，1925—1966），美国笑星，言论自由运动偶像，爱在即兴节目中爆粗口讽刺时事，多次因猥亵表演罪被捕，死于吸毒。迪伦在1981年为他创作了同名纪念歌曲。

2 梅贝尔（maybelle），可能指梅贝尔·卡特（Maybelle Carter，1909—1978），美国乡村女歌手，卡特家族演唱团成员。

3 E. E. 卡明斯（1894—1962），美国现代诗人，以语言创新闻名，如不使用大写字母、词类活用、别出心裁的诗行排列等。《狼蛛》也可算是一个“E. E. 卡明斯之类”的实验作品。

4 参见《新约·马太福音》27:35，耶稣被钉十字架时，士兵抓阄瓜分了他的衣服。

5 “哟嗬嗬，来瓶朗姆酒”（yo ho ho & a bottle of rum），出自史蒂文森小说《金银岛》（*Treasure Island*,1883）中的海盗歌《亡灵宝藏》（“Dead Man’s Chest”）。

6 温暖（warming），音近“警告”（warning）。

7 约德尔（yodeling），来回快速变换真假嗓音的民歌唱法。据说歌手“约德尔牛仔”布里特(Elton Britt,1913—1972)在潜泳时练唱。

8 捕狗队（dog catcher），戏指最底层官僚。伦尼·布鲁斯可以把人笑死。

9 黑兹尔（Hazel），参见迪伦歌曲《黑兹尔》（“Hazel”，1974）。

10 狮子坑（the lion’s den），参见《旧约》故事：先知但以理被国王扔进狮子坑，上帝差遣使者封住狮子的口，让他不受伤害。也出自苏格兰同名民谣。

11 起锚（anchors away），可能指美国海军军歌《起锚歌》（“Anchors Aweigh”，1906），作曲者查尔斯·齐默曼（Charles A. Zimmermann，1861—1916）和鲍勃·迪伦本名同姓。

12 她手指上的鱼（the fish in her finger），可能指英式小吃炸鱼条（fish fingers）。

13 约翰·李·胡克（John Lee Hooker，1912—2001），美国蓝调歌手，民谣界的电吉他先驱之一，乐风较随性，说话口吃。迪伦初到纽约时做过他的暖场乐手。

14 小莎莉（Little Sally）的名字常见于儿歌游戏。

15 参见迪伦歌曲《瘦人歌》：“因为这里正有事情发生 / 但你却不知道是什么 / 对不对，琼斯先生？”

16 山地摇滚（rockabilly），一种融合了山地民谣（hillbilly）等音乐元素的早期摇滚乐形式，猫王普雷斯利即其代表。

17　阿尔·卡彭（Al Capone，1899—1947），美国黑手党头目，绰号“刀疤脸”（Scarface），他的形象在大量文艺作品中出现。迪伦在自传《编年史》中说他既不有趣也不英勇，冷冰冰的，像一条鲫鱼，从不独自活动，根本不配有个绰号。

18　巴纳姆（P. T. Barnum，1810—1891），美国马戏团老板，被誉为“最伟大的演艺人”。

19　“语词即对象”（words are objects），参见美国当代哲学家蒯因（Willard Van Orman Quine，1908—2000）著作《语词和对象》（*Word and Object*，1960）。

20　罗伊·阿卡夫（Roy Acuff，1903—1992），美国歌手，被誉为“乡村音乐之王”，主要用小提琴伴奏。

21　好心的圣医者（Good St. Doc），可能指圣路加，《新约》中《路加福音》和《使徒行传》的作者，他原来的职业是医生。

22　庞蒂亚克（Pontiac，1720—1769），北美印第安酋长，曾领导了五大湖区印第安人反英大暴动。

23　H. G. 威尔斯（H. G. Wells，1866—1946），英国作家，以科幻小说闻名，如《隐身人》。

24　约翰布朗（john brown），可能指美国废奴运动领袖约翰·布朗（John Brown，1800—1858），因暴动失败被绞死。

25　铃鼓之日（the day of the Tambourines）一句，参见迪伦歌曲《铃鼓先生》：“带我远行吧，乘上你的飞旋魔法船……”

26　杰瑞·李·刘易斯（Jerry Lee Lewis，1935— ），美国歌手，因1958年与年仅13岁的表妹结婚而轰动一时，并因此被电台网封杀，他的现场演唱非常狂野，被称为“摇滚乐第一大狂人”。

Advice to Hobo's Model

58 paint your shoes delilah–ye walk on white snow where a nosebleed would disturb the universe...down these narrow alleys of owls an flamenco guitar players, jack paar an other sex symbols are your prizes–check into the bathrooms where bird lives for when he comes flying out with a saber in his wing–a country music singer by his side–digesting a carrier pigeon...ye just might change your style of fornicating, sword swallowing–ye just might change your way of sleeping on nails–paint your shoes the color of the ghost mule–the paper tiger's teeth are made of aluminum–youve a long time to Babylon–paint your shoes delilah–paint them with a sponge

look! like i told you before, it doesnt
matter where it's at! there's no such
thing. it's where it's not at that you
gotta know. so what if tony married his
mother! what's it got to do with your life?
i really have no idea why youre so unhappy.

给模范盲流的忠告

涂涂你的鞋吧黛利拉[1]——你走在白雪地上哪怕一滴鼻血都会扰乱宇宙……走进猫头鹰和弗拉明戈吉他手们的这些狭窄巷道[2]，杰克帕尔[3]及其他性感明星都是你的奖赏——核查大鸟[4]住过的那些卫生间当时他在翅膀上挂着长刀飞了出来——他身边有个乡村音乐歌手——正在消化一只信鸽……你也许会改变你通奸、吞剑的风格——你也许会改变你在钉床上睡觉的方式——涂涂你的鞋吧用幽灵骡子的颜色——纸老虎的利牙是铝制的[5]——你有大把时间去巴比伦——涂涂你的鞋吧黛利拉——用一块海绵来涂

瞧！就像我以前说的，不论它
在哪里都没关系！根本没有这种
东西。它在哪里都不是你
非要知道的事情。托尼娶了他
老母又怎样！跟你的生活有关吗？
我真搞不明白为什么你那么不开心。

perhaps you ought to change your line of
work. you know. like how long can someone
of your caliber continue to paint pencil
59 sharpeners...see you next summer, good to
know youre off the wagon.

premeturely yours,

Funka

也许你要改变一下你的工作
行当。你懂的。要是能有
你这样的才具谁还会继续画那
卷笔刀呢……明年夏天见，很高兴
知道你又开戒了。

你永永的，
<u>疯卡</u>

注　释

1　黛利拉（delilah），参见《旧约·士师记》16:4–22，力士参孙被他的情妇大利拉（Delilah）出卖。另参见迪伦歌曲《墓碑蓝调》。

2　“狭窄巷道”（narrow alleys），与上文的“扰乱宇宙”（disturb the universe）一语分别出自艾略特诗《J. 阿尔弗雷德·普鲁弗洛克的情歌》（*The Love Song of J. Alfred Prufrock*，1920）中“我是否该说，我已在黄昏穿过狭窄街道”（Shall I say, I have gone at dusk through narrow streets）一句，和“我是否敢于 / 扰乱宇宙”（Do I dare/Disturb the universe）一句。

3　杰克·帕尔（Jack Paar，1918—2004），美国深夜脱口秀节目主持人。

4　大鸟（bird），可能指美国爵士乐手查理·帕克（Charlie Parker，1920—1955）的绰号。

5　赫鲁晓夫在回应中国指责苏联对美国绥靖时说：“把帝国主义称为纸老虎的人应该记住纸老虎有核武器牙齿。”

A Blast of Loser Take Nothing

jack of spades–vivaldi of the coin laundry–wearing a
hipster's dictionary–we see him brownnosing around
the blackbelts & horny racing car drivers–dashing to &
fro like a frightened uncle remus...on days that he gets
no mail he rises early, sticks paper up the pay phones &
cons the bubble gum machines..."the world owes me a
living" he says to his half–hawaiian cousin, the half–wit,
joe the head who is also planning to marry a folksinger
next month–"round & round, old joe clark" is being
recited from the steps of the water & light building as
jack ambles by with a case full of plastic bubbles–things
look well for him: he can imitate cary grant pretty good.
60 he knows all the facts why mabel from utah walked out
on horace, the lightingman from Theatre Altitude. he
has even stumbled onto a few hairy secrets of mrs. Cunk,
who sells fake blisters at the world's fair–plus being able
to play a few foreign legion songs on the yoyo & always
managing to look like a grapefruit in case of emergency...
he brags about his collection of bruises & corks & the
fact that he pays no attention to the business world. he
would rather show his fear of the bomb & say what have
you done for freedom than to praise an escaped mental

输家通失狂欢会

黑桃杰克——投币洗衣房的维瓦尔第[1]——揣着一本嬉普士词典[2]——我们看到他在巴结那些黑带&色眯眯的赛车手们——来&回冲杀像一个受惊吓的雷木斯大叔[3]……在他没收到邮件的日子，他就早早起床，给投币电话贴纸&欺骗泡泡糖售卖机……“世界欠我一个生活”他告诉他的半夏威夷、半智人士老表大头乔，此人也计划下个月跟一个民谣歌手结婚——“转啊&转啊，老乔克拉克”[4]在供水&供电大楼的台阶上被吟诵而杰克提着一个塞满塑料泡泡的箱子慢慢溜达——在他看来一切顺利：他可以模仿加里格兰特[5]惟妙惟肖。他知道所有真相为什么来自犹他州的梅布尔会抛弃贺拉斯，来自高峰剧院的灯光师。他甚至撞破了坎克夫人的秘密，她在世界博览会上卖冒牌水疱——加上能够用悠悠球演奏几首外籍军团歌曲&遇到紧急情况总是努力做出一副葡萄柚的模样……他吹嘘他收藏的淤肿&瓶塞&他实际上对工商界毫无兴趣。他宁可表露他对炸弹的恐惧&说说你为自由付出了什么而不是赞美一个逃逸的精神病患那种在

patient who pissed on the floor of junior's delicatessen–
jack of spades, with his axe, the record player. with his
companion, the menu. & his destination, a piece of
kleenex–never touches the cracks on the sidewalk–"jack"
says his other cousin, Bodeguard, half danish & half
surfer, "how come you always act like Crazy, jackie
gleason's friend? i mean wow! aint there enough sadness
in the world?" jack walks by in a flash–he wears ear
plugs–from the steps of the water & light building, the
band, after knocking all the juice out of their horns,
begin to play on my papa...jack, shocked, takes a second
look, raises his hand in a nazi salute. a woodsman,
walking by with an axe, drops it. a D.A.R. woman
flies off the handle. looks at jack. says "in some places,
you'd be arrested for obscenity" she doesnt even hear
the band...she falls down a sidewalk crack/ the band
leader, paying no attention, does a slight curtsy, sneezes.
points his wand at the classical guitar...a street cleaner
61 bumps into jack & says & i quote "o.k. so i bumped into
you. i dont even care. i got me a little woman at home.
i know a good radiator down the block. man, i aint
never gonna starve. would you like to buy a pail?" jack,
amazed, rearranges his collar & heads off to the bell
telephone hour. which is located beyond the next cop
car...he passes a hot dog stand. a sauerkraut hits him in
the face...the band is playing malaguena salerosa–the
D.A.R. woman pops out of the sidewalk, hears the band,
screams, starts doing the jerk. the street cleaner steps on
her...jack hasnt eaten all day. his mouth tastes funny–he
has his unpublished novel in his hand–he wants to be a

朱尼尔熟食店地板上撒尿的人——黑桃杰克，提着他的斧子，电唱机。领着他的同伴，菜单。&他的目的地，一张纸巾——从不沾惹人行道上的那些裂缝——他的另一个老表保膘，半丹麦裔&半冲浪员，说，“杰克，你的动作怎么总像老疯儿，杰基格里森[6]的朋友？我是说真牛！这世界的忧伤已经够多了不是吗？[7]”杰克的脚步一闪而过——他戴着耳塞——从供水&供电大楼的台阶，乐队把他们喇叭里的汁水敲干净了，然后开始演奏我的老爸[8]……杰克被震住了，又多看一眼，举起他的手敬纳粹礼。一个林里人，提着斧子走过，丢下它。一个革女会[9]的娘们怒不可遏。看着杰克。说“在有些地方，你这就是犯猥亵要给抓进去的”她都没听乐队……她掉进一个人行道裂缝/乐队指挥不理不睬，只微微屈膝，打喷嚏。把指挥棒点点古典吉他……一个街道清洁工撞到了杰克&说&我引用如下“好吧是我撞你了。我才不在乎。我屋里还有个婆姨等我呢。我知道楼那边有个散热器好使。哥们，我永远不会饿疯了。你要不要买一个桶？[10]”杰克被唬住了，整整他的衣领&调头去听贝尔电话时段[11]。就在另一辆警车那边……他经过热狗摊。一头酸白菜直砸到他的脸上……乐队演奏马拉加美人[12]——革女会娘们从人行道蹦了出来，听着乐队，尖叫着，开始跳抽抽[13]。街道清洁工一脚踩她身上……杰克一整天都没吃东西了。他那嘴里的味道真够呛——他把他没出版的小说捧在手里——他想当明星——但他终

star–but he gets arrested anyway

hi y'all. not much new happening.
sang at the vegetarian convention
my new song against meat. everybody
dug it except for the plumbers neath
the stage. this one little girl,
fresh out of college & i believe
president of the Dont Stomp Out the
Cows division of the society. she tried
to push me into one of the plumbers.
starts a little chaos going, but you
know me, i didnt go for that not one
little bit. i say "look baby, i'll sing
62 for you & all that, but just you dont
go pushing me, y'hear?" i understand
that theyre not gonna invite me back
cause they didnt like the way i came on
to the master of ceremony's old lady, all
in all, i'm making it tho. got a new song
against cigarette lighters. this matchbook
company offered me free matches for the rest
of my life, plus my picture on all the
matchbooks, but you know me, it'd take a
helluva lot more'n that before i'd sell out–

究还是被抓进去了

大家好。没什么新鲜事。
我在素食者大会上唱
反对吃肉的新歌。人人
都喜欢除了舞台底下的那些
管子工。这个小小丫头，
才刚出校门&我相信
协会的<u>不许践踏</u>
<u>奶生</u>分部主席。她还老想
逼我去做一个管子工。
开头有点小混乱，但你
知道我的，我压根不会
那样做。我说“瞧好了宝贝，我给你
唱上一曲&诸如此类，但你不能
再逼我，听到没？”我明白
他们不会再请我回去
因为他们不喜欢我那样去勾搭
晚会主持人的老太太，不管
怎么说，我还就那么干。又写了首新歌
是反对打火机的。这家火柴
公司为我下半辈子提供免费的
火柴，还有在所有火柴盒上
印我的头像，但你懂我的，这可是
比我从前卖的高了老鼻子去了——

see you around nomination time

your fellow rebel

kid tiger

获得提名的时候再见

你的叛匪同党

老虎崽

注 释

1 维瓦尔第（Antonio Vivaldi，1678—1741），意大利神父，作曲家，小提琴演奏家。参见迪伦《重访61号国道》唱片文案。

2 嬉普士词典（hipster's dictionary），指美国爵士乐手凯布·卡洛威（Cab Calloway，1907—1994）著《嬉普士词典》（*Hepster's Dictionary: Language of Jive*，1939），其中收录了黑人爵士乐界的行话俚语。

3 雷木斯大叔（Uncle Remus），出自美国作家哈里斯（Joel Chandler Harris，1848—1908）寓言故事中一个爱讲故事的老黑人。

4 老乔克拉克（old joe clark），出自美国传统民谣《老乔克拉克》（"Old Joe Clark"），伍迪·格思里曾唱过。

5 加里·格兰特（Cary Grant，1904—1986），美国著名影星，以英俊潇洒而闻名。

6 杰基·格里森（Jackie Gleason，1916—1987），美国著名喜剧演员，在电影《江湖浪子》（*The Hustler*，1961）中扮演"明尼苏达胖子"一角广受好评。

7 可能出自英国作家E. M. 福斯特小说《看得见风景的房间》（*A Room with a View*，1908），是资产阶级小姐露西安于现状时的心声，参见巫漪云译本，上海译文出版社2007版第34页。

8 《我的老爸》（"My Papa"），20世纪50年代流行歌曲，源自德国。

9 美国革命女儿协会（Daughters of the American Revolution，D.A.R.），美国老牌保守组织。

10　英国传统童谣《杰克和吉尔》中有两人提水的情节。

11　贝尔电话时段（The Bell Telephone Hour），美国电台古典音乐节目，由贝尔公司赞助。又指越战美军刑讯手段。

12　《马拉加美人》（“Malagueña Salerosa”），20 世纪 50 年代流行歌曲，源自墨西哥。

13　抽抽舞（jerk）兴起于 1964 年。

making love on maria's friend

yawn to foxy queenie school teacher–gone, decatur
& entering the pink highway–your black mongrel
vagabond, your rat from Delphi–now he shall tattle
63 on your nauseous bra–your hair in chains & speak TU
CAMINO while your El Paso ideals, they celebrate ES
TERCIOPELO they leave your gruesome body–your
structure falling, you listen for a lazy siren & some young
Spaniard to buy your wounds, your pregnant drawl...yawn
to queenie of the Goya painting seeking poor Homer
QUEDATE CONMIGO while the dikes break & count
your number & Baby Mean crying NO PREDENDAS
while author Fritz from your industrial south yelling
what's this all about & get the hell home, queenie & you,
queenie, the spider–the sweat web's got you–you beg
your arms to move–you pray to be righteous–you look
for postcards & teddy bears for payoffs–the partisans,
they laugh CON TUS PIERNAS & the boys with brown
rags, they whisper of the bust & already they have Leo
the Sneak & Doc's gonna have to leave by noon–St. Willy
hides in the pawnshop PARA QUEENIE you need
not fear & nobody's chasing–you want to be held LA

跟玛丽亚的朋友做爱[1]

向狐狸精奎妮老师打个哈欠——走了走了，迪凯特[2]&进入粉红公路——你的黑皮杂种流浪汉，你的德尔斐耗子——现在他怕是在瞎掰你的邋遢胸罩——你的锁链长发&说起**你的道路**[3]而你那些埃尔帕索[4]楷模，他们颂扬**丝般顺滑**他们丢开你受束缚的肉体——你的身架倒落，你留神听着一声懒懒的警笛&有个年轻的西班牙佬来收买你的创伤，你的意味深长的拖腔……向戈雅画中寻求可怜荷马的奎妮打个哈欠**与我同行吧**而堤坝溃决&清点你的数目&辣手宝贝大叫**不要假装**而作家弗里茨从你的南方工业区嚷嚷这都是怎么回事儿&滚你妈的老家去，奎妮&你，奎妮，蜘蛛——那汗臭的网罗套住了你——你乞求你的胳膊能挪开——你祈祷要行得正直——你寻找明信片&泰迪熊作回报——党徒们，他们取笑**你的大腿**&小伙子们披着褐色破布，他们嘀咕着胸围&他们早已经逮到了溜子里奥&多克到中午就必须得离开了——圣威利躲在当铺里**等奎妮**你不用怕&没有人在追——你想要被捉住**错误的女人**&挖空你的钱包——

ERRONEA DAMA & dig into your purse–forget your
pupils & pay for your partner & botheration–the shadow
of your boss, it is your felony–author Fritz would like to
suck your toe–your holiday be gone soon & vanishing like
your life LA CHOTA the grass cuts your feet & Socrates'
Prison is your goal AHI VIENEN you are the wrong
lady–you threaten nobody–spend your money on health
food & you shall be run over by a truck–they'll put a tag
on you–send you home to Fritz–Fritz will cry for a week
64 & marry your nurse–the dikes will curl their mouths
but you'll still be the wrong one TODOS SON DE LA
CHOTA live now...live before you board your Titanic–
reach out, Queenie, reach out–feel for equal saggy skin &
believe this dark playboy licking ink from your notebook–
see the cages & screaming ghosts & you with the gall to
think that ruins are buildings...take your bloody glands
& medallion & make love once freely–it means nothing
so wear a top hat–travel on a slow ship back to your guilt,
your pollution, the kingdom of your blues

hi. watcha doing? how's the new religion?
feel any different? gave it up myself. just
couldnt make all the auctions and frankly,
i's running out of bread. you know how it
is, like about that little old lady in the
back building all the time pointing telling
me that God is watching. you know, like for a
while there, i's scared to take a shit. anxious

忘了你那些学生吧&付钱给你的伙伴&讨厌鬼——你老板的影子，那是你的重罪——作家弗里茨会乐意给你舔脚趾的——你的假期马上就结束了&像你的生命那样消逝**羊羔**草叶割破你的脚&苏格拉底的牢狱是你的目标**他们过来了**你是那个错误的女人——你吓唬不了谁——把你的钱花在健康食品上&你应该被一辆卡车碾死——他们会给你挂上标签——送你回家给弗里茨——弗里茨会哭上一个星期&跟你的护士结婚——堤坝会噘起它们的嘴巴但你仍旧会是那个错误的人**都是羊羔而已**现在活着……活在你登上你的泰坦尼克之前——伸手啊，奎妮，伸手啊——去抚摸同样松弛的皮肤&要相信这个漆黑的花花公子从你的笔记本上舔墨水——看看那些笼子&尖叫的鬼魂&你带着恼恨把那些废墟视为建筑……带上你那身血糊糊的腺体&奖章&自由自在地做一次爱——戴上大礼帽也没什么特别的——乘着一条慢船回归你的罪孽，你的污染，你的蓝调王国

嘿。干啥呢？那个新宗教怎么样？
觉得有点不同？我自动放弃了。真是
无法干完所有的拍卖而且说实话，
我的面包快吃光了。你知道是怎么
回事，就像那个小老太太住在
后楼里整天都跟我指指点点
说上帝在看着。你懂的，就像刚才
还在那儿，我要被吓出屎来了。切盼

to get together with you. i know you dont wear bow ties anymore but i'm interested in other aspects of your new faith too. by the way, are you still in the keyhole business? cant wait to talk to you

bye,
your buddy,
Testy

能与你一聚。我知道你已经不再戴
领结了但我对你的新宗教的其他方面
同样很感兴趣。另外，你是否
还干钥匙孔的买卖？真等不及想
跟你谈谈

回见，
你的哥们，
<u>老烦</u>

注　释

1　标题原文为小写，是本书唯一的小写标题。

2　迪凯特（Decatur），可能指美国伊利诺伊州城市，林肯的起家之地，或拉斯维加斯的主干道迪凯特大街（Decatur Boulevard）。

3　本章黑体字部分原文均为西班牙语。

4　埃尔帕索（El Paso），美国得克萨斯州城市，毗邻墨西哥，由马提·罗宾斯（Marty Robbins，1925—1982）演唱的同名乡村歌曲是1959年的大热门。参见迪伦歌曲《现在她是你的爱人了》（"She's Your Lover Now"，1966）："每一个纠结的人都在爬城堡的旋梯 / 但我不在你的城堡之中 / 真的，我完全不记得圣弗朗西斯科 / 我根本想不起埃尔帕索 / 你不必对我忠贞 / 我也不想让你悲伤 / 没什么难的 / 如果你不想跟我在一起，那就走吧？"

Note to the Errand Boy as a Young Army Deserter

wonder why granpa just sits there & watches yogi bear? wonder why he just sits there & dont laugh? think about it kid, but dont ask your mother. wonder why elvis presley only smiles with his top lip? think about it kid, but dont ask your surgeon. wonder why the postman with one leg shorter'n the other kicked your dog so hard? think about it kid, but dont ask any mailman. wonder who ronald reagan talked to about the foreign situation? think about it kid, but dont ask any foreigners. wonder why the mechanic, whose wife shot herself with a gun she got from his best friend, hates castro so much? wonder why castro hates rock n roll? think about it kid, but dont ask no roll. wonder how much the man who wrote white christmas made? think about it, but dont ask no made. wonder what bobby kennedy's really got against jimmy hoffa? think about it, but dont ask no bobby. wonder why frankie shot johnny? go ahead, wonder, but dont ask your neighbor...wonder who the carpet baggers are? think, but dont ask no carpet. wonder why youre always wearing your brother's clothes? think about it kid, but dont ask your father. wonder why general electric says

给一个身为年轻逃兵的跑腿小子的短信

想知道为什么爷爷老坐在那儿&看瑜伽熊[1]吗？想知道为什么他老坐在那儿&一笑不笑吗？自己琢磨一下孩子，别去问你老妈。想知道为什么埃尔维斯普雷斯利只用他的上嘴唇笑吗？自己琢磨一下孩子，别去问你的外科医生。想知道为什么那个邮差一条腿比另一条腿短一截的踢起你的狗来那么狠吗？自己琢磨一下孩子，别去问任何邮递员。想知道跟罗纳德里根[2]谈论国外局势的是哪位吗？自己琢磨一下孩子，别去问任何外国人。想知道为什么那个机械师，就是他老婆从他好友那儿搞来手枪然后自杀了的，他为什么那么恨卡斯特罗[3]吗？想知道为什么卡斯特罗恨摇滚乐吗？自己琢磨一下孩子，别去问不摇的。想知道那个写雪白圣诞[4]的人挣了多少吗？自己琢磨一下，别去问没挣着的。想知道波比肯尼迪[5]到底抓住了吉米霍法什么吗？自己琢磨一下，别去问不懂波比的。想知道为什么弗兰姬要枪杀约翰尼[6]？琢磨去吧，想一想，但别去问你的邻居……想知道提包客[7]都是些什么人吗？琢磨一下，别去问不提包的。想知道为什么你总是要穿你兄弟的衣服吗？自己琢磨一下孩子，

that the most important thing for a family to do is stick
together? think about it kid, but dont ask no together...
66 wonder what is paydirt is? go ahead, wonder...wonder
why the other boys wanna beat you up so bad? think
about it kid, but dont ask nobody

yes. ok. i guess youre a pumpkin.
yes, it's true i referred to you as "that
chinese girl" you have a right to
be angry. but what i want to know
is just what have you got against
the chinese anyway?
maybe we can still work
it out
properly yours,
prince goulash

别去问你老爸。想知道为什么通用电气说一个家庭最重要的事情是团结？自己琢磨一下孩子，别去问不抱团的……想知道大发横财是什么吗？去琢磨吧，想想……想知道为什么别的孩子都想狠狠揍你一顿吗？自己琢磨一下孩子，别去问任何人

对。好。我猜你是个南瓜宝贝。
对，我确实把你称为“那个
中国姑娘”你有权利
生气。但我只想弄明白
你到底为什么会反感
中国人？

也许我们还是可以搞
清楚
你专有的，
炖肉王子

注　释

1　瑜伽熊（Yogi Bear），1961 年汉纳－巴伯拉（Hanna-Barbera）公司推出的动画片形象。

2　罗纳德·里根（Ronald Reagan，1911—2004），原为电影演员和知名电视主持人，曾任美国演员协会（SAG）主席，1964 年发表演讲力挺美国共和党总统候选人巴里·戈德华特，1966 年成功当选加利福尼亚州州长。

3 参见迪伦歌曲《汽车惊魂噩梦》（“Motorpsycho Nightmare”，1964）。

4 《雪白圣诞》（“White Christmas”，1942），美国 20 世纪最流行的歌曲之一，作者欧文·伯林（Irving Berlin，1888—1989）。

5 波比肯尼迪（bobby kennedy），指罗伯特·F. 肯尼迪（Robert F. Kennedy，1925—1968），绰号“波比”（Bobby），是约翰·F. 肯尼迪的弟弟，曾任美国司法部长、国会参议员，曾指控美国卡车司机公会（IBT）及其主席吉米·霍法（Jimmy Hoffa，1913—1975）劳工欺诈和有组织犯罪，当时的调查组叫“抓住霍法”。

6 在美国传统民谣《弗兰姬和约翰尼》（“Frankie and Johnny”）中，弗兰姬杀死了偷情的丈夫或男友约翰尼，自己也被打入死牢。由猫王埃尔维斯·普雷斯利主演的同名电影于 1966 年春上映。

7 提包客（carpetbagger），原指美国内战结束后涌到南方被占地区大捞一票的北方人，讽刺外来的投机分子。畅销小说《提包客》（*The Carpetbaggers*，1961）及同名热门电影（1964）是“性解放”时代的重要作品。

Taste of Shotgun

the roar of our engines promises us cover–we wear
choking pants & are slaves to appetite–we get stoned
67 on joan crawford & form teeming colonies & die of
masculine conversation...Marcellus, wearing khaki when
madness struck him, immediately filed suit against an
illegitimate son belonging to someone else–Josie said
everybody at the trial came with a blowgun...Tom Tom
made Melodius hate him, then jumped from a window–
we are all alike & place scorpions neatly in our insides–
we take pills thru the ass–we praise faggot missionaries
& throw homosexuals into phenomenon gutters...in the
winter a blackface musician announces he is from Two
Women–he spends his free time trying to peel the moon
& he's here to collect his eight cent stamp–Marguerita
the pusher, wheeling a cartful of Thursday up Damaen's
Row yelling "cockles & muscles," kills him for getting
in the way of her appetite...the rewards are few on
Chemical Isle–little girls hide perfume up their shrimps
& there are no giants–the warmongers have stolen all
our german measles & are giving them to the doctors to
use as bribes–i stayed awake for three hours last nite with
Pearl–she claimed to have walked by a rooming house i

霰弹枪的滋味

我们的轰隆引擎给我们提供掩护——我们穿上束身裤&都是食欲的奴隶——我们痴迷琼克劳馥&组建繁庶的殖民地&渴求雄性对话……马塞卢斯[1]，犯魔怔的时候就穿卡其制服，他立刻起诉了别人家的一个私生子——乔西[2]说每个出庭的人都带着吹箭……通通鼓致使旋律美憎恨他，然后跳出了窗户——我们都相差不离&在内心里巧妙地藏着一只蝎子——我们从屁眼吃药——我们赞美基佬宣教使团&把同性恋都投进现象阴沟……在冬天有一个黑面乐手宣告他来自两个女人[3]——他把闲暇时间都花在试图给月亮剥皮[4]&他来这里收集他的八分钱邮票——玛格丽塔[5]小贩[6]，推着满车的星期四[7]上达曼恩路吆喝“蛤蚌&肌肉，”[8]因为挡了她的饕餮之路就把他宰掉……化学岛上薪资微薄——小姑娘们在她们的小虾米藏起香水&那里没有巨人——战争贩子已盗走我们所有的德国麻疹[9]&把它们送给医生用来行贿——我昨晚有三个小时不眠不睡地陪着珍珠——她声称她曾路经我从前住过的寄宿

once lived in–we had nothing in common, me & Pearl–
i shared her boredom & had nothing to give her–i was
drunk & entertained myself...we wish to make journeys
& use everything excpt our feet & we meet tongue tied
broken vulgar geeks with gorilla handshakes & drunken
Hercules waits for us on our beds & we must salute him
& he says that the new helicopters have arrived & "this
68 is your geek" & "you will take your orders from him"
yes the rewards are few here but there are no oaths to
take nor mental strokes–excpt for the self conscious
insanity brought in by hunters with radios wearing
religious clothes, all goes well...Angola being bombed
this morning, i right now am happy with nausea–my head
is suffocating–i am gazing into the big dipper with silver
buttoned blouse in my nostrils–i'm glad Marguerita's all
right–i Do feel expensive

i am leaving my kid on your
doorstep, if you're so hot, you'll
see that he gets taken care of.
after all, he's your kid too. i
expct to see him in about twenty
years, so you better do a good
job. i am going into the mountains
to find work. i am taking along
the food. remember luv, keep the
stove clean & watch the gas tank

屋[10]——我们没有任何共通之处，我&珍珠——我分享她的无聊&没有任何东西给过她——我喝醉了&自娱自乐……我们希望能去旅行&可借助一切除了我们的脚&我们以大猩猩式握手结识那些舌头打结巴的粗鄙怪咖&醉醺醺的赫拉克勒斯在我们的床上等待我们&我们必须向他敬礼&他说新的直升机都已抵达&“这就是你的怪咖”&“你会从他那儿接受指令”是的此地薪资微薄但没有誓言要遵守也没有神经抽风——除了配着无线电穿着宗教服装的猎人们带进来的那些自我意识错乱者，全都过得好好的……安哥拉今早上被炸了[11]，我立刻乐滋滋地犯了恶心——我的脑袋要窒息了——我用银纽扣罩衫塞在鼻孔里凝望着北斗星——我很高兴玛格丽塔安然无恙——我当真觉得昂贵

我把我的孩子留在你家
门道，要是你够辣，你会
保证他得到细心照料。
毕竟，他也是你的孩子。我
预计大概二十年后再来看
他，所以你最好好好干。
我这就要进山里边去
找工作了。我身上带着
吃的。记得爱，保持
炉灶清洁&留神煤气罐

yours

louie louie

你的

路易路易[12]

注　释

1　马塞卢斯（Marcellus，前268—前208），罗马帝国名将、执政官。另，在莎剧《哈姆雷特》开场，有一个名叫马塞卢斯的哨兵看到了先王的幽灵，并上报给哈姆雷特的好友霍拉旭。

2　在美国女权主义西部片《乔西传奇》（*The Ballad of Josie*，1967）中，乔西误杀她的家暴丈夫，在庭上获判无罪，后又推动妇女投票招致男性乡民不满，由多丽丝·黛主演。

3　意大利电影《两个女人》（*Two Women*），1961年的热门影片，讲述二战时期女性的苦难，由索菲亚·罗兰主演。

4　试图给月亮剥皮（trying to peel the moon），参见迪伦歌曲《请你爬出窗户来好吗？》（“Can You Please Crawl Out Your Window?”，1965）：“他的样子多诚恳，他的感觉是这样吗？ / 试图给月亮剥皮并暴露它。”

5　玛格丽塔（Marguerita），参见埃尔维斯·普雷斯利歌曲《玛格丽塔》（“Marguerita”，1963），歌词大意：我曾像吉卜赛人一样自由，不驯，当我突然看到玛格丽塔燃烧的目光，就像火中的飞蛾被她捕捉，她的双唇命我作她的囚徒，百依百顺的奴隶，她的手轻轻一触，便俘虏了我，迷醉了我。

6　下文出自爱尔兰传统民谣《莫莉马隆》（“Molly Malone”），歌词大意：在美丽的都柏林，姑娘们漂漂亮亮，有个少女名叫莫莉，她每天推着车子走街串巷叫卖，“蛤蚌和贻蚌，新鲜啦，新鲜啦”，她是个鱼贩子，她的父母也是这样叫卖，她死于伤寒，没有谁能拯救她，这就是莫莉的结局，但她的灵魂仍在街巷里一路叫卖。皮特·西格、宾·克罗斯比等人唱过这首歌。

7 “星期四”（Thursday），音近“饥渴”（thirsty）。

8 “肌肉”（muscles），音同“贻蚌”（mussels），两者源出同一个词；另，也音近下文的“麻疹”（measles）。

9 德国麻疹，即风疹，主要危害孕妇和婴儿，1962—1965年在欧美大流行，纽约有1%的新生儿被感染。

10 寄宿屋（rooming house），参见英国民谣《在寄宿舍》（“At the Boarding House”）：“在我曾住过的寄宿舍里，所有东西都变旧了。”

11 1966年，争取民族独立的安哥拉各派力量正式分裂，后来爆发内战。文中也可能指美国1965年起对北越实施的战略轰炸。

12 路易路易（louie louie），出自《路易路易》（“Louie Louie”，1957），美国热门摇滚蓝调歌曲，1963年经金斯曼乐队（The Kingsmen）翻唱，误打误撞而大火，次年又惹起美国联邦调查局的调查风波。

Mae West Stomp (A Fable)

69 train goes by every nite the same old time & he, same old man, sits looking into a rosary which reads "i told you so" while rocking back & forth thinking about his eldest son, Hambone, who's in jail for life–buying beer for the kids & murdering the grocer with a pocket comb–this same old man, with nothing but a bathtub full of memories consisting of: a few Baby Huey for President buttons–a deck of cards with the aces missing–some empty deodorant bottle–a pamphlet of egyptian slogans–three pant legs that dont match & a hollow lynch rope... sits in a candy wrapper chair muttering day in court–day in court–i'll get it yet–my day in court–a dapper young gentleman with chapped lips rubbed them on the old man's neck today–the little old man is planning revenge just as the same old time train shakes his whistler's mother painting off the wall & it gooses him to...day in court–i'll get it yet–yesterday was not so good either–a fox left him in a clump of mud & some little pest let him have it right in the kisser with a mixture of bamboo, barley & rotten ice cream–there he sits wishing he could get thru to the president–the little old man's bowels ache so he opens the window to breathe some good fresh air–

梅韦斯特跺脚舞（寓言一则）

列车总在每晚同一个老时间开过&他，每晚同一个老头，坐在那儿一边看玫瑰经上面写道“我早跟你说过会这样”[1]一边前前&后后地摇晃着想念他的大儿子火腿畳[2]，他要在牢里蹲一辈子了——帮小孩买啤酒&用一把小梳子谋杀食杂店主——这个同样的老头一无所有除了浴缸里满满的回忆，包括：几枚鸭宝宝休伊当总统[3]纪念章——一副缺了A的扑克牌[4]——香体露空瓶子若干——一本埃及口号小册子——三条不齐的裤腿&一根空荡荡的绞索……坐在一把糖纸靠椅上喃喃着庭审日[5]——庭审日——我总会有的——我的庭审日[6]——今天有个潇洒的年轻绅士把他皲裂的嘴唇在老头的脖上摩擦——当小老头盘算着复仇在同样的老时间列车震得他的惠斯勒[7]妈妈图画掉下墙来&它冲他轰轰……庭审日——我总会有的——昨天也不是那么好——有只狐狸把他丢在一摊烂泥&某种小虫虫让他狠狠啃了满嘴子糊巴巴的竹子、大麦&烂冰淇淋——他坐在那儿期望着他能够联系上总统——小老头的肚子痛了所以他打开窗呼

he inhales deeply–there is a line full of wet underwear–used tires–dirty bed sheets–hats–chicken feathers–an old watermelon–paper plates & some other garments–johnny drumming wind–an indian, passing thru on his way to st. louis, is standing neath the old man's window–"amazing" he says as he looks up & sees all this stuff on the clothesline suddenly get sucked into a hole...next day, the rent collector comes to get the rent–finds that the old man has disappeared & that the room's full of garbage–the lady who owns the clothesline, she reports theft to the robbery department–"all my valuables have been stolen"–she mutters to the inspector–the train still goes by at the same old time & johnny drumming wind, he gets picked up for vagrancy–the rent collector looks around–steals a broken coocoo "i think i'll give it to my wife" he says–his wife, who is six feet tall & wears a fez, & who, at the minute, by weird circumstance, is riding by on that same old time train–all in all, not much happens in chicago

i'm not saying that books are
good or bad, but i dont think
youve ever had the chance to find
out for yourself what theyre all
about–ok, so you used to get B's
in the ivanhoe tests & A minuses
in the silas marners...then you
wonder why you flunked the hamlet

吸点新鲜空气——他深深地吸纳——前面的一根绳上挂满湿内裤——旧轮胎——脏床单——帽子——鸡毛——老西瓜——纸餐碟&一些其他服装——约翰尼咚咚鼓着风——有个印第安人，一路去圣路易斯，正站在老头的窗户下边——“太神奇了”他边说边仰头张望&看见晾衣绳上的这一堆玩意儿突然被卷进一个窟窿……第二天，收租人来要房钱——发现老头已经不见了&屋里满是垃圾——那根晾衣绳的女主人向反盗分局报案——“我所有值钱的东西都被偷了”——她对督察抱怨道——列车依旧在同一个老时间开过&约翰尼咚咚鼓着风，他因流浪罪[8]被逮着了——收租人四处张望——偷一个破咕咕“我想我可以拿去送给老婆”他说——他老婆身高一米八&戴一顶土耳其圆毡帽，&而她这时，好巧不巧地，正乘在那同一个老时间的列车上——总的来说，芝加哥没什么大事情

我可没说过书是
好还是坏，我只是觉得
你凭自己很难有机会
搞清楚它们到底都在说些
什么——好的，所以，你考艾凡赫[9]
总是得B&考织工马南[10]
能拿到A减……接着你又
纳闷为什么考哈姆雷特

exams–yeah well that's because one
hoe & one lass do not make a spear–
71 the same way two wrongs do not make
a throng–now that youve been thru
life, why dont you try again...you
could start with a telephone book–
wonder woman–or perhaps catcher in
the rye–theyre all the same & everybody
has their hat on backwards thru the
stories

see you at the docks
helpfully yours,
Sir Cringe

会挂科——哈，那是因为一
锄&一妞得不出一矛来——
同样地，两个错误得不出
一群人物——现在你已经看过了
生活[11]，不妨再多试一下……你
可以从电话号簿开始[12]——
神奇女侠——也可以看麦田
守望者——它们都一样&在故事里
人人都把他们的帽子
反戴[13]

码头上见
你乐意效劳的，
谄媚爵士

注 释

1 出自《新约·约翰福音》16:1："我已将这些事告诉你们，使你们不至于跌倒。"另，阿瑞莎·富兰克林早期歌曲有《我早跟你说过会这样》（"I Told You So"，1962）。

2 火腿骨（Hambone），出自美国同名传统歌谣，大意：火腿骨火腿骨你在哪里？我周游世界很快就回来。回来之后你要做什么？我要沿着铁路转一转。

3 鸭宝宝休伊（Baby Huey），派拉蒙影业在20世纪50年代推出的卡通形象，不如迪士尼漫画中唐老鸭的小外甥辉儿（Huey Duck）出名。当时的美国副总统汉弗莱（Hubert H. Humphrey，1911—1978）也被称为"休伊"。

4　一副缺了A的扑克牌（a deck of cards with the aces missing），参见迪伦歌曲《满眼忧伤的低地女士》："你那副缺了J和A的扑克牌"（And your deck of cards missing the jack and the ace）。

5　《庭审日》（*Day in Court*，1958—1965），美国广播公司的一档电视连续剧。

6　我的庭审日（my day in court），意即有机会发表自己的观点。

7　惠斯勒（James McNeill Whistler，1834—1903），美国著名画家，代表作有《艺术家的母亲》（1872）。另，"whistler"也可理解为：鸣汽笛者。

8　流浪罪（vagrancy），美国曾有反流浪法，条文模糊，可执行范围很广，后因违宪逐渐取消或明细化。

9　《艾凡赫》（*Ivanhoe*，1820），英国作家沃尔特·司各特长篇历史小说，中译本又名《撒克逊英雄传》。

10　《织工马南》（*Silas Marner*，1861），英国女作家乔治·爱略特长篇现实小说。马南的悲苦故事让收信人有同感，故能考高分，但他不同意最后的幸福结局，故未得满分，至于其他帝王将相的故事，收信人则考不好或挂科。

11　可能指美国知名画报《生活》（*Life*），该刊在20世纪60年代中期逐渐从巅峰走向衰落，1972年底停刊。

12　朗诵电话号簿是当时美国先锋文艺圈的一种游戏。

13　人人都把他们的帽子反戴（everybody has their hat on backwards），出自塞林格小说《麦田里的守望者》。

Black Nite Crash

aretha in the blues dunes–Pluto with the high crack
laugh & rambling aretha–a menace to president
as he was jokingly called–go–yea! & the seniority
complex disowning you...Lear looking in the window
dangerous & dragging a mountain & you say "no i
am a mute" & he says "no no i've told the others you
72 were Charlie Chaplin & now you must live up to it–
you must!" & aretha saying "split Lear–none of us got
the guts for infinity–take your driving wheel & split...
& aretha next–she's got these hundred Angel Strangers
all passing thru saying "i will be your Shakti & your
outlaw kid–pick me–pick me please–ah c'mon pick
me" & aretha faking her intestinal black soul across
all the fertile bubbles & whims & flashy winos–Jinx,
Poet Void & Scary Plop all skipping to hell with their
bunnies where food is cheaper & warmer & Nucleur
Beethoven screaming "oh aretha–i shall be your
voodoo doll–prick me–let's make somebody hurt–draw
on me whoever you wish! ah pretty please! my bastard
frame–my slimy self–penetrate unto me–unto me!"
Scholar, his body held together by chiclets–raw beans
& slaves of days gone by–he storms in from the road–

黑夜撞击

阿瑞莎在蓝调沙丘——普鲁托[1]嘎嘎放声大笑&闲游的阿瑞莎——对于被人戏称的总统是个捣蛋鬼——冲啊——耶！&前辈优越感抛弃你……李尔望着险恶的窗户&拖动一座大山&你说“不我是个哑巴”&他说“不不我已经告诉别人你是查理卓别林&现在你必须不负众望啊——你必须！”&阿瑞莎说“起开吧李尔——我们谁都没有无穷的胆量——把好你的驱动轮&起开吧……&阿瑞莎接着——她已经让这一百个天使陌生人全都通过了说“我愿做你的夏克提[2]&你的法外小徒[3]——挑我吧——求你挑我——啊快来挑我吧”&阿瑞莎假扮着她的肠道黑灵魂横渡那所有丰饶的泡沫[4]&冲动&闪亮亮的酒鬼们——灾星、空虚诗人[5]&惊恐扑通全都跟他们的兔女郎蹦向地狱那里饭菜更便宜&更暖和&核能贝多芬嘶吼“哦，阿瑞莎——我愿做你的巫毒娃娃——戳我吧——让我们给某人造成伤害——在我身上随便你画一个谁！啊美人求求你！我的杂种身材——我的蔫巴自我——捅穿我吧——捅穿！”学究，他的身体被芝兰裹成一团——生鲜豆子&

his pipe nearly eaten "look! she burps of reality" & but
he's not even talking to anybody–a moth flies out of
his pocket & Void, the incredible fall apart reminds
you once more of america with the dotted line–useless
motive–the moral come on & silver haired men hiding
in the violin cases...on a mound of phosphorus &
success stands the voluptuous coyote eagle–he holds
a half dollar–an anchor sways across his shoulders
"good!" says Nucleur Beethoven "good to see there are
some real birds around" "that's no bird–that's just a
thief–he's building an outhouse out of stolen lettuce!"
signs aretha–Sound of Sound–who really doesnt give
a damn about real birds or outhouses or any Nucleur
73 Beethoven–approval, complaints & explanations–they
all frighten her–she has no flaws in her trumpet–she
knows that the sun is not a piece of her

the audio repairman stumbles
thru the door with "sound is sacred–
so come in & talk to us" written on
the back of his shirt

旧日年华的奴隶们——他从大路上猛冲进来——他的烟斗快要吃光了“瞧！她打着现实的饱嗝儿”&但他甚至不跟任何人说话——他的衣兜里飞出一只蛾子&空虚，那不可思议的崩散又再次让你想起虚线勾勒的美国——无用的动机——道德登场[6] &银发男子们躲在提琴箱里……在一大堆白磷上&凯旋矗起妖艳的土狼老鹰[7]——它抓住半美元[8]——它的肩头上晃悠着一只铁锚“多好呀！”核能贝多芬说“能在这儿看到真正的鸟儿们飞来飞去多好呀”“那不是鸟——那只是一个贼——他在用偷来的莴苣搭一间厕所！”署名阿瑞莎——声音的声音——她确实毫不在乎真正的鸟儿或厕所或任何核能贝多芬——赞同、抱怨&解释——他们都惊到她——她的小号声里没有一点瑕疵——她知道太阳不是她的那一份

音响修理工磕磕绊绊
穿过大门，他的衬衣背后
写着“声音是神圣的——
进来吧&我们谈谈”

注 释

1 普鲁托（Pluto），古希腊神话中的冥王，也是爱伦·坡恐怖小说《黑猫》（1843）中的猫，以及迪士尼动画片中米老鼠的宠物狗的名字。

2 夏克提（Shakti），印度教的母神，性力的象征。

3 《法外小徒》（*Outlaw Kid*），美国系列漫画书。

4 可能戏拟爱神维纳斯，生于海沫，踏着贝壳渡海而来。

5 空虚诗人（Poet Void），可能戏拟古罗马诗人奥维德（Ovid）。

6 康德以降的近代唯美主义一般认为，审美或艺术是一种无关道德价值、无关逻辑概念、非功利性的直觉观照，但另一方面，美又被视为道德属性的象征。

7 美国印第安人传说，大洪水淹没了世界，只剩下老鹰和土狼，老鹰把土狼叼到最高的山巅，洪水退后，土狼下山察看，发现土地都已经干了，老鹰为土狼找了一个河中女子做老婆，并教他们生儿育女，于是人民重新繁盛。

8 1964 年版的 50 美分银币正面为先总统肯尼迪头像，背面为美国鹰徽纹章。

Hostile Black Nite Crash

on this abandoned roof or pagoda stool they place you & you hear voices saying things like "titen 'm up Joe–keep 'm titened up" & then Orion looking evil & he wipes you off & keeps you clean & Familiar Face himself "i heard you been eating some eggs? any truth to that?" & Orion licking his flesh & trouble in mind blues & shades of fire hydrants...YOU–the fire hydrant & Beau Geste, a fire hydrant–failures completely & walking to Gibraltar & trying to find your energy–
74 get your kicks & shadow box your language...Faust from the garden–Emancipation Anne, who looks like a hungarian deer & Chump with a brain like an iceberg all imitating Africa...Dead Lover who hitchhikes & brags & says he's going to Carthage & he keeps repeating "when i die" but then his mind goes black & blue & methodist butter erupting & Twinkle Clown with arabic lettering on his forehead wanting everybody to experience his fright "you must experience my fright to be my friend!" so says he to Lucy Tunia, whose vegetarian legs shine like mahogany & who comforts Twinkle Clown in his fits when he has no harem... Zing & Orion stutters & coughs & SHAZAMMM–

恶意的黑夜撞击

在这撂荒的屋顶或宝塔坐凳上他们把你安置&你听见各种说话的声比如“丕快把他绑紧了——牢牢地绑紧了”&然后奥赖恩一副邪性样&他给你擦拭&让你保持洁净&熟面孔本人“我听说你吃了鸡蛋？是不是真的？”奥赖恩舔舔他的肉身&心中的烦恼蓝调[1]&那些消防栓的阴影……**你**——消防栓&翩翩君子[2]，一个消防栓——彻底失败&步行去直布罗陀&想要寻找你的能量——祝你一路顺风[3]&把你的语言装进玻璃展柜……来自乐园的浮士德——解放者安妮，她长得好像一只匈牙利的鹿[4]&大笨头扛着一个冰山脑袋完全模仿非洲……死灵爱人[5]搭便车&吹牛皮&说他要去迦太基&他老在念叨“到我死的时候”但是他的心灵渐渐青一块&紫一块&循道宗黄油喷射[6]&眨眼小丑用阿拉伯文写在额头上想让每个人都体验到他的恐惧“你必须体验到我的恐惧才能做我的朋友！”他这样告诉露西图尼亚[7]，她的素食大腿如红木一般锃亮&她抚慰着大笑的眨眼小丑在他没有妻妾[8]的时候……嗖&奥赖恩[9]结结巴巴&咳嗽&**沙赞姆**[10]——鸦

the opium ghost neath the ferris wheel–on the side of the highway–where nobody can stop–where he can cause no trouble–where the show must go on...this is where He wishes to die–He wishes to die in the midst of cathedral bells–He wishes to die when the tornadoes strike the roofs & stools "so much for death" he will say when he dies

the newsboy comes in the back door–
his big toe sticks thru his shoe–he
carries a piece of peeling with a
number on it–he makes a phone call–
then he blows his nose

片鬼在摩天轮之下——在公路道旁——在那里没有谁能停留——在那里他引不起任何麻烦——在那里表演必须继续……这就是他希望的死亡之地——他希望死在大教堂的钟鸣当中——他希望死在飓风席卷那些屋顶&坐凳的时候“死到头了”他会在死的时候这样说

报童从后门进屋来——
他的大脚趾冒出鞋头——他
拿着一块果皮上面
有个号码——他打电话——
然后他擤擤鼻涕

注　释

1　《心中的烦恼》（“Trouble in Mind”，1924），美国爵士乐蓝调老歌。

2　《翩翩君子》（*Beau Geste*，1966），英国作家P.C.雷恩以北非法国外籍军团为背景创作的冒险小说，该书在1966年被美国环球影业改编成同名电影《壮烈千秋》。

3　祝你一路顺风（get your kicks），出自《祝你一路顺风在66国道》（“Get Your Kicks on Route 66”，1946），美国爵士乐蓝调老歌。

4　在匈牙利传说中，匈诺和马果两兄弟在打猎时发现一只银色的神鹿，他们追呀追呀追到乐文地，在那里他们遇到两个公主，分别娶妻生子，发展成后来的匈族和马扎尔族两大支系。

5　死灵爱人（Dead Lover），出自法国浪漫主义诗人、作家戈蒂耶的同名短篇小说《死灵爱人》（*La Morte amoureuse*，1836），大意讲一个神父和女吸血鬼的奇情故事。

6　循道宗黄油喷射（methodist butter erupting），参见美国传统民谣《循道宗馅饼》（“Methodist Pie”）。

7　露西·图尼亚（Lucy Tunia），戏拟美国华纳公司的系列动画片《乐一通》（*Looney Tunes*）。

8　妻妾（harem），指阿拉伯贵族的后宫嫔妃；音近哈莱姆（Harlem），纽约曼哈顿北部的黑人区，荷兰殖民地时期命名为新哈勒姆（Nieuw Haarlem），20 世纪 20 年代以这里为中心的黑人艺术及文学兴起被称为“哈莱姆文艺复兴”。

9　“嗖 & 奥赖恩”（Zing & Orion），原文戏拟宾·克罗斯比的歌曲《唱一首小歌》（“Zing a Little Zong”，1952）。

10　沙赞（Shazam），美国老牌漫画《神奇队长》（*Captain Marvel*）中英雄变身的咒语。

Unresponsible Black Nite Crash

the united states is Not soundproof–you might think that nothing can reach those tens of thousands living behind the wall of dollar–but your fear Can bring in the truth...picture of dirt farmer–long johns–coonskin cap–strangling himself on his shoe–his wife, tripping over the skulls–her hair in rats–their kid is wearing a scorpion–the scorpion wears glasses–the kid, he's drinking gin–everybody has balloons stuck into their eyes–that they will never get a suntan in mexico is obvious–send your dollar today–bend over backwards...or shut your mouths forever

> the bully comes in–kicks the newsboy
> you know where–& begins ripping away
> at the audio repairman's shirt

免责的黑夜撞击

合众国不是隔音的——你可能以为任何东西都无法触动那几万住在美元高墙背后的人——但你的惧怕却能够引出真相……图画中的庄稼人——秋裤——浣熊皮帽——他踮着脚尖把自己勒死——他的老婆，在满地骷髅上磕磕碰碰——她的头发垫着老鼠[1]——他们的小孩戴一只蝎子——蝎子戴着眼镜——那小孩，他在喝金酒——人人都有气球戳进他们的眼里[2]——他们绝不会在墨西哥晒日光浴这是显然的——今日内寄出你的美元——使尽办法吧你……不然就永远闭嘴

恶棍进屋来——踢踢报童
你知道在哪儿——&动手撕掉
音响修理工的衬衣

注　释

1　老鼠（rats），也指假发垫。

2　参见《新约 · 马太福音》7:3–5：“为什么看见你弟兄眼中有刺，却不想自己眼中有梁木呢？你自己眼中有梁木，怎能对你弟兄说，‘容我去掉你眼中的刺’呢？你这假冒为善的人！先去掉自己眼中的梁木，然后才能看得清楚，去掉你弟兄眼中的刺。”

Electric Black Nite Crash

76 nature has made the young West Virginia miners not want to be miners but rather get this '46 Chevy–no money down–take to Geneva…hunting for the likes of escape & Lord Buckley & Sherlock Holmes about to be his mother turning to Starhole the Biology Amazon saying "i dont want to be my mother!" & e.e. cummings–spell it right–wrapping his leftover chicken bones in a pig tail belonging to Bronx Baby No. 2 & she thinks the world's coming to an end & tries to organize a rally & her 320 pound Frenchman who sticks his tongue out at her father–he dont want no part of it–"i dont wanna go to no San Quentin! i'm not a criminal–i'm a foreigner & i cant help it if you dig e.e. cummings but me–like ah said–i'm just a foreigner" & she throws all these leftover chicken bones into his face & some celebrities passing by–they witness the whole thing & take down the serial numbers…Mona carries a lone ranger advertisement on her left front breast–Mona's cousin–this 320 pound Frenchman–he resembles Arthur Conan Doyle…Mona–she resembles a sexy Buddha & always looks like she's standing over the Golden Gate…she dont dig e.e. cummings–she digs Fernando Lamas–i am on a black train going west–there

电声的黑夜撞击

天性已使得年轻的西弗吉尼亚矿工们不肯再做矿工宁可去搞一辆46年款雪佛兰——定金全免——开到日内瓦……猎捕各种逃亡者&巴克利老爷[1]&夏洛克福尔摩斯快要成了他的妈妈变成星洞[2]而亚马逊生物学说“我不想成为我妈妈！”&e.e.卡明斯——要拼写正确——把他吃剩的鸡骨头裹在属于布朗克斯宝贝2号的猪尾辫里&她认为世界即将走到尽头&试图组织一场集会&她的320磅法国佬朝她爸爸吐舌头——他不想成为其中一员——“我可不想进圣昆丁[3]！我不是罪犯——我是个老外&如果你着迷e.e.卡明斯而不是我那我就帮不上了——就像俺说的——我只是个老外”&她把所有这些吃剩的鸡骨头都砸到他的脸上&有几个名流经过——他们目睹了整个事件&记下序号……蒙娜在左前胸上挂着孤胆奇侠的广告——蒙娜的老表——这个320磅法国佬——他好比亚瑟柯南道尔……蒙娜——她好比一位性感的佛陀&那模样总是像她跨在金门海峡上……她不着迷e.e.卡明斯——她着迷费尔南多拉马斯[4]——我坐一趟

is no aretha on the desert–just–if you want–memories
of aretha–but aretha teaches not to depend on memory–
there is no aretha on the desert

77 the stripper comes in wearing an
engagement ring–she asks for lemonade,
but says she'll settle for a sandwich–
the newsboy grabs her–yells "lord have
mercy"

黑火车[5]去西部——荒漠上没有阿瑞莎——只有——如果你愿意——阿瑞莎的回忆——但阿瑞莎教人不要依赖回忆——荒漠上没有阿瑞莎

脱衣舞娘来时戴着一枚
订婚戒指——她要柠檬水，
却说她也能接受三明治——
报童拽住她——大叫“求主
垂怜”

注　释

1　巴克利老爷（Lord Buckley，1906—1960），美国笑星，迪伦很喜欢他的节目。

2　星洞（Starhole），戏拟夏洛克·福尔摩斯（Sherlock Holmes）。

3　圣昆丁（San Quentin），加利福尼亚州立监狱所在地，位于旧金山附近，以其死牢闻名。

4　费尔南多·拉马斯（Fernando Lamas，1915—1982），阿根廷影星。

5　黑火车（black train）是美国民谣的常见意象。

Somebody's Black Nite Crash

from entire Mexico & gay innocence once comes Satan
of Autumn–from the gentleness & barbarian bebop
& lonesome rooms where you must put a nickel in the
parking meter–into the arms of notorious daughters–
daughters who get social poems published in bazaar &
fashion magazines & wonder of adventure–beer barrel
polkas & eat goofballs "why didnt HUAC get custer?" say
some "how did robert burns escape hitler is what i'd like
to know!" say the smarter ones–all the hipster T–bone
heads & wheel chair Marxists wishing to be in Kansas
City '51 & Satan of Autumn & his friend, I DONT
78 KNOW YOU, gnawing farts in the farmlands & coming
back & telling everybody & then I DONT KNOW YOU
finally coming to the conclusion "what good's it all to
tell everybody about anything–they all got alibis?" &
then Montana coming & Aztec Landlords themselves–
their atomic fag bars being looted & Bishops disguised as
chocolate prisoners & the empty Barbary Coast haunted
houses where the bureaucrats–the dreamy Huxley hanger
oners–the New Awake with money & no place else to
go & the ex cop who writes verse & thinks of himself as
a salami & Gabby–the crippled horror from Telegraph

某人的黑夜撞击

从整个墨西哥&快乐无邪每当遇到秋之撒旦——从文雅&野蛮比波普乐&那些寂寞房间你必须给停车表投一个硬币——进入臭名女儿们的怀抱——女儿们搞出交际诗发表在芭莎&时尚杂志&历险奇遇——啤酒桶波尔卡[1]&吃傻瓜药“为什么**非美调查委员会**[2]不抓卡斯特？”有人说“我想知道的是罗伯特彭斯[3]怎样逃离希特勒！”另一个更聪明的说——所有的嬉普士丁骨[4]脑袋&轮椅马克思主义者们但愿在51年的堪萨斯城[5]&秋之撒旦&他的朋友，**我不认识你**，在农田里咬牙切齿地放屁&转回来&告诉每个人&然后**我不认识你**终于得出结论“把什么事情都告诉每个人又有什么好处——他们都会找借口？”&然后蒙塔纳来了&阿兹特克地主们本人——他们的原子基佬酒吧被打劫&主教们假扮巧克力囚犯&空荡荡的巴巴利海岸[6]鬼屋出没官僚——梦想家赫胥黎跟班们——新觉醒要花钱&没地方可去&前警察开始写诗歌&把自己想成一条熏肠&盖比——来自电报大道[7]的跛脚神经病但有谁要听这个呢——有谁当真

Avenue but who wants to hear of this–who really wants to hear of this?" who wants to hear anything? we just a part of a generation! just one mangy grubby part!" said I DONT KNOW YOU one day to Satan & it was autumn "you mean like the hula hoop happening?" "no–like the crucifixion happening!" "like the Modern beat?" "like the beat of a peach tree"...both Satan & I DONT KNOW YOU–they skip thru the New York race track–all the typical renaissances & a blond that looks like ezra pound & they go right into Summer–without winter–seeing them so unsuffered, Lu with a crew cut, one of the chicks that write the big fat writings–her mouth hangs open–some beggar comes out of his hovel & hangs a hair from her lip–a streetcar crashes...but all in all–nobody really cares

the chamber of commerce all come in–
each member carrying hand grenades–
79 everything turns into blood–excpt for
the jukebox, a stranger wearing a––
calendar, & a postcard of a greek
building...which the owner of the
place has left on top of the radiator
by mistake/ the play now begins...it
is all in the past...i will not be
so insulting as to write it for you

要听这个呢？“有谁要听点什么吗？我们只是一代人的一部分！只是一个肮脏丑陋的部分！”有一天**我不认识你**这样告诉撒旦＆那是在秋季“你是说像呼啦圈[8]那样的发生？”“不——像钉十字架那样发生！”“像现代节拍？”“像一棵桃树的节拍”……撒旦和**我不认识你**两人——他们一蹦一蹦过了纽约跑马场——全都是典型的文艺复兴＆一个酷似埃兹拉庞德[9]的金发白人＆他们直接走进夏季——没有冬——看到他们都安然无恙，露剪个平头，就是写了长篇大论的雏儿们中的一个——她的嘴巴咧着——有个乞丐走出他的窝棚＆挂着一根头发在她的嘴唇上——有一辆电车撞击……但总的来说，没有谁当真在乎

商会全都进来了——
所有成员攥着手榴弹——
一切都变得血腥——除了
点唱机，一个陌生人披着件——
日历，＆希腊建筑
明信片……是那个地方的
主人搞错了留在散热器
顶上／现在表演开始……这
都是过去的事了……我不会
那样无礼地都写给你看

注　释

1　啤酒桶波尔卡（beer barrel polkas），出自源自捷克的二战流行歌曲《啤酒桶波尔卡》（“Beer Barrel Polka”）。

2　众议院非美活动调查委员会（House Un-American Activities Committee，HUAC），美国反共机构，1975 年撤销。

3　罗伯特·彭斯（Robert Burns，1759—1796），著名的苏格兰民族诗人。

4　丁骨是上等牛排肉。可能指“丁骨瘦子”（T-Bone Slim，1880—1942），美国左翼作家、工运领袖，他创作的抗议歌曲在当时重新受到推崇。另，“丁骨”沃克（T-Bone Walker，1910—1975），美国蓝调歌手，电吉他先驱之一；walker 意即行走者，与轮椅相反。

5　1951 年 7 月，堪萨斯河域洪水泛滥，50 万人转移。

6　巴巴利海岸（Barbary Coast）一带是旧金山的文化娱乐中心、红灯区、同性恋聚居地。

7　电报大道（Telegraph Avenue），位于加州大学伯克利分校附近，是 20 世纪 60 年代反文化运动的主要场所。

8　呼啦圈在 1960 年前后开始风靡美国及西方世界。

9　参见迪伦歌曲《荒凉路》。

Seems Like a Black Nite Crash

between the shrieking mattress in the kitchen & Time, a mysterious weekly–Tao–a fingertip on his chin, his knees knocking together–Tao–he shows the inside of his mouth to a column of faces "does this mean you must take a nap today?" & Phil Silvers eating a banana–he is inside of the column of faces–Tao is quiet & Phil pokes Duff the Hero–a miser from the Aegean Sea–a vast desert in his head–he has plenty of self confidence & lets yokels test bombs in his brain–" "love is a ghost thing" says Duff "it goes right thru you" Tao strains–he looks almost pornographic "some tonsils!" says Phil, who now wears long suspenders & tells Duff to keep up the self confidence "self confidence is deceiving" says Mr. O'toole–a husband of questionable virtue "it gives people without balls a sense of virility" "does your wife own a cow?" says Phil, who has now turned into an inexpensive Protestant ambassador from Nebraska & who speaks with a marvelous accent "what do you mean does my wife own a cow?" "are you from Chicago then?" asks the ambassador...Tao's face–meanwhile–becomes so big–it disappears "where'd he go?" says Duff–who's

看似一场黑夜撞击[1]

在厨房的尖叫床垫&时代，一份神秘周刊之间——道——他的一个指尖抵着下巴，膝盖啪地并拢——道——他向一列面孔展示他的嘴巴内部“这意思是说你今天必须打个盹儿了？”&菲尔西尔沃斯[2]吃着香蕉——他在那一列面孔之中——道很安静&菲尔捅捅英雄达夫——来自爱琴海的财迷——他的脑袋里长了一个大沙漠——他有着丰富的自信&任由乡巴佬们在他的脑子里试验原子弹——“爱情是个鬼东西”达夫说“它从你身上穿透而去”道紧张了——他那模样简直就是色情片“有些扁桃腺！”菲尔说，现在他系着吊裤带&叫达夫要保持自信“自信就是欺诈”奥图先生[3]——这个操守可疑的丈夫说“它能让没卵子的人长点硬气”“你老婆有没有一头奶牛？”菲尔说，他现在已经变成一个来自内布拉斯加的廉价新教徒大使&说起话来满口子绝妙的口音“你问我老婆有没有奶牛是什么意思？”“那你是不是从芝加哥来的？”大使问……与此同时——道的面孔越来越庞大——它消失了“他上哪儿了？”达夫说——他

not so much of a hero anymore but rather a jolly youth
that hates degenerates & is supposed to be in school
anyway...Mr. O'toole–falls out of his chair "i must
find some railroad tracks–i must put my ear to the
tracks–i must listen for a train"–the column of faces–
all together now–a munching chorus "DONT GET
KILLED NOW"–repeat–"dont get killed now"...yes
& between this mattress shrieking & that mysterious
weekly lay the slave counties–Doris Day gone & Pacific
fog–a Studebaker in twilight–crash–& breaking down
the honkytonk doors & strange left handed moonmen–
from Arkansas & Texas & vagabonds with girlie
magazines from Reed College–cellars & Queens–
they all shouting "watch me Tao–watch me–i'm high–
watch me now!"...that lonesome feeling–paralyzing–
that lonesome feeling–or aretha–my mama didnt raise
no fool–i have nothing new to add to that feeling...
81 slide on vomit–better'n working with a shovel–Reject–
God Bless Holy Phantomism & damn the farewell
parties–statistic books–the politicians...the column of
faces–all together now–raising the flag & staring up
to a hole in it–chanting "it's halloween' can Tao come
out & play?"–getting no reaction & shouting louder–
all in unison now–"IT'S HALLOWEEN...CAN TAO
COME OUT & PLAY?"

give up–give up–the ship is lost: go
back to san bernardino–stop trying to
organize the crew–it's every man for

可不再有那么多英雄气概了现在只是一个憎恨堕落的快乐青年&反正应该去上学的……奥图先生——从椅子掉了下来“我必须找到些铁轨——我必须把耳朵贴在铁轨上——我必须听火车来”——那一列面孔——现在都聚拢了——发出吧唧吧唧的合唱“**别找死啊**”——重复——“别找死啊”……是的&在这床垫尖叫&那神秘周刊之间坐落着蓄奴县——多丽丝戴离去&太平洋大雾——昏暗中一辆斯图贝克[4]——撞击——&崩掉酒馆大门&那些奇怪的左撇子月球人——从阿肯色&得克萨斯&流浪汉们看着里德学院弄来的美女杂志——那些地窖&女王——她们都在大喊“看看我呀道——看看我——我好嗨哟——快看看我呀！”……那种孤独感——麻痹——那种孤独感——或者阿瑞莎——我老妈可不是养蠢货的——对那种感觉我没有什么新东西要补充了……在呕吐物上滑溜——好过用铲子干活——拒绝——上帝保佑神圣幻象派&诅咒送行宴——统计手册——政客们……那一列面孔——现在都聚拢了——升上旗帜&注视着那上边的一个孔——唱道“万圣节将至道能不能出来&玩玩？”——没有反应&喊得更大声了——现在都齐唱了——**“万圣节将至……道能不能出来&玩玩？”**

放弃——放弃——船已经没了：回
圣贝纳迪诺[5]去吧——不要再试图
招募船员——每个人都是为了

himself–are you a man or a self? when
the coast guard gets there, stand up
proudly & point–dont be a hero–everybody's
a hero–be different–dont be a conformist–
forget about all those sea shanties–just
stand up & say "san bernardino" in a deep
monotone...everybody will get the message

your benefactor
Smoky Horny

自己——你是一个人还是一个自己？
等海岸警卫队过来了，傲慢地站在
那儿&指指点点——不充英雄——人人
都是英雄——你要不一样——不做遵从者——
忘掉那所有的水手歌谣——只需
站在那儿&说“圣贝纳迪诺”，以低沉
单调的声音……所有的人都会收到消息

你的恩主

欲火中烧

注　释

1　标题参见迪伦歌曲《约翰娜幻象》的最初版本《看似一场驱逐》（“Seems Like a Freeze-Out”）。

2　菲尔·西尔沃斯（Phil Silvers，1911—1985），美国笑星。

3　奥图先生（Mr. O'Toole），可能指彼得·奥图（Peter O'Toole，1932—2013），英国演员，反战人士，以影片《阿拉伯的劳伦斯》（1962）成名。参见迪伦歌曲《干净整洁的孩子》（“Clean-Cut Kid”，1985）。

4　斯图贝克（Studebaker），美国汽车厂牌，1966 年停产。

5　圣贝纳迪诺（San Bernardino），美国加州南部小城。

Chug A Lug—Chug A Lug Hear Me Hollar Hi Dee Ho

82 he was propped in the crutch of an oak tree–looking down –singing "there's a man going round taking names" indeed–i nod howdy–he nods howdy back "well he took my mother's name–lef' me there in pain" i, who am holding a glass of sand in one hand & a calf's head in the other–i look up & say "are you hungry?" & he say "there's a man going round taking names" & i say "good nuff" & keep walking–his voice rings thru the valley–it sounds like a telephone–it is very disturbing–"you need anything up there?"– "i'm going to town" he shakes his head "well he took my sister's name & i aint never been the same" "right–o" i say–tie my shoelace & keep walking–then i turn & say "if you need any help getting down, just you come to town & tell me" he doesnt even hear–"well he took my uncle's name & you know he wasnt to blame" "groovy" i say & continue my way to town...it couldnt've been more'n a few hours later when i happened to be passing by again–in the spot where the tree was, a lightbulb factory now stood–"did there used to be a guy here in a tree?" i yelled up to one of the windows–"are you looking for work?" was the reply...it was then when i decided that marxism did not have all the answers

咕咚咕咚听我吼声嗨嘀嗬[1]

他被撑在一棵橡树的枝杈上——往下看——唱着“有个人到处转悠点名”[2]的确——我点头问好——他也点头问好“啊他点了我妈妈的名字——让我痛苦不堪”我一只手里端着一杯沙子＆另一只手里是牛犊脑袋——我抬头看看＆说“你饿了吗？”＆他说“有个人到处转悠点名”＆我说“很好了”＆继续走——他的声音在山谷里回荡——就像电话铃——真是烦人——“你在上边需要帮忙吗？”——“我要进城”他摇摇头“啊他点了我姐姐的名字＆我完全变了样”“不错嘛”我说——系好鞋带＆继续走——然后我转身＆说“如果你要人帮忙下来，你就进城＆告诉我”他根本没听——“啊他点了我伯父的名字＆你知道他无可指摘”“棒极了”我说＆继续向城里走去……还没过几小时我又恰巧路过——就在那棵树的地方，现在是一座灯泡厂——“这儿从前有个家伙爬在树上吗？”我对着一扇窗户嚷道——“你是不是来找工作？”便是回复……就是在那个时候我确定西马也没有全部答案

83 why are you so frightened of
being embarrassed? you spend a lot of
time on the toilet dont you? why
dont you admit it? why are you so
embarrassed to be frightened?

your uncle
Matilda

为什么你要那样惧怕
受窘呢？你花了大量的
时间在厕所上对吧？为什么
你就不承认？为什么你要
那样窘迫于惧怕呢？

你的伯父
玛蒂尔达[3]

注 释

1 “咕咚咕咚”（Chug a Lug-Chug a Lug），出自美国乡村歌手罗杰·米勒（Roger Miller，1936—1992）歌曲《咕咚一口闷》（“Chug-a-Lug”，1964）。“吼”（hollar，holler），常指美国黑人传统民谣的一种劳动号子。“嗨嘀嘀”（Hi Dee Ho，Hi-De-Ho）则是美国黑人爵士乐歌手凯伯·凯洛威（Cab Calloway，1907—1994）在20世纪30年代成名的招牌唱法，曾拍过多部同名音乐电影。

2 “有个人到处转悠点名”（There's a man going 'round taking names），出自铅肚皮在20世纪30年代录制的同名传统民谣，这个人可能指死神，他点了我父母姐妹的名字，任我徒伤悲。参见迪伦歌曲《什么东西着了，宝贝》（“Something's Burning, Baby”，1985）：“有个人到处骂大街”（There's a man going 'round calling names）。

3 玛蒂尔达（Matilda），一般是女名。

Paradise, Skid Row & Maria Briefly

fatty Aphrodite's mama–i bend to you...& with sex mad
eternity at my vegetable shadow–i, wiping my hands on
the horse's neck–the horse burping & you of the Indiana
older brother–he who whips you with his belt & you who
does not look for reason to your torture & i want your
horizontal tongue–within Reflex–the perfect doom &
these cruel nitemares where brickmasons introduce me
to hideous connections & Marx Brothers grunting NO
QUIERO TU SABIDURIA & your thighs be half awake
& me so Sick so Sick of these lovers in Biblical roles–"so
84 youre out to save the world are you? you impostor–you
freak! youre a contradiction! youre afraid to admit youre a
contradiction! youre misleading! you have big feet & you
will step on yourself all the people you mislead will pick
you up! you have no answers! you have just found a way
to pass your time! without this thing, you would shrivel
up & be nothing–you are afraid of being nothing–you
are caught up in it–it's got you!" i am so Sick of Biblical
people–they are like castor oil–like rabies & now i wish
for Your eyes–you who does not talk any business &
supplies my mind with blankness QUIERO TUS OJOS &
your laughing & your slavery...there be no drunken risk–

天堂、陋巷&玛丽亚简述

肥肥阿芙洛狄忒的老妈——我向你鞠躬……&以我的蔬菜阴影上的淫欲疯狂永恒——我，在马脖子上擦拭着双手——马匹打嗝儿&你有印第安纳老哥——他用皮带抽你&你不为自己受折磨找理由&我想要你的平面舌——在反光镜中——那完美的宿命&这些残酷的夜魔有砖瓦匠指引我看到丑恶的关联&马克斯兄弟[1]咕哝我**不要你的智慧**[2]&你的大腿半梦半醒&我好恶心好恶心这些圣经人物中的情侣——“所以你就出来拯救世界对吗？你这冒牌货——你这怪胎！你是一个矛盾！你害怕承认你是一个矛盾！你在误导！你有大脚丫&你会踩翻你自己那些被你误导的人会把你捡起来！你没有答案！你不过是找着了一种打发时间的方式！没了这个，你就会瘪掉&毫无价值——你是害怕你毫无价值——你被这种想法套住了——它抓住你了！”我真的好恶心那些圣经中人——他们就像蓖麻油——就像疯狗&现在我希望得到你的眼睛——你是不谈什么生意的&给我的头脑提供空虚**我想要你的眼睛**&你的欢笑&你的奴役……不会有酒

i am an intimate Egyptian–say good–bye to the marine

hi–just arrived–terrible trip–this
little man carrying a white mouse
stared at me the whole way–jesus he
was a handsome man–are there any good
lawyers around? will look you up shortly –
have to eat first

sincerely yours,
Froggy

醉风险——我是一个亲密的埃及人——向水兵说再见

嘿——我刚到——可怕的旅行——这
个拎着一只白鼠的小男人
一路上老是盯着我——耶稣啊他
曾是个大帅哥[3]——这附近有没有
好律师？很快就去找你了——
先吃点东西

你诚挚的，
小青蛙

注　释

1　马克斯兄弟（Marx Brothers），美国笑星组合，流行于20世纪上半叶。

2　本章黑体字部分原文为西班牙语。

3　出自美国诗人E. E. 卡明斯的《野牛比尔》："耶稣啊 / 他曾是个大帅哥 / 我想知道的是 / 你觉得你的蓝眼睛男孩怎样，死神先生。"

A Punch of Pacifist

85 Peewee the Ear, whose mouth looks like a credit card–him & Jake the Flesh–along with Sandy Bob from Pecos–theyre leading the white elephant to water somewhere between wichita falls & el camino real–it's late in the day & no word from Saigon is in yet–along comes jerry mc boing–boing's daughter–Liza the Blimp–riding on a two dollar bill belonging to Goose John Henry, negro medicine man from Denver, who plays folk songs for kicks & speaks french for a living–onward then when Brown Dan, the creep cop–who likes to kill bullfrogs & whose boss keeps saying "he's got a bad knee but you oughta see him run, babe, you oughta see 'm run & chase them little chink lovers when they come down the river"–anyway Brown Dan–he comes snooping for the strangers with his flunky known simply as Little Stick, who carries a burnt hat pin & two pieces of kotex in case of emergency... they meet up with the crew at a clearing resembling a fisherman's dwarf...Jim Ghandi, the welder, is overlooking from his window–& yells something like "aw reet ye sons a vermits–draw ye now or shut ye mouths frever" just as the chick spreads her legs into the intersection & lets loose with the bumble seed grease, but nobody sneezes–she

反战人士的一拳

小不点伯嚼，嘴巴跟一张信用卡似的——他&大肉杰克——会同来自贝可斯[1]的桑迪鲍勃[2]——他们牵着白象[3]去威奇托瀑布[4]&国王大道[5]之间的某处饮水——当时天色已晚&还是没有西贡的任何消息——又会同了杰里麦克啵音啵音[6]的女儿——飞艇莉萨[7]——乘着一张两美元钞票[8]，这属于母鹅约翰亨利，从丹佛来的黑人巫医，[9]他会唱民谣寻开心&讲法语讨生活——走着走着正好碰到布朗丹，那个变态警察——他喜欢杀牛蛙&他的老板总是说“他伤了膝盖但你还是能看到他奔跑，宝贝，你还是能看到他奔跑&追逐那些到河边来的中国小妞”——反正布朗丹——他来是要打探陌生人，他的跟屁虫，人称小棍儿，带了一根烧焦的帽针&两块卫生巾以备不时之需……他们在一个酷似渔人矮头[10]的空地上汇合了团队……焊工吉姆甘地从他的窗户望出来——&嚷着像是“嘿嘿狗崽子们——快滚要不就永永[11]闭嘴”这时小娘们摊开大腿进入交叉准心&倾泻巴拉巴拉种籽油，但没有谁打喷嚏——她开始叫嚷她老爸是谁谁，但是这也不起

begins to yell about who her father is, but this doesnt work
either...her fat two dollar bill falls dead from a bullet–"the
86 flag of tex's ass is upon ye" screams Jim Ghandi & the
chick immediately takes to the hills–Peewee drops his
cookies as up drives an XKE with Sandy Bob's cousin,
Sandy Slim, who shows everybody his pictures of Nasser
& says "hold it boys, i know all about these things–i used
to work in the edsel factory" taking advantage of the
confusion, Little Stick steals the white elephant...nobody
notices–not even Brown Dan, who by this time is busy
beating Jake the Flesh to death with a hacksaw–all in all,
the situation in viet nam is very disturbing

who wants to be noticed anyway? only you,
who believes what suits you, could speak
so badly of thelonius baker–what'd he
ever do to you anyway besides get his
name in the papers? dont you know that
everybody wants to pick a moron for you–
dont concern yourself with all this
pettiness–it will all pass–think big–
youve seen the sign–all in all, tho,
youre a pretty good guy–stay clean–
dont waste your money on haircuts–see you
at the drugstore

your highness,
Gumbo the Hobo

效……她的肥肥两美元钞票被一颗子弹打中摔死了——“得克萨斯傻死的旗帜插着你们”[12] 吉姆甘地大叫＆小娘们立刻跑进山里——小不点丢了他的甜饼驾着一辆XKE[13] 载上桑迪鲍勃的老表桑迪瘦子，他到处跟人炫耀他的纳赛尔照片[14] ＆说“瞧好了小子，我可知道所有这一切事情——我曾在埃德赛工厂[15] 干过”趁着一片混乱，小棍儿偷走了白象……谁都没注意，包括布朗丹，他这一次是忙着用钢锯也要把大肉杰克活活揍死——总而言之，越南的局势非常乱

谁又想被人注意呢？只有你，
相信什么适合你，才能那样
过分地数落塞洛尼厄斯贝克[16]——他
到底对你做了什么呢除了把他的
名字印在报纸上？你知不知道
人人都想挑一个白痴给你——
不要为这种鸡毛蒜皮让自己
太操心了——都会过去的——想大点——
你已经看见征兆——反正，总之，
你是一个好小伙子——保持本色——
不要浪费金钱去理发——下次
在药店见

你的王子
流浪者秋葵汤

注 释

1 贝可斯河（Pecos）流域位于美国南部新墨西哥州和得克萨斯州一带。

2 桑迪·鲍勃（Sandy Bob），美国民谣《在魔鬼尾巴上系个结》（“Tying a Knot in the Devil's Tail”）唱的其中一个牛仔。

3 白象（white elephant），东南亚的瑞兽，在英语中常比喻代价高昂但毫无用处的玩意儿。

4 威奇托瀑布（Wichita Falls），美国得克萨斯州城市。

5 国王大道（El Camino Real），西班牙人在美洲殖民地修建的道路系统，至今仍在一些老地名中有保留。文中可能借以对比“胡志明小道”。

6 杰拉德·麦克“啵音啵音”（Gerald McBoing-Boing），美国1950年同名动画片中的一个小男孩，他不（会）说话，弄出各种声音来表达，后来成为电台有名的神童音效师。另，杰里（Jerry）也是同时期动画片《猫和老鼠》（*Tom and Jerry*）中老鼠的名字。波音公司（Boeing）是当时最先进的B-52“同温层堡垒”战略轰炸机的生产商。

7 这几句穿插了爵士乐老歌《莉萨》（“Liza”，1929），原词大意：月光映照河水，莉萨快来与我相会，天色已昏暗，但你的微笑将驱走我所有的阴霾，我们就要跟布朗牧师约好日子，去定下你将属于我的那个日子。另，飞艇（blimp），常指胖子。

8 2美元纸币很少使用，于1966年8月停印。

9 《灰鹅》（“Grey Goose”）、《约翰·亨利》（“John Henry”）、《巫医》（“The Medcine Man”）等均为美国传统民谣的经典曲目，铅肚皮都曾唱过。

10 渔人矮头（fisherman's dwarf），音近“渔人码头”（fisherman's wharf）。

11 永永（frever），音近“永远”（forever）。

12　得克萨斯傻死的旗帜插着你们（the flag of tex's ass is upon ye），戏拟美国老歌《得克萨斯的眼睛》（"The Eyes of Texas"，1903），歌词大意：得克萨斯的眼睛注视着你，你无法躲避，不要设想你能够逃脱，无论夜晚还是凌晨，直到大天使吹响号角。

13　XK-E，英国捷豹汽车公司在 20 世纪 60 年代推出的中高端跑车系列，造型时髦，评价甚高。

14　纳赛尔（Nasser），可能指贾迈勒·阿卜杜·纳赛尔（Gamal Abdel Nasser，1918—1970），时任埃及总统，1956 年成功收复苏伊士运河。

15　埃德赛（Edsel），美国福特汽车公司在 1958 年推出的中端车型，但遭遇惨败，沦为笑柄。另，福特公司并没有为该车型安排专门工厂生产线，导致品控混乱。

16　塞洛尼厄斯贝克（thelonious baker），混合了两个著名爵士乐演奏家的名字，塞洛尼厄斯·蒙克（Thelonious Monk，1917—1982）和切特·贝克（Chet Baker，1929—1988）。

Sacred Cracked Voice
& the Jingle Jangle Morning

87 go on–flutter ye mystic ballad–ah haunting & Tokay jittery ye be like the mad pulse–the mad pulse of child–the children of ring around the rosy & wandering poets over India–the jugglers who call you by the wrong name & title you wounded kitten–it is that easy for they know no fairy tales...in the modal tuning–a pontiac is parked without a leg to stand on–Plague the Kid–crusading in the blues dimension, he–hitchhiking the pontiac–brooding over the highway & searching for Joker–or perhaps the devil's eight drummer "down with enthusiasm!" says Plague "it is all temporary! away with it!" & Lord Randall playing with a quart of beer–Fanny Blair dragging a judge–Willy Moore, a shoemaker, who counts his thumbs with a switchblade along with Sir James, the dunce, who wears a stovepipe when he goes out on the town–Matty Groves, who secretly at midnight tries to chop down the church steeple with Edward, who cuts hedges for his wages & last but not least–Barbara Allen–she smuggles Moroccan cinders into Brooklyn twice a month & she wears a sheet–she takes many penicillin shots "anything temporary can be used for money reasons" says Plague &

神圣破锣嗓＆叮当咣当的早晨[1]

继续吧——扑动你神秘的歌谣——啊萦绕不去＆托凯[2]惊惊颤颤的你就像狂乱的脉搏——孩子的狂乱脉搏——那些绕啊绕玫瑰[3]的孩子们＆漫游在印度各地的诗人们——杂耍师都叫错了你的名字＆称你为受伤的猫咪——他们轻易就相信没有童话存在……以调式定弦[4]——停放的庞蒂亚克[5]没有一条腿站得住——瘟疫小子——在蓝调空间里东征西讨，他——在路边搭上那辆庞蒂亚克——对着公路思虑重重＆寻找小丑[6]——也有可能是魔鬼的八鼓手“打倒狂热！”瘟疫说“世事无常！终将消散！”＆兰德尔老爷[7]耍着一夸脱啤酒——芳妮布莱尔[8]拖着一个法官——威利穆尔[9]，一个鞋匠，他用弹簧刀打发时间还有詹姆斯爵士[10]，蠢货，他进城的时候戴着烟囱帽[11]——马蒂格罗夫斯[12]半夜里偷偷出去要劈掉教堂的尖塔，伙同爱德华[13]，他砍篱笆挣工钱＆最后但不是最次要的——芭芭拉艾伦[14]——她每个月两次把摩洛哥煤渣偷运到布鲁克林＆她穿一身床单——她打很多针青霉素“凡无常之物皆可为金钱所用”瘟疫说＆所有这些人——随便

88 all these people–call them what you will–they believe him–yesterday i talked to Abner for forty minutes–he, Abner–cursed out East Texas, tomatoes & tin pan alley–he didnt talk to me–he talked into a mirror–i did not have the courage to crash or shatter myself...when i left him, i met Puff–Puff had nothing but bad words for unemployment, Wrigley's Spearmint & Rabelais–i slapped myself in the face–he told me i was crazy & my only regret being that i could not fart thru my mouth–i walked away into a dimestore...what i speak of is the crazy unspeakable microphone & great flower celebration–it is not phony vision but rather friendly dark–behold the dark–your strength–the darkness "the matrimony of self & spinal dream" says Plague the Kid & we buy him a boxcar–Hysterical–melody in the Hysterical–as opposed to the music which offers every sound to make life existable excpt that of silence... Houdini & the rest of the ordinary people taking down puckered Jesus posters out there on 61 highway–Midas putting them back up–in the throne sinks Cleo–she sinks because she's fat...this land is your land & this land is my land–sure–but the world is run by those that never listen to music anyway–"enthusiasm is music which needs a flashlight to be heard" so says Plague

sorry to say baby but you ARE hung up
arent you? you know like suppose everybody
89 DOES tell you youre like sabatchead
dajapeeled...you know what happened to him

你怎么叫他们——他们都信他——昨天我跟阿伯纳谈了四十分钟——他，阿伯纳——咒骂东得克萨斯、番茄&锑盘巷[15]——他不搭理我——他跟镜子说话——我没有勇气去砸烂或粉碎我自己……离开他之后，我遇见扑忽[16]——扑忽一无所有只剩下满口关于失业的坏话，白箭口香糖&拉伯雷——我抽了自己一耳光——他告诉我说我疯了&我唯一的遗憾就是我不能用嘴巴放屁——我转头走进一家杂货铺……我要说的是一个不可言说的癫狂麦克风&盛大的鲜花庆典——那不是冒充的幻象而是温柔的黑暗——快看那黑暗——你的力量——那黑暗“自我&脊髓梦幻的联姻”瘟疫小子说&我们给他买一个车皮——歇斯底里——那歇斯底里的曲调——与之相反的是音乐所呈现的每一个声响都令生命得以存在而非沉寂……胡迪尼[17]&其余的平民百姓在61号国道[18]把皱巴巴的耶稣招贴画全都撕掉——弥达斯[19]又把它们贴回去——宝座上陷没着克丽奥[20]——她之所以陷没是因为太胖了……这片土地是你的土地&这片土地是我的土地[21]——那确实——但世界却由那些根本不听音乐的人来运转——“狂热就是一种要打电筒才能听见的音乐”瘟疫如是说

真不想说宝贝但你**确实**太牵肠挂肚
不是吗？你知道就像好比每个人
都来告诉你说你就像破鞋脑袋
已然剥皮……你知道被人读完之后

after everybody read him–yeah he went
right up on the shelf...let me know if
you could use a horse tamer or a good
worried mind...

your meatman
Shorty Cookie

他遭遇了什么——哈他直接就
被妥妥地束之高阁……请告诉我
你是否懂得使用驯马师或者
适度的忧虑之心……

你的肉贩子
墩墩饼

注　释

1　标题参见迪伦歌曲《铃鼓先生》："嘿！铃鼓先生，为我奏一曲 / 我还不想睡，也没有什么地方可去 /……在这叮当咣当的早晨，我愿意追随着你。"

2　托凯（Tokay），一般指葡萄酒名。

3　《绕啊绕玫瑰》（"Ring around the Rosy"，"Ring a Ring o'Roses"），英语传统儿歌和游戏，类似"编花篮"。

4　调式定弦（modal tuning），吉他等弦乐器的一种非标准调音法，比如把所有的琴弦都调到一个音级，不区分大小调性，弹奏某些简单和弦或特殊声效。另，据下文也可理解为汽车的改装、升级、调试等。

5　庞蒂亚克（Pontiac），美国通用汽车公司旗下的中端品牌，在当时备受好评。

6　小丑（Joker），美国老牌漫画《蝙蝠侠》中的大反派。

7　兰德尔老爷（Lord Randall），出自同名英国传统民谣，大意讲妈妈不断追问儿子兰德尔为什么不对劲，最后才知道他在晚会上被自己的爱人投了毒，已经快要死去。迪伦歌曲《暴雨将至》即受《兰德尔老爷》的影响。

8　芳妮·布莱尔（Fanny Blair），出自同名英国传统民谣，大意讲一个囚犯临死前坚称自己被冤枉，没有强奸11岁的小姑娘芳妮。

9　威利·摩尔（Willie Moore），出自20世纪同名美国民谣，大意讲威利和安娜相爱，但父母不同意他们结婚，后来安娜投河自尽，威利孤苦一生。

10　詹姆斯爵士（Sir James），出自英国传统民谣《玫瑰詹姆斯爵士》（"Sir James the Rose"），大意讲杀人犯詹姆斯四处躲藏，但被情人出卖了行踪，最后死在仇家的长矛下。

11　在学校惩罚差生或捉弄笨小孩时，会给他戴一顶纸筒尖尖帽。

12　马蒂·格罗夫斯（Matty Groves），出自同名英国传统民谣，大意讲少年马蒂在教堂勾搭上一个贵妇，他们被捉奸在床，马蒂死于决斗，贵妇也被丈夫杀死。

13　爱德华（Edward），出自同名英国传统民谣，大意讲妈妈不断追问儿子爱德华为什么剑上滴血，原来他已经杀死了父亲，准备抛弃一切逃往远方，任由家产荒废、妻儿乞食，他只给妈妈留下来自地狱的诅咒。

14　芭芭拉·艾伦（Barbara Allen），出自同名英国传统民谣，大意讲芭芭拉狠心拒绝了病危的追求者，但两人先后死去，他们的墓树交缠成同心结。迪伦1962年唱过这首歌。

15　锑盘巷（Tin Pan Alley），位于纽约百老汇附近，在二战前曾是音乐人和相关产业的聚集区，因此成为旧时代流行音乐的代名词。

16　扑忽（Puff），出自1963年的热门歌曲《神龙扑忽》（"Puff, the Magic Dragon"），大意讲神龙扑忽和小男孩杰基·佩帕原是纵横四海的玩伴，但男孩渐渐长大，忘却了年少时的奇想，神龙失去了朋友，也失去了勇气，它忧伤地躲进洞穴，从此不再玩耍。

17　哈利·胡迪尼（Harry Houdini，1874—1926），美国魔术师，以逃脱术享誉世界，晚年致力于揭露通灵术、招魂术、降神术以及各种宗教迷信的骗局。

18　61 号国道（Highway 61），纵贯美国南北的大道，从新奥尔良经孟菲斯、圣路易斯抵达芝加哥，很多老民谣歌手曾沿途旅行，迪伦的家乡就在这条路的北段。参见鲍勃迪伦歌曲《重访 61 号国道》。

19　在古希腊神话中，吕底亚的国王弥达斯（Midas）听到太阳神阿波罗和牧神潘的音乐比赛，他认为潘的芦笛要优于阿波罗的竖琴，阿波罗大怒，把弥达斯的耳朵变成驴耳朵。弥达斯用高高的王冠遮住耳朵，理发匠发现了这个秘密又不敢声张，只能对着河边一个土洞诉说，后来河边长出的芦苇都吹着“国王长了驴耳朵”。另一个故事讲弥达斯获得了金手指的神通，所触之物都变成黄金，但因此失去了人生幸福，比喻嗜财如命的大富翁。

20　克丽奥（Cleo），可能指埃及艳后克丽奥帕特拉（Cleopatra），或克丽奥·布朗（Cleo Brown，1907—1995），美国爵士乐女歌手、钢琴家，1953 年退出乐坛，成为修女。

21　这两句出自伍迪·格思里的代表曲目《这片土地是你的土地》（“This Land Is Your Land”，1940）。

Flunking the Propaganda Course

strange men with belly trouble & their pin up girls: zelda rat–crooked betty & volcano the leg–here they come–theyre popped out & theyve been seen crying in the chapel–their friend, who says that everybody cries alot–he's the congressional one & carries the snapshots–his name is Tapanga Red–known in L.A. as Wipe 'M Out–he coughs alot–anyway they walk in–it's very early & they ask for black mongrels apiece–jenny says "why not roll'm?" "theyre cops!" says a little boy who just climbed a mountain & who's learned how to smell in the circus–jenny retires to the pinball machine–steam getting thicker–zelda rat asks for second black mongrel–please make it hot–one of the men, he dangles a watch in front of her face "it's late–zeld babe–it's late" & zelda's face turns into a measle & she says "i'm allergic"–a ringing sound & she say "oh look–that girl over there is getting free balls"–trying to get jenny's attention, one of the men, he asks "anything bothering you?" jenny replies "yes–whatever happened to Orval Faubus?" & the man quickly drops the subject–his eye swollen he pushes one of the hot mongrels down poor zelda's dress–asks now does she

宣传课挂科

那些陌生人带着一肚子毛病&他们的海报女郎：泽尔达耗子——滑头贝蒂&长腿火山——他们大驾光临——他们砰地冒出来&他们曾被人看见在礼拜堂哭泣[1]——他们的朋友说每个人都哭得很厉害——他是国会的人&带着照片——他名叫塔潘加红人[2]——在洛杉矶人称抹杀者——他咳得厉害——总之他们进来了——天还很早&他们点了黑杂种每人一杯——珍妮说“怎么不捞了他们？”“他们是警察！”一个刚刚爬过山的小男孩说&他懂得怎样在马戏场上闻味道——珍妮回到弹球机前——蒸汽越来越浓——泽尔达耗子又点了一杯黑杂种——要热的谢谢——其中有个男的吊着一块表在她面前晃悠“天晚了——泽尔达宝贝——天晚了”&泽尔达起了一脸疹子&她说“我过敏”——铃声响起&她说“瞧嘿——那边那妞儿打通关了”为了吸引珍妮注意，其中有个男的问她“你是不是有麻烦？”珍妮答道“是啊——奥瓦尔福伯斯[3]究竟遭遇了什么？”&那人立马就放下话题——他的眼睛红肿他把其中一杯热的黑杂种打翻

wanna nother one–everybody breaks into stitches excpt someone who's talking to a window & jenny, who's busy racking up balls...the man who looks like an adam's apple–i think he belongs to crooked betty–he goes thru his stool–volcano–she wraps him in the national insider–everybody reads him–jenny tilts the machine–the man's dead–just then, the congressional one, he pulls out a luger he says a kraut give to him during the war which is a goddamn lie, & begins to shoot up the barbecue beef signs...the radio plays the star spangled banner–next day, a young arsonist, with a turtle on his head & his hands on his hips & his backbone slipping, sees me walking the donkey on the east side–"saw you with jenny last nite–anything happening there?" i say "oh my God, how can you ask such a thing? dont you know there are starving kids in
91 china?" he say "yes, but that was last nite–today' a new day" & i say "yeah–well that's too bad–i still aint gonna tell you nothing about jenny" he calls me an idiot & i say "here take my donkey if it'll make you feel any better–i'm on my way to the movies anyway" it is five minutes to rush hour–a strange transaction of goods takes place on third avenue–the supermarket explodes from malnutrition–God bless malnutrition

i dont care what bob hope says–he
aint going with you nowhere–also, john
wayne mightve kicked cancer, but you
oughta see his foot–forget about those

在可怜的泽尔达的裙子上——问她还想不想要再来一杯——所有人都笑出褶子除了有一个正对着窗户说话&珍妮在忙着上分……那个男的长得像一块喉结——我想他是滑头贝蒂的人——他从自己的凳子中穿了过去——火山——她把他裹进国家内幕[4]——人人都读他——珍妮摇晃弹球机——那人死了——这时，那个国会的家伙拔出一把鲁格手枪他说是一个德国酸菜佬在战场上给他的真他妈吹牛，&开始射击烧烤牛肉招牌……电台播放星条旗永不落——第二天，有个年轻纵火犯头上戴着龟壳&两手叉在屁股上&他腰椎滑脱，他看见我在东区遛驴子——“昨晚看到你跟珍妮了——在那儿干嘛呢？”我说“上帝啊，你怎么问这种问题？你不知道在中国还有很多孩子忍饥受饿吗？”他说“没错，但那是昨晚嘛——今天是新的一天”&我说“是啊——那真是糟透了——但我还是不想告诉你任何有关珍妮的事”他叫我傻瓜&我说“我的驴子给你了如果能让你好过些的话——我反正是打算去看电影的”还差五分钟到高峰时间——在第三大道发生一场奇怪的货物交易——超级市场从营养不良中爆发——上帝保佑营养不良

我才不管鲍勃霍普[5]说什么——他
不会带你去任何地方——还有，约翰
韦恩[6]或许能打败癌症，但是你
应该看到他的脚——忘掉那些

hollywood people telling you what to do–
theyre all gonna get killed by the indians–
see you in your dreams

lovingly,
plastic man

好莱坞演员叫你该怎么怎么做的吧——
他们迟早都要死在印第安人手上——
我们梦里见

爱你的，
塑胶人

注　释

1 《在礼拜堂哭泣》（"Crying in the Chapel"，1953），美国流行福音歌曲，1965 年猫王凭翻唱此曲重新走红。

2 塔潘加（Tapanga），一种非洲砍刀，书中指洛杉矶附近的一个小镇、艺术村托潘加（Topanga），以及芝加哥蓝调吉他手"坦帕红人"（Tampa Red，1904—1981），他对摇滚乐影响极大。

3 奥瓦尔・福伯斯（Orval Faubus，1910—1994），1955—1967 年连任美国阿肯色州州长，1957 年 9 月派遣国民警卫队阻止黑人学生进入小石城中央中学就读。

4 国家内幕（the national insider），美国 20 世纪 60—70 年代有同名花边新闻小报。

5 鲍勃·霍普（Bob Hope，1903—2003），美国著名笑星、主持人，有"路"系列喜剧片，如《香港之路》（*The Road to Hong Kong*，1962）。

6 约翰・韦恩（John Wayne，1907—1979），美国著名影星，以硬汉形象闻名，1964 年被诊断出肺癌，切除了左肺及 4 根肋骨。他从影前是橄榄球运动员，因伤退役。

Ape on Sunday

92 ZING & they throw him thru the door & he lands in truck–he gets out somewhere on the Mobile line & says "the war's going fine–aint it paleface?" & immediately makes a friend..."it's nice to have friends aint it shitbrain?" this makes a stronger tie & both of 'm together–they go beat up some male secretary who works for a jockey... UNTOUCHABLE–they walk thru the streets of France & poison the dogs & when they get back–both receive medals for bravery "it's nice to have medals aint it monsterass?" they cannot be separated these two friends...they are invited to speak at religious & college gatherings & finally become board members of the rootbeer industry "it's nice to have all the rootbeer you can drink aint it fishturd?" an ABSOLUTE bond that cannot be broken...one day one of the friends discovers that he's never been doing any of the talking...he inquires about it but gets no response–he murders the other friend & some young punk around town–he gets put in jail for 90 years...everything wouldve been overlooked but John Huston–& i do mean John Huston–he made a Bible movie out of it & changed all the names–also there was nothing in the plot of course about the rootbeer stand–other'n that–it was a full drag "i was expecting to see a bit of Mobile"–

星期天的猿猴

嗖&他们把他扔出门外&他落在卡车里——他在开往莫比尔[1]的某个地方下来&说“这一仗打得够爽——对吧白皮佬？”&马上就交起朋友来……“交朋友很开心是不是，猪脑袋？”这话更加拉近了关系&两人凑到一块——他们胖揍了某个为骑师工作的男秘书……**不可触摸**[2]——他们走过法兰西的街道&给狗下毒&他们回来的时候——两人都获得英勇勋章“戴勋章很开心是不是大驴怪？”他们没法分开这两个老友……他们应邀在宗教&大学集会上演讲&最终成为根汁汽水公司的董事会成员“喝根汁汽水喝到饱很开心是不是鱼粪？”一个牢不可破的**绝对**友谊……有一天一个老友发现他从来没做过传闻中的那些事……他去打听但是没有回音——他谋杀了另一位老友&城里的某个小阿飞——他被判90年徒刑……一切都会被忽视除了约翰休斯顿[3]——&确实是约翰休斯顿——他据此拍了一部圣经片&改了所有人的名字——而且剧情当然一点都没提那根汁汽水的事——除此之外——全是瞎扯“我期待能看一眼莫比尔”

said Princess "i was really expecting to see a bit of Mobile"–
Princess is an ape–she usually goes to movies on Sundays

93

look you asshole–tho i might be nothing but
a butter sculptor, i refuse to go on working
with the idea of your praising as my reward–
like what are your credentials anyway? excpt for
talking about all us butter sculptors, what else
do you do? do you know what it feels like to
make some butter sculpture? do you know what
it feels like to actually ooze that butter around
& create something of fantastic worth? you said
that my last year's work "The King's Odor" was
great & then you say i havent done anything as
great since–just who the hell are you talking to
anyway? you must have something to do in your
real life–i understand that you praised the piece
you saw yesterday entitled "The Monkey Taster"
about which you said meant "a nice work of butter
carved into the shape of a young man who likes
only african women" you are an idiot–it doesnt
mean that at all...i hereby want nothing to do
with your hangups–i really dont care what you think
of my work as i now know you dont understand it
anyway...i must go now–i have this new hunk of

公主说“我真的很期待能看一眼莫比尔”——公主是一只猿猴——她通常星期天去看电影

瞧你那臭屁股——也许我不过是
一个黄油雕塑家，我拒绝再迎合
你的赞美就是我的奖赏这样的观念——
难道你有什么资历证书吗？除了
对我们黄油雕塑家说三道四，你还会
干点什么？你知道做成一个黄油雕塑
是什么感觉吗？你知道真正地挤出黄油
&造出价值非凡的东西是什么感觉吗？你
　　原说
我去年的作品“王者之气”是
杰出的&现在你又说我再也没做出那样
杰出的东西——你他妈到底在跟谁
说话？你在现实生活中肯定也有你的
事情做——我能理解你昨天看了
那尊“猴子品尝师”之后发出的赞美
你的意思是说“一件好的黄油作品
就是要雕出一个只喜欢非洲婆娘的
青年男子的形象”你就是个蠢货——这根本
不搭界……因此我不想跟你的执念
有任何瓜葛——我真不在乎你怎么看
我的作品反正我知道了你根本就不懂……
我必须走了——我还有这一大块新到的

margarine waiting in the bathtub–yes i said
MARGARINE & next week i just might decide
to use
cream cheese–& i really dont care what you
think of my experimenting–you take yourself
too seriously–youre going to get an ulcer &
go into the hospital–they'll put you in a
94 ward where you cant have any visitors–you'll
go right off your nut–i really dont care anymore–
i am so bored with your rules & regulations
that i might not even talk to you again–just
remember tho, when you evaluate a piece of
butter, you are talking about yourself, so
you'd just better sign your name...see you,
if youre lucky, at mrs. keeler's cake festival

yours

Snowplow Floater

p.s. youre my friend & i'm trying to help you

collision

boss aint it awful the way
they make you look at things
as if you were inside of a toilet–
their toilet!

人造黄油在浴缸里等着呢——对我说的就是
人造黄油&下周我就可以定下来使用
奶油干酪了——&我真的不在乎你怎么
看待我的实验——你把你自己
太当回事——你这样会得溃疡的&
快上医院吧——他们会把你送进一个
绝对无人探视的病房——直到你
沤坏了脑壳——我就真的什么都不在乎了——
你的那些规则&条条框框把我给烦得
都不想再跟你说话——但你要
记住，在你评价一个黄油雕塑的时候，
你不过是说你自己，那样
你最好签上你的名字……下次见，
如果你走运的话，就在基勒太太[4]的糕饼大
　　会上

你的
雪犁浮浪子

另，你是我的朋友&我是想帮你

对撞

老板这样吓不吓人[5]
他们教你盯着些东西
就像你蹲在厕所里边那样——
她们的厕所！

these sadistic nurses–they speak
to me as if i was a finger–
i lay in this bed unprotected &
the fellow next door–he must
be a Zulu–the doctors cant
stand him
& he gets no visitors–the
Sister says he's irreligious but
i just think he gags alot
boss three bodies got shipped out
this morning–Lady Esther said that
they went to the hunting ground–
Cronie said that they never were
worth much anyway & St. Crockasheet
said abracadabra–Lady Esther is
the cleaning lady & she was
mopping up the beds when i woke
up...there was some candle wax
on the window–Cronie said not
to touch it

there is a sign in the hall that reads "Quiet"–
it waits for no one–i think that is
what makes people different than
signs

这些嗜虐的护士——她们对我
说话时就好比我是一根手指[6]——
我躺在这张无遮无盖的床上&
隔壁房间的那个家伙——他肯定
是个祖鲁人——连医生都
受不了他
&他无人探视——嬷嬷
说他是不敬神的但
我觉得他只是塞得太撑了
老板今天早上三具尸体已经
运走了——埃丝特女士[7]说
他们去了打猎场——
克罗尼说他们根本
就没那么值钱&圣狗屁连篇
念念有词——埃丝特女士是
一个清洁工&当我
醒来的时候她正在擦洗
床铺……有些蜡烛油
滴在窗户上——克罗尼说别
碰它

大厅上有一块标牌写着"静"——
它不等待任何人[8]——我想就是
这一点造成了人与标识之间的
区别

i say to him "they'll get you"
& he say "no" & i say "& if they
dont get you, you'll get yourself"
& he say "you got bad manners &
i go to church & nobody's gonna
get me" & then some guys wearing
parachutes come in & give him
a wiff of mint & hand him a
peacock feather & then they slit
his throat...i looked out the
96 window & saw this car stop–it
had a bumper sticker saying
"Vote, Goat" & a man got out &
wiped his feet on a doormat–
he carried a book of Aesop's Fables
& then Lady Esther came in again
& cleaned up the mess–i turned
on the radio but all that was
happening was the news

boss aint it fierce the way that one
woman with the Persian monkey treated
the other woman with the Alley monkey?
Claudette came to see me last nite–

我对他说“他们会抓到你的”
&他说“不会”&我说“&如果他们
没抓到你，你也会抓自己”
&他说“你不讲礼貌&
我去教堂&没有谁要来
抓我”&这时有几个兵背着
降落伞走进来&喷了他
一口薄荷气&交给他一根
孔雀毛&然后他们切开
他的喉咙……我望着窗户
外边&看见这辆车停住——它
在保险杠上有张贴纸说
“我选山羊”，[9] 一个人下了车&
在门垫上刮刮他的鞋——
他拿着一本《伊索寓言》
&这时埃丝特女士又进来了
&把垃圾打扫干净——我打开
收音机但前面发生的
那些事就是新闻了

老板这样够厉害吗就像一个
养波斯猴子的女人对待
另一个养胡同猴子的女人？
克劳黛昨晚过来看我——

she doesnt own a monkey & she couldnt
get it–then at the same time, the nurse
came in & said "it's raining cats &
dogs outside–is it too much for you
to bear ha ha?" i couldve swallowed her

tonite i dance with Strawberry, the
bloody clothes wife–i say her head,
if necessary, would crack like an egg
& she damns me–if i thank her
then she calls me a whore so there's
no way out...my mind is with the kitchen
workers but when they catch spiders &
97 pull their legs off & laugh–it usually
wakes me up...i am sick of people
praising Einstein–bourgeois ghosts–
i am sick of heroic sorrow

as soon as i get out of here
i'm going to my blood bank
& make a withdrawal & go
to Greece–Greece is beautiful
& nobody understands you
there

她没有养猴子＆她也搞不到
一只——就在那个时候，护士
进来了＆说“外面大雨下得鸡飞＆
狗跳——对你来说是不是实在
难以承受哈哈？”我差点没吃了她

今晚我的舞伴是草莓[10]，一个
穿血红裙的婆娘——我说她的脑袋
很有可能会像鸡蛋那样被砸碎
＆她骂我——如果我感谢她
她就把我叫做婊子这样就
没出路了……我的思维紧跟着那些厨房
帮工但在他们抓蜘蛛的时候＆
拔掉它们的腿脚＆大笑——这声音
经常吵醒我……我最恶心有人
赞美爱因斯坦——资产阶级幽灵——
我最恶心英雄的哀伤

只要我一离开这儿
我就去找我的血液银行
＆提款＆然后去
希腊——希腊很美
＆那里没人理解
你

the janitor with a glass eye–
he's all right–at least he
minds his own business–he
tells me that Shakespeare's relatives
killed his ancestors–& that now
his brothers wont read Shakespeare...
he says that he used to ride to
church on a ox & when they sold
the church, he sold the ox...
the janitor, he's ok...Lady
Esther says that he aint never
gonna amount to much but i
never speak to Lady Esther &
what does she know about people
with glass eyes anyway?
98 my bosom feels like the
grave diggers have been at
it all nite...tomorrow
if i'm lucky, i'll have breakfast
in Heaven...some crazy fishhook dangles
thru my window–i might as well
get up & walk on my forehead–
i might as well lose all my tickets...
i wish there was something i
wanted as badly as this fishhook

那个镶了玻璃眼珠的门房——
他很好——起码他
重视他的职业——他
告诉我说莎士比亚的亲戚
杀了他的祖先——&所以现在
他家的兄弟都不会去看莎士比亚……
他说他从前常骑着一头牛
上教堂&后来教堂被卖掉了
他也卖掉了那头牛……
门房不错的……埃丝特
女士说他绝不可能
有啥了不起但我
从不跟埃丝特女士说话&
她对镶了玻璃眼珠的人
又能有什么了解呢?
我的胸部感觉就像有
掘墓人在里面整夜整夜地
挖着……明天
如果走运，我就可以在天堂
吃早餐……我的窗户挂着某种
疯狂的鱼钩——看来我还是
起床吧&用额头走路——
看来我还是丢了所有的票票……
但愿还能有些东西是我
极度想要的就像这枚鱼钩

wants to express itself

dear mister congressman:
it's about my house–some time
ago i made a deal with a syrup company
to advertise their product on the side
facing the street–it wasnt so bad at
first, but soon they put up another
ad on the other side–i didn't even
mind that, but then they plastered
these women all over the windows with
cans of syrup in their arms–in exchange
the company paid my phone & gas bill &
bought a few clothes for the tots–i told
the town council that i'd do most anything
just to let some sun in the house but they
said we couldnt offend the syrup company
99 because it's called Granma Washington's
Syrup & people tend to associate it with
the constitution...the neighbors dont help
me at all because they feel that if anything
comes off my house, it'll have to go on theirs
& none of them want their houses looking like
mine–the company offered to buy my house as
a

想要表现它自己

尊敬的议员先生：
我要说我房子的事——不久
前我跟一家糖浆公司签约
在当街的立面上给他们
做广告——事情刚开始还
不坏，但很快他们在另一面又
贴了个广告——我根本都没
在意，但他们把每个窗户
都糊满了怀里抱着糖浆罐头的
女人像——作为交换
公司付我的电话费&煤气费&
买了些衣服给小孩——我上报给
市政局说我已经想尽了办法
只求能有点阳光照进屋里但是他们
说我们不能得罪那家糖浆公司
因为它叫做华盛顿奶奶牌
糖浆&人们都习惯把它联想到
国家体制……邻居们也都不肯
帮我因为他们觉得如果什么事情
离了我的房子，就肯定要轮到他们家
&他们都不想自己的房子落得像
我家那模样——公司出价要买我的房子做
永久广告牌，但上帝啊，我的根都

permanent billboard sign, but God, i got my
roots here & i had to refuse at first–now they
tell me some negroes are moving in down the
block–as you can see, things dont look
too good at the moment–my eldest son is
in the army so he cant do a thing–i
would appreciate any helpful suggestion–
thank you

yours in allegiance
Zorba the Bomb

扎在这儿&我立刻就拒绝了——现在他们
又告诉我说有一帮黑人要搬进
这条街来——你看，事情到这一步
就不怎么好了——我的大儿子
在部队所以他什么也做不了——我
企盼您能给予宝贵意见——
谢谢

您忠诚的

炸弹佐巴[11]

注　释

1　莫比尔（Mobile），美国亚拉巴马州南部港口城市，原为法国殖民地；"mobile"也有运动、活动的意思。参见迪伦歌曲《又被困在莫比尔听孟菲斯蓝调》（"Stuck Inside of Mobile with the Memphis Blues Again"，1966）。

2　不可触摸（UNTOUCHABLE），可能出自美国警匪连续剧《铁面无私》（*The Untouchables*，1959—1963）。

3　约翰·休斯顿（John Huston，1906—1987），美国著名导演，有影片《圣经：创世记》（*The Bible: In the Beginning*，1966）。

4　基勒太太（mrs. keeler），可能指英国舞女克莉丝汀·基勒（Christine Keeler，1942—2017），曾同时与英国陆军大臣和苏联驻英使馆武官有染，丑闻于1963年曝光，间接导致英国保守党在次年大选丢失了政权。

5　出自美国幽默作家"侯爵大人"（Don Marquis，1878—1937）的讽刺诗《执拗的瓢虫》（"The Froward Lady Bug"，1913）。后文

多处与“侯爵大人”的讽刺诗有关。

6 手指(finger),俚语中又作“扒手”“告密者”“卑鄙的人”之意。

7 埃丝特女士(Lady Esther),美国化妆品厂商,二战前后曾赞助几个有名的电台栏目。

8 它不等待任何人(it waits for no one),有英谚:“时间不等人。”

9 我选山羊,亦即跳出驴党、象党二选一的框框。

10 出自美国早期流行歌曲《乐队开始演奏》(“The Band Played On”,1895),又名《草莓红金发美人》(“The Strawberry Blonde”),同名电影曾获1941年奥斯卡最佳音乐片奖。

11 佐巴(Zorba),出自希腊著名作家尼科斯·卡赞扎基斯的长篇小说《希腊人佐巴》(*Zorba the Greek*,1946),同名电影于1964年上映。

Cowboy Angel Blues

100 meanwhile back in texas–beautiful texas–Freud paces back & forth–struggling with his boot & trying to finish his Vermouth–"fraid you got the wrong idea Mr. Clap–if i was you, i'd give in & go chop those trees down for my mother–after all, there's a little mother in all of us" "yes but i mean why do you think i do it? why do you think i intentionally set fire to my bed everytime she asks me to cut down those trees? why?" "yes–well–Mr. Clap–perhaps it is the womb calling–you know–perhaps when you were a little boy, you heard a tree falling & the sound of it went WOOOOM & now as you are older–everytime you hear that sound–in one form or another of course–you just want to–oh shall we say–light it up?" "yes that seems logical–thank you very much–i feel to go chop those trees down now" "ah but remember son–a tree falling in the forest without any sound has nobody to hear it!" "yes–well–i shall be there then–i shall not burn my bed anymore" "good–let me know of your progress & if anything drastic comes up–here–take these pills–by the way, you should call your mother 'Stella' just to show her that you mean

牛仔天使蓝调[1]

而此刻回到得克萨斯——美丽的得克萨斯[2]——弗洛伊德来来&回回踱步——跟他的靴子作斗争&努力喝完他的苦艾酒——“恐怕你的头脑想错了克拉普先生——我要是你的话，我就让一步&去帮我妈妈把那些大树都劈掉砍倒——毕竟，我们每个人心中都有一个小妈妈”“没错但我想说的是为什么你认为我会那么干？为什么你认为每次她叫我去砍那些树的时候我就会故意放火烧我的床？为什么？”“是啊——哈——克拉普先生——也许那是子宫的呼唤——你懂的——也许在你还小的时候，你听见一棵树倒下&那声音响着**唔姆**[3]&现在你长大了——每当你听到那个声音——当然是以这样或那样的形式——你就想——哦我们应该说——把它点燃？”“没错这很合逻辑——非常感谢——我觉得现在就该把那些大树砍掉”“啊但是孩子你要记住——有一棵树在森林里倒落得无声无息就没有任何人能听见！[4]”“是啊——哈——我应该去那儿——我不会再烧我的床了”“好啊——要让我知道你的进步&如果有什么强烈

business–oh & while youre at it, could you chop me
some firewood please?" "yes–all right–thank you
very much again–excuse me sir–are you having some
trouble with your boot?" "no–no–my leg's just getting
101 a little hairier–that's all"...get back to this beautiful
texas & dont swap that cow–Corpus Christi aflame–
common thieves–maggots & millionaires trading sons
& dollars & rolling back chumps–the black gypsy lady
& Buddy Holly himself into the tanks & voids held
up to Scrawny Horizon by Lee Marvin & the forty
thieves BRILLIANT & Sancho Panza Remembered
like in an Arabic moonbook & Malcolm X Forgotten
like a caught fish & wonder–ah wonder just what–
just what That means...Lovetown so pathetic & the
grown men crying–the winds are anchored here &
you do not disturb these tears nor rivers–you do
not take baths in the abandoned bathtubs but rather
mix electric herbs & be watchdog to the Great
White Mountain...Funky Phaedra–in the center of
a No Disturb sign & Black Ace singing–she tries to
outstare a bowl of money–she–as they say–has one
foot in the grave–the apprentice clown, Tomboy, at
her feet–he's known professionally as Rabbit Rough
& plays a homemade steel guitar–when loaded,
he really bites into it–Weep the Greed is watching
the happening from a caved-in mare & he lights a
cigarette with one of his stolen wanted posters..."love
is magic" says Phaedra–Funky Phaedra–Rabbit dont
say nothing–Weep the Greed says "go to it gal!" "love
is wonderful" says Phaedra "get 'm, stranger!" says

反应——拿着——吃这些药——另外，你应该叫你妈妈‘斯特拉’[5]好让她看到你是当真的——哦&等你去到那儿的时候，也劈点柴火给我好吗？”“行——没问题——再次感谢你——请原谅先生——你的靴子是不是有问题？”“没有——没有——只是我的腿有点发毛——就那么回事”……回到这美丽的得克萨斯[6]&不要换那头牛——燃烧的圣体[7]——惯偷——蛆虫&百万富翁交易儿孙&金钱&木头往回滚——黑吉卜赛女士[8]&巴迪霍利[9]本人进入坦克&虚空被李马文[10]捧上瘦巴巴的天际&四十大盗[11]**光彩夺目**&被纪念的桑丘潘萨[12]如在阿拉伯月历&被遗忘的马尔科姆X[13]像一条网中鱼&诧异着——啊就是诧异着——就是那个是什么意思……爱情小镇好悲惨&成年人在哭泣——风向在这里抛锚&你不扰乱这些泪水或河流——你不在被人遗弃的浴缸里沐浴只爱混合电子香草&给大白山[14]做看家犬……疯起的菲德拉[15]——在请勿打扰标牌&黑老A[16]的歌声中央——她努力直视大碗钱财——大家都说——她已经一只脚踏进坟墓——见习丑角假小子，在她的脚边——他被行内人叫做粗毛兔子&在弹一把自制的钢吉他[17]——要是喝飞了，他真能大咬一口——贪婪的麦鸡正从一匹累塌了的母马观看这情形&他用一张他的贼赃通缉令点了根烟……“爱是魔法”[18]菲德拉——疯起的菲德拉说——兔子不作声——贪婪的麦鸡说“来吧姑娘！”“爱是奇妙无比”菲德拉说“抓住啊，陌生人！”贪婪的麦鸡说——

Weep the Greed–Phaedra takes off her stetson–five
bunnies & a nickel shot full of holes jump out "which
way's laos?" says one of the bunnies "some trick!" says
102 Weep the Greed–"love is that gliding feeling" "yipee!
& i'll be a coonbong!" says Wee the Greed "love is
gentleness–softness–creaminess" say Phaedra–who is
now having a pillow fight–her weapon, a mattress–
she stands on a deserted marshmallow–her foe, some
Unitarian who's fallen off one a them high sierras
& lived to tell about it–he holds a fascist pint of
yogurt "love is riding a striped mare across the orgy
plains on barbarian sunday" screams Rabbit Rough,
the apprentice clown–this is the first thing he's said
all day & now he hesitates–Phaedra–meanwhile–
is getting beaten in the fight–"sure it is" says Weep
the Greed "& then your mare ends up like this one–
then you put your arm in a sling–your feet in a vault
& then you get a job working for a camel–right?"
Phaedra–totally wiped out from the fight–she comes
crawling back–seizes Rabbit–pulls his shirt off–
twists his arm behind his back & throws him into the
windmill–Weep the Greed gets busted by the Padres
& all the wanted posters fly over the united states–
the mare gets confiscated & held without bail...Mr.
Clap–meantime–makes another visit to Freud "only
rich people can afford you" he says "only rich people
can afford all art–isnt that the way it is?" "isnt that
the way it always has been?" says Freud "ah yes" says
Mr. Clap with a sigh–"by the way–how's the mother?"
"oh she's ok–you know her name's Art–she makes a

菲德拉脱下她的牛仔帽——五只小兔＆一枚千疮百孔的硬币蹦出来“去老挝怎么走？”其中一只小兔说“好把戏！”贪婪的麦鸡说——“爱是那种滑动的感觉”“太棒了！＆我要做个机灵鬼！”贪婪的麦鸡说——“爱是温柔——体贴——像奶油一样”菲德拉说——她正在打枕头仗——她的武器，一张床垫——她站在一块废弃的棉花软糖上——她的敌人，某些一神论者他们从高高的山脊跌落＆又活了过来讲这故事——他端着一品脱法西斯酸奶“爱是骑着花斑母马在野蛮人的星期天穿过那纵欲的原野”见习丑角粗毛兔子大叫——这是他整日里说的第一句话＆现在他支支吾吾——菲德拉——与此同时——被打得满地找牙——“那确实”贪婪的麦鸡说“＆然后你的母马到头来也跟这个一样——然后你给胳膊吊上一条三角巾——你的双脚踩进墓室＆然后你找了一份活计去给骆驼打工——对不对？”菲德拉——被打得丢盔卸甲——她慢慢爬回来——捉住兔子——扯掉他的衬衫——把他的胳膊扭到背后＆把他扔进风车磨坊——贪婪的麦鸡被随军牧师们制服了＆所有的通缉令飞遍全美国——母马被没收＆不得保释……克拉普先生——与此同时——又一次去拜访弗洛伊德“只有富人才供得起你”他说“只有富人才供得起各种艺术——难道不是这样吗？”“难道不是一直都这样吗？”弗洛伊德说“没错啊”克拉普先生叹道——“另外——你妈妈好吗？”“哦，她很好——你知道她的名字叫艺术——她赚了很多

lot of money" "oh?" "yes–I've told her all about you–
you must come to the house some time" "yes" says
Freud with a martha raye type grin "yes–perhaps i
103 will"...Phaedra pounding her knuckles into a piece of
water–scratching her snake bites–a getaway car goes
by consisting of: three lying hunters off the Brazos
River–two window–peeking mothers each holding
some decayed pictures of lili st. cyr–a side order of
bacon–some underprivileged bonus babies shot full
of dexedrine–a painter with a plate on his face–one
barbell–Dracula smoking a cigarette & eating an angel–
the ghost of cheetah, madame nhu & bridey murphy
all wrapped in toothpaste–a box of magic wands & one
innocent bystander...needless to say–there is no more
room in the car–Phaedra scowls & she bellows "love
is going PLUMB INSANE" & wine bottle breaking–
texas exploding & dinner by the sea–ship commanders
with perfect features–theyre seen–theyre seen by
truckdrivers–the truckdrivers complain of hijacking
& see these ship commanders riding stallions into the
howling Gulf of Mexico & here comes Phaedra "love is
going plumb insane"...she is walking by Mr. Clap–who
is smiling–he wears his cap inside out–he's eating good
fruit–HE'LL be all right–Mr. Clap–he'll be all right

dear buzz:

i want the bibles marked up thirty percent–

to justify the markup, i want free hairbrushes

given away with each bible–also, the chocolate

钱”“啊？”“没错——你的事情我都已经告诉她了——你必须找个时间来家里”“好的”弗洛伊德带着玛莎雷伊[19]式的咧嘴笑说道“好的——我也许会去的”……菲德拉把拳头砸进一摊水里——挠着她的蛇咬伤口——逃亡飞车一路上满载：布拉索斯河边闲躺的三个猎人——两个在窗前窥看的妈妈各自捧着些莉莉圣西尔[20]的腐朽照片——小碟熏肉——几个失去特权的奖金宝贝[21]满肚子右旋安非他命——一个脸上挂着图版的画家——一副杠铃——德古拉抽着烟&嚼着一个天使——猎豹之灵，蹂夫人[22]&布莱蒂墨菲[23]全都裹在牙膏里——整箱的魔法杖&一个无辜的旁观者……不消说——车里根本没地方了——菲德拉绷着脸&她怒吼“爱是要**疯狂透顶**”&红酒瓶破碎——得克萨斯爆炸&海滨晚餐——仪表堂堂的船长们——他们被看见——他们被卡车司机看见——那些卡车司机控诉劫匪&眼看这些船长骑着种马进入咆哮的墨西哥湾&菲德拉驾到“爱是要彻底疯狂”……她身边是克拉普先生——笑眯眯的——他戴着一顶里朝外的帽子——他在吃好果子呢——**他会**[24]一切顺利——克拉普先生——他会一切顺利

亲爱的小嗡嗡：
我要把圣经涨价百分之三十——
为了显得合理，我要给每本圣经
附送一把免费梳子——此外，巧克力

jesuses should not be sold in the south...one
104 more thing, concerning the end of the world
game–perhaps if you had some germ warfare for
it you could sell it for twice as much–things
kinda stormy round here–office in turmoil–
secretary wiped out recently–guess what happened
to the pictures of the pres? yeah well some
joker drew a earring on him in the original print
& somehow it slipped by the production staff–
needless to say, we couldn't get rid of any
of them around here that's for sure, so we had
to ship them all to puerto rico–thing worked
out ok tho–distributors down there said they
went like hot cakes...almost as fast as the
red white & blue hamburger sets–oh–i meant to
tell you, i think if you made the "I voted for
the winner" buttons triangle shaped, they might
go a little faster...by the way, i did tell you
to send the "i'm a beatles eater" handkerchiefs to
the dominican republic & Not to england–fraid you
made a little mistake there, buzzy boy! like i
said, office in turmoil–got a new kid but he fell
in the water cooler right away...he's suing us for
teeth damage–lotza problems

see you in the cafeteria

耶稣不应该在南方销售……还有
一件事，关于这场世界游戏的
终局——如果你能为之发动细菌战
也许你能卖上两倍那么贵——这里的
情况有点波澜——办公室乱成一团——
秘书最近被搞掉了——猜猜总统的
那些肖像遭遇了什么？啊哈，有些个
捣蛋鬼在原作上给他画了一个耳环
&制作部门不知怎的竟然没看出来——
不消说，我们这里肯定是没办法
处理掉任何一张的，所以我们只好
把它们都运去波多黎各——事情
进展顺利——那边的经销商说这些肖像
卖得好抢手……简直跟红白&蓝汉堡[25]
套餐一样畅销——哦——我是想
告诉你，我觉得如果你把“我选
赢家”纪念章做成三角形的，那样会
好卖一些……另外，我都告诉过你了
把“我是披头士食用者”手帕发到
多米尼加共和国&不是英国——恐怕你
在此处犯了小错误，嗡嗡小子！如我
所说，办公室乱成一团——新招了个家伙但他
立刻就掉进冷饮水机里边……他还要我们赔偿
牙齿损害费——麻烦一大堆

餐厅再见

bosom buddy,
syd dangerous

知心兄弟，
危险的悉德

注　释

1　牛仔天使，亦即自由、流浪或堕落的天使。参见迪伦歌曲《伊甸园之门》（“Gates of Eden”，1965）：“牛仔天使骑着 / 四条腿的森林乌云 / 用他的蜡烛照射太阳。”另参见美国流行小说《午夜牛郎》(*Midnight Cowboy*,1965),讲一个得州男妓在纽约挣扎的故事。

2　《美丽的得克萨斯》（“Beautiful Texas”，1933），美国乡村音乐老歌，作者奥丹尼尔（W. Lee O'Daniel，1890—1969）早年是有名的电台主持人，后任得克萨斯州州长、参议员，1960 年在民主党总统候选人提名中曾击败林登·约翰逊。

3　原文“WOOOOM”，音近“womb”（子宫）。

4　出自英国哲学家乔治·贝克莱（George Berkeley，1685—1753）在《人类知识原理》（*The Principles of Human Konwledge*，1710）中提出的命题的衍生版本：如果一棵树在森林里倒落但没有人听见，它有没有发出声音？

5　斯特拉（Stella），可能指斯特拉·阿德勒（Stella Adler，1901—1992），美国女演员、教育家，开办演艺学校，借鉴斯坦尼斯拉夫斯基教学法，培养了马龙·白兰度、朱迪·加兰、伊丽莎白·泰勒等大批明星，被誉为“演艺之母”。

6　回到这美丽的得克萨斯（get back to this beautiful texas），参见伍迪·格思里歌曲《哆唻咪》（“Do Re Mi”，1940）：“喂，你最好回到美丽的得克萨斯、俄克拉何马、堪萨斯、佐治亚、田纳西。”

7　圣体（Corpus Christi），也可指得克萨斯州海滨城市科珀斯克里斯蒂。

8　黑吉卜赛女士（the black gypsy lady），参见迪伦歌曲《伊甸园之门》（1965）："摩托车黑圣母 / 两轮吉卜赛女王 / 和她银亮镶钉的魅影。"

9　巴迪·霍利（Buddy Holly，1936—1959），美国早期摇滚歌手，1959 年 2 月 3 日在巡演路上他和乐队一起死于空难，被称为"音乐死亡日"。在霍利死前两天，17 岁的迪伦近距离聆听了他的演唱会。

10　李·马文（Lee Marvin，1924—1987），美国演员，在影片《女贼金丝猫》（*Cat Ballou*，1965）中分饰正反派两个人物广受好评。

11　丘吉尔把 1921 年（开罗）中东殖民地会议的代表们称为"四十大盗"。

12　桑丘·潘萨（Sancho Panza），意即"猪肚皮"，堂吉诃德的侍从。

13　马尔科姆·艾克斯（Malcolm X，1925—1965），美国黑人运动领袖。另，美国学者玛格丽特·克拉普（Margaret Clapp，1910—1974）著有《被遗忘的第一公民》（*Forgotten First Citizen: John Bigelow*，1947）。

14　大白山（Great White Mountain），不详，可能指纽约百老汇的剧院聚集区，因灯火通明被戏称为"大白路"（Great White Way）。

15　菲德拉（Phaedra，淮德拉），古希腊神话中英雄忒修斯的第二个妻子，她爱上了继子希波吕托斯，遭到拒绝后自杀，并给忒修斯留言说希波吕托斯奸污了她，忒修斯因此咒杀希波吕托斯。参见迪伦歌曲《我要做你的爱人》（"I Wanna Be Your Lover"，1966）："菲德拉心如明镜 / 躺在草地上 / 她把一切都搞砸了，她垮掉了 / 因为她太过表露，但你不同 / 我想做你的爱人 / 我想做你的男人 / 我不想做她的，只想做你的。"

16　布莱克·艾斯（Black Ace，1905—1972），美国得克萨斯蓝调歌手，以夏威夷吉他为乐器。

17　钢吉他（steel guitar），一般指横置弹奏的夏威夷吉他、平板吉他。

18　参见《新约·哥林多前书》13:4-8："爱是恒久忍耐，又有恩慈；爱是不嫉妒，爱是不自夸，不张狂，不作害羞的事……爱是永不止息。"

19　玛莎·雷伊（Martha Raye，1916—1994），美国女笑星、歌手，绰号"大嘴"（Big Mouth）。

20　莉莉·圣西尔（Lili St. Cyr，1918—1999），美国著名脱衣舞女。

21　奖金宝贝（bonus baby），指直升全美职棒大联盟并获得丰厚条件的运动新秀。

22　瑈夫人（Madame Nhu，1924—2011），南越前总统吴廷琰的弟媳，担任第一夫人角色，因吴氏兄弟被政变推翻而流亡。

23　布莱蒂·墨菲（Bridey Murphy，1923—1995），一个据称拥有前世记忆的美国妇女，曾名噪一时。

24　他会（HE'LL），原文拼法同"hell"（地狱）。

25　夹着红白蓝三色食材以象征美国国旗的汉堡包被称为"爱国汉堡"。

Subterranean Homesick Blues & the Blond Waltz

105 let me say this about Justine–she was 5ft.2 & had Hungarian eyes–her belief was that if she could make it with Bo Diddley–she could get herself straight–now Ruthy–she was different–she always wanted to see a cock fight & went to Mexico City when she was 17 & a runaway castoff–she met Zonk when she was 18–Zonk came from her home town–at least that's what he said when he met her–when they busted up, he said he never heard of the place but that's beside the point–anyway these three–they make up the Realm Crew...i met them exactly at their table & they took 2 years of sanction from me but i never talk much about it myself–Justine was always trying to prove she existed as if she really needed proof–Ruthy–she was always trying to prove that Bo Diddley existed & Zonk he was trying to prove that he existed just for Ruthy but later on said that he was just trying to prove he existed to himself–me? i started wondering about whether anybody existed but i never pushed it too much–especially when Zonk was around–Zonk hated himself & when he got too high he thought everybody was a mirror

地下乡愁蓝调[1]&金发圆舞曲

让我来说说贾丝汀——她身高 1 米 58 &有一双匈牙利眼睛——她的信念是如果她能跟博迪德利[2]一起干——她就能把自己理顺——现在讲露西——她不一样——她一直想看一场斗鸡& 17 岁的时候就离家出走&去了墨西哥城——她认识阿肿的时候才 18 岁——阿肿也来自她的家乡——起码刚认识的时候他是这么跟她说的——后来他们闹崩了，他说他从没听说过那个地方但这无关紧要——反正这三个人——他们组成领域乐团……我正好在餐桌上认识他们&他们从我这儿拿了 2 年的特许但我本人从来不大说这件事——贾丝汀一直在努力证明她的存在就像她当真需要一个证明似的——露西——她一直在努力证明博迪德利的存在&阿肿则是在努力证明他只为露西而存在但后来又说他只是在努力证明他为自己而存在——我？我都开始纳闷到底有没有谁是存在的不过我从没往深处琢磨——尤其是阿肿还在的时候——阿肿讨厌自己&他嗑太高了之后就会把每个人都当成一面镜子

106 one day i discovered that my secrets were puny–i tried to build them up but Justine said "this is the Twentieth Century baby–i mean you know–like they dont do that anymore–why dont you go walk on the street–that'll build up your secrets–it's no use to spend all these hours a day doing it in a room–youre losing living–i mean like if you wanna be some kinda charles atlas, go right ahead... but you better head off for muscle beach–i mean you just might as well snatch jayne mansfield–become king of your kind & start some kind of secret gymnasium"... after being ridiculed to such a degree–i decided to leave my secrets alone & Justine–Justine was right–my secrets go bigger–in fact they grew so big that they outweighed my body...i hitchhiked a lot in those days & you had to be ready–you never knew what kind of people you were gonna meet on the road

i sang in a forest one day & someone said it was three o'clock–that nite when i read the newspaper, i saw that a tenement had been set aflame & that three firemen & nineteen people had lost their lives–the fire was at three o'clock too...that nite in a dream i was singing again–i was singing the same song in the same forest & at the same time–in the dream there was also a tenement blazing...there was no fog & the dream was clear–it was not worth analyzing as nothing is worth analyzing–you learn from a conglomeration of the incredible past–
107 whatever experience gotten in any way whatsoever–controlling at once the present tense of the problem–more

有一天我发现我的那些秘诀不经用了——我使劲想让它们再强大起来但贾丝江说“这都二十世纪了宝贝——我说你懂的吧——它们再也没效果了——为什么你不到街上走走——那样才能让你的秘诀变强大——整天耗在屋里做这些是没有用的——你这是浪费生命——我是说如果你想成为大力神查尔斯[3]那样的人，那就上吧……但你最好去肌肉海滩[4]——我是说你不如干脆去绑了简恩曼斯菲尔德[5]——成为你们那帮人的王者&创办某种秘诀健身房”……既然被嘲笑到这样的程度——我决定抛开我的那些秘诀&贾丝江——贾丝江说得对——我的秘诀越长越大——实际上它们已经大得超过了我的身体……我那段时间搭了很多趟便车&你必须做好准备——你没法知道你在路上会碰见什么样的人

有一天我在森林里唱歌&有人说是三点钟——那天晚上我在读报，我看到一座廉租公寓被烧着了&三个消防员&十九个人失去生命——火灾也是三点钟……那天晚上我在梦中又唱了起来——我在同一座森林&同一个时间唱着同一首歌——在梦里也有一座廉租公寓熊熊燃烧……没有烟雾&梦里是清晰的——这不值得分析因为没什么值得分析的——你从一大堆不可思议的过往学到东西——不管得到怎样的经验反正不管怎样——立刻控制住问题的现在时态——多少有点像罗伊罗杰斯&扳机[6]的关系，按目前的西方标准来说是不可能发生

or less like a roy rogers & trigger relationship of which under present western standards is an impossibility–me singing–i moved from the forest–frozen in a moment & picked up & moved above land–the tenement blazing too at the same moment being picked up & moved towards me–i, still singing & this building still burning...needless to say–i & the building met & as instantly as it stopped, the motion started again–me, singing & the building burning–there i was–in all truth–singing in front of a raging fire–i was unable to do anything about this fire–you see–not because i was lazy or loved to watch good fires–but rather because both myself & the fire were in the same Time all right but we were not in the same Space–the only thing we had in common was that we existed in the same moment...i could not feel any guilt about just standing there singing for as i said i was picked up & moved there not by my own free will but rather by some unbelievable force–i told Justine about this dream & she said "that's right–lot of people would feel guilty & close their eyes to such a happening–these are people that interrupt & interfere in other people's lives–only God can be everywhere at the same Time & Space–you are human–sad & silly as it might seem"...i got very drunk that afternoon & a mysterious confusion entered into my body–"when i hear of the bombings, i see red & mad
108 hatred" said Zonk–"when i hear of the bombings, i see the head of a dead nun" said i–Zonk said "what?"...i have never taken my singing–let alone my other habits–very seriously–ever since then–i have just accepted it–exactly as i would any other crime

的——我唱着——我走出森林——在一瞬间就被吓傻了&被拎起来&在地面上拖走——燃烧的廉租公寓也在同一时刻被拎了起来&拖向我这边——我，仍在唱着&这幢房子仍在燃烧……不消说——我&房子相遇&它顿时一停，然后又开始动——我，唱着歌&房子燃烧着——我就在那儿——千真万确——当着烈火熊熊歌唱——我对这火灾真是无能为力——你看——不是因为我懒或者喜欢围观大火——而是因为我&火灾两者的确都处在同一个时间但我们并不在同一个空间——我们唯一相通的就是我们存在于同一个瞬间……我对于站在一旁唱歌不会有任何罪恶感因为如我所言被拎起来&拖到那儿不是出于我的自由意志而是出于某种难以置信的强力——我跟贾丝汀说过这个梦&她说“没错啊——很多人对这样的情形都会觉得有罪&闭上他们的眼睛——这些人扰乱&干涉了其他人的生活——唯有上帝才能于同一时间&空间无处不在——你只是人——也许这显得很悲哀&愚蠢”……我那天下午喝得大醉&一个玄奥的困惑进入我的身体——“我听见爆炸的同时，还看见红色&疯狂的仇恨”阿肿说——“我听见爆炸的同时，还看见一个死修女的脑袋”我说——阿肿说“什么？”……我从来不把我的歌当回事——更别提我的其他爱好了——很认真地——从那以后——我只是接受它——正如我会接受其他罪恶一样

the soldier with the long beard says go ask questions my son but the shaggy orphan says that it's all a hype–the bearded soldier says what's a hype? & the shaggy orphan says what's a son? the taste of bread is common yet who can & who cares to tell someone else what it tastes like–it tastes like bread that's what it tastes like...to find out why Bertha shouldnt push the man off the flying trapeze you dont find out by thinking about it–you find out by being Bertha–that's how you find out

let me say this about Justine–Ruthy & Zonk–none of them understood each other at all–Justine–she went off to join a rock n roll band & Ruthy–she decided to fight cocks professionally & when last heard from, Zonk was working in the garment district...they all lived happily ever after

where i live now, the only thing that keeps
the area going is tradition–as you can figure
out–it doesnt count very much–everything
around me rots...i dont know how long it has
been this way, but if it keeps up, soon
109 i will be an old man–& i am only 15–the only
job around here is mining–but jesus, who wants
to be a miner...i refuse to be part of such
a shallow death–everybody talks about the middle
ages as if it was actually in the middle ages–

大胡子士兵说我的孩子过来问你几个问题但长毛孤儿说尽吹牛——胡子士兵说什么叫吹牛？&长毛孤儿说什么叫孩子？面包的味道很寻常但谁又能&谁又有兴趣告诉别人它是什么味道——它的味道就是面包那样的味道呗……要探究为什么伯莎[7]不会把那个男的从高空秋千[8]推下去你就不能靠思维去探究——你必须要成为伯莎——这样你才能探究出来

让我来说说贾丝汀——露西&阿胂——他们根本就没有点相互理解——贾丝汀——她后来去加入了一支摇滚乐队&露西——她决定从事职业斗鸡赛&而根据最新消息，阿胂在时装街区上班……从此他们都过上了幸福的生活

我现在住的地方，唯一让这个地区
保持运转的东西就是传统——正如你想象的
那样——这不算太要紧——我周围的
一切都在腐烂……我不知道它这个样子
已经多长时间了，但如果它继续下去，很快
我就要变成一个老头——&我才 15 岁——这
　　一带
唯一的工作就只有采矿——但耶稣啊，谁又想
去当矿工……我拒绝成为这种轻如鸿毛的
死亡的一分子——每个人都在谈论中
世纪就好像这当真处在中世纪似的——

i'll do anything to leave here–my mind
is running down the river–i'd sell my
soul to the elephant–i'd cheat the sphinx–
i'd lie to the conqueror...tho you might
not take this the right way, i would even
sign a chain with the devil...please dont
send me anymore grandfather clocks–no more
books or care packages...if youre going to
send me something, send me a key–i shall
find the door to where it fits, if it takes
me the rest of my life

your friend,
Friend

我会千方百计离开这里——我的头脑
正随着大河流向远方——我要把我的灵魂
卖给大象——我要戏弄狮身人面兽——
我要哄骗征服者……哪怕你也许
不肯好好认识这一点，但我还是会
和魔鬼签一家连锁店……请不要
再给我寄老爷钟表——也不要
书籍或爱心包裹……如果你打算
给我寄点什么，就寄一把钥匙——我会
找到那一扇配得上它的大门，即便
这会耗尽我的余生

你的朋友，

彭友

注　释

1　标题参见迪伦歌曲《地下乡愁蓝调》。

2　博·迪德利（Bo Diddley，1928—2008），美国歌手，摇滚乐先驱。参见迪伦歌曲《发自别克 6 型》："她不会让我紧张，她不会说个没完 / 她走路活像博·迪德利而且她不需要拄拐杖。"

3　大力神查尔斯（Charles Atlas，1892—1972），美国健美运动明星、大众偶像。

4　肌肉海滩（Muscle Beach），美国加州圣莫尼卡海边的一处露天锻炼场，现代健美运动的发祥地之一。

5　简恩·曼斯菲尔德（Jayne Mansfield，1933—1967），美国

女影星、性感偶像，死于车祸。参见迪伦《统统带回家》唱片文案，及诗《大学以外的选择》（“Alternatives to College”，1965）。

6　罗伊·罗杰斯（Roy Rogers，1911—1998），美国西部片影星、乡村音乐歌手，他的马“扳机”（Trigger，1934—1965）出演过多部电影，他的妻子黛尔·埃文斯（Dale Evans，1912—2001）也是著名影星、歌手。

7　伯莎（Bertha），可能指一头名叫伯莎的母象（Bertha the Elephant，1944—1999），美国马戏明星。

8　参见老歌《高空秋千》（“The Flying Trapeze”），大意讲自己心爱的姑娘却情钟荡高空秋千的男子。

Furious Simon's Nasty Humor

110 i had a dream
that the cook
leaned
& shook
his fist over the
balcony & said yes
to the people
yes the people
& he said this
to the people
"i want four cups of stormtrooper–
a tablespoon of catholic–five hideous paranoids–
some water buffalo–a half pound of communist–
six cups of rebel–two cute atheists–
a quart bottle of rabbi–one teaspoon of
bitter liberal–some antibirth tablets–
three fourths black nationalist–
a dab of lemon cock powder–

暴火西蒙的黄段子

我做了个梦
有个厨师
倚在
阳台上
&挥着
拳头&向
人民说是的
是的人民[1]
&他对人民
这样说
"我要四杯冲锋队——
一大勺天主教徒——五份骇人偏执狂——
再来些水牛——半磅共产党——
六杯叛匪——两个俏皮的无神论者——
一夸脱瓶的拉比——一茶匙
苦味自由派——再来些打胎片——
四分之三黑人民族主义者——
一点点柠檬公鸡粉——

some mogen david capitalists & a whole lot
of fat people with extra money"
then the cook's helper
appeared
& cleared his throat & then he
said to the people yes the
111 people
"also we'd like a mocking bird
& some maids in milking–some raped
college students & a drenched hen–
two turtle gloves
& a partridge & a gin & a pear tree"
i awoke from this dream
in the state of fright–then jumped out of bed &
ran for the kitchen–crashed thru the door &
slammed on the light/fell on my
bended knees &
thanked God
that there was nothing new in
the ice box

dear Puck,
traded in my electric guitar for
one you call a gut one...you can play
it all by yourself–dont need a band–

再来些大卫星[2]资本家＆一整个
外快滚滚的大胖子”
然后厨师的助手
出场了
＆清清喉咙＆然后他
向人民是的人民
说
“另外我们还想要一只反舌鸟[3]
＆一些挤牛奶的村姑——几个被强奸的
大学生＆一只湿淋淋的母鸡——
一双无指手套
＆一只鹧鸪＆一瓶金酒＆一棵梨树”[4]
我从梦中醒来时
惊恐万分——跳下床＆
跑到厨房——闯进门去＆
砸开灯／跪下
我的膝盖＆
感谢上帝
冰箱里
没有任何东西是新鲜的

亲爱的小鬼头，
我的电吉他跟你换了
一把所谓肠弦的[5]……你可以
自己随便弹——不需要乐队——

eliminates all the fighting except of
course for the other gut guitar
players–am doing well–have no idea of
what's happening but all these girls
with moustaches, theyre going crazy
over me–you must try them sometime–
weather is good–threw away all my lefty
frizzell records–also got rid of my
112 parka–you can keep my cow as i now am
on the road to freedom

see yuh later aligator
Franky Duck

以避免所有争斗当然除了
其他的肠弦吉他手
之外——我干得不错——没意识到
发生了什么只知道这些姑娘
长了胡子，她们都为我
疯狂——你有机会必须试试她们——
天气真好——扔掉我那些左手
弗里兹尔[6]唱片吧——还有我的
风雪大衣——你可以留着我的奶牛因为我
　　已经
走在通往自由的路上

再见了短吻鳄[7]

老鸭弗兰基

注　释

1 “人民，是的，人民”，出自卡尔·桑德堡（Carl August Sandburg，1878—1967）长诗《人民，是的》（*The People, Yes*，1936）。

2 大卫星（Magen David），即六角星犹太标志。

3 反舌鸟（mockingbird），象征被践踏的纯真无辜者，参见美国作家哈珀·李的长篇小说《杀死一只反舌鸟》（*To Kill a Mockingbird*，1960）。

4 这段话戏拟英语传统圣诞歌曲《圣诞十二日》（“The Twelve Days of Christmas”）：“圣诞节第十二天，我的真爱送给我礼物……八个挤牛奶的女佣……四只鸣叫的鸟儿 / 三只法兰西母鸡 / 两只

斑鸠鸟 / 还有一只梨树上的鹧鸪。”

5 传统的提琴、吉他等弦乐器使用羊肠弦。

6 左手弗里兹尔(Lefty Frizzell,1928—1975),美国乡村音乐歌手。

7 《再见，短吻鳄》(“See You Later, Alligator”)，美国早期摇滚歌曲,1956 年走红。歌中离心离德的恋人将对方称为挡道的鳄鱼。

I Found the Piano Player Very Crosseyed But Extremely Solid

he came with his wrists taped & he carried his own
coat hanger–i could tell at a glance that he had no need
for Sonny Rollins but i asked him anyway "whatever
happened to gregory corso?" he just stood there–he
took out a deck of cards & he replied "wanna play some
cards?" to which i answered "no but whatever happened
to jane russell?" he flapped the cards & they went sailing
all over the room "my father taught me that" he said "it's
called 52 pickup but i call it 49 pickup cause i'm shy three
cards–haw haw aint that a scream & which one's the
piano?" at this gesture, i was relieved to see that he was
human–not a saint mind you–& he wasnt very likable–but
nevertheless–he was human–"that's my piano over there"
113 i say "the one with the teeth" he immediately rambled
over & he stomped hard across the floor "shhhhhh" i said
"you'll wake up my No Pets Allowed sign" he shrugged
his shoulders & took out a piece of chalk–he began to
draw a picture of his kid on my piano "hey now look–
that aint what's wrong with my plano–i mean now dont
take it personally–it's got nothing to do with you, but my
piano is out of tune–now i dont care how you go about it
but fix it–fix it right" "my kid's gonna be an astronaut"

我发现钢琴师是个斗鸡眼但非常结实[1]

他来时在手腕上缠着胶布&他还扛着他自己的衣帽架——我一眼就能看出他不需要桑尼罗林斯[2]但我还是问他"格雷戈里柯索[3]到底遇到了什么？"他只是傻站着——他掏出一沓扑克&他说"要玩牌吗？"我对此答道"不玩但是珍妮拉塞尔到底遇到了什么？"他弹起扑克牌&它们满屋子乱飞"我爸爸教我的"他说"这叫52式捡牌[4]但我叫它49式因为我差了三张牌——啃啃赶快尖叫吧&谁才是钢琴？"从他这个姿势，我安心地看到他是个凡人——不是一个圣徒你要注意——&他也不很讨人喜欢——但不管怎样——他是个人——"那是我的钢琴"我说"它长了牙齿的"他立刻就浪荡过去&他狠狠踩过地板"嘘"我说"你会惊醒了我的宠物禁入牌牌"他耸耸肩&掏出一截粉笔——他开始在我的钢琴上画他的孩子"嘿瞧啊——是不是我的钢琴出了岔子——我说我不是跟你作对——这跟你一点关系都没有，只是我的钢琴都跑调了——我可不在乎你要搞些什么反正现在给我修好它——修好为止""我的孩子要做宇航员""我

"i should hope so" says me "& by the way–could you
tell me what happened to julius larosa?" a picture of
abraham lincoln falls from the ceiling "that guy looks
like a girl–i saw him on Shindig–he's a fag" "how wise
you are" says i "hurry & fix my piano willya–i have this
geisha girl coming over at midnight & she digs to jump
on it" "my kid's gonna be an astronaut" "c'mon–get
to work–my piano–my piano–c'mon it's out of tune"
at this time, he takes out his tool & starts to tinkle
on a few high notes–"yeah it's out of tune" he says
"but it's also 5:30" "so what?" i say most melancholy
"so it's quitting time–that's so what" "quitting time?"
"look buddy i'm a union man..." "look yourself–you
ever heard of woody guthrie? he was a union man too
& he fought to organize unions like yers & he dug
people's needs & do you know what he'd say if he knew
that a union man–an honest–to–God union man–was
walking out on a poor hard traveling cat's needs–do
you know what he'd say d'yuh know what he'd think?"
"all right i'm getting sick of you sprouting out names
114 at me–i never hearda no boody guppie & anyway..."
"woody guthrie not boody guppie!" "yeah well anyway
i dont know what he'd say, but tomorrow–now if you
want a new man tomorrow–like you can just call up &
the union'll send you over one gladly–like i dont care–
it's just another job to me buddy–just another job to
me" "WHAT! you dont even take any pride in your
work? i cant believe this! do you know what boody
guppie would do to you man? i mean do you know
what he'd think of you?" "i'm going home–i hate it

希望如此”我说“&另外——你能不能告诉我朱利叶斯拉罗萨[5]到底遇到了什么？”一张亚伯拉罕林肯肖像从天花板掉下来“这哥们像个小妞——我在大舞会[6]上见过他——他是个基佬”“你真聪明”我说“赶快&把我的钢琴修好——这个艺伎妞儿今天半夜会过来见我&她就喜欢扑上去”“我的孩子要做宇航员”“别扯了——干活——我的钢琴——我的钢琴——快点它都跑调了”这一次，他搬出了他的工具&开始敲几个高音——“哈确实跑调了”他说“但也5点半了都”“那又怎样？”我郁闷不已地说“就是下班时间呀——就是这样”“下班时间？”“哥们你瞧我是工会成员……”“瞧好你自己吧——你听说过伍迪格思里吗？他也是工会成员&他为着组织你们这样的工会而奋斗&他懂得人民的需要&你知不知道他会怎么说如果他知道有一个工会成员——无愧于上帝的工会成员——对一个困苦无助的可怜人的需要竟然不屑一顾——你知不知道他会怎么说你知不知道他会怎么想？”“好了我真的很烦你老是跟我冒出一堆人名来——我从没听说过什么古里古屁&反正……”“伍迪格思里不是古里古屁！”“哈好吧反正我不知道他会怎么说，但明天——如果你现在想明天另换一个人——你打个电话就可以了&工会很乐意为你派人过来——跟我没关系的——反正我又不止这一份活计哥们——我有的是活计”“**什么！**你竟然对你的工作一点自豪感都没有？我真是难以置信！哥们你知不知道古里古屁会对你

here–it's just not my style at all & anyway i never heard of any coody puppie" "boody guppie, you miserable bosom–not coody puppie & get out of my house–get out this instant!" "my kid's gonna be a astronaut" "i dont care–you cant bribe me–i'm bigger'n that–get out–get out"...after he leaves i try playing my piano–no use–it sounds like a bowling alley–i change my No Pets Allowed sign to a Home Sweet Home sign & wonder why i havent any friends...it starts to rain–the rain sounds like a pencil sharpener–i look out the window & everybody's walking around without a hat–it is 5:31–time to celebrate someone's birthday–the piano tuner has left his coat hanger behind...which really brings me down

unfortunately my friend, you shall not get
the information you seek out of me–i, my
good man, am not a fink! none of my relatives
115 are or have been related to benedict arnold
& i myself despise john wilkes booth–i dont
smoke marijuana & my family hates italian
food–none of my friends like black & white
movies & again myself, i have never seen a
russian ballet–also, i have started an organization
to turn in all people that laugh at
newsreels–so: could you please stop those
letters to the district attorney saying that

做什么？我是说你知不知道他会怎么想你？”“我要回家了——我讨厌这里——这根本不是我的风格&反正我从没听说过什么狗里狗屁”“是古里古屁，你这可怜虫——不是狗里狗屁&给我滚出去——马上滚！”“我的孩子要做宇航员”“干我屁事——你哄不了我——我懂得很——滚蛋——滚蛋”……他离开之后我试着弹我的钢琴——没用——听起来就像一路咣当的保龄球道——我把我的宠物禁入牌牌换成了美好家庭牌牌&纳闷为什么我一个朋友也没有……下雨了——雨声像一个卷笔刀——我往窗外看去&人人都不戴帽子到处走——5 点 31 分——到了庆祝某人生日的时间——钢琴调音师把他的衣帽架落下了……这让我郁闷得很

真遗憾我的朋友，你不会从我这儿
得到你想要的消息——我的先生，我
不是一个线人！我所有的亲戚都不
是也不曾跟本尼迪特阿诺德[7]有关系
&我本人鄙视约翰威尔克斯布思[8]——我不
抽大麻烟&我们家人都讨厌意大利
风味——我的朋友没有谁喜欢看黑&白
片&再说我本人，我从来没看过
俄国芭蕾——还有，我创办了一个组织
专门捉拿那些嘲笑新闻纪录片
的人——所以：麻烦你不要再

i know who murdered my wife–my principles
  are
at stake here–i would NOT sacrifice them for
one moment of pleasure–i am an honest man

yours in growth,
ivan the bloodburst

写信给地方检察院说
我知道是谁杀了我妻子——我的原则
申明如下——我绝不会为了一时的快乐
而牺牲原则——我是个正派人

你成长中的，
爆血伊万

注　释

1　迪伦很喜欢法国导演弗朗索瓦·特吕弗（François Roland Truffaut，1932—1984）的影片《射杀钢琴师》（*Shoot the Piano Player*，1960）。

2　桑尼·罗林斯（Sonny Rollins，1930— ），美国爵士乐萨克斯手。

3　格雷戈里·柯索（Gregory Corso，1930—2001），美国诗人，“垮掉派”核心成员之一。

4　开玩笑把整副扑克牌乱扔叫傻孩子去捡，并声称考验他是否识数。

5　朱利叶斯·拉罗萨（Julius La Rosa，1930—2016），美国流行歌手。

6　《大舞会》（*Shindig!*，1964—1966），美国电视综艺节目。

7　本尼迪克特·阿诺德（Benedict Arnold，1741—1801），美国独立战争时期的著名叛徒。

8　约翰·威尔克斯·布思（John Wilkes Booth，1838—1865），美国话剧演员，刺杀林肯的凶手。

The Vandals Took the Handles (*An Opera*)

to South Duchess County comes Them & Woolworth's
Fool & triumphant alice toklas, the National Bank in
short sleeves & the regulars–the sincereful regulars–
116 House on its final kick–still breeding & a cellarful of
imaginary Russian peasant girls holding triangles–the
triangles are real–House on Doomstown, an academy–
a priest with his winnings from Reno coming in on a
parachute... "integrate the house!" "only if you wish to
live where youre not wanted" "then bomb the house!"
"only if you wish to live there by yourself" "what do
you suggest then?" "it's a pointless house–leave it
alone–it is not happy within itself–it breeds disaster–
it forces you to learn things that have nothing to do
with the outside world & then it kicks you out there–
the house dont need you–why should you be so low as
to need it–leave–go far away from the house" "no, my
friend, your way of thinking is called giving up" "do as
you wish, your way is called losing–it's not even a way
of thinking" the priest leaves with his eyes downward–
he is examining the rocks but he's forgotten that his
parachute has already been used once...alice toklas lays
on a grassy knoll & blesses a flower "oh the enemy–

破坏狂拆掉了把手[1]（歌剧一部）

南达奇斯县[2]迎来他们&伍尔沃斯傻瓜[3]&凯旋而归的爱丽丝托克拉斯[4]，穿短袖的国民银行&老主顾——忠实的老主顾们——议会死到临头——还能生养&满地窖的想象的俄国农村小妞们捧着三角尺[5]——这些三角尺是真实的——末日城议会，一座学院——有个牧师带着他从雷诺[6]赢来的钱财乘降落伞来临……“要整合议会！”“除非你希望活在你不想要的地方”“那就炸掉议会吧！”“除非你希望你自己一个人活着”“那你有什么建议？”“这是个没用的议会——别管它了——它自己也很郁闷的——它养育灾难——它迫使你去学那些跟外部世界毫无干系的东西&然后它把你一脚踢到外边——议会不需要你了——为什么你还那么卑屈地需要它呢——走吧——离开这议会越远越好”“不，我的朋友，你的思维方式就叫做放弃”“你爱怎样就怎样吧，你的方式叫做失败——这甚至不是一种思维方式”牧师垂着眼睛离开了——他在考察岩石但他忘了他的降落伞已经用过一次……爱丽丝托克拉斯躺在绿茵茵的草坡[7]&祝

beware of the enemy–the enemy is santa claus!"...the flower doesnt need her–the flower needs rain

we sat in a room where Harold, who called himself "Lord of dead animals," was climbing down from a ladder & he said "friend or doe? friend or doe?" he wore a black shawl & someone said that he experimented in the depth of mirrors–Poncho was very startled & screamed "i'll give you a friend or doe, you freak!" & banged him with a judo chop
117 & stuck his head thru the ladder–"shouldnt done that" said a very manly girl who came down the chimney "he's very sullen but he's a good cat–does anybody want a piece of bread?" Poncho said that he wanted a piece of kidney–i said i wanted a piece of separate...the girl began to cry

in the photographs–you see the sand at Nice & Tangier & all the medicine men looking elegant & then out come the radar slaves–each one wanting to be an apostle & they carry the electrograms–we call them Employment & each one says things like "haul away ho" & "heave 'm johnny" & "I dont dig harry james at all!" & Hefty Bore, a leftover horror from the beat generation & a dubious health freak saying to his bewildered birdgirl, WeeWee the Dyke, "oh c'mon–it wouldnt cost you nothing to tell everybody that i'm the hippest person you ever met–c'mon–i do lots of things for you!" & WeeWee saying "but i never see anybody–you never let me see anybody!" & then Olive, who once started a streetfight over Carl Perkins' eyes & now builds laugh machines for rich

福一朵花儿“哦，敌人——要当心敌人——敌人就是圣诞爷爷！”……花儿并不需要她——花儿需要雨露

我们曾坐在一个房间，自称“万兽死灵之王”的哈罗德从梯子爬下来&他说“是友是驴？是友是驴？”他蒙着黑披肩&有人说他在镜室的深处做实验——蓬丘非常惊愕&大叫“我来给你是友是驴，你这怪胎！”&用一招柔道劈砍把他撂倒&把他的脑袋塞进梯档——“不要这样”一个非常爷们相的姑娘从烟囱爬下来说“他非常阴郁但他是个好人——有人想要一块面包吗？”蓬丘说他想要一块肾——我说我想要一块个人财产……姑娘就开始哭了

在照片上——你看到尼斯&丹吉尔的沙滩&所有温文尔雅的医学人士&然后出现那些雷达奴隶——个个都想成为传道者&他们拿着电描记图——我们称他们为雇员&一个个说起话来都是“拖啊嘀嘿”&“扛起来呀约翰尼”[8]&“我根本不鸟哈利詹姆斯[9]！”&超无聊，一个来自垮掉一代的残余吓人精&一个可疑的健康怪胎对他那晕头转向的鸟儿姑娘拉子嘘嘘说“哦说嘛——快告诉大家我是你见过的最嬉皮的人，这又不花费你什么——快呀——我为你做了那么多！”&嘘嘘说“但我从没见过人——你从来不让我见人！”&还有奥利弗，有一次干架他还揍过卡尔帕金斯[10]的眼睛&现在为富裕民主党人

democrats–he brings in the equipment & you get taken
across a narrow bridge where hundreds of tourists follow
& sail lead weight records at your feet & they place you in
a giant bus horn & voices yelling "i want that one–i want
that one!" Madame Remember appears & she takes away
your photographs & all that's left in the outside world is
your hand–little babies bite it & mothers are screaming
118 SCREAMING "yes–he can have my vote–i'll vote for
him any day"...now youre a plastic vein–youve vanished
inside of a perfect message–historic phone calls come
thru to your belly & curious tabernacles move slowly thru
your mind–hitchhiking–hitchhiking unashamed thru
the goofs of your brain–your ideals are gone & all that
remains are the cutup photographs of you standing in
the supermarket–the bus still runs but now you take cabs
with the jungle boys...Egotist shows you his diary & he
says "I've learned to be silent" & you say "youve learned
nothing–youve just said something"

the good folks around here, they got plenty of questions–they beat elephants to death with candy sticks–"a white bear is a crazy bear" say the thieves who really are not thieves but rather plain people who dont expect their friends to get sick so they'll need them–there is an illness on the mountain & a polio lily grew out of a green purse last Sunday–a dangerous nickel lays on the town square... everybody watches to see who'll pick it up...TO SEARCH IS TO NEGLECT & VIOLENT LUCK IS STAMPEDE & there's a bunch of us around here but we only pick up dollars

制造欢笑机器——他带了设备过来&你得以通过一条窄桥[11]有几百游客跟随其后&带着你双脚上记录的铅锤上路&他们把你放进一个巨大的班车喇叭&大声嘶鸣“我要那个——我要那个！”回忆夫人来了&她拿走你的照片&在整个外部世界只剩下你的手——小宝宝们在啃它&妈妈们在尖叫**尖叫**“对——他可以赢得我的选票——随时我都会投给他”……现在你是一条塑料血管——你已经消失在一个完整信息的内部——历史性的电话都打进你的肚子&古怪的帐幕[12]都在你的思维中缓缓移动——搭车——搭个没羞没臊的小便车穿过你头脑的愚钝——你的理想一去不返&剩下的只是你站在超市里的照片剪切[13]——班车还在开但现在你跟丛林小子们打出租车……自我主义者向你展示他的日记&他说“我已学会沉默”&你说“你已学会个屁——你刚刚就在说话”

这一带的好心人，他们提了一大堆问题——他们用棒棒糖将大象殴打致死——“白熊就是疯熊”盗贼们说，他们其实不是真的盗贼而是普通人，这些人并不希望他们的朋友遭灾染疾，那样他们就会需要他们——在山区有一种病&上个星期天从绿色钱包里长出一棵脊髓灰质炎百合[14]——中心广场上搁着一枚危险的硬币……人人都在观望着谁会捡起来……**探究即忽略&厄运来汹汹**&在这周围我们有一大帮人但我们只会捡大票子

here lies bob dylan
murdered
119 from behind
by trembling flesh
who after being refused by Lazarus,
jumped on him
for solitude
but was amazed to discover
that he was already
a streetcar &
that was exactly the end
of bob dylan

he now lies in Mrs. Actually's
beauty parlor
God rest his soul
& his rudeness

two brothers
& a naked mama's boy
who looks like Jesus Christ
can now share the remains
of his sickness
& his phone numbers

鲍勃迪伦长眠于此
被身后
颤栗的肉体[15]
谋杀而死
凶手遭到拉撒路拒绝之后[16]
就扑上他
以求个清净独处
但惊讶地发现
他已经变成
一辆电车＆
这样的结局正适合
鲍勃迪伦

他如今安息在现实太太的
美容院
上帝抚慰他的灵魂
＆他的鲁莽

两个兄弟
＆一个赤裸的好妈宝
长得好像耶稣基督
现在可以分享他的病痛
的遗体
＆他的电话号码

there is no strength
to give away–
everybody now
can just have it back

here lies bob dylan
demolished by Vienna politeness–
which will now claim to have invented him
the cool people can
now write Fugues about him
& Cupid can now kick over his kerosene lamp–
boy dylan–killed by a discarded Oedipus
who turned
around
to investigate a ghost
& discovered that
the ghost too
was more than one person

South Duchess County importing pyramids & scavengers by the truckload & Cousin Butch–he leaves now & then to make three dollars a nite telling about the flying saucers… a warmonger–Antonio–working day & nite in a garage–he smuggles pad locks to the olympic swimmers & hires out women for the baseball players–he's very quiet & very fashion conscious–he knows his religious geography–he's

再也没有力量
可奉送——
现在每个人
都可以将它拿回

鲍勃迪伦长眠于此
毁于维也纳礼节[17]——
他们现在可以声称发明了他
冷静人士现在
可以写有关他的赋格曲
&丘比特现在能踢翻他的煤油灯——
小鲍迪伦——丧命于被遗弃的俄狄浦斯
后者曾四处
转悠
调查一个幽灵
&发现
那幽灵同样
要多过一个人

南达奇斯县进口金字塔&满车的食腐动物&屠户老表——他已经走了&然后去讲飞天盘的故事一晚上赚三块钱……有个战争贩子——安东尼奥——在修车场没日&没夜苦干——他帮奥林匹克游泳队偷运挂锁&给棒球选手找女人——他非常安静&非常有时尚感——他知道他的宗教地理学——他在训练他的孩子成为大猩猩&然

training his kid to be a gorilla & then he will rent him out for people's closets–he says his right hand holds war but his left hand holds a wet paranoid smile...the peacemonger–Roach–when last seen–was chasing a train–he says that his right hand hold peace but his left hand was seen holding
121 a doorknob & a meathook...South Duchess County in bandages & little Lady Suntan trying to analyze the Albino terrorists...South Duchess County–pure as visions & uneducated–shall exist past the deadly complements to it–past its lack of holidays & past the possible

you cant fool me–i'm too smart–you
were on that subway train when that
kid got knifed–you just sat there–you
were on the street when that black car
drove up & tossed some form in the
river–you turned around & walked to a
phone & pretended you had someone to call...
you were also there when they castrated
that poor boy in public–you cant fool me–
youre not so tough–sure, you took a big
stand on juvenile delinquency–you said to
run all the hoods out of town–oh youre so
brave–sure, you say youre patriotic–you
say youre not scared to drop any H bomb &
show everybody that you mean what you say

后他会把他租出去给别人关进衣柜——他说他的右手握着战争但他的左手握着一个潮湿的偏执狂微笑……和平贩子——洛奇——上次被人看见——正在追火车——他说他的右手握着和平但他的左手被看见握着一个门把手&肉钩子……南达奇斯县扎着绷带&小晒黑女士努力分析白化病恐怖分子[18]……南达奇斯县——幻象般纯洁&未受教育——应历经那些要命的补充部分——历经它的劳苦无休&历经可能性

你没法糊弄我——我太聪明了——你
坐在那趟地铁里的时候那个
小孩挨了刀子——你就坐在那儿——你
走在大街上的时候那辆黑色轿车
开过来&把某种东西抛进了
河里——你转过身&走到
电话亭&假装你要打给某某人……
也是你在那儿的时候他们正当众
阉割一个可怜小子——你没法糊弄我——
你没那么厉害——的确，你对少年
违法行为立场强硬——你说过要
把所有阿飞都赶出城——哦你可真
威风——的确，你说你是爱国者——你
说你根本不怕扔一个什么氢弹&
让所有的人都知道你是说话算话的

but you dont say anything excpt that youre
not scared to drop any H bombs–how can you
say that my kids must learn from a good
example? they can learn from a bad example
just as well–they can learn from you as well
as me–you cant have me under your thumb
122 anymore–not because i'm too squirmy, but because
your hands are made of water…when you wish
to talk to me, let me know ahead of time–i'll
have a bucket waiting…just because your wife
is pregnant, youve no license to meddle in mine
or my friends' affairs–ask your wife if she
remembers me

yours faithfully
Simon Dord

p.s. you probably remember me as
Julius the Honk

但你却不肯说别的只会说你根本
不怕扔一个什么氢弹——你怎能说
我的孩子都必须跟着好榜样
学？他们跟着坏榜样学也
是可以的——他们可以跟你学也可以
跟我学——你再也不能把我按在你的大拇指
底下——不是因为我太难弄，而是因为
你的手是用水做的……如果你希望
跟我说话，要让我提前知道——我会
拿一口大桶来等着……就因为你老婆
怀孕了，你也没有特权来干涉我
或者我朋友的事情——问问你老婆是否
还记得我

你忠实的

西蒙多德

又及，你可能会把我记成

大喇叭朱利斯

注　释

1　标题参见迪伦歌曲《地下乡愁蓝调》最后一句："水泵不工作了 / 因为破坏狂拆掉了手柄。"另在前文《吉他之吻》中，水泵房看守被希特勒谋杀了。

2　达奇斯县（Dutchess County）是纽约的卫星城。

3　伍尔沃斯（Woolworth's），美国"一元店"连锁便利超市品牌。

1960 年，四个黑人大学生在“仅限白人”的伍尔沃斯超市餐吧台前静坐半年，试图迫使商场停止种族歧视，他们的行动引发大量关注和效仿，成为民权运动的标志事件之一，但该商场直到 1965 年才正式取消歧视政策。

4 爱丽丝 · 托克拉斯（Alice B. Toklas，1877—1967），美国先锋派女作家格特鲁德·斯泰因（Gertrude Stein，1874—1946）的情人，晚景凄凉。

5 迪伦家祖辈是俄裔犹太移民。两个三角构成大卫星（犹太标志）。

6 雷诺（Reno），美国内华达州城市，以便于离婚和赌场而闻名。

7 1963 年 11 月 22 日，美国总统 J.F. 肯尼迪在得州达拉斯市迪利广场遇刺身亡。美国哥伦比亚广播公司（CBS）插播特别新闻快报，主播沃尔特 · 克朗凯特根据合众国际社（UPI）通讯说枪击来自一个“绿茵茵的草坡”（grassy knoll）。

8 “拖啊啃嘿”&“扛起来呀约翰尼”（“haul away ho” & “heave ’m johnny”），出自传统水手号子《南澳大利亚》（“South Australia”）。“扛起来呀约翰尼”（heave’m Johnny）参见老歌《扛起来呀，我的约翰尼》（“Heave Away, My Johnny”）。

9 哈利·詹姆斯（Harry James，1916—1983），美国爵士乐小号手。

10 卡尔 · 帕金斯（Carl Perkins，1932—1998），美国歌手，早期摇滚先驱。

11 犹太人谚语 :“整个世界就是一条非常窄的桥，但重要的是不要被恐惧吓到。”

12 帐幕（tabernacles），《旧约》中犹太先民在荒野流浪时的中心大帐篷，内有约柜等圣物。

13 剪切（cut-up），美国垮掉一代作家威廉 · 巴勒斯从超现实主义风格发展出的一个实验写作概念，迪伦受其影响。

14 脊髓灰质炎百合（polio lily），原文戏拟礼来制药（Eli Lilly）的公司名，1955 年大力推广脊髓灰质炎疫苗。

15　参见莎士比亚戏剧《理查三世》第五幕第三场中，暴君被死者幽灵诅咒的最后恐惧："灯火烧蓝，死亡之夜来临。冷汗滴落我颤栗的肉体，我在恐惧什么？我自己？这里没别人。理查爱理查，只有我和我。这里有凶手吗？没有。对，我就是凶手。逃吧！逃离我自己？以免我来复仇。我自己向自己复仇？"另参见《旧约·诗篇》119:120："我因惧怕你，肉就发抖，我也怕你的判语。"

16　《新约·路加福音》16:19-31，财主下地狱被火烧，乞丐拉撒路上天堂躺在先灵的怀抱，财主乞求拉撒路用指头尖沾点水，给他凉凉舌头，但遭到拒绝。

17　维也纳是欧洲古典音乐的故乡和精神分析学的圣地。

18　"晒黑"（Suntan），戏拟"苏丹"（Sudan）、"撒旦"（Satan）；"白化病"（Albino），戏拟"阿拉伯"（Arabian）。

A Sheriff in the Machinery

Fringe–the boy lunatic–conceived on an Ash
Wednesday when Scrounge meets Suckup girl–now
Scrounge, he's twisted–he's completely wacked–ever
since a midget (who turned out to be a child actor
smoking a cigar) stomped on him like a balloon,
Scrounge just aint never been the same–it's been
123 said that he paralyzed his hometown soda jerk & if
he didn't like you, he'd turn the jerk loose on you–
to my knowledge, this never happened...Suckup
girl–her nosejob keeps dripping & she has to carry a
gardener along when she goes to parties–she is talking
to Bishop Freeze, who asks her "whaja thinka that
Monet painting? i mean i just got done spending five
days reading Kierkegaard–alone in a room baby–just
me & Kierkegaard–yeah–& the first thing i see when
i come outa there is that painting–well! flip? lemme
tell you did i flip? i mean did you dig the wisdom in
that goddamn forehead? did you dig the crumbs in
the chick's smile?" "yes i found it extremely...i found
it extremely..." "monographic?" says Scrounge trying
to help her out & put the make on her "yes & also i
found it voluptuously interesting" when Bishop Freeze

机关里的一个县警[1]

边缘人——那个疯小子——受孕于一个圣灰星期三[2]，当时老花子认识了跪舔妞——现在老花子他都抽傻了——他完全废了——自从有一个侏儒（后来发现只是个抽雪茄的儿童演员）把他像气球一样踩爆，老花子就再也不是同一个人——有人说他玩残了他家乡的汽水小哥&如果他不喜欢你，他会放那小哥出来干死你——据我所知，这种事从没发生过……跪舔妞——她整过形的鼻梁一直在下垂&她去舞会的时候只好带上一个园丁——她在跟急冻人主教说话，他问她"你搅得莫奈的那幅画咋地样？我是说我刚花五天时间读了克尔凯郭尔——独守空房啊宝贝——就我一个人&克尔凯郭尔——是啊——&当我走出房间的时候第一眼看到的就是那幅画——啊！神经？让我告诉你我神不神？我是说你能搞懂那该死的前额里边的智慧吗？你能在鸡仔的微笑里搞到面包屑吗？""是啊我觉得这实在是太……我觉得这实在是太……""专题研究吗？"老花子说，他想帮她脱身&跟她搞一把"是的&我也觉得这性感有趣"急冻人

goes home, Suckup comes over to Scrounge & thanks
him "dont mention it" says Scrounge who unbuttons his
shirt & shows her his name signed on his stomach "had
that done in Kadalawoppa last year–that's in Mexico you
know" "oh that's donkey country–i know it very well–
the beaches are extremely fantastic–i hear the fuzz are
down there now tho" "yeah baby the fuzz come in about
last Christmas–the scene now is in the jungle" "would
you like to go for a ride on my stallion–we'll drop the
gardener off" "yeah baby sure–then maybe we'll come
back & shoot the bull" "all right–sounds wizzy–i got my
gun & we can talk about Kadalawoppa & everything"
"Kadalawoppa yeah & did you ever know Puny Jim down
124 there?" "no but what about Lupe d'Lupe–did you know
him–he's a retired coffee expert–comes from the coast?"
"yes–oh my god–yes i did–i found him extremely uh...
extremely..." "he's a natural baby–he's a natural–a meth–
head but he's all beautiful–he's the one that showed
me that the jungle was there" "yes me too–i found him
extremely interesting"...nite falls now & Scrounge takes
Suckup girl by the leg–she rearranges her mouth & they
both go out the back door looking at the moon...Fringe
is conceived

a greasy fat newspaper lays on Roger's counter–Roger, the owner of Cafe de la All Nite–a spanish all nite restaurant–is sad for the first time in 9 months–his mother has disappeared in Paris & he fears now that all those frenchmen might have their fun over what they think is her dead body...roger glances thru the

主教回家之后，跪舔妞就去找老花子&感谢他“别客气”老花子一边说一边解着衬衫&向她展示他肚皮上签着他的名字“去年在卡达拉沃帕做的——在墨西哥你懂的”“那个驴蛋乡下呀——我熟得很——那海滩真是极端梦幻了——但我听说条子已经把那儿抄了”“没错宝贝去年圣诞节前后条子就进去了——现在地方已经改到了丛林里”“你愿意骑我的种马去跑上一圈吗——我们撇开那园丁”“当然了宝贝——以后也许我们可以回去&猎野牛”“好啊——太棒了——我有枪&我们可以谈卡达拉沃帕&什么都可以”“卡达拉沃帕嘛&你认不认识那边的瘦鬼吉姆？”“不知道那鲁皮德鲁皮呢——他是个退休咖啡专家——从海边过来的,你认识吗？”“认识呀——哦上帝——我真的认识——我觉得他实在太嗯……实在太……对”“他是自然之子——他是自然的——虽然脑子溜冰了但他优美无比——就是他告诉我丛林在那边”“我也是——我觉得他极端有趣”……现在天黑了&老花子抱起跪舔妞的大腿——她重新摆好她的嘴巴&他们两人从后门出去看月亮……边缘人受孕

一张油腻腻的报纸摊在罗杰的柜台上——罗杰，通宵咖啡厅店主——就是个西班牙通宵饭馆——9个月来头一次有人说泣[3]——他的妈妈在巴黎失踪了&他现在担心那些法国佬会拿他们认为是她的尸体的东西来找乐子……罗杰扫了一眼腻油油的报纸上的新闻——好莱坞

facts of the fat greasy newspaper–a tiger stampede in hollywood–annette & frankie avalon found in pacific ocean–hands tied behind their backs–footage of bugs bunny documentary found in the lungs of tom mix, whom everybody thought was dead but showed up as a boxtop–rebels attack Walgreen's in Fantasia–dictator wires for more candy–U.S. sending in marines & arnold stang–in Phoenix, man eats his wife at 2 in the afternoon–FBI investigating/ bomb explodes in norman mailer's pantry–leaves him color blind–big shakeup in sports department–ed sullivan & Freshkid, a relative of Prince Rainier & visiting this country as a guest of Cong Long, a grandson of Huey Long–seen escaping with catchers' mitts–contact lenses & dope tablets–Bishop Sheen very disturbed–when asked for opinion–just stated "i cant believe it–i cant believe this could happen to ed–it mustve been the company he's been keeping lately"–william buckshot junior writing oriental cookbook–is very upset that he's lived after falling off diving board with no water in the pool–walter crankcase arrested in Utah for lifting candles–when questioned, he calmly explained that he needed them to listen to some early little richard records–Doctor Sponge, inventor of deer poison & snap crackle & pop cereal–willing to take case for slight fee/ little girls spray chancellor erhard with goose fat on his arrival from miami–president lets embarrassing fart at banquet table–blames it on the eggs–stock market takes worst dive in years–in gary, indiana, colored man shot twenty times thru the head–coroner says cause of

有一只老虎脱逃——安妮特&弗兰克阿瓦隆[4]在太平洋现身——双手被绑在身后——兔巴哥[5]纪录片的连续镜头在汤姆米克斯[6]的肺里寻到，人人都以为他已经死了但却作为盒盖封面出现——叛匪在梦幻城[7]袭击了沃尔格林药房——独裁者来电索要更多糖果——美国派出陆战队&阿诺德斯堂[8]——在凤凰城，一男子在下午2点吃了他老婆——联邦调查局介入／诺曼梅勒[9]家餐具室炸弹爆炸——导致他色盲——体育部人事大震荡——埃德苏利文[10]&新鲜小子，兰尼埃亲王[11]的亲戚&应休伊朗[12]的孙子孔朗邀请访问这个国家——被人看到逃脱时带着捕球手们的手套——隐形眼镜&大麻药片——希恩主教[13]非常烦扰——在被询问见解时——只是声明“我无法相信——我无法相信埃德会遭遇这种事——肯定是因为他近来接触的那帮人”——写东方菜谱的小威廉巴克雷子[14]——很心烦他从跳板掉进没有水的游泳池之后的生活——沃特曲轴箱[15]在犹他州因举烛台被捕——在讯问时，他冷静地解释说他要用这些蜡烛来听小理查德[16]的早期唱片——海绵博士，毒鹿药&酥酥脆脆&嘎嘣玉米片[17]的发明者——给点小钱就可以接洽／小姑娘们在艾哈德总理[18]从迈阿密抵达时给他喷洒肥鹅油——总统在宴会桌前放出尴尬臭屁——归咎于鸡蛋——股市创下多年来最大跌幅——在印第安纳州加里市[19]，一有色男子头部中二十枪——法医称死因不明……城里没有好电影看&招聘广告栏只有一种工作——**诚聘**：实诚男子一

death is unknown...no good movies playing in town & only one job in the want ads–NEEDED: a honest man to be rag picker for friendly family–must be sturdy–preferably a basketball player–must have a love for children–couch & a toilet–wages to be discussed–phone TOongee 1965...Roger puts down his greasy paper & who should come in but Scrounge the Suckup girl–it is early morning & they are not lovers anymore–they are customers

126 9 months later, Fringe is born–he wears short pants–goes to college–gets a job for a war magazine–he marries a nice plump girl whose father is a natural winner/ Fringe meets more & more people–he goes on a diet & then he dies

to my students:
i take it for granted that youve all read
& understand freud–dostoevsky–st.
michael–confucius–coco joe–einstein–
melville–porgy snaker–john zulu–kafka–
sartre–smallfry–& tolstoy–all right then–
what my work is–is merely picking up where
they left off–nothing more–there you have
it in a nutshell–now i'm giving you my
book–i expct you all to jump right in–
the exam will be in two weeks–everybody

人为友善家庭捡垃圾——须身强体健——篮球运动员为佳——须爱护孩子——沙发&马桶——薪金面议——请致电 TOongee 1965……罗杰放下那张油腻报纸&除了老花子跟跪舔妞没谁会来了——大清早的&他们不再是恋人了——他们是顾客

9 个月后,边缘人出生——他穿短裤了——上大学了——在战争杂志找了份工作——他娶了个漂亮的胖妞，她爸爸是天生赢家 / 边缘人认识了更多&更多人——他开始节食&后来他死了

同学们：

我想大家应该都已经读过
&理解弗洛伊德——陀思妥耶夫斯基——圣
米迦勒——孔夫子——可可乔[20]——爱因斯坦[21]
——
梅尔维尔——蛇人波吉[22]——祖鲁的约翰[23]
——卡夫卡——
萨特[24]——小鱼苗[25]——&托尔斯泰——那好
吧——
我的工作就是——仅仅是把他们停住的地方再
接下去——此外无他[26]——你们可以
一言以蔽之——现在我给大家发我的
书——我希望你们都能投入进来——
考试将在两个星期后进行——每个人

has to bring their own eraser.

your professor

herold the professor

都必须自带橡皮。

你们的教授

赫罗德教授[27]

注　释

1　机关（machinery），机器、国家机器，另参见本书第 1 章：在床垫（mattress）守候大审判的肥胖县警们。

2　圣灰星期三（Ash Wednesday），参见前文《浮驳船上的玛丽亚》："一个荒废的冰柜纸箱里，小男孩们在圣灰星期三为战争 & 为天才做好了准备。"

3　原文为"sad"，音近"said"（说起）。

4　安妮特·弗奈斯洛（Annette Funicello，1942—2013），弗兰克·阿瓦隆（Frankie Avalon，1940— ），美国青春偶像组合，20 世纪 60 年代因"海滩派对"系列电影而走红。

5　兔巴哥（Bugs Bunny），美国华纳公司推出的动画片形象。

6　汤姆·米克斯（Tom Mix，1880—1940），美国电影明星，老一代西部片代表人物。

7　梦幻城（Fantasia），参见迪士尼动画《幻想曲》（*Fantasia*，1940）。

8　阿诺德·斯堂（Arnold Stang，1918—2009），美国笑星，配音演员。

9　诺曼·梅勒（Norman Mailer，1923—2007），美国作家，他不喜欢鲍勃·迪伦，曾说，如果鲍勃·迪伦是个诗人，那我就是棒球选手。

10　埃德·苏利文（Ed Sullivan，1901—1974），美国电视综艺节目主持人。1963 年迪伦因政治嘲讽歌曲被删而拒绝参加他的节目。

11　兰尼埃三世（Rainier III，1923—2005），摩纳哥君主。

12　休伊·朗（Huey Long，1893—1935），美国政客，被认为实行独裁，死于刺杀。

13　富尔顿·希恩（Fulton Sheen，1895—1979），时任纽约副主教，以在广播和电视上传道而闻名。

14　小威廉·巴克利（William F. Buckley Jr.，1925—2008），美国保守派作家、媒体人，文笔犀利。

15　沃尔特·克朗凯特（Walter Cronkite，1916—2009），美国哥伦比亚广播公司晚七点新闻主持人，因现场报道肯尼迪遇刺案成为美国最受欢迎的主播。书中将他的姓氏挪揄为“曲轴箱”（crankcase），可指扭曲、乖戾、奇思怪想、疯话连篇或妙语连珠等。另参见迪伦歌曲《黑钻石湾》（“Black Diamond Bay”，1976）。

16　小理查德（Little Richard，1932—2020），美国歌手，早期摇滚明星。

17　酥酥、脆脆和嘎嘣（Snap, Crackle and Pop），美国家乐氏公司（Kellogg's）系列方便早餐的卡通形象和广告歌。

18　路德维希·艾哈德（Ludwig Wilhelm Erhard，1897—1977），时任西德总理，1966 年下台。

19　加里市（Gary），由美国钢铁公司（USS）建立，拥有当时全球最大钢铁厂，但已走向产业衰退，有色人种居民比例约占全市一半，1967 年选出了美国最早的黑人市长之一。1962 年热门音乐电影《音乐人》（*The Music Man*，1962）的男主角、骗子教授哈罗德·希尔声称自己是加里人，有插曲《加里，印第安纳》（“Gary, Indiana”）。

20　《可可乔》（“Koko Joe”, 1958），美国流行歌曲，据说作者“小子波诺”（Sonny Bono，1935—1998）写下这首歌时才 16 岁。

21　爱因斯坦，参见迪伦歌曲《荒凉路》。

22　蛇人波吉（porgy snaker），出自 1959 年美国热门音乐电影《波吉和贝丝》（*Porgy and Bess*），主人公波吉是一个瘸腿跪行的黑人乞丐，反映了底层男女的悲惨爱情。另，英语传统儿歌《乔吉·波吉》（“Georgie Porgie”），原词大意讲小坏蛋乔治偷偷亲吻女孩子，把她们吓哭，然后他又跑掉了。另，美国民谣蓝调歌手“蛇人”戴夫·雷（Dave “Snaker” Ray，1943—2002），迪伦早年曾在他家听碟学歌。

23 约翰·查德（John Chard，1847—1897），英国殖民军中尉，在祖鲁战争（1879 年）中因率领工程兵 150 人抵御数千祖鲁军队的进攻而获得最高勋章。以他为主人公的英国电影《祖鲁》（*Zulu*）是 1964 年的热门片。

24 1964 年，萨特拒绝接受诺贝尔文学奖。

25 《小鱼苗》（“Small Fry”），美国流行歌曲，1938 年在热门电影《棠棣歌声》（*Sing You Sinners*）中由宾·克罗斯比演红。

26 参见迪伦《统统带回家》唱片文案：“成功毫无意义，我不想成为巴赫、莫扎特、托尔斯泰、乔希尔、格特鲁德斯泰因或詹姆斯迪恩，他们都死了，伟大的书都被写过了，伟大的话都被说过了。”

27 赫罗德教授（herold the professor），参见前注电影《音乐人》中的骗子教授哈罗德。

False Eyelash in Maria's Transmission

127 maria–she's mexican–but she's american as Howling Wolf–"my worried mind, it annoys me! i cant take my rest! i'm disgusting!" says her brother, who sneaks across the border & gets drunk on skinny whores & Turkish gas–"maria needs a shot" says King Villager "she needs a shot of a very bored God"–the rest of the villagers sing a song that sounds like "oh the days of forty–nine" in a Welsh accent & Adlai Stevenson starting a riot on the mountaintop...maria once nailed coffins for a living–"i will bust a plateglass window over Adlai Stevenson's head!" says her brother very drunk on Turkish gas "i will prove to him that he too is a masochist–i shall make him bend like a woman & wish he was on a freight train to Frisco"–a marine with his finger nibbled–Josephine–whose grandfather died at Shiloh–stabbed maria once & hid her clothes–she was arrested on an incest charge...King Villager, who is slowly dying of cancer, polishes his noisy beard now & mutters "cops–progress–american monuments" & "nothing matters" maria has made love with a beggar recently–he was disguised in flamboyant tinfoil–they made it in a saddlebag–she can run a mile in 5 days

玛丽亚变速箱中的假睫毛[1]

玛丽亚——她是墨西哥人——但她跟啸狼[2]一样是美国人——“我心里那个愁啊，叫我烦得要死！我根本都睡不了！直犯恶心！”她的兄弟说，他摸过了边界&沉迷于那些瘦巴巴的婊子&土耳其煤气——“玛丽亚需要来一针”村民之王说“她需要一针非常厌烦的上帝”——其余村民唱起一首歌，听来像是威尔士口音的“哦四九年的日子”[3]&阿德莱史蒂文森[4]在山顶上发动暴乱……玛丽亚曾经靠钉棺材谋生——“我要把一扇平板玻璃窗砸到阿德莱史蒂文森头上！”她那个沉迷土耳其煤气的兄弟说“我要证明他也是个受虐狂——我会叫他服帖得像个女人&但愿他已经爬货车去了旧金山”——有个陆战队员啃着手指——约瑟芬——她的爷爷死在示罗[5]——她曾经刺伤玛丽亚&藏起她的衣服——她因乱伦罪被捕……村民之王受着癌症的煎熬，他正在润饰他那俗艳的胡须&嘀咕着“警察——进步——美国纪念碑”&“什么都无所谓”玛丽亚最近跟一个乞丐做爱了——他包裹着亮闪闪的锡箔——他们在马鞍袋里边干——她

point 9 & the traveling roadshow that comes thru the town once a year respects her for it

128 maria's father lays dead on the hill–rich pimps–humanity & civilization walk over his grave to show her that they mean business...she is not going on any goodwill tours this year–there is a false eyelash in her transmission... there is not many places she can taste

this is my last letter–i've tried to
please you, but i see now that you have
too much on your mind–what you need is
someone to flatter you–i would do that, but
what would be the worth? after all, i
need nothing from you–you are so much
tied up in, though, that you have turned
into a piece of hunger–while the mystics
of the world jump in the sun, you have
turned into a lampshade–if youre going to think,
dont think about why people dont love each
other–think about why they dont love
themselves–
maybe then, you will begin to love them–if
you have something to say, let me know, i'm
just around the corner, located by the flight
controls–take it easy & dont scratch too
much–watch the green peppers & i think
youve

可以5点9天跑一英里&每年一度穿过城里的巡回路演为此向她致敬

玛丽亚的爸爸死在小山上——有钱的皮条客们——人性&文明踩过他的坟墓向她表明他们是当真的……她今年不打算再搞什么亲善之旅——她的变速箱里边有一个假睫毛……没有太多地方能让她品味

这是我最后一封信——我以前老想
讨好你，但现在我觉得你
脑子里的东西太多——你需要的是
有个人奉承你——我可以那样做，但
那样值得吗？说到底，我
对你一无所求——你实在太多
纠葛，所以你已经变成了
一块饥饿——当世界的
神秘论者在阳光下蹦跳，你已经
变成一个灯罩——如果你打算思考，
不要思考为什么人们不能彼此
相爱——要思考为什么他们不爱自己——
那样，也许你就开始爱他们了——如果
你有什么要说，请告诉我，我就
近在眼前，由飞控中心给我
定位——放松点&不要那样
紧张了——看看绿胡椒吧&我想你已得到了

had enough popcorn–youre turning into an
addict–
as i said, there's simply nothing i can give
you excpt a simply–there is nothing i can take
129 from you excpt a guilty conscience–i cant give
nor take any habit...see you at the masquerade
ball

tormentedly
water boy

足够的爆米花——你正在变成瘾君子——
我说过，根本没有什么东西是我能给予
你的除了一句话——没有什么东西是我能
从你那里拿走的除了犯罪感——我不能给予
也不能拿走任何嗜好……化装舞会上
见

苦恼不堪的
送水哥[6]

注　释

1　标题参见迪伦《统统带回家》唱片文案：“我的诗是用一种经过非诗性变形的韵律写成的，除以穿孔耳朵、假睫毛，减去那些用描述性空洞的优美诗行不断互相折磨的人。”

2　啸狼（Howlin' Wolf，1910—1976），美国黑人蓝调歌手。

3　《四九年的日子》（“The Days of Forty-nine”），美国传统民谣，原词指 1849 年。

4　阿德莱·史蒂文森（Adlai Stevenson II，1900—1965），美国民主党人，演说家，时任美国常驻联合国代表。

5　示罗（Shiloh），希伯来语原意：和平安宁之地，在《旧约》中是古以色列建立耶路撒冷之前的宗教中心，供奉着约柜。1862 年 4 月，美国南北战争的一场重要战役在田纳西州的示罗教堂附近爆发，双方伤亡两万多人，北军取得惨胜。

6　送水哥（water boy），出自同名美国传统民谣。

Al Aaraaf & the Forcing Committee

now the anarchist–we call him Moan–he takes us & Medusa–she carries the wigs–Moan carries the maps–by noon, we're in Abyss Hallway–there are shadows of jugglers on the wall & from out of the Chelsea part of the ceiling drops Monk–Moan's boy–Medusa going into a room with two swords above the door–some removable mirrors inside–Medusa disappears...Lacky, a strange counterpart of the organization–he comes out of the room carrying a mirror–both swords above the door fall down–one sticks into the floor–the other slices him in half...Monk, typical flunky & writer of eccentric gag lines to tell yourself if youre ever hung
130 up in the Andes–he leads us into a room with Chinese sayings that all read "a penny slaved is a penny is a penny is a penny"...there is a gigantic looking glass & Monk immediately disintegrates...after lunch, you hear a punch of rocks & car accidents over a loudspeaker & Chang Chung–some transient & a professional extra sensual bum without any pride or shame & he's selling rebel war cries & "how to become a birth control pill' pamphlets–"invent me a signature" says Mom "i must go sign some papers concerning the zippers of

阿尔阿拉夫[1]&军事委员会

下面讲无政府主义者——我们叫他莫安——他载上我们&美杜莎——她带着假发——莫安带着地图——中午的时候，我们来到深渊门厅——戏法师们的影子投在墙壁上&从切尔西[2]的天花板坠下和尚——莫安的小子——美杜莎走进一个在门上悬着两柄剑的房间——里边还有些活动的镜子——美杜莎消失了……拉奇，该组织的一个奇特对应物——他拿着一面镜子从房间出来——门上的两柄剑掉落——有一柄插进地板——另一柄把他切成两半……和尚，典型的马屁精&奇文怪句作家要告诉你本人你是否过于执着安第斯山[3]——他把我们领进一个房间那里的中文名言都写着"苦干一分钱是一分钱是一分钱是一分钱"[4]……那里有面巨大的镜墙&和尚立刻就解体了……午餐后，你听见一片轰隆的落石&车祸在扩音器传来&张钟——某个过客&一位专业的超感官流浪汉他没有任何荣誉或羞耻感&他在兜售军事叛乱口号&"怎样成为一颗避孕药"小册子——"帮我编造一个签名吧"妈妈说"我必须去签署一些有关真理拉链的

truth" "zippers of truth!" says Chang Chung "there is no truth!" "right" says Moan "but there are zippers" "very sorry–velly solly–it is my mistake–it's just that i'm wearing huge shoes today that's all" "dont let it happen again" says Moan, staring down to his own shoes...down the hallway now in a wheelchair comes Photochick–she is the flower of Moan & she's eating a cowpie

Grady O'lady comes in–gives everybody the nod & wants to know where she can get a maid–"dig henry miller?" she asks kind of snaky like–"you mean that fantastically dead henry miller? the real estate agent henry miller?" "what you mean?" say Grady O'lady "henry's not a real estate agent–he's a cavedweller–he's an artist–he writes about God" "i'm thinking of another henry miller–i'm thinking of the one that wears a tulip in his crotch & writes about cecil b. de mille's girls... O'lady takes an orange out of her pocket "got this in the Aztec country–watch me now
131 boys" she takes the orange & squeezes it very gently & slowly–then she rips it open madly & snarls & it oozes & dribbles down her mouth–all over her shirt–more–more she's all covered in orange–Moan comes in with his art critic–Sean Checkshit & both of them–they start discussing a shipping deal "Junior Bork has just finished his novel on World War I–speaks very good for our side & we must remember not to use it for toilet paper" "i'm going to use it for toilet paper" says Photochick "explain yourself!" says Moan & Photochick explains that one

文件”“真理拉链！”张钟说“根本没有真理！”“正确”莫安说“但是有拉链呀”“非常抱歉——灰墙爆线——都是我的错——就怪我今天穿了双大码鞋子就是这样”“下次不要这样了”莫安说着，低头看看自己的鞋……现在照相小妞[5]坐着轮椅到门厅来了——她是莫安的花儿&她在吃一泡牛屎饼

老太君奶奶驾到——向大家点点头&想知道她去哪里才能找个女仆——“懂不懂亨利米勒？”她有点狡黠地问——“你是说那个死得匪夷所思的亨利米勒？那个房产经纪人亨利米勒？”“你说什么呢？”老太君奶奶说“亨利可不是房产经纪人——他是个穴居人——他是个艺术家——他在写上帝”“我想到另一个亨利米勒了——我想到有一个在裤裆上插着郁金香&写过塞西尔 b. 德米尔[6]的姑娘们……老太君从兜里掏出一个橘子[7]“在阿兹特克乡下得了这个——都瞧好了小子们”她抓着橘子&非常轻柔&缓慢地压挤它——然后她死命将它掰开&嗥叫着&它汁水横流&从她嘴里淌下来——滴满她的衬衫——继续滴着——滴着，她全身都被橘汁包裹了——莫安来时带着他的艺术批评家——肖恩查个屎&两人一块——他们开始讨论一桩航运买卖“小博克刚写完一本讲第一次世界大战的小说——给我们这边说了很多好话&我们一定要记得不能用来擦屁股”“我正打算用来擦屁股呢”照相小妞说“请解释清楚！”莫安说&照相小

person's truth is always someone else's lie & Moan he starts whipping her with his map & she starts crying & walks into a room with mirrors & blows up–"now back to this shipping deal" says Moan, who turns around to find Sean Checkshit on the floor with Grady O'lady & theyre both covered in orange "tell me more about this henry miller" says Sean "oo ah isn't it wonderful" says Grady O'lady

in Ponce de Leon land–the union leader–Stormy Leader–is on exhibition fighting a lady wrestler...out of his past appears Insanely Hoppy screaming & dancing Screaming–pouting "the world belongs to the woikas–the woikas–none of you want to be woikas–none of you–none of you could make it–none of you" "shut up!" says Moan, who comes in the room unnoticed "shut up– i've got a backache & anyway it's workers not woikas!" "the world is his–it's his that looks like a walrus & moves about like
132 a walrus & has to sleep with a wife that feels like a walrus & he's forced to be a walrus for a buncha nagging kids & he goes to nagging walrus ball games & plays poker with a bunch of walruses & then he's driven into the earth & buried with a walrus in his mouth–i dare not say enough about him–he lives in his armpit & he hates you–he has no need for you–you clutter his life–you are lucky to be hanging around in his world–you have no choice excpt to walk naked–why be so honorable about it–why be so honorable about sleeping with pigs?" CRASH "put that boy in with proverb writers–but give him a bad review

妞解释说一个人的真理肯定是另一个人的谎言&莫安他就用他的地图猛抽她&她开始哭&走进一个装满镜子的房间&爆发了——“现在继续谈那桩航运买卖”莫安说着，转身发现肖恩查个屎的正跟老太君奶奶滚在地板上&两人都裹满了橘汁“再跟我讲讲这个亨利米勒吧”肖恩说“噢哟很精彩是不是”老太君奶奶说

在庞塞德莱昂[8]之地——工会领导人——暴风领袖——在表演跟一个女摔跤手搏斗……从他的过往冒出了疯喜狂乐尖叫着&舞蹈着尖叫——嘟囔着——“世界属于老动着——老动着——你们谁都不想成为老动着——谁都不想——你们谁都不能做到——谁都不能”“闭嘴！”莫安说，没人注意他进了房间“闭嘴——我腰痛得很&反正是劳动者又不是老动着！”“世界是他的——是他的，他长得像只海象[9]&走起来像只海象&还必须跟一个摸上去像只海象的老婆睡觉&他为了一帮聒噪的小孩被迫去做一只海象&他去参加聒噪的海象顶球比赛&跟一帮海象打扑克&然后他被撵进了泥土&嘴里含着海象一起埋葬——关于他我不敢说太多——他住在他的胳肢窝里&他恨你们——他对你们一无所求——你们干扰他的生活——你们很幸运能在他的世界里厮混——你们除了赤裸裸行走没有别的选择——为什么还那么引以为荣——为什么跟一群猪猡睡觉还那么引以为荣？”**咣当撞击**“把那小子跟格言作家放一块——但要给他一个恶

& say that he beat his wife & ate pork–say that he ate meat on Friday–say anything–just get him out of here till he's ready for training"...a lost pony express rider peers out from the trap door–he is carrying a picture of a long corridor & he sort of blows out his words when he talks "you are all fools! you cant add! you can count to a million but none of you–none of you–can see the sum total of the ground on which you stand on" Darling the Hypocrite immediately lights a fire to the floor & People Gringo pounds his fist on a book & says that rocking chair & watermelon are the same word only with different letters...St. Bread from the riot squad–entering with his chess pieces & a hilarious hard on & he laughs too

mother say go in That direction & please
do the greatest deed of all time & say i say
133 mother but it's already been done & she say
well what else is there for you to do & i say
i dont know mother, but i'm not going in That
direction–i'm going in that direction & she
say ok but where will you be & i say i dont
know mother but i'm not tom joad & she say
all right then i am not your mother

prince hamlet of his hexagram–sheik of unsanitary angels–he rides on a bareback instrument–exact factor concerning the reality of grandstand–Taj Mahal & Clytia's

评&就说他打老婆&吃猪肉——说他在星期五吃肉——随便怎么说——总之叫他离开这儿除非他肯接受训练”……有个迷路的驿站骑手从活板门往外偷看——他正扛着一幅绘有长廊的图画&他的说话就像要把词语轰出来——他说“你们都是蠢货！你们根本不识数！你们能从一数到一百万但是你们谁都不能——谁都不能——算出你们脚下这块地的总数”亲爱的伪君子立刻放火去烧地板&人民的外国佬重拳捶打一本书&说摇摇椅&西瓜只是拼写不同的同一个词……来自防暴队[10]的神圣面包——领着他的棋子们进来&一片滑稽的雄起&他也笑了

妈妈说你要走那个方向&每时
每刻你都要积德行善&说我说
妈妈但早都有人做过了&她说
那这样你还有什么能做的&我说
我不知道妈妈，但我不想走那个
方向——我想走那个方向&她
说好吧但你要去哪儿&我说我不
知道妈妈但我不是汤姆约德[11]&她说
行啊那我就不是你妈妈

戴六角星[12]的哈姆雷特王子——不讲卫生天使们的酋长——他骑上一台裸背器械[13]——关系到大看台现实性

sundial missing–this exact factor missing...nevertheless–the bubbling under does not disturb him–Lilith teaches her new husband, Bubba, how to use deodorant–also she teaches him that "stinky doo doo" means nasty filth & both of these teachings together add up to Bubbling Under Number One...Obie Doesnt–whose eyes are waxed & that they say lives in a world of his own–he keeps repeating "these aint normal people are they? are they? oh my God–pass the crackers–these arent normal people are they? hello hello can you hear me?" "yes yes it's true–they are–they are the normal people" says prince–who gives Obie a little tickle–makes him laugh "but remember–it's like the boogie man told the centaur when the centaur invaded the territory of the Giant Mother Geese, 'you dont have to be around those people'–by the way, i've
134 heard you live in a world of your own" "yes it's true" says Obie "& i also dont go to birthday parties" "very good" says the prince "keep up the good work"...about this bareback instrument–sometimes the prince is sure he's on it but not so sure he's riding on it–at other times, he's sure he's riding on it, but not so sure it's bareback–at odd moments, the prince is sure that he's riding on something bareback but not so sure it's an instrument...all his daily adventures, unsuccessful potatoes & other pirates try to pin him down to Certainality & put him in his place once & for all "care to arm wrestle?" say some–"youre a phony–youre no prince!" say the smarter ones who go into bathtubs & ask for the usual...the prince sees many jacks & jills come tumbling down "funny how when you look, you cant find any pieces to pick up" he says this

的精确系数——泰姬陵[14] & 克吕提亚[15] 的日晷丢失——这个精确系数丢失……尽管如此——锅底冒泡[16] 并未干扰他——莉莉丝[17] 在教她的新丈夫笨巴怎样使用香体露——而且她还教他"臭便便"意即肮脏污秽&这两堂课合起来就是锅底冒泡第一名……奥比不肯[18]——他的眼睛像打过蜡&他们说他活在一个自我的世界里——他不断重复着"这些都不是正常人对不对？对不对？哦上帝呀——把脆饼递过来——这些都不是正常人对不对？喂喂你听得见吗？""的确如此——他们是——他们是正常人"王子说着——他给奥比来了个小咯吱——让他笑了起来"但要记住——就像人头马入侵大鹅妈妈们的领土时夜魔怪对人头马说的，'你不一定非要跟那些人周旋不可'——而且，我曾听说你活在一个自我的世界里""的确如此"奥比说"&我也不去生日晚会""非常好"王子说"继续保持好状态"……对于这台裸背器械——有时候王子能确定他在上面但不确定是否骑着——又有些时候，他能确定他骑在上面，但不确定它是不是裸背——偶尔还有些时候，王子能确定他正骑着某种裸背的东西但不很确定它是不是一台器械……他日复一日的历险，不成功的土豆&其他海盗们试图把他限定于确实性&让他摆正自己的位置一了&百了"喜欢扳腕子吗？"有人说——"你就是个假货——你不是王子！"更聪明的人们这样说着便走进浴缸&要求按常规……王子见到许多杰克&吉尔滚滚掉落"看这些真是有趣，你都没法

usually once a day to his bareback instrument–who never talks back–most good souls dont

it is not that there is no Receptive for anything written or acted in the first person–it is just that there is no Second person

MAMMOTH NOAH & the orient marauders all on the morality rap & Priest of Harmony in a narrow costume–he's with the angels now & he says "all's useless–useless" & Instinct, poet of the antique zenith–putting on his hoofs & whinnying "all's not useless–all is very signifying!" & the insane pied piper stealing the Queen's Pawn & the conquering war cry "neither–neither" & jails being cremated & jails falling & newly arrived spirits digging–digging their fingernails–their fingernails into each other...Goal–Hari Cari & the Cruel Mother teasing at your harmless fate...the sight of george raft–richard nixon–liberace–d.h. lawrence & pablo casals–all the same person–& struggle–struggle & your weapons of curls blowing & Digging–Digging Everything

aretha–known in gallup as number 69–in
wheeling as the cat's in heat–in pittsburgh
as number 5–in brownsville as the left
road, the lonesome sound–in atlanta as

找到一块能捡起来的碎片”这话他通常每天都要跟他的裸背器械说上一次——它从不搭话——大多数好灵魂都不会

并不是说难以接受任何以第一人称书写或行使的东西——只因为没有第二人称

猛犸象诺亚&东方劫匪们都在吹嘘道德&和谐牧师穿着紧身衣——他现在跟天使们一块了&他说“全都没用——没用的”&本能，上古鼎盛时期诗人——扬起他的蹄子&嘶鸣“全都并非没用——全都意味深长！”&发神经的花衣魔笛手[19]偷掉王后的卒子[20]&胜利的战叫“都不——都不”&监狱被焚毁&监狱倒塌&新近到来的灵魂们在挖——用指甲——用他们的指甲互相对挖……射门——切腹自杀&残酷妈妈[21]戏弄你那无辜的命运……一眼望去乔治拉夫特[22]——理查德尼克松——利伯拉切——d.h. 劳伦斯&巴勃罗卡萨尔斯[23]——全都是同一个人——&斗争——斗争&你的卷毛飘飘的武器&挖——挖一切[24]

阿瑞莎——在盖洛普[25]她名为69号——在
惠灵[26]是叫春猫——在匹兹堡
是5号，在布朗斯维尔[27]是走左边的[28]
路，是孤独之声[29]——在亚特兰大是

dont dance, listen–in bowling green as
oh no, no, not again–she's known as horse
chick up in cheyenne–in new york city she's
known as just plain aretha…i shall play
her as my trump card

i would like to do something worthwhile like perhaps plant a tree on the ocean but i am just a guitar player–with no absurd fears of her reputation, Black Gal co–exists with melody & i want to feel my evaporation like Black Gal feels her co–existence…i do not want to carry a pitchfork

136 prince hamlet–he's somewhere on the totem pole–he hums a little shallow tune "oh killing me by the grave"–aretha–lady godiva of the migrants–she sings too…there are a lot of historians under the totem pole–all pretending to be making a living–there's also a lot of spies & customs agents–the popes dont quit & the artists live in the meantime–the meantime dies & in its place comes the sometimes–there is never any real sometime & the customs agents & spies usually turn into star ice skaters on a winter vacation & they brood about the meantime/ they usually dont know anybody under the totem pole excpt their elders…San Francisco freezing & New York neath spells of Poe & famous barbarians "you can make it if you have nothing" lips prince to a spaghetti dinner–wasting away on a slushy rink–belonging to nobody &

别跳舞，听歌——在滚球绿地[30]是
哦不，不，不要再来了——在夏延族[31]
她被称为小母马——在纽约城她
就直接地称为阿瑞莎……我应该把她
当成我的王牌来打

我也想去做些有价值的事情比如在海洋上种一棵树但我只是一个吉他手——对她的盛名没有荒唐的恐惧，黑妹[32]与旋律共存&我要感受我的蒸发就像黑妹感受她的共存……我可不想扛着一把草叉

哈姆雷特王子——他高在图腾柱上的某处[33]——他哼哼着一支无力的小曲“哦用坟墓把我杀死”[34]——阿瑞莎——移民们的戈黛娃夫人——她也在歌唱……图腾柱下围着很多历史学家——都假装是在谋求生计——还有很多间谍&海关密探——教皇们没有退位——艺术家们在同一时间活着——同一时间死去&在它的位置出现了某些时间——但那里从来未有过什么真正的某些时间[35]&海关密探&间谍们通常在寒假里就变成溜冰明星&他们默默怀念同一时间/他们通常不认识那图腾柱下的任何人除了他们的上级……旧金山冻结了&纽约笼罩在爱伦坡&著名蛮族的魔咒之下“如果你一无所有你就可以做到”对着一碟意面晚餐念叨王子——在泥泞的溜冰场上日渐憔悴——不属于任何人&伐木工们来了“我在寻

the lumberjacks are coming "i'm searching–i'm searching
for some kind of meaning!" says Jug the Lady, an escaped
werewolf–she wears a chrome head piece & has been
studying Yugoslavia for the past ten months–she has a
built–in jukebox on her motorcycle "your mind is small–
it is limited–what kind of sense must you need?" says
prince "i want to be on the totem pole too" she confides
"the lumberjacks are coming" says prince & then he takes
out his shirt tail & begins to draw circles on the air "there
are magnets on this shirt tail & they all pick up pieces
of minute–now you see–i've got something to do–why'n
you go see this fellow–Moan is his name–he'll straighten
137 you–& if he cant–he knows someone that can" one of
Jug's friends, a drummer who doesnt drum but rather just
drops his sticks on the drums–comes out of the bushes–
rather a sadist type & whose entire wardrobe consists of
a marine's uniform & a washed out nurse's outfit–he yells
"i'm looking for a partner–gimme some secrets!" & then
there's two little boys playing & one says "if i owned the
world, each man would have a million dollars" & one
says "if i owned the world–each man would have the
chance to save the world once in his lifetime"...prince
hamlet of his hexagram–he pulls a train & makes love to
miss Julie Ann Johnson "i said gimme some secrets–i'm
just the usual beer" says this drummer & prince carves
Memphis–London & Viet Nam into the pole "there are
only a few things that exist: Boogie Woogie–highpowered
frogs–Nashville Blues–harmonicas walking–80 moons
& sleeping midgets–there are only three things that
continue: Life–Death & the lumberjacks are coming"

找——我在寻找某种意义！”水壶女士，一头脱逃的狼人说——她戴着一顶镀铬头盔&已研究南斯拉夫长达十个月[36]——她的摩托车上有一台内置点唱机“你的头脑太小——它是有限的——你一定要得到哪种知识呢？”王子说“我也想到图腾柱上去”她直言道“伐木工都来了呀”王子说&然后他抽出他的衬衫下摆&开始对着空气划圈圈“这件衬衫下摆有万磁力&它们可以收拢所有零碎的时刻——你看——我已经有事情要做了——为什么你不去看看这个家伙——他名叫莫安——他会给你摆平的——&如果他办不了——他知道谁能办”水壶有个朋友，一个鼓手他不打鼓只是让鼓槌落在鼓面上——出自丛林——有点虐待狂的派头&他的全套行头不过是一件陆战队制服&一件洗旧的护士大褂——他大嚷“我在找一个搭档——给我透点机密吧！”[37]&当时有两个小男孩在那儿表演&一个说“如果我拥有世界，每个人都会得一百万”&一个说“如果我拥有世界——每个人在他的生命中都有机会拯救世界一次”……戴六角星的哈姆雷特王子——他拖着一列火车[38]&跟朱丽安约翰逊[39]小姐做爱“我说给我透点机密吧——我只是个普通啤酒”这个鼓手说&王子在柱子上雕刻孟菲斯——伦敦&越南“只有几样东西是存在的：布吉乌吉[40]——高能跳跳蛙——纳什维尔蓝调——口琴漫步[41]——80个月亮&熟睡的小矮人——只有三样东西是持久的：生命——死亡&伐木工来了”

注 释

1 阿尔阿拉夫（Al Aaraaf），出自爱伦·坡早期同名长诗（1829）。

2 切尔西（Chelsea），可能指纽约切尔西饭店（Hotel Chelsea），迪伦以及很多文艺界人士是那里的常客。

3 安第斯山即南美洲，彼时正在发生革命。

4 “苦干一分钱是一分钱是一分钱是一分钱”（a penny slaved is a penny is a penny is a penny），混合了英国谚语“节省一便士就是赚得一便士”和美国先锋派作家格特鲁德·斯泰因（Gertrude Stein）的名句“玫瑰是一朵玫瑰是一朵玫瑰是一朵玫瑰”。

5 照相小妞（Photochick），参见迪伦1965年纽波特民谣音乐节宣传册文案《剪掉我的头顶》（“Off the Top of My Head”），她的嘴唇上别着胡佛纪念章，不能开口。

6 塞西尔·德米尔（Cecil B. DeMille，1881—1959），美国电影导演，好莱坞元老级人物。

7 有关亨利·米勒和橘子的叙述见前文《电影明星嘴里的沙子》。另参见迪伦诗作《11个简要墓志铭》（“11 Outlined Epitaphs”，1964）：“亨利米勒站在乒乓球桌的另一头，不停地谈论我。”

8 胡安·庞塞·德莱昂（Juan Ponce de León，1474—1521），西班牙探险家、殖民先驱，在佛罗里达半岛被印第安人击败身死。

9 参见迪伦歌曲《就像个女人》（“Just Like a Woman”，1966）：“她做派就像个女人，是的 / 她做起爱来就像个女人，是的 / 她有欲火就像个女人 / 但她心碎却像个小女孩。”

10 防暴队（the riot squad），参见迪伦歌曲《荒凉路》：“防暴队坐立不安 / 他们需要有地方可去……”

11 汤姆·约德（Tom Joad），美国作家、1962年诺贝尔文学奖获得者约翰·斯坦贝克的长篇小说《愤怒的葡萄》（*The Grapes of Wrath*，1939）的主人公，他出狱后和家族一起离乡背井前往加利福尼亚讨生活，他的妈妈是家中主心骨，最终汤姆又因杀人被迫逃亡，他向妈妈发誓，无论去到哪里都会坚持抗争。参见伍迪·格思里歌曲《汤姆·约德》。

12　六角星（hexagram），此处可能指美国警察系统的某种徽章，如洛杉矶县警为六角星徽中间有一头熊；一般指犹太标志大卫星、秘教标志所罗门封印等；中国《易经》的六十四卦象在西方也被称为“hexagram”。

13　裸背器械（bareback instrument），摩托车，如不配鞍鞯的机器马，哈姆雷特王子骑哈雷摩托（Harley-Davidson）。参见迪伦歌曲《像一块滚石》：“你从前常骑镀铬的骏马和你的外交官出游。”另，“bareback”也指不带套性交，后文有暗示。

14　泰姬陵的墓主玛哈皇后（Mahal）结婚 19 年生育 14 个子女，38 岁死于难产。

15　克吕提亚（Clytia），古希腊神话中的一个海仙女，苦恋着太阳神赫利俄斯，死后化作向阳花。

16　“锅底冒泡”（Bubbling Under），亦即将近沸腾、接近成功，也是美国《公告牌》每周单曲 100 强之外另设的潜力榜。

17　莉莉丝（Lilith），犹太传说中的大女妖，据说是亚当的第一个妻子。

18　奥比不肯（Obie Doesnt），出自美国山地摇滚歌曲《奥比多比》（“Ooby Dooby”，1955），由罗伊·奥比逊（Roy Orbison，1936—1988）唱红。

19　发神经的花衣魔笛手（the insane pied piper），参见迪伦歌曲《墓碑蓝调》：“把花衣魔笛手关进监狱，把奴隶们养肥 / 然后把他们派遣到丛林。”

20　王后的小卒（the Queen’s Pawn），国际象棋中，王后前面的那个兵叫“后兵”。参见迪伦歌曲《只是别人棋局中的一个小卒》（“Only a Pawn in Their Game”，1964）。

21　《残酷妈妈》（“The Cruel Mother”），英语传统民谣，大意讲妈妈在林中产下私生子，将他杀死、埋葬，回到家又看见有孩子在玩耍。另，哈姆雷特的妈妈格特鲁德王后也是一个“残酷妈妈”。

22 乔治·拉夫特（George Raft，1901—1980），美国演员，以反派形象出名。

23 巴勃罗·卡萨尔斯（Pablo Casals，1876—1973），西班牙大提琴家。

24 挖（digging），也意为理解，喜欢，发现。

25 盖洛普（Gallup），美国新墨西哥州城市，印第安人聚居地，很多西部片在这里拍摄。迪伦早年曾吹嘘，他 7 岁时就离家出走，在盖洛普长大。也可能指盖洛普民调。

26 惠灵（Wheeling），美国西弗吉尼亚州城市，靠近匹兹堡。也可能指旋转、轮盘赌等，参见迪伦专辑名《自由飞旋的鲍勃·迪伦》（*The Freewheelin' Bob Dylan*，1963）。

27 布朗斯维尔（Brownsville），美国得克萨斯州港口城市，位于美国大陆领土最南端，对岸就是墨西哥；美国还有多个同名城镇。迪伦后与萨姆·谢泼德（Sam Shepard）合作时，将《帝国滑稽剧》中未采用的、向格思里致敬的《新丹斯维尔女孩》加以改编利用，写成《布朗斯维尔女孩》（“Brownsville Girl”，1986）。

28 出自美国哲学家纳尔逊·古德曼（Nelson Goodman，1906—1998）的“问路难题”：在陌生路口有个本地人，他要么是骑士要么是流氓（要么只说真话要么只说假话），他只会回答“是”或者“否”，你应该怎样问路才能得到想要的答案？你不必管他是好人坏人，你只需问：“你是否在当且仅当左边的路通往正确目标时才是一个骑士？”衍生版本：“你是不是能够断言左边的路通往布朗斯维尔的那一类人？”

29 孤独之声（the lonesome sound），美国蓝草乡村歌曲的一种唱法，大意指高声调、失声跑调地唱出心中的凄楚郁闷。

30 滚球绿地（Bowling Green），纽约市曼哈顿金融区的一个街心小花园。

31 夏延族（Cheyenne），北美印第安人部族，在文化上以太阳舞仪式闻名。

32 黑妹（Black Gal），参见铅肚皮 1940 年代同名歌曲，源自美国传统民谣《松林下》（“In the Pines”）。

33　早期基督教有一种柱顶苦修士（stylite）长期在高柱顶上斋戒、布道；荷马史诗中，奥德修斯叫水手把自己绑在桅杆上抵抗塞壬海妖的魅惑歌声。参见尼采《查拉图斯特拉如是说》（1883）第29章《狼蛛》：“朋友们，把我紧紧绑在柱子上吧，我宁可做柱顶苦修士，也不愿（因狼蛛的毒）飞旋起舞……”另参见兰波（Arthur Rimbaud，1854—1891）诗《醉舟》（“Le Bateau ivre”，1871）：“当我在无情的大河漂流，/ 我不再感到纤夫的指引，/ 吵嚷嚷的红种人已将他们捉来当成靶子，/ 赤条条地钉在彩柱上。”

34　“哦用坟墓把我杀死”（oh killing me by the grave），戏拟三角洲蓝调之王罗伯特·约翰逊（Robert Johnson，1911—1938）的老歌《说教蓝调》（“Preachin' Blues”，1936），原词大意：蓝调是卑鄙的心疼病，就像肺痨，一步步把我杀死（killing me by degrees）。另参见迪伦歌曲《今夜你在那里？（穿过黑热之旅）》（“Where Are You Tonight? [Journey Through Dark Heat]”，1978）：“胡闹和疾病正一步步把我杀死。”

35　亦即，艺术家们活跃的那个时代，那个“同一时间”已经逝去了，现在也许在不确定的“某些时间”还会有艺术家，但实际上那种“时间”并不真的存在。

36　指十月怀胎。

37　上帝保存电汇机密，胡佛保存国家机密。

38　美国乡村音乐歌手约翰尼·卡什（Johnny Cash，1932—2003）的歌曲《伐木工》（“Lumberjack”，1960）中有长达1分钟的火车音效和念白。

39　《朱丽·安·约翰逊》（“Julie Ann Johnson”），美国黑人传统民谣，由铅肚皮演唱成名，有多个录音版本，3分钟加长版混合了伐木歌，说道：“现在斧头落下，小伙们要唱朱利安约翰逊，让你知道节奏会继续不停，哪怕斧头落下，你现在没听见，但他们马上砍回来……斧头砍回来了，砍啊砍啊。”

40　布吉乌吉（Boogie Woogie），一种快节奏的爵士乐钢琴曲式。

41　口琴漫步（harmonicas walking），不详，或可参见本书第1章开头的“疗救那些尖酸懦夫、骸骨&往故的口琴大军”（harmonica battalions）。

译后记

好一头八臂琴魔

《狼蛛》及青年鲍勃·迪伦的纯文学创作

or

They'll stone you when you're playing your guitar[1]

罗　池

1　出自迪伦歌曲《雨天的女人们第 12、35 号》（"Rainy Day Women #12 & 35"，1966）。

这是文学吗？：*I put down my robe, picked up my diploma*[1]

《狼蛛》，鲍勃·迪伦作品，是20世纪后半期在地球表面上最难以定位、最不知所云的奇著之一。有人说这是一本“小说”，有人说是“散文诗”，有人叫它“实验写作”，当然还有很多人斥之为“failed”（失败之作），或“bullshit”（狗屁不通），也就等于说，它根本不属于“文学”。

至于评价，众说纷纭，在互联网平台[2]还算马马虎虎，但在评论界，除了一笑而过之外，最多也就一笔带过：很多大部头的迪伦传记、论著对它实在避不开，只好随手应付，完成任务了事。《狼蛛》问世已有五十余年，迄今为止，能认真对它予以较正面论述的作者在全世界最多可能就十几个，而且他们基本都带着一点跟人争吵的架势。

文坛从来不缺少争吵，可以吵到要开除你的“坛籍”。2016年诺贝尔文学奖获得者鲍勃·迪伦所招致的强烈质疑，就是近年来在国际范围内影响最广的事

1　出自迪伦歌曲《蝗虫之日》（“Day of Locusts”，1970）。

2　在Goodreads网站，《狼蛛》英文版有2921个投票（截至2019年9月14日），平均得分为3.26（满分5），其中五星18%，四星23%，三星32%，二星17%，一星8%，https://www.goodreads.com/book/show/132025.Tarantula。

件之一。多位诺奖前辈羞与迪伦同席，巴尔加斯·略萨（Mario Vargas Llosa）说："我不认为他是个好作家。诺奖是给作家的，不是给歌手的。"奥尔罕·帕慕克（Ferit Orhan Pamuk）指出："是的，我非常失望。……我认为很多作家在那一天受到了伤害。"索因卡（Wole Soyinka）称，给迪伦颁奖是"为了打破成规而打破成规……真是荒唐"。[1] 在相关报导中，甚至有言论把院士丈夫性侵、高层大乱斗和迪伦获奖并列为瑞典文学院的三大丑闻，令"公信力大减，让桂冠失色，这些污点必定难以轻易洗去"。[2] 以上只是刊载在 2019 年一张中国报纸上的消息而已。

说来话长，这位摇滚天王头戴着惹人争议的光环已是长达半个世纪的老故事。早在五十多年前他就凭借歌词赢得了"诗人"荣誉，支持者为他奉上"穿牛仔裤的荷马""唱片上的华兹华斯""可乐世代的乔伊斯""点唱机上的布莱希特""诗人的诗人"这样的耀眼桂冠，但几十年来，也一直不断有资深评委坚持灭灯否决我们的歌手迪伦晋级"诗人"资格，正方反方的笔仗足以编出一大部精彩纷呈的厚书。

如 1965 年 11 月，在美国常青藤联盟院校英文系大

1　康慨，《沃莱·索因卡公开发难：鲍勃·迪伦获诺贝尔奖真是荒唐》，《中华读书报》，2019 年 3 月 13 日 04 版。

2　康慨，《霍拉斯·恩达尔退出诺贝尔委员会，瑞典学院宣布重启诺贝尔文学奖》，出处同上。

学生中进行的一项调查显示，鲍勃·迪伦压倒罗伯特·洛厄尔（Robert Lowell）、索尔·贝娄（Saul Bellow）、诺曼·梅勒（Norman Mailer）等名家，被新一代知识青年选为当代美国作家之首。这件事在主流文学界引起不小的震荡，《纽约时报》还做了后续报道。诗坛巨擘 W. H. 奥登（Wystan Hugh Auden）对迪伦敬谢不敏："我恐怕对他的作品一无所知。但无所谓了——我要读的东西实在太多。"路易斯·辛普森（Louis Simpson，1964 年普利策诗歌奖获得者）不以为然："我根本就没觉得鲍勃·迪伦是个诗人；他就是个艺人——诗人这个词现在简直任谁都可以用了。"[1] 对这个话题，诺曼·梅勒很干脆地说了一句名言："如果迪伦是个诗人，那我就是棒球选手。"[2] 而迪伦也不是省油的灯，他在《狼蛛》中这样回敬梅勒："诺曼梅勒家餐具室炸弹爆炸——导致他色盲——体育部人事大震荡。"[3]

知名乐评家罗伯特·克里斯戈（Robert Christgau）历来就很不感冒任何歌星——包括鲍勃·迪伦——的"诗人"头衔。当然克里斯戈本身就不喜欢美国现代口语诗，

---

1 Thomas Meehan, "Public Writer No.1?", *New York Times Magazine*, Dec. 12, 1965, http://movies2.nytimes.com/books/97/05/04/reviews/dylan-writer.html. 关于这场论争综述见 Shelton, p. 162，参见中译本，第 415—416 页。主要引用书目见文末。

2 Shelton, p. 234.

3 Dylan 1971, p. 124.

他认为金斯堡（Allen Ginsberg）更像个野人，还把摇滚乐诗潮归入“刻奇”（kitsch，媚俗，媚雅）。他说：摇滚歌词不是诗（也许）——

> 诗是靠读或者念的。歌是靠唱的。……再重复一遍：迪伦是唱作人，不是诗人。他最成功的那些作品也仅仅只有极少数——如《别想二次，都没事》《就像个女人》——能够在书页上立得住。纯属例外而已。……迪伦的唯一创新就是他在唱歌，这是一种控制所谓“语感”的好方式，但远还谈不上“现代诗的一大革命”。他或许开创了些不错的东西，但现代诗歌一直进展顺利，谢谢。[1]

不用谢。

但必须指出，在歌手鲍勃·迪伦的另一面，他确确实实也是一个标准的现代诗人。迪伦可谓笔耕不辍，他的早期代表性诗作主要以“文案”的形式随唱片一起发表。其实，单单这些“文案”拿到任一家文艺书店，出版一两本常规的小诗集都绰绰有余，但他不是太忙就是太懒，后来干脆罢手不玩了。而文坛、学界也好，歌迷、乐评人、传记家也好，对迪伦的纯文学创作基本没有给

---

1 Robert Christgau, “Rock Lyrics Are Poetry (Maybe)”，原载 *Cheetah*, Dec. 1967，引自作者个人网站 https://www.robertchristgau.com/xg/music/lyrics-che.php。

予足够的艺术关注，大家都围着他的歌词打转转（虽然歌词也是广义的诗）。就连迪伦的支持者、当年执美国新先锋之牛耳的安迪·沃霍尔（Andy Warhol）也曾说："如果迪伦变成一个不弹吉他的诗人，还说那些同样的东西，是不会有效果的；但是当诗歌冲上十大金曲的时候你就不能忽视它了。"[1]

不奇怪，印在纸上的迪伦诗作既然没有登上某个文化工业排行榜的实力，就大概率要领受全方位的"忽视"。尤其《狼蛛》，迪伦的第一本"纯文学"书籍，这部实验文体作品如此极端、彻底地在先锋异途上狂奔，完全的 freewheelin'（自由不羁），都不照顾一下普通读者的感情，结果就成了他名下最饱受争议的一个"什么玩意儿"，直接被打入冷宫。但迪伦对这类问题却相当犀利地反问：

你怎么看这些诗？

恐怕你得去找个学者来问问。

但你怎么说？

但我怎么说？那我也得去请教学者。它们是诗歌，或者它们不是诗歌……这真的很重要吗？

---

1 Warhol, pp. 146–147.

对谁才那么重要？[1]

鲍勃·迪伦写的那些文学东西在评论圈里长期不受待见，难道都是他临时瞎搞出来，甚至嗑药嗑出来的吗？真不是。迪伦年轻时的写作量一直非常大，随时写，随地写，窝在汽车后座里写，一边跟朋友聊天还能一边写，打字机色带一卷接一卷。然而，最后正式、半正式发表为歌词和诗文的仅是其中的一小部分，而且迪伦还对千挑万选出来的作品极不满意。悔其少作，他就不是那种愿意凑数的人。

虽然已公开的迪伦手稿数量有限，但我们仍可以通过他的歌曲创作和不断修订的过程明显地看到迪伦的文学匠心。如他在1965—1966年的巅峰时期，除了三张正式专辑之外，还留下一大堆录音，现已正式整理发行的就有《尖锋1965—1966》（*The Bootleg Series Vol.12: The Cutting Edge 1965–1966*[*Collector's Edition*]）十八张CD、《1966巡演现场录音》（*The 1966 Live Recordings*）三十六张CD，大多数曲目都是同一首歌重重复复的不同版本，改来改去，改来改去，证明了迪伦那份一丝不苟的艺术要求。

有趣的是，尽管迪伦（作为歌手以及作家）

1 Dylan 2008, p. vii.

的概念和用语对我们当年的耳朵而言如同时刻不停的马刺，驱策着一代人的急躁，但他在实际工作中却吹毛求疵。他试验每一个词、韵律、音调的分寸，一连几个小时、几天，直到他满意为止。他像诗人一样工作——这种方式他后来就不再有了——但他要处理的问题比［正统诗人所面对的］格律或对句要复杂得多：他必须将它与音乐融合，在不同的试唱中又完全变了个样，直到一切结合起来成为完成的作品。[1]

那么，这位很用功、很用心，乃至吹毛求疵的鲍勃·迪伦，当他转身于书页，只作为诗人或作家而存在的时候，他在文学创作方面的水平到底怎么样？好吧，他确实很喜欢写东西，很热爱文艺，但是，这样就算得上一个文学家吗？

迪伦就是如此不断地被反对者提出这样仿佛万世不易的问题，在诺贝尔奖获奖感言中，他毫不退让地表示：

我首先想到莎士比亚，这位大文豪。我猜想他会把自己看作戏剧家。创作文学的念头不会进

1　Mikal Gilmore, "Why Bob Dylan Is a Literary Genius", *Rolling Stone*, Dec. 9, 2016, https://www.rollingstone.com/music/music-features/why-bob-dylan-is-a-literary-genius-105108.

入他的头脑。他的文字为舞台而写。用于口述而非阅读。……我敢打赌，莎士比亚头脑中最不可能思考的就是“这是文学吗？”……即便在四百年后，有些事情也未曾从未改变。我一直没有闲暇来问自己：“我的歌是文学吗？”所以，我要感谢瑞典文学院，不仅花时间考虑这个问题，而且，最终，做出了如此精彩的回答。[1]

迪伦又把球踢回去了。到目前为止，这是最精彩的回答。

见习诗人：*He's an artist, he don't look back*[2]

年少的鲍勃·迪伦，原名罗伯特·艾伦·齐默曼（Robert Allen Zimmerman），1941 年生于一个俄裔正统犹太人家庭，在明尼苏达州的工业城市希宾（Hibbing）长大。这个曾兴盛一时的采矿中心，美国的铁岭（Iron Range），已日渐萧条没落，在少年的眼中，它处处流露

1 “Banquet Speech by Bob Dylan”，Dec. 10, 2016，引自诺贝尔奖官网，https://www.nobelprize.org/prizes/literature/2016/dylan/25424-bob-dylan-banquet-speech-2016/。

2 改写自迪伦歌曲《她属于我》（“She Belongs to Me”，1965）。

着闭塞、颓败的气息。迪伦曾多次写到他对于故乡生活的精神分析，如在《狼蛛》中：

> 我现在住的地方，唯一让这个地区
> 保持运转的东西就是传统——正如你想象的
> 那样——这不算太要紧——我周围的
> 一切都在腐烂……我不知道它这个样子
> 已经多长时间了，但如果它继续下去，很快
> 我就要变成一个老头——&我才15岁——这一带
> 唯一的工作就只有采矿——但耶稣啊，谁又想
> 去当矿工……我拒绝成为这种轻如鸿毛的
> 死亡的一分子——每个人都在谈论中
> 世纪就好像这当真处在中世纪一样——
> 我会千方百计离开这里——我的头脑
> 正随着大河流向远方……[1]

幸运的是，迪伦家在街上经营电器商店，收音机、电视机、电唱机，便利的现代视听装备给他打开了一道通往广阔音乐天地的侧门。而且希宾当时还拥有当年矿老板巨资兴建的"土豪"级公立学校，设施一流，师资雄厚，藏书丰富，连音乐厅都富丽堂皇。他的妈妈说：

1 Dylan 1971, pp. 108–109.

鲍勃静悄悄地待在楼上当了十二年的作家。他把所有的书都看过了。他买漫画也只买那种有意义的，像“经典名著绘本”。他经常泡图书馆。我不知道他喜欢哪些作者，我们几乎不谈作家。我们只会说笑和聊天。[1]

总之，我们的鲍勃同学成了希宾镇上有名的文艺特长生，十岁的时候他就懂得写诗作为礼物送给父母，惠而不费。其中，《父亲节献诗》（“For Father's Day”）的开头还模仿了一段饶有趣味的电器说明书文风：

这份礼物只献给我爸
打高尔夫球或在家坐着的时候使用。
他可以在饭后，或在开汽车的时候使用，
他可以在休息或出远门的时候使用，
我知道我爸是世界上最好的。[2]

迪伦早在中学时代就已经开始有了文学自觉，给自己诗歌本中的习作打分：“好诗”“差诗”，但鲜少示人，只给父母看过。他每天都窝在房间里鼓捣文艺爱好，却

---

1 Shelton, p. 39，参见中译本，第 91 页。

2 Shelton, p. 35，参见中译本，第 78 页。

让父母忧心忡忡。他的妈妈又说了：“写这些诗，你是要到死了以后才会被人发现的。……诗歌又不能当饭吃。……你不能一天又一天就这样坐在那里发呆、做梦、写诗来过活。我真担心他到头来成了一个诗人！你知道我说的是哪种诗人吗？就是没有抱负、只为自己写作的那种。在我们那时候，诗人就是没有工作、没有抱负的人。”在迪伦即将离家去上大学时，妈妈还语重心长地唠叨他：“波比，为什么你不做点有用的事情呢？……别再老是写诗了，求你。去学校要学点建设性的东西吧。拿个学位。”[1]

迪伦于 1959 年夏进入州城明尼阿波利斯，文艺青年扎堆的大学城真正打开了他的当代文学视野。他在文青圈子里搜刮市面难觅的唱片、最新潮的垮掉派作品，而且不惜做出窃书不算偷之类的糗事。“我直到高中毕业才真正开始写诗。在大概十八岁的时候我发现了金斯堡、加里·施耐德（Gary Snyder）、菲利普·惠伦（Philip Whalen）、弗兰克·奥哈拉（Frank O’Hara）这一批诗人。然后我又回头去读法国的诗人，兰波（Arthur Rimbaud）和弗朗索瓦·维庸（François Villon）。”[2]

迪伦像一块疯狂的海绵。据学弟爆料，明州大学图书馆每一本兰波的书背后的借书条都有齐默曼的名字，

1 Shelton, p. 40，参见中译本，第 92 页。

2 Heylin, p. 138.

英文版、法文版都有，还用同样的墨水乱划杠杠。[1]艾伦·金斯堡多次提到，对大学生迪伦影响最大的诗人是凯鲁亚克。

> 迪伦本人说过在1959年给他打开诗歌大门，并激励和促使他立志成为一个诗人的那本书，是凯鲁亚克的《墨西哥城蓝调》(*Mexico City Blues*, 1959)。……当时[1975年11月]我们站在凯鲁亚克墓前，拍他[迪伦]的电影《雷纳多和克拉拉》(*Renaldo and Clara*)。他从我的手上拿过《墨西哥城蓝调》然后开始朗诵，我说："你对这本书怎么看？"他说："1959年在圣保罗[2]有人借给我一本，[我当时还看不大懂，现在才更明白，但那时]它轰开了我的头脑。"我说："为什么？"他说："它是第一本用我自己的[美国]语言对我说话的诗集。"所以迪伦作品中那些亮闪闪的意象珠串(chains of flashing images)，比如"摩托车黑衣圣母两轮吉卜赛女王和她的银光扣钉幻影情人"，它们就是借鉴了凯鲁亚克的亮闪闪的意象珠串以

1 Mark Spitzer, "Bob Dylan's *Tarantula*: An Arctic Reserve of Untapped Glimmerance Dismissed in a Ratland of Clichés", 原载 *Jack Magazine*, Issue 7, Oct. 2003，转引自迪伦官网 https://www.bobdylan.com/news/new-take-tarantula。

2 明尼阿波利斯都会圈的一部分。

及自发性写作。[1]

多年后，纽约佳士得拍卖行以七万八千美元的高价售出一件迪伦大学时期的诗歌本：封面题为《无标题诗》（*Poems Without Titles*），共十六张手写册页，每首诗都有署名“Dylan”或“Dylanism”。这一组习作滑稽、泼辣，有来自垮掉派诗人格雷戈里·柯索（Gregory Corso）的明显影响，对于未满二十岁的大学生来说堪称老练，其中甚至还非常在行地戏谑了 T. S. 艾略特（T. S. Eliot）的《普鲁弗洛克情歌》，还有詹姆斯·乔伊斯（James Joyce）的《芬尼根氏维客》：

我想我看见汉弗莱[2]尿尿
在一碗热番茄汤里边
他边尿我边瞧着
我边瞧边等着
我边等着边看见整个社会

---

1 Seth Goddard，“The Beats and the Boom: A Conversation with Allen Ginsberg”，原载 *Life*, Jul. 5, 2001，综合转引自伊利诺斯大学现代美国诗歌网站 http://www.english.illinois.edu/maps/poets/g_l/ginsberg/interviews.htm。

2 汉弗莱，指休伯特·汉弗莱（Hubert Humphrey，1911—1978），曾任明尼阿波利斯市长，时任联邦参议员、党鞭，在《狼蛛》时期为美国副总统；也指乔伊斯小说《芬尼根氏维客》同名主人公（Humphrey Chimpden Earwicker）。

……

我觉得他就像一个
白痴儿硬要在暗处阅读詹姆斯乔伊斯
然后出于某种乌漆墨黑的信念
他尿了四十日又四十夜——
然后大战爆发了
整个社会都饿得要死
然后就像他突然飙尿一样
他突然尿停了
他说“五旬节快乐”[1]

这份手稿表明，此时的迪伦已有志于成为一个具有正式身份的现代诗人，他初窥门径，并给自己确定了沿用至今的笔名。

但这还不够。这些还不足以构成一个迪伦。博览和泛听，从古希腊到后现代，单靠正统文学以及依附正统而来的所谓先锋文学（如垮掉派），还无法集齐龙珠，召唤神龙。我们现在都知道，迪伦是从美国传统民谣、蓝调中掘出了他的第一桶和第 n 桶金，但在当时，二战后的保守年代，那些具有强烈的民本意识、左翼色彩的野生吟游文化传统已接近断档、失传。迪伦需要跳出金

1　引自佳士得官网 https://www.christies.com/lotfinder/Lot/bob-dylan-poems-without-titles-4598803-details.aspx。

斯堡、凯鲁亚克为代表的新先锋派之外，另辟蹊径，重新接上美国人民文学的任督二脉，才能打通这一关。

在迪伦卖唱的比萨店，有个姑娘问他有没有听过伍迪·格思里（Woody Guthrie），他当然听过，“一点点”，而姑娘哥哥的唱片收藏中竟然有十二张格思里的碟子。他被格思里的嗓音和歌词迷倒，那完全是直击人心的另一种音乐。随即，大概1960年9月，他借到了伍迪·格思里的自传小说《奔向荣光》（*Bound for Glory*, 1943），这本书在当时很罕见。于是，一种全新的言语方式把迪伦震住了。该书开篇第一章正好发生在迪伦的家乡，各种肤色的流浪汉们挤在货运列车上经过明州北部，这些都是迪伦曾习见的事实，而格思里用非正统的行文把美国底层社会生猛麻辣的俚语表现得淋漓尽致。原来，文学也可以这样！他开始模仿书中流浪汉、外省失地农民、黑人劳工们的用语方式，如简略的快速拼写，灵活的常用词，错乱的蹩脚语法，双重否定（ain't no）表示强烈否定，外语移民口音等等。

在类似题材中，《奔向荣光》对青年迪伦的影响要比《在路上》重大得多，他迫不及待地想占据格思里的一切，想成为另一个格思里。从阶级分析上讲，以垮掉派为代表的新先锋作家多是衣食无忧、温文尔雅的名牌大学高材生（柯索、奥洛夫斯基等极少数几个例外），他们的艺术革新仍局于沙龙（salon）、咖啡馆（café）、写作班（workshop）。虽然迪伦的家境还行，高考成绩也不错，但他在明尼苏达大学基本就没怎么上过课，他早年卖唱的馆子也够不上先锋派们时常光顾的比波普（bebop）爵士乐酒吧那种档次。

不过，如果迪伦真是聪明乖宝宝的话，他也许会绕过凯鲁亚克和格思里，走上另一条按部就班的金光大道：如果他在明大得到驻校诗人艾伦·塔特（Allen Tate）、约翰·贝里曼（John Berryman）的名师指点，那就是另一个故事、另一种成功了，但也许没有那么精彩。而现时空的故事版本中，诗人阿德里安娜·里奇（Adrienne Rich）在十年后（1969 年）给已成为摇滚巨星的迪伦扳回了这一局：

> 一种新语言正在那些操着英语的美国人头脑中演化出来。其他国家都拥有自己的本土语言以及词典的安全保障，而美国人必须从外来的基本元素中改良出他们自己的语言。……莎士比亚的英语和一些 [美国] 游方艺人的副歌在此相逢，互相致敬、互相传习，……英国（美国）语言。谁能完全理解它呢？在这个时代也许只有两个人：鲍勃·迪伦和约翰·贝里曼。[1]

---

1 Adrienne Rich，原载 *The Harvard Advocate*, Spring 1969，综合转引自新版贝里曼诗集导言：John Berryman, *The Heart Is Strange: New Selected Poems*, Farrar, 2014, p. xxviii；John Berryman, *The Dream Songs: Poems*, Farrar, 2014, p. xxv。

总之，十九岁那年，迪伦自己找到了自己的导师，把垮掉派的先锋性与格思里的人民性相接合，他要承续现代吟游诗人的传统，如格思里所言：

> 我听见一道词语洪流在我身体里奔腾，几百首歌、几百本书都写不完。我知道我听来的这些词语不是我自己的私人财产。我是从你们［人民］那里借来它们的。……你们的创作和我的创作手挽着手，我们的记忆永不分离。我从你们的生活的创作中借来我的生活。我能感到你们的能量在我身上涌动，也看到我的能量在你们身上。也许曾有人教你们用“诗人”这个名字来称呼我，但我并不比你们更是一名诗人。……你们才是诗人，你们每天的谈话就是我们的最佳诗人的最佳诗作。我不过是某种职员或社会风气的品尝者，我的工作室在人行道上，在你们的大街、你们的田地、你们的公路以及你们的房屋。[1]

1961 年 1 月，迪伦决定弃学从艺，背着一把吉他走向了“荣光之路”。明尼阿波利斯已无可留恋，旧金

1　Woody Guthrie,“The People I Owe”(1946)，综合转引自 Shelton, p. 65, 151，参见中译本，第 163、385 页。

山、洛杉矶也没有更大的吸引力，因为他知道格思里一直在纽约养病，或许还因为纽约更热闹又路途更近，总之，他要去纽约看望格思里。2 月初，他终于如愿以偿见到了偶像，不久便以格思里接班人的身份在纽约民谣界落下了脚跟。

纽约纽约：
It's alright, Ma, I'm only typing[1]

纽约超级大都会的视野远远比大学城还要辽阔。漂在纽约，迪伦的饕餮诗欲可以肆虐了。他疯狂听碟、疯狂阅读、疯狂打字，押韵的歌词，不押韵的口语诗或分行散文，有整有零的纸头满天飞。

1963 年，迪伦开始进入创作的旺盛期。他的个人演唱会（4 月 12 日）节目单上刊载了（伪）自传诗《我在偷闲一刻的生活》（"My Life in a Stolen Moment"），而最后一个节目是诗朗诵《对伍迪·格思里的最后想法》（"Last Thoughts on Woody Guthrie"）。迪伦发表的第一批诗作多为青春自述，还明显露出格雷戈里·柯索的垮掉派文风和伍迪·格思里的脱口蓝调（talking blues）歌

1　改写自迪伦歌曲《没事的，妈妈（我只是在流血）》["It's Alright, Ma (I'm Only Bleeding)"，1965]。

词互相混合搅拌得不够均匀的痕迹，散漫拖沓的口语诗甚至有沦为分行散文的危险。

《我在偷闲一刻的生活》中的这一段有很多传记家喜欢引用：

希宾是一个美好的旧城
我 10、12、13、15、15½、17 和 18 岁就逃离它
我每次都被人抓住送回家除了这一次
我写的第一首歌给我妈妈题为“给妈妈”
我写在五年级作业上老师给打了个 B+
我 11 岁就开始抽烟中间只停过一次
　　好歇一口气
我不记得我爸妈是否爱唱歌
至少我不记得跟他们交流过什么歌曲
我进了明尼苏达大学念书
　　那个冒牌文凭我从没拿过
我去上科学课但挂科了因为拒绝观察
　　一只兔子死亡
我被英文课开除因为使用四个字的词
　　在论文中描述英文老师
我在传播学课也没及格因为每天点名
　　都说我没能来

我的西班牙语倒很好但那是我早就懂的了[1]

迪伦很清楚地定义过自己的跨界性：

> 我能唱的东西，我叫作歌。我不能唱的东西，我叫作诗。我不能唱但是又太长不成其为诗的东西，我叫作小说。但我的小说没有通常的故事线。它们写的是我在特定时间特定地点的感受。[2]

他甚至还号称他正在写三本小说，可惜，从来没人见过。他的艺术发展是狂飙猛进的，很快他就找到了自己的腔调（voice）。1963 年的鲍勃 · 迪伦跟主流或先锋的诗坛都还不挂边，但在歌坛他是备受欢迎的创作能人，他写的歌曲（如《风中吹响》）由同行唱红，他的口语诗或分行散文在各种民谣报刊和演唱会海报、节目单上大量刊登；此外，他还应邀为朋友们的新唱片封套或歌词本撰写诗文，称为“文案”（liner notes，jacket notes），琼 · 贝兹还有彼得、保罗和玛丽三重唱等多位民谣同行的唱片都用过他的文案。

1　Dylan 1985, p. 70.

2　Nat Hentoff, “*Freewheelin' Bob Dylan* (jacket notes)”, Columbia, 1963.

写给“民谣女王”琼·贝兹的文案[1]可算得上迪伦的新版自述，他在更广阔的想象剧场空间里重新构筑了一个“纽漂”文青的精神史。这首三百行长诗的前段象征性地回顾了他的旧日时光，中间部分围绕“美”的观念展开一个心理自传，同时也是对新女友的浪漫表白。

[……从前我是铁路边上一个粗暴、苦闷、自闭的孩子……]

我最初的膜拜是“美”这个词
因为铁路的线条并不美
它们乌漆墨黑一片邋遢的颜色
满是烂臭、煤烟和灰尘
而我就用这些标准来评判美
只要它是丑的就接受它
只要我能用手抓得到
因为那时我只理解这些
还说“啊这是真实”

[……后来我遭到幻灭，“美”变成羞耻，我恨不得将它抛弃……]

再后来到了纽约
年纪渐长我用自己的话语说

1 “Joan Baez in Concert, Part 2（jacket notes）”，又名“Poem to Joannie”，1963 年 11 月随唱片发行。

“真正的美就藏在裂缝和路沟之中
身穿着裙袍满是尘灰和污垢”
我在一个个窟窿里寻找它
然后迎头扑进它的胸怀
在它耳边把歌曲轻唱
亲吻它的嘴唇拥抱它的腰身
在它的身体里四处巡游
在它的肚皮上昏昏沉睡
像盲目的恋爱中人莽撞地飞翔
我在我创伤的深处发出呐喊
“替我和家人说话的歌喉
是肮脏不堪的阴沟声响
因为它只有这样我才能触到
只有这样的美我才能感受”

[……我认识了许多人，唯有一人向我证明男孩仍在成长……]

一位姑娘和我有很多共同点
她喜欢我乱弹一气的孤独之歌
那“迷人的歌喉”我以前从没听过
人们说“一物有一物的美”
作家写道“神奇万籁”
但我说“我讨厌那种声音
真正的美是丑陋的，哥们
那些爆裂、震荡、破碎的声音

就是我所理解的真正的美”

[……我固于偏见，对她总有隔阂，但她用温柔打开我的心扉……]

啊多么愚蠢狭隘可悲

我曾以为“美”不过是

丑陋和污秽的东西

但它其实是一根魔杖

指挥和挑逗着我的思维

它知道只有它才能有感觉

知道我是毫无机会的

它愚弄我把它当成我的双手

去把握和理解事物

[……我不再受愚弄，因为我在姑娘的歌声里听到真实的微风……]

它蕴藏圣歌和奥义

而奥义极为复杂难懂

不可能用手用脚或指尖

去理解或解答

而且它不应被冠上一个下流的名字

[……如果再回到铁路边，我将开朗乐观，但依旧叛逆……][1]

---

1 Dylan 1985, pp. 78–85.

迪伦的分行体太受同行们欢迎了，以至于欠下很多笔债，他在一篇文案的开头就说："我不是唱片文案作家——决不曾是、决不将是、决不愿是。"署名："鲍勃·迪伦／满脑子暴雨和饿痛。"[1]

1964年他已星途闪耀，就很少给外面写东西了，而他最出色的诗作当然留给了自己的唱片，主要包括《时代正在改变》《鲍勃·迪伦的另一面》《统统带回家》《重访61国道》等专辑。直到1973年，迪伦才把歌词和诗选一起汇编成书，按各个唱片专辑分章节，可以说，他的确是一个真正的"唱片诗人"。[2]

组诗《11个简要墓志铭》("11 Outlined Epitaphs")，即《时代正在改变》唱片文案，1964年1月发行，全文共十一首八百多行，可视为迪伦的第一本诗集。"在迪伦为第三张专辑写下《11个简要墓志铭》的时候，他已经把民谣和垮掉派诗歌结合到一起了。"[3]

《墓志铭》组诗中包括迪伦的"保留节目"自传诗(#2)，以及抒情夜歌（#10），都很出色，但在那个特定时代，更令人印象深刻的是他的政治诗。第一个墓志铭是一位死于枪击的无名牺牲者的自述，自然叫人联

1　引自"新世界"乐队歌手个人网站 http://cantorbob.com/new_world.html。

2　迪伦诗作主要收录在：*Writings and Drawings*（1973）及 *Lyrics, 1962—1985*（1985）；后来新版的迪伦歌词集均未正式收入诗作。

3　Shelton, p. 74，参见中译本，第186页。

系到同一专辑中的歌曲，如《只是棋局里的一个小兵》（“Only a Pawn in Their Game”）[1]、《海蒂·卡罗尔的孤独死亡》（“The Lonesome Death of Hattie Carroll”）等，但与歌词不同，它的风格是“简要”的。

我完蛋
在黄昏时分
盲目捶打蒙布
气喘吁吁
结结巴巴
怒火冲天
往哪走？
到底是做错了什么？
谁放哨？
谁战斗？
在什么窗户背后
我才至少
能听见有人从晚餐桌上
抬头问
“我刚听见外边有人是吗？”
[……死者被绘成油画、海报被人吹捧，过后

1 《小兵》歌词中有：“他将在他的墓旁看到碑石长存，他的名下刻着简单的墓志：只是棋局里的一个小兵。”

又被扔进垃圾堆……]

“他什么时候还会睁眼？”

“他是谁？你知道吗？他是个疯子

他从来都不睁眼的。”

“但他总会想念这个凡尘世界吧”

“不！他只活在他自己的世界”

“哎呀那他肯定就是个疯子”

“对他是个疯子”[1]

作品发表时，J. F. 肯尼迪总统刺杀案（1963 年 11 月 22 日）仍在持续轰炸着全美国的神经。在这种语境下，《墓志铭 #1》的刺激性极为强烈，而第七首的政治挑衅意味就更加熏眼刺鼻了。

有个俄国人长着三颗半红眼睛

五根燃烧的触角

拖着甜菜色的铁球脚镣

要把细菌偷偷倒进

我的可乐机

“烧掉边境的所有树桩”

那些性饥渴的变态佬

在清晨时鼓吹战争

1 Dylan 1985, p. 106.

“往天空投毒这样飞机就过不来了”
装备爱国盾牌的
桦木色骑士们大叫
[……]
扎紧武装带吧
枪手先生
再去买几个新螺栓
因为你的脖子
没有右翼
或左翼……
只有上翼
和下翼[1]

专辑《鲍勃·迪伦的另一面》(1964年8月发行)的文案组诗《一些其他类型的歌……》(“Some Other Kinds of Songs...”),也是十一首,共约九百行,算是他的第二本诗集,并首次正式标注出:Poems by Bob Dylan(鲍勃·迪伦诗作)。这批作品更加广阔,“如同他的歌曲扩展了诗,他的诗也扩展了他的音乐……《一些其他类型的歌》更深入地记录了迪伦在口头音乐上的实验以及他通常难以捉摸的世界观。其风格是印象派的和超现实的”[2]。

---

1 Dylan 1985, pp. 111–112.

2 Shelton, p. 159,参见中译本,第407页。

第三首写给金斯堡（诗中很明显，因为他们都是犹太家庭出身的叛逆）：先是讲两人下象棋，谁输谁就要学爬爬，然后他们海阔天空地闲聊社会见闻、犹太人处境、身份标牌等等，“我”想到长羽毛的小男孩死在后院、被查禁的亨利·米勒跟“我”打乒乓球、记者追问“我”对共产党和人性的看法、“我”说我操他妈的非美活动委员会和CIA、但她只想要“我”说她想要“我”说的她能理解的话、她追逐“我”想查明“我”的标牌（星座），然后“我”——

我带艾伦金斯堡去认识奇幻
伟大美妙的艺术家但是禁止入内
木牌钉得死死随处都可看到。
驱离。传染坏疽和
原子弹。两个极端的存在只
因为那里有人想要
利润。男孩失去视力。成为
飞行员。人们捶打自己的
胸膛以及别人的胸膛并
解释圣经以适应他们自己的
目的。遵奉只是一个被曲解的词
如果耶稣基督本人能来
看看这些街道，那基督教
就要从头再来一遍。站

在万物发源地。昆虫
游玩在它们自己的世界。长蛇
滑动穿过树丛。蚂蚁沿着草叶
来来往往。海龟和蜥蜴
在沙地走出各自的路。一切
都在爬行。一切……
而一切仍在爬行[1]

第五首是一个长诗，从约书亚率领以色列人攻打耶利哥的圣经战争故事开始，说到在布鲁克林大桥上有一个人要投河自尽，“我”和很多人都在围观，就像看马戏，但“我”突然看不下去了，因为“我”认识到，在“我”内心深处是真的想看到他往下跳。“我”逃离麻木、无聊的人群，变成惊惶的鱼，在一条条河流、街道上乱窜，沿路看到纽约城的种种幻觉和异象：

不他们做不到
从他们岸边
我进入他们的河流
（我想知道他跳了吗
我真的好想知道他跳了吗）
我转身

1　Dylan 1985, p. 147.

要离开河流
离开河流
再继续向前
我掉转头
却发现
我在另一条河流上
[……]
（那家伙跳了吗？）
聪慧的蜘蛛
在第六大道拉网
点四五左轮枪
探出它们的
肚脐眼
我这辈子
第一次
自豪地感到
我从来没读懂
任何一本经典名著
（但为什么我硬是想去看
那个可怜的灵魂呢？）[1]

迪伦的未刊手稿还有庞大存量。近年他或者他的出

1 Dylan 1985, p. 150.

版商突然翻出一个名为《好莱坞照片修辞学》(*Hollywood Foto-Rhetoric*)的 1964 年旧稿，让读者意外惊喜。这还是迪伦迄今第一次正式出版的“常规”诗集单行本。这组作品的灵感来自他的合作伙伴、摄影师巴里·范斯坦(Barry Feinstein)的好莱坞纪实照片，迪伦给它们编出故事，像冷峻的默片字幕。其中一些短诗是迪伦少有的，如第三首，写一个裸模在棚内拍照，另一个女子在棚外抽烟：

从屋外边
看进去
手指摆动
门廊穿着长裤
耷拉着
并不排斥
在爱情和选择上
一切可行
但宝贝要小心
遮住窗户的情感
也别忘了
带包烟
因为你很可能
就会发现
在屋外的人

走向更远

而屋内的人

只走向另一个[1]

作为他的自我道路选择，大概从1964—1965年开始，迪伦的创作渐渐开始弥漫某种恣意又任性的犬儒、末日论、虚无主义的气息，三言两语难以概括。这些因素导致他的文字（歌词以及诗作）虽然貌似有着透明、洗练的措辞，简简单单的句法，但越来越倾向于意象晦涩、线索错综，充满了许多剧场式的片段细节，常叫读者迷失其中，难以把握这位作者要表达什么，要走向哪里。他的“诗艺特权”（poetic licence）的经营范围不限于静态的、固化的纸上写作，他是那个站在屋外的人，他会走向更远。

熔融和引爆：*He's lookin' for the fuse*[2]

在相当程度上，每一个诗人都是被其他诗人激发出来的。他们先是阅读，然后交游，“其交游也，缘义而

---

1 Dylan 2008, p. 10.

2 出自迪伦歌曲《墓碑蓝调》（“Tombstone Blues”，1965）。

有类”[1]，然后再碰撞出火花。不然就很容易变成迪伦妈妈说的那样，死了以后才被人发现。不过，青年迪伦毫不“社恐”，他有庞大的朋友圈，并从中获益良多。

迪伦文学生涯的第一个贵人是伍迪·格思里，1961年初通过打入格思里亲友团，他迅速在纽约民谣界立下根基。比如，他袭用和发扬了一套纯美国的俚语正字法，像接头暗号一样，在以歌迷为代表的听觉系受众中打开局面，赢得一个基本盘。

> 像使用小写字母、去掉撇号、省略化拼写等实验手法，迪伦是在追随 E.E. 卡明斯（我们在高中语文都读过，而且迪伦在《狼蛛》中还多次提及他），另外也是想显得更新潮、先锋、高深莫测。至于用古怪拼写来表示发音，迪伦是在追随马克·吐温、约翰·斯坦贝克，尤其是伍迪·格思里。在《奔向荣光》中，格思里确实非常善于用拼写来传达方言俚语，尤其是写到他在货运车皮里遇见一大堆南腔北调的流浪汉的时候。[2]

除格思里之外，青年迪伦还疯狂吸收了丰盛的美国

1 《荀子集注》，王先谦编，中华书局，1988年，第234页。另有版本作“……缘类而有义”。

2 Pichaske, p. 313.

传统民谣 / 蓝调的美学营养，如：卡尔·桑德堡的诗人歌曲以及他采编的《美国歌谣集》[1]、哈利·史密斯收录的全套《美国民间音乐选》[2]、罗伯特·约翰逊（Robert Johnson）和“老妈”雷尼（Ma Rainey）等等前辈歌手的老蓝调。多年来，研究者们更多地关注到布莱克、兰波以及布莱希特、垮掉派等正统的“文学”资源如何影响了迪伦的创作，但对于活在书籍之外的美国口述传统、吟游文化、民谣历史、蓝调美学等等，这些东西又是怎样塑造了一位自命为“鲍勃·迪伦”的伟大艺术家，学界所做的努力还不够恰如其分。类似情况也发生在托马斯·沃尔夫（Thomas Wolfe）、凯鲁亚克等等许多热情拥抱音乐、并带着敏锐耳朵来码字的古今中外写作者身上。

在领取诺贝尔奖时，迪伦坦言：

> 听完所有早期民谣艺人的歌，你开始唱自己的歌，模仿那些俚语（vernacular）。你会将它内在化。……你听出所有微妙之处，你学会了所有细节。你便知道它说的都是些什么。掏出手枪，收回兜里。在车流中疾驰，在黑暗处讲话。你知道

1 Carl Sandburg, ed., *The American Songbag*, 1927, 1950.

2 Harry Smith, ed., *Anthology of American Folk Music*, Folkways Records, 1952.

晃腿老李是坏人，弗兰娅是个好姑娘。你知道华盛顿是资产阶级城市，你听到天启者约翰，看见泰坦尼克沉没在一条泥泞的小溪。你和爱尔兰流浪汉、垦殖园奴工们成为伙伴。你听见沉闷的鼓声和低哑吹奏的笛音。你曾眼看荒淫的唐纳德老爷用刀刺向他的妻子，你的许多同志都裹上了白亚麻布。我把这些俚语都记下。我知道它的修辞。一点都没忘——乐器、技巧、诀窍、秘传——而且，我还知道它历经过多少荒凉的路才走来。我能够把它和时日之流再完全连接起来，一起前行。当我开始自己写歌的时候，民谣行话（folk lingo）是我所掌握的唯一词库，我就用它。[1]

迪伦的第二个文学贵人是艾伦·金斯堡，以及垮掉派核心和周边的先锋文学圈子。其实，在大学时期（1959—1961 年），迪伦对垮掉派有过一轮先扬后抑的情感变化，然后他选择了民谣和格思里这边。格思里的影响“一直存在于第一、第二、第三张专辑，但到了第四张，它就有点疲沓了”。[2]“迪伦似乎是想把民谣的激

1 “Bob Dylan Nobel Lecture”, Jun. 5, 2017，引自诺贝尔奖官网，https://www.nobelprize.org/prizes/literature/2016/dylan/lecture/。

2 Heylin, p. 179.

进和垮掉派作家的文学练达结合起来。”[1] 经过几年来的艺术探索，当迪伦从民谣挺进摇滚，试图用电吉他摧毁传统歌迷的听觉习惯，新的艺术决断又摆在他面前。迪伦在“自传”《编年史：第1卷》（*Chronicles：Volume One*，2004）中总结道：

> 我想我［最初］是在寻找《在路上》里边读到的东西——寻找大城市，寻找它的高速和喧响，寻找艾伦·金斯堡所谓的“氩气点唱机世界”。也许我一辈子都生活在它里面，我不知道，但没有人这样说过。劳伦斯·费林盖蒂（Lawrence Ferlinghetti），垮掉派诗人之一，称之为“塑料马桶坐垫、卫生棉条和计程车的接吻不掉色的世界”。这也很有意思，但格雷戈里·柯索的诗《炸弹》更加到位而且更能抓住时代的精神——整个荒废的完全机器化的世界——到处忙乱嘈杂——大堆的货架要洗，纸箱要摞。我可不想把我的希望寄托在那里。在创作上你没法对它多做些什么。反正，我［后来］进入了一个平行宇宙，那里遵循的是更加古老的原则和价值观，那里的行为和美

1 “Interview with Allen Ginberg (8/11/96)”，引自乔治华盛顿大学国安档案解密网站，https://nsarchive2.gwu.edu//coldwar/interviews/episode-13/ginsberg3.html。

德是老派的……它不是用纸餐碟端上来的。民谣音乐是一个在更辉煌维度上的现实。……它非常真实，比生活本身还要忠于生活。它是生活的放大版。民谣音乐是我的存在所需的一切。但问题是，它还不够。它太旧了，跟时代的状况和潮流失去了适当联系。它有一个庞大的故事但却难以让人理解。而一旦我溜出边界之外，我的六弦琴就像变成了水晶魔法杖，我便能前所未有地驱动事物。[1]

其实，迪伦初到纽约时在煤气灯咖啡馆（Gas Light Café）驻唱，那里曾为垮掉派诗人们的聚会和朗诵场所，后来仍是纽约新一代文艺青年的一个打卡热点；但直到1963年圣诞节，迪伦才见到漫游世界归来的垮掉派领袖金斯堡，两人很快成为“狐朋狗友”。当时的垮掉派运动也亟待补充新鲜血液，因为巴勒斯、凯鲁亚克、卡萨迪和柯索等几员干将的明星效应已日渐褪色，或淡出江湖；同时，喜新厌旧的文化舆论兴奋点转向更热门的新民谣和摇滚乐，而社会思潮也已演进到了更为激烈、紧迫的政治问题。也许是在这样的情境下，金斯堡和迪伦互相在对方身上找到了碰撞的火花。金斯堡需要吸收更接美国地气的新血，而迪伦则需要“再入”，重新与

1 Dylan 2004, pp. 235-236，参见中译本，第235—236页。

垮掉派的先锋美学找回联系方式。[1]

前引中提到的“氢气点唱机”（hydrogen jukebox），出自金斯堡的杰作《嚎叫》（*Howl*，1956）：

> 他们整夜沉没于比克福餐厅的深海灯光然后浮出
> 　　水面在荒凉的弗加齐酒馆傻坐一个馊啤酒下
> 　　午，听着末日在氢气点唱机上噼啪作响[2]

这是金斯堡的一个著名的“跳省并置”（elliptical juxtaposition），政治和音乐的并置，戏拟氢弹（hydrogen bomb）。他在访谈中说：

> 问题是怎样触及思维的不同部位，它们同时存在着，同时进行着各自的联想，那就一并选取两者的要素，比如：从爵士乐、点唱机等等，我们得到点唱机；然后政治、氢弹，我们有了氢，于是你就看到了“氢气点唱机”。它实际上在瞬间压缩了一系列的东西。[3]

1　有关迪伦与金斯堡以及垮掉派的交往综述，见 Wilentz, pp.48–84，参见中译本，第 55—95 页。

2　Ginsberg, p. 134，参见中译本（上），第 188 页。

3　“Allen Ginsberg, The Art of Poetry No. 8”，*Paris Review*, Spring 1966, https://www.theparisreview.org/interviews/4389/allen-ginsberg-the-art-of-poetry-no-8-allen-ginsberg/.

1965年的鲍勃·迪伦已扬弃了单线条的抗议民谣、时事歌曲，带着电声乐队走向融合创新。当被激怒的民谣歌迷指责迪伦投奔摇滚乐就是向商业利益出卖了灵魂，金斯堡用点唱机的典故为迪伦大力辩护：

> 迪伦是出卖给上帝了。也就是说，他的大法力是尽可能广泛地传布他的美。有一种艺术挑战就是看看伟大的艺术能否在一台点唱机上完成，而他证明这是可行的。[4]

而作为“点唱机首席诗人”，迪伦当然拥有他的“神器”。如《狼蛛》一开篇，他还戏拟了荷马以来的古典史诗传统，高声召唤他的黑皮肤非裔美国缪斯，“阿瑞莎／水晶点唱机圣歌＆生哥儿女王”[5]，他乞求后现代的诗神赐予无上的灵感。

金斯堡陆续带迪伦认识了一大票新先锋诗人，迪伦也带金斯堡进了摇滚青年的圈子。这些交往不仅是人和人的相遇，更是风格和风格的相遇，绝非一堂单向度的文学课。诗人迈克尔·麦克卢尔说：

4　金斯堡在1965年12月迪伦伯克利演唱会后答记者问，转引自Heylin 2003, p. 223。

5　Dylan 1971, p. 1.

如果有学者对诗歌和摇滚浪潮的会聚做一番深入分析，那么列侬、凯鲁亚克、迪伦和金斯堡之间的对照会很有意思。整个事情要从 1950 年代的诗人们说起。那是一场“炼金术生理学”（alchemical-biological）的实践运动，而非文学的。[……从垮掉派到披头士、迪伦然后又到垮掉派……] 有着来来回回互相反应的广阔空间。[1]

迪伦用自己的唱作实践经验在怎样捕捉和运用声音方面给这些严肃文学的诗人们提供实打实的建议，他赞助金斯堡购买了一台专业级的德国产 Uher 牌小型录音机，金斯堡称之为“写作新法宝”，利用它完成杰作《威奇托涡旋经》（“Wichita Vortex Sutra”，1966），进一步加强了口语诗、朗诵诗的人声音乐性探索。迪伦还送给麦克卢尔一把自鸣筝（autoharp），说他应该把诗作先唱出来，后来麦克卢尔和“大门”乐队主唱吉姆 · 莫里森（Jim Morrison）成为好友和合作伙伴，也许与此不无关系。麦克卢尔说：

鲍勃 · 迪伦 1966 年初送给我的那把自鸣筝在

---

1 Michael McClure,“Bob Dylan: The Poet’s Poet”, *Rolling Stone*, Mar. 14, 1974, https://www.rollingstone.com/music/music-news/bob-dylan-the-poets-poet-190445/.

壁炉架上搁置了六个礼拜我才捡起来弹弄它。一把黑色的具有魔力的自鸣筝。我怕音乐，从前总是觉得自己根本没有乐感——顶多只会欣赏。鲍勃曾问我喜欢弹什么乐器（我当时写些歌词）。我就脱口而出：自鸣筝，虽然我对自鸣筝到底长什么样子其实毫无概念。想必是在我的肯萨斯童年时代有农人弹奏过吧。

1965 年的旧金山诗人都很穷啊，这真是一件感人的礼物，而且它让我从此致力音乐。写歌词是很有意思的，或许也是一种使用韵律的新方式。摇滚对一切人都具有相互吸引力；不管我们是诗人、印刷工还是雕塑家都一起加入这场共同的部落群舞，它是我们大家都有份参与的一种形式。[1]

而迪伦也在 1964—1965 那两年的观念碰撞中迎来了一个文学大转型。1965 年两张专辑《统统带回家》《重访 61 国道》中的文案，以及同时期的其他诗文作品，如《去掉我的头顶》（“Off the Top of My Head”）、《大学之外的选择》（“Alternatives to College”）等，表明迪伦似乎已经玩腻了回车键，开始转向某种不分行的拼贴式的半叙事散文诗，其中既有波德莱尔、兰波以降的法

1　Michael McClure，出处同前。

国象征主义传统的承续，也有垮掉派及其他美国新先锋写作技法的发挥，同时也从未丢弃民谣/蓝调的平民美学色彩和底层关怀基调，还有他一贯的虚无主义和叛逆精神。

迪伦的《统统带回家》文案（1965年2月发行）就是这样一篇艺术宣言（manifesto）。

> 如果有人认为诺曼梅勒比汉克威廉斯更加重要，那无所谓。我没有争议而且我从来不喝牛奶。我宁愿去做标准口琴支架也不想讨论阿兹特克人类学/英语文学。或联合国的历史。我接受混乱（chaos）。我不确定它是否接受我。我知道有些人害怕炸弹。但有些人却害怕被发现他手持一本现代电影杂志。而经验教导我们沉默才最令人害怕[……]伟大的书都被写过了。伟大的话全都被说过了/我只想给你勾画一下某个时候在这附近出现的事情。尽管我本人也不是很理解到底是发生了什么。我只知道我们有一天都会死而死亡并不会停止这个世界。我的诗用一种非诗性变形的韵律写成/除以穿孔耳朵。假睫毛/减去那些不断互相折磨的人。描述性空洞的优美哼叽诗行——有时通过黑墨镜去看，以及其他形式的心理爆炸。一首歌是能够自己行走的东西/我被称为歌曲作者。一首诗是一个赤裸的人……有些人说我是一

个诗人[1]

迪伦在这个时期的作品形式，实验散文诗，跟后来的《狼蛛》实际上已经没什么差别了。如《重访 61 国道》文案（1965 年 8 月发行），全文如下：

慢车上时间并无干涉 & 在阿拉伯路口等大白堆子，一个报社的人 & 他身后是一百不可避免者由山岩 & 石块构成——奶油法官 & 小丑——玩具屋里野蛮玫瑰 & 可定者简简单单地生活在他们的野生动物的奢华中……秋天，她的鼻梁上架着两个零，在争论太阳是黑的或巴赫跟它的暴乱一样著名 & 说她本人——而非俄耳甫斯——是个有逻辑的诗人“我是个有逻辑的诗人”她大叫“至于春天？春天只是开了个头！”她企图招惹奶油法官的妒忌便跟他讲脚踏实地的人们 & 当宇宙喷发时，她指点慢车 & 祈求下雨祈求时间干涉——她并不极端肥胖只是有些进行性的不开心……一百不可避免者隐藏他们的预言 & 来到酒吧 & 喝 & 醉，以他们极为特殊的清醒方式 & 这时汤姆杜力，这类人你总以为你曾经见过，他和大白堆子一路溜达进来，一百不可避免者都说“那人是谁呀看上

1　Dylan 1985, p. 182.

去那么白？”&酒保，一个好人，&一个在头脑里养野牛的人，他说，“我不知道，但我确定我曾在什么地方见过另一个人”&这时保罗萨金特，来自第四大街的便衣人士，在凌晨三点钟进来&把所有人都震得难以置信，没人真的生气——大多数人只生了一点文盲&罗马，一百不可避免者之一和约翰夫人悄悄嘀咕“我早说会这样”……野蛮玫瑰&可定者正豪放地抛飞吻给卡纳比街六角星破鞋&给所有神秘少年人&奶油法官正在写一本书关于梨子的真实意义的书——去年，他写过一本讲南北战争名犬的&现在他有假牙&没孩子……当奶油见到野蛮玫瑰&可定者的时候，他的介绍人正是了无生气——了无生气是个大敌&总穿一件嬉屁裤——他非常嬉皮……了无生气在介绍每个人的时候说“去拯救世界吧”&“要介入！这是关键”&诸如此类&野蛮玫瑰朝可定者打个眼色&奶油走开了用三角巾吊着胳膊嘴里唱着“夏天啊&生活多悠闲”……小丑出场了——塞了一个口衔在秋天的嘴里然后说“有两种人——简单人&正常人”这照常引得沙坑里发出爆笑&大白堆子打个喷嚏——晕倒了&扒开秋天的口衔&说“你叫秋天是什么意思，缺了你就没有春天了吗！你个蠢货！缺了春天，才没有你呢！你到底怎么想的？？？”这时野蛮玫瑰和可定者过来

&踢他的脑瓜&涂他粉红色因为他是个冒牌哲学家——然后小丑过来大叫“你这个冒牌哲学家！”&跳到他的头上——保罗萨金特过来了还穿着一套裁判服&有个读完了所有尼采的大学小子过来&说“尼采从来不穿裁判服”&保罗说“你想买衣服吗，小子？”&然后罗马&约翰离开了酒吧&他们往哈莱姆走去……我们今天唱的是大扫荡帮——大扫荡帮并购、持有、运营发神经工厂——如果你不知道发神经工厂在哪里，敬请向右走两步，擦擦你的牙&去睡觉……主题是——尽管毫无意义——要做点什么给漂亮陌生人……漂亮陌生人，维瓦尔第的绿夹克&神圣慢车

你是对的约翰科恩——夸西莫多是对的——莫扎特是对的……我不能再说眼睛这个词了……我一说到眼睛这个词，就好像我是在说我依稀记得的某人的眼睛……没有眼睛——只有一系列的嘴巴——嘴巴万岁——你的屋顶——如果你还没知道的话——已经毁掉了——眼睛是浆质体&你在这方面也是对的——你真走运——你不用操心眼睛&屋顶&夸西莫多之类的问题。[1]

“另一面”的鲍勃·迪伦，一个青年诗人，已完全

1 Dylan 1985, pp. 209–210.

"成型"。对这个问题一直都有人说好说坏。其实，迪伦本人一直最喜欢调侃他作为"诗人"的身份，除了扮酷和反讽之外，可能还出于两个原因：一、他认为在职业文士之外，歌手、艺人、笑话家以及所有进行真诚表达的普通人，都是诗人；二、他不喜欢被限定在一个文绉绉、土渣渣的标签上，但舆论似乎总要给他戴一顶桂冠，实在让他受不了。也许他很清楚，单凭那几年间的歌词和零散诗文，他还称不上一个伟大诗人，所以，何必呢，他宁可俏皮地说自己是个吊秋千、走钢丝的艺人。[1]

> 艾伦·金斯堡是我唯一认识的作家。其他的作家我可没有太多敬意。如果他们真要想，那他们得先唱出来。我不愿意自称为一个诗人可不仅是因为我愿意自称为一个"抗议歌手"。那些人总想把我归进一个范畴，跟一大堆让我厌烦的人放在一起。我就是不想进入他们的范畴。我不想糊弄任何人。[2]

如果真要归入一个范畴，迪伦还是愿意和金斯堡他们为伍。权威性的《垮掉派便携读本》在《同行者》("Other

1　迪伦在访谈中经常自嘲为各种马戏团艺人，如：1965 年 8 月访谈，Cott, p. 52。

2　1966 年 3 月访谈，Shelton, p. 242，参见中译本第二册，第 200 页。

Fellow Travelers”）一章中收入了鲍勃·迪伦的《风中吹响》《时代正在改变》和《暴雨将至》三首歌词以及《狼蛛》（节选两章），[1] 分量不少。纽约民谣老将戴夫·范容克（Dave Van Ronk）对迪伦在垮掉派的地位有一段推介：

> 鲍勃基本上是垮掉一代的产物。迪伦的确是跟凯鲁亚克同一窝的人。你再也不会看到他这样的了。鲍勃刚好在[时代的]尾巴尖儿上抓住了垮掉派诗歌。他超越了他们所有人，也许除了金斯堡。但鲍勃是个迟到者而且不会有接班人，就像他的名字也不会有接班人了。[2]

慢车开来：*The words that are used for to get the ship confused* [3]

三十岁以前，迪伦都没出过一本“文学著作”，这对于一个诗人来讲的确不算什么美事。尽管早在1963年秋，他就曾与劳伦斯·费林盖蒂见面，商量在旧金山

1 Charters, pp. 371–379.

2 Shelton, p. 79，参见中译本，第201—202页。

3 出自迪伦歌曲《大船入港时》（“When the Ship Comes In”，1964）。

垮掉派重镇——城市之光书店（City Lights）出版一本迪伦作品，列入著名的口袋诗人丛书，和金斯堡、凯鲁亚克、柯索们的诗集在一起。这多好呀！但直到 1964 年 4 月迪伦还没有交稿，他写了一封分行诗体长信给费林盖蒂解释[1]：

微风从西部吹来而我正准备动身
明天去法国。要翻遍我所有的裤袋
才能搜罗东西寄给你。
因为我现在正忙着毁灭我做过的
一切（我甚至把旧打字机砸成碎片把钢笔
都烧成一个个塑料小雕像）
我知道我这段时间的某一天会把东西给你寄
　　去的。
我要做的就是写完它然后寄给你。[2]

这首书信诗写得非常漂亮，像在飞一样，但迪伦终究没能兑现诺言。此外，还有《好莱坞照片修辞学》，也是同时期的另一个半途而废的原定书稿[3]——迪伦不是太忙就是太懒，而且总是悔其少作。结果他的经纪人

1　Heylin, p. 140.

2　引自城市之光官网 http://www.blogcitylights.com/2013/02/05/beat-letters/。

3　Heylin, p. 141.

阿伯特·格罗斯曼（Albert Grossman）替这个交稿拖延癌晚期患者另行决定商业计划，和大牌的麦克米伦出版公司签订了一单大合同。两年后，迪伦总算身体诚实地为新合同交出了一本另起炉灶的新书：《狼蛛》。

其实，如果按城市之光的口袋诗人丛书规格，一般就巴掌大的短方形小开本，正文有个四五十页到百来页就可以了。最典型、最有名的巴掌小诗集，如，金斯堡的《嚎叫及其他》（*Howl and Other Poems*，1955），满打满算不过五十六页。基本上，迪伦的《11 个简要墓志铭》加《一些其他类型的歌……》就绰绰有余，势头好还可以再出第二、第三本，这样精悍，但动能相当强劲。即便是《狼蛛》这样野心更大的作品，如果放在城市之光，或者更主流一点的新方向（New Directions）、克诺普夫（Alfred A. Knopf）甚至兰登集团（Random House）等专业文艺出版社，那也许会是另一种局面。不能不说，在这个抉择上，作为青年诗人的鲍勃·迪伦已经被他的流行音乐经纪人主宰了，没有走向“人迹更少的那条路”。摇滚天王与小清新书店绝缘了，这可谓“生涯规划”上的一个典型（失败）案例。

《狼蛛》会是一本怎样的书？在迪伦头脑中，它还是非常清晰的。他在 1965 年 3 月的一个访谈中说：

你有本书要出来了。是说什么的？书名呢？

暂时，叫 *Bob Dylan Off the Record*（《不可录

的鲍勃·迪伦》)。但他们跟我说已经有很多书用过“off the record”(非正式,私底下)这个标题。这本书其实是不能取名的,它就是它那种书。我也准备给它写点评论。

为什么写书而不是歌词呢?

我已经写过一些超常规的歌词了,就像一大组韵诗,这类的——但我还没有真正有机会写一部完全自由的歌。嘿,你懂不懂剪切(cut-ups)?我说,就像威廉·巴勒斯(William Burroughs)?

对,有个人在巴黎出了一本没有页码的书。书就装在一个盒子里边,你当空一抛,它怎样落下来,你就怎样读它。

对,就那样。因为那就是它的方式,总之。好了,我要写这本书是因为里边有很多的东西是我不可能唱出来的……各种拼贴(collages)。我唱不出来是因为它太长或者太超出常规了。我只能跟一些真正懂的人一块玩。因为对于大多数听众——不管他们从哪来、他们够不够上道——我觉得它都会完全失效。它没有韵律,都是剪切,什么都没有,只是一些即兴发生的,都是词语的。

那你写这本书是要说些东西了?

对,但确实没有任何深刻的见解。这本书不

想开始也不想结束什么。

但你有东西要说。你是想说给某人听的呀。

对，我说给我自己听。而且，我很走运，因为我可以把它放进一本书里。现在别的人很快也能看到我对我自己说的话了。[1]

大概数易其稿，迪伦用一年多时间基本完成了新书。在 1966 年 3 月巡回演出的航班上，迪伦一边摆弄着《狼蛛》的校样，一边跟老友罗伯特 · 谢尔顿打趣。

他［迪伦］对《狼蛛》即将为正统文学界、被严肃诗人所接受有什么看法呢？“首先，”他饶有兴趣地说，“你先要明白，你是不是要为诗人和文学界来写作——”他停了一会“我觉得诗人是任何一个不会自称为诗人的人。任何人只要自称为诗人就不可能是一个诗人。他们不过是沉湎于他们先辈的传奇以及他们对于虚假故事的历史知识。然后他们大概还以为他们略高一等。刚开始有人称我为诗人的时候，我说：‘哦，帅呆了，被称为一个诗人真是帅呆了！’但这对我一点好处都没有，真的。这并不能让我更幸福。嘿，我也

1 1965 年 3 月访谈，Cott, pp. 48–49。

喜欢说我是一个诗人。我当真愿意把自己设想为一个诗人，但我就是做不到，因为所有的懒虫都被称为诗人了。”那谁是诗人呢？金斯堡？“他是一个诗人，”迪伦回击，“成为一个诗人并不一定意味着你非要在纸上写字不可。你知道我的意思吗？从旅馆楼梯走下来的那些卡车司机当中就有一个是诗人。他一说话就像个诗人。我是说，除此之外，一个诗人还需要做什么呢？诗人，……诗人，老头，死亡，腐朽，就像罗伯特·弗罗斯特诗中的那些树木和枝条那样的人，但这不是我要说的那种。”[1]

在那一日的谈话里，迪伦意气飞扬，正处于他的巅峰云端。但在鲜花着锦、烈火烹油的升腾中，crash（撞车）！迪伦坠入了一个幽深的不应期。在1966年的夏天，他什么都要做，什么都不想做，什么都想做好，什么都做不满意，什么都想重来，但什么都不愿再来一次。强行达到激越之后的陡然消沉，像淹没在泥石流中的泰坦尼克号。《狼蛛》的修订工作也随即告吹，在戛然间不告而吹，甚至没有一个“answer is blowin' in the wind”。

关于《狼蛛》被弃置的问题，鲍勃·迪伦在低潮时期兴致阑珊地告诉记者，当初，他不知怎么地脑子“瓦

1　Shelton, p. 242，参见中译本第二册，第199—200页。

特”[1]了，就跟大牌出版商签订一笔巨额合同，但其实连一点稿子都还没有，结果事情就变成欠了他们一本书。

……总之，我就这样欠了他们一本书了。

于是我就坐下来，说：“没问题，我以前多么多事情都能做成，写一本书也没什么难的。”于是我就坐下来给他们写一本书，在酒店房间和各种地方，加上我还搞了一堆其他纸张，穿插别人写过的东西，然后我用一个星期就把它拼凑起来，寄给他们。

没过多久我就收到回件要我做校对了。我拿到回件然后我说：“俺滴肾裂，这东西是我写的？我不能把它放出去。”你懂我的意思吧？“我不能把它放出去。别人把它买回家根本就看不懂的。”我说，“我必须给它做点修改。”我告诉他们，然后就动手修改。我告诉他们我在改进。

他们正急着要这本书。他们才不管它是什么样子。那边的人都在说，“他是詹姆斯·乔伊斯重生”，还有“第二个杰克·凯鲁亚克”，他们还说什么“荷马再世”……他们都只顾着满脑子的胡言乱语。

他们只想卖书，这就是他们想要的一切。其

1 上海方言，意为坏掉。

他都不相干……我知道的——我认为他们也肯定知道，他们是做这行的。我知道，我是无关紧要的。连我都知道了，那他们呢？他们只是在玩我。还有我的书。

然后我又写一本新的。我自己觉得满意了才寄过去。他们看到之后说："嘿，这是另一本书呀。"我说："是的，但这本更好。"他们说："那行，我们就印这本吧。"他们就印了出来，并寄回给我校对。于是我开始校对——刚看了第一段——我就知道我不能够任由它那样。所以我去巡演的路上随身都带着这一堆东西。我准备全部重写一遍。扛着打字机满世界跑。拼命地追赶他们给我说定的出版截稿日期。他们都把我逼到墙角落了。很多从未谋面的人。所以到最后，赶着赶着截稿日期，一直在写，直到我的摩托车翻了。[此前]那段时间，我研究了各种不同的印本，以及我想要他们怎样印这本书。我还研究了很多当时的诗人……我在想象中有一种能给我带领方向的书……而且我在各种事情上都用了一些。

然而，它还不是书；它仅仅是按照合同交付出版商去印行的东西。懂吧？然后我的摩托车就翻了，也让我摆脱了这一切，因为我再也不管它了。就现在的情况来说，我可以写一本书。但是我要先写出来，然后再交给他们。你懂我的意思吧？[1]

于是，《狼蛛》的出版经过就是一趟很慢、很慢，绕着大弯开过来，一趟神那个圣的慢车。它1965年预告，1966年宣传，然后“咣当”，一个黑暗撞击就停摆了。然后，过了五载，不知是什么东西的推动，据说在迪伦要求下，或是对盗印版坑钱砸锅的反击，总之，直到1971年5月，《狼蛛》正式版由麦克米伦出版社发行。这些在“出版人前言”（见本书）已经做了解释，或者是言不由衷的辩解。

该前言没提到的是，在《狼蛛》迟到的这五年中间发生了多少事情，比如还有一个历史性的1968年呢！这几年里，摇滚乐艺术和产业的狂飙突进，滚石（Rolling Stone）、平克·弗洛伊德（Pink Floyd）、杰斐逊飞机（Jefferson Airplane）、感恩而死（Grateful Dead）、大门（The Doors）、地下丝绒（The Velvet Underground）、黑色安息日（Black Sabbath）随手列举……连迷幻的调调都快过时了，歌迷们正在向往更震撼和直接的重金属。一个全新的多元共和在1970年代初已经欣欣向荣，而鲍勃·迪伦先生，只是凌霄阁里面叫下一代俄狄浦斯们敬拜瞻仰的先辈伟人。这一波新“摇滚诗人”什么都敢做，

---

1 “Interview with Jann S. Wenner”, *Rolling Stone*, Nov. 29, 1969, Cott, p. 156–157.

什么都敢写，甚至直接用强力撕扯、考验着市民朋友们敏感的神经末梢。仅就文学 / 文字而言，时代正在改变，且已然改变了，但《狼蛛》却一点没改。迪伦抓住了垮掉一代的尾巴，但《狼蛛》一书却不幸掉出了 1960 年代的尾巴——它那曾经的“摇滚文学”已经过时了。

瞬间沧桑啊，笔者这种“吃瓜看戏”的代入感主要来自迪克斯坦（Morris Dickstein）的那本《伊甸园之门：六十年代美国文化》(*Gates of Edens*, 1977) 中的一句话：

> Never were the sixties more over than on those illusory occasions when it seemed that nothing had changed.
>
> 六十年代的结束最明确无疑地体现在那些似乎一切依然照旧的虚幻时刻。[1]

但毕竟是老牌流量带货，《狼蛛》的销量不坏，然而反应就很不咋地。在麦克米伦 1971 年版的“出版人前言”中，作者的口气相当勉强，甚至都不曾署名。[2]而且它的护封勒口上写道：

---

1 Dickstein, p.184，译文引自中译本，第 185 页。

2 该前言的执笔人应为麦克米伦责编鲍勃 · 马克尔（Bob Markel），他一直负责这个项目。

> 这是一部活力与想象之作，一场穿越我们生活和时代的奇异之旅。你也许会把它多读几遍，因为它是不容易让人一眼就看懂的。它遍布着文字游戏，以及才华的峰峦和幽默的原野。它既有简单的真实也有复杂的真实；它非常感伤但有时又滑稽得叫你不禁大笑出声。[1]

这等于警告读者：这本书是看不懂的，而且很搞笑，大家可以买来看看，但千万别认真对待，如无特殊爱好，就不要深究了，都是为了生意，请多多体谅……（对照"出版人前言"来看，您认为是不是就这样的一个效果？）

公司宣发部门似乎也"放羊"了：他们仅照例在各报末版刊登些豆腐块软文，原先说好的整合营销推广活动根本没有发生。迪伦本人更神龙见首不见尾，他一直躲在远郊的隔音地下室，忙着磨练他的音乐新转机。至于畅销书业界必备的巡回见面、朗诵、签售会什么的，都不存在。炒作，有啊，但是是负面的，大小媒体和论家、写手们对这本东西进行冷嘲热讽，到今日还戏谑不休（不过，我们也正好可以通过早年的那些酷评，"理中客"地了解一下西方专业读者的最初观感。详见下章。）。

《狼蛛》完稿时，迪伦二十五岁；《狼蛛》正式出版时，他三十岁。也许，他过量地消耗了青春，然后又过

1　护封文案，*Tarantula*, Macmillan, 1971.

早地步入了中年。从 1966 年夏天过后那几年，迪伦本想做一个安安静静的美男子，但事情并不如意。上一张专辑《自传》（*Biograph*，1970）得分超低，被乐评人格雷尔·马尔库斯评为："这是什么鬼？"（What is this shit?）[1] 新专辑《新的早晨》（*New Morning*，1970）刚挽回一些名声，又在《狼蛛》上被批评圈和歌迷界大泼冷水。但是可忍，迪伦亦可忍，他已经"一点儿也不在意"（didn't care anymore）了。对于《狼蛛》，迪伦已经"悔其少作"到了极致，他干脆摆出一副"管生不管养"的态度，至今也未见松口的迹象。

从早产的盗印本开始，《狼蛛》就成了没有继承权的不受待见的私生子，几乎全靠"饭圈"里的少数"干爹"灌水养活。它真的就像黑巫师的"邪典"膜拜物（cult item），只有一些超级粉丝在歌迷小杂志和互联网新闻组、专业论坛上自娱自乐，但在外界几乎毫无声息。

迪伦年轻时最擅长反讽调侃，年长之后更加成熟圆润，关于《狼蛛》他已不愿再谈，但他在三十六岁那年说过的一句很意味深长的中肯话语，值得一提：

> 艺术是幻觉的永恒运动。艺术的最高目的在

1　Greil Marcus, "Self Portrait No. 25" , *Rolling Stone*, June 8, 1970, https://www.rollingstone.com/music/music-album-reviews/self-portrait-107056/.

于激发。除此之外你还能做什么？除此之外你还能对别人做什么呢，除了激发他们？[1]

一地鸡毛：*Come writers and critics who prophesize with your pen*[2]

其实，很多实至名归的大作家也曾被人一路取笑过来，迪伦绝对不算最倒霉的那一个，但《狼蛛》确实不走运。它的盗印本洛阳纸贵，而正式版却碰了个满头包，这首先是一场营销公关的灾难。

如《柯克斯书评》（专为新书上市写写软文的中庸刊物），就在第一时间发出了快评：鲍勃·迪伦的《狼蛛》是一堆垃圾。

> 《狼蛛》，1966 老款，延宕五年后正式发行，无疑仍会再次令我们困惑和费解；现在，当我们已经习惯了《纳什维尔天际线》的甜美平庸和《新早晨》的清晰明了，迪伦却再次重访 61 国道，在美国的垃圾场里东翻西捡，在"利伯拉切的田园"

1　1977 年 12 月访谈，Cott, p. 211.

2　出自迪伦歌曲《时代正在改变》（"The Times They Are A-Changin'"，1964）。

上抛洒他的超现实主义便便。……他舞动着滑动着，在我们能理解、领会或破译那些象征符号之前绝不会停止。迪伦的景象里充斥着破碎、变形的物件，像游乐园的哈哈镜馆。……一大片形象与意义相脱节的弹幕向我们齐射而来：它是一个巨大的拼图游戏，而你只能靠自己把那些碎片凑合到一起。它们当然都对不上；它们都译不出："请帮我翻译这个事实，钹锣鼓博士……我想知道的事实是这个：是不是希特勒曾说过这话？戴高乐？匹诺曹？林肯？阿格妮丝穆尔黑德？戈德华特？蓝胡子？"都错了，是鲍比·齐默曼。[1]

而辛辣的摇滚乐评家罗伯特·克里斯戈给《狼蛛》献上了长篇的盖棺定论，发表于很大牌的《纽约时报书评》，总之三个字——"非文学"：

鲍勃·迪伦的《狼蛛》正式登场不是一个文学事件，因为迪伦并非文学人士。文学是从书籍出来的，而迪伦并不打算将他的最重要著作让人去读。即便他曾有此打算，但他五年前把那些拼凑《狼蛛》的碎片从出版社撤回也说明他改变了

---

1 *Kirkus Review*, May 10, 1971, https://www.kirkusreviews.com/book-reviews/bob-dylan-3/tarantula-2/.

主意。当然，很有可能，现在他又再次改变主意了——对于迪伦，谁知道呢。不过，最大的可能是，他那难以捉摸的性子才是这本书的真正出人意料的收获。一个著名公共艺术家被他的广大受众所追逐，这本身就是他生涯中一个无所不在的主题，而《狼蛛》盗印版被那些自命的迪伦学家和内行的黄牛贩子在大街上、在柜台底下叫卖不过是这一主题的变奏而已。但现在迪伦准许本书发行（不是黄牛价，这值得一提）也就等于承认他那永不停息的隐私权战斗已经失败。很简单，他的手已经为他的拥趸所迫使了。他现在已是一个作家，管你喜不喜欢。

断言迪伦不属于文学史，并不是把他排除在艺术传播或语言的历史之外。正相反。一个唱作人不像诗人或小说家那样使用语言，因为他遣词造句要适应更强烈、更官能化的效果；一个选择用大众传媒来做工作的艺术家，跟一个必须依照自己的手段、意图和对象作出判断的艺术家，是完全不同的。这显而易见。但迪伦的选择远远超出了它们本身的理论准绳——它们敏锐反映了现代主义的死胡同，各种艺术，尤其文学，在那里沉沦于自命不凡的崇智主义和精英做派。

……实际上，迪伦的歌迷若想知道《狼蛛》究竟什么样子，只需参照一下《重访61国道》的文案即可。基本技巧就是这样：含糊的故事，活动着历史人物和传说中的或匿名的角色，以省略号和破折号作标点，充满了醒目但又不知所云的离题话，每章都压上一封与前文没有明显关联的虚构书信。就这样，朋友们。这本书就是一连串类似这样的碎片。大多数都似乎毫无联系，只不过有几个显著的人物，如名为阿瑞莎的，重复出现。我能想到的文学先例唯有《赤裸的午餐》，当然更一般来说，这本书如果努力攻读也能让人联想到许多文学。但如果你不是迪伦信徒的话，我就要问，它值得这样努力吗，而且请别说我是门外汉——正是鲍勃·迪伦促使我提出这样的问题。

最奇怪的是，迪伦通过歌曲创作表现的文学自夸倒无可非议，但他对文学作为一门专业的态度却矛盾重重，甚至根本就是敌意。……迪伦借用了文学的技巧——最主要是用典、双关、象征以及幻想——他显然是热爱语言的，但他鄙视那种量身剪裁的高雅斯文。他的很多歌曲似乎沿袭前人，但（比如《狼蛛》）它们并非袭自具体某个人。那些明显的相似者或“影响”——布莱克、惠特曼、兰波、塞利纳——只参与了他的方法和个性：了不起的土豪新贵，堂皇的瞎扯淡。他像一个迷醉于辞藻的大学生那样把自己狂写成天才，战后一代人的杂乱文化——从达芬奇到连环漫画，从 T. S. 艾略特到查理·里奇[1]——就是他唯一的传统。……迪伦也许是个糟糕的诗人,但他[的歌词]有头等的聪明。

……也许是文学催生了迪伦神话，但却是摇滚乐养育了它。我们能记住那些名句是因为我们一遍又一遍地听过，经常不是真正在听，而是在吸收那种非诗性变形的韵律。或许《狼蛛》也含有类似的宝石，但我们根本不可能知道它藏在哪里，因为《狼蛛》不是一张专辑。精彩的文字，搞笑的段子，以及沉闷、朦胧、有趣的内容和蹩脚的末世论修辞，应有尽有。……这本书会在 A. J. 韦伯曼[2]的迪伦索引中占有一席之地而且无疑会成为一个膜拜对象，但那不过是返祖。还是去买他的唱片吧。[3]

但《狼蛛》之所以差评如潮，更应归咎于迪伦在那个时期的消极态度，因而引发其他人比如编辑、记者、评论家的消极对待。他仿佛一颗过度燃烧了的红巨

1　查理·里奇（Charlie Rich，1932—1995），美国乡村音乐歌手。

2　韦伯曼（A. J. Weberman，1945— ），一个超级狂热的“迪伦学家”，翻垃圾桶找线索，常被视为神经病。

3　Robert Christgau, “The answer, my friends, is still blowin’ in the wind” , *New York Times*, June 27, 1971. https://www.nytimes.com/1971/06/27/archives/tarantula-by-bob-dylan-137-pp-new-york-the-macmillan-company-395.html.

星（red giant），在一系列事件中，既耀眼又虚弱，让所有的人都看得出来。英国摇滚歌手大卫·鲍伊（David Bowie）当时有一首《献给鲍勃·迪伦的歌》（"Song for Bob Dylan"，1971），也许代表了圈中人对迪伦的复杂情绪。

> 你曾坐在一百万双眼睛的背后
> 告诉他们该怎么观看
> 后来我们错失了你的思想列车
> 你的图画全都属于你自己
> 当困境袭来，我们恐惧联合
> 胜过害怕孤独
> ……
> 听听这首歌，罗伯特·齐默曼
> 尽管我不认为我们会相遇
> 但请转告你的好友迪伦
> 若他愿意俯瞰一下这条老街
> 就告诉他我们已经丢失了他的诗歌
> 所以我们就在墙壁上面写：
> 归还我们的团结
> 归还我们的家人
> 你是所有国家的流亡者
> 不要任由我们去顺应他们的理智[1]

---

1 David Bowie, "Song for Bob Dylan", *Hunky Dory*, RCA, 1971.

当年，也有少数评论家为迟来的《狼蛛》说了好话。他们早在盗印本时期就是迪伦新小说的忠实拥趸，但他们对正版上市又隐约抱有敌意，因为多年来迪伦商业团队的律师一直在追杀他们。

伊莱亚·卡茨在1969年就分析了盗版《狼蛛》的地下社会学，复印本的复印本的复印本在长毛嬉皮士们的手里不断卖掉、租掉，好像禁药一样可以当硬通货使用。人们认为它是遭到政治封杀的“革命”艺术，强行赋予其一种其实很娱乐化的传奇色彩，但迪伦确实有权阻止它的出版。《狼蛛》已藏匿在先锋之中，但终会回来，无论正版或盗版，都窘困和激惹着我们。[1]

在《狼蛛》官方版发行之际，戴维·沃利热情洋溢地赞美这位二十五岁早熟天才的梦幻之作：虽然神奇复印机已改换新的形式，“他们”或许用玻璃纸和塑料膜捉拿了“他”的灵魂，作者和出版商在查禁那灵动的手指，但这本书已深潜到后世的时区，多年后，这部表现扭结思绪和苦痛情感的地下杰作将重新被人认识。[2]

---

1 Elia Katz, “*Tarantula*: Dylan’s unpublished novel”，原载于 *Carolina Quarterly*, Vol. 21, Iss. 3, Fall 1969，转引自 https://search.proquest.com/openview/e8012b96db77536720bff1e33fc1d921/。

2 David Walley, “Life, Death & Lumberjacks—Bob Dylan, Poet”，原载 *Zygote Magazine*, 1971，转引自作者专栏，http://newpartisan.squarespace.com/home/life-death-lumberjacks-bob-dylan-poet.html。

在《狼蛛》面前，众多大腕遭遇了想象力和共感力的双重挫败，殊不知，这本备受鄙夷的小书实际上是“迪伦的实验室”[1]。但时至今日，哪怕为《狼蛛》说一句好话仍会被视为是反常之举，毕竟这本书如此难以卒读，谁要声称能读得有滋有味，那肯定是扯淡——这种看法“未必毫无道理”。[2]

保罗·威廉斯认为，《狼蛛》的遭遇一点都不奇怪，这归咎于迪伦的自不量力。

> 迪伦试图要成为他并不是的那种人。他不是一个写书的作家。但他却怀着一种强烈欲望要写书、写小说；或许是因为他在这条路上的早年努力遇到过挫折，到了《狼蛛》时期，迪伦的写作表现出他对自己所从事的写书这种形式的轻蔑，就好像在说：“这根本就是狗屁形式，我要通过炸烂它、颠覆它来证明这一点，要彻底打破它的界限。”这可不是他在写歌、录唱片、登台演唱时所具有的精神。在那里，他是真正革命的，发自内心的，所突破和扩展的是他得心应手并且敬重和热爱的歌曲形式。[3]

---

1 Bell, p. 375，参见中译本，第 391 页。

2 Bell, p. 350，参见中译本，第 366 页。

3 Williams, p. 171.

跨界之难，对迪伦来说可能更难在他的一时豪情万丈，又一时兴致阑珊，他浪漫到“漫浪”。放下吉他的时候，迪伦太“文青”，太自我，太不职业，太无可救药，而且太不走运。他不像安迪·沃霍尔，玩什么成什么，拍拍脑袋就跨媒、跨界，且轻轻松松进入各门类艺术史。在后现代文化史上，他们两人看起来很像，而且还很熟，但实际上，他们可能是两个世界的人。迪伦的根子还是扎在美国吟游诗人的传统之中，“那里遵循的是更加古老的原则和价值观，那里的行为和美德是老派的”。要理解迪伦的文学追求，也许要从老派美国开始，而这些兴趣点太容易被电声乐器的直击效果给压制了。

另一方面流行文化对迪伦的娇宠也在助长这位天才青年的坏毛病。澳大利亚诗人、唱作人克利弗·詹姆斯在早年就观察到迪伦现象中暗藏的“癌”：

> 他那些自由不羁的语言学发明，即便在最精彩的时候，一直存在着某些致命的超离因素要逃出具体感知的规训：迪伦也乐得享受连自己都不知所云的语言。他对自己的创作无法做出分辨，哪些是振聋发聩的概念，哪些是故作姿态的概念，哪些是能量饱满的形象，哪些是哗众取宠的形象。长期以来对迪伦的一切都不加批判地予以追捧，其实是把癌细胞当成身体的一部分来赞美，只要两者还能一同发育，这倒不成问题，但是当癌细胞

的激增而导致身体发生萎缩的时候，麻烦就大了。[1]

二十五岁的迪伦在《狼蛛》中爆燃，但激起火花寥寥。三十五岁时，他又重整旗鼓，召集所有人马，使尽浑身解数，自编、自导、自演、自剪了一部长达四个多小时的实验电影《雷纳多和克拉拉》(*Renaldo and Clara*, 1978)，但同样被烂番茄淹没，而且情况远比《狼蛛》更惨烈，然后旋即又同样被这位任性的艺术家弃若敝履，甚至未被收入官网（bobdylan.com）。直到回忆录《编年史：第1卷》，迪伦才成功重建了一个靠谱作家的形象。该书备受好评，迪伦也相当开心，甚至乐于承认自己对“写书”这种事不是很在行：

> 大多数评论音乐的人，对于演奏是怎么回事根本一无所知。但说到我写的书，如果我认为“那些给这本书写评论的人根本不懂他们究竟在谈什么”，那就自欺欺人了。他们懂得怎样写书，他们比我要懂得多。对这本书的评论，有些简直叫我拍案称奇——写得太好了。我看乐评就从来没有

---

1 Clive James, “Bob Dylan: Bringing Some of It All Back Home”, 原载 *Cream*, Sept. 1972，收入 Hedin, pp.104–105。

这种感觉，真的。[1]

对他来说，写书远比写歌更有挑战性。

写歌，是我能够做、懂得做而且需要做的事情。要是有谁写一本书出来我就惊奇了。我在歌曲里边也使用许多隐喻和象征，但它们是以旋律的价值为准。显然，写一本书稿的时候你就不能那样做了，必须要有文学意义。我不得不调整我的想象力；我不能再海阔天空、东拉西扯。我不能说我喜欢这个过程。我写歌的时候，它只在我的头脑里边停留一个比较短的时间，我也不一定非要把它跟下一首歌联系在一起。我一边写歌的时候，我会觉得自己还在过着生活。但是要写这样一本书[《编年史》]，你就必须在真正停止生活一段时期之后才能做。你要用打字机努力把它定在纸上。我不是说我就像点着一盏油灯来写书那样，但我确实感觉，我在把自己关闭起来。[2]

---

1 Jonathan Lethem, "The Genius and Modern Times of Bob Dylan" , *Rolling Stone*, Sept. 7, 2006, https://www.rollingstone.com/music/music-news/the-genius-and-modern-times-of-bob-dylan-237203/.

2 Edna Gundersen, "Dylan Chronicles His Journey" , *USA Today*, Oct. 4, 2004, https://usatoday30.usatoday.com/life/books/news/2004-10-04-dylan-main_x.htm.

迪伦在文学创作上最难解决的问题可能是，他野心太大，而相对的耐心却太小。十五年过去了，传说中的《编年史》“第 2 卷”乃至“第 3 卷”似乎还遥遥无期。迪伦从来不喜欢文学编辑或“天才捕手”[1] 来提携或干预他的创作，但他又像从事音乐一样要对文学反复试唱、排练、编配、重混……直到满意为止，要么就是直到把他自己也搞烦了，不玩了。

> 我一直在断断续续地写着。但《编年史》完全是我自己的事。我恐怕我不会有一个真正的编辑。这是一个庞大的工作。我不担心怎么写，但是要不断重读，还有为重读而消耗的时间——这些才是我的困难。[2]

---

1 参见美国影片《天才捕手》（*Genius*，2016）。

2 Andy Greene, “Bob Dylan Working on ‘Chronicles’ Sequel”, *Rolling Stone*, Sept. 14, 2012, https://www.rollingstone.com/music/music-news/bob-dylan-working-on-chronicles-sequel-188881/.

爱乐魔虫：

Intellectual spiders weave down sixth avenue[1]

当弹吉他的人竟然要插手文学绝对领域，他已预感且预设了自己会成为一个张牙舞爪的毛绒绒小怪兽，会给衣冠楚楚的高雅读书人和搔首弄姿的老派歌迷们带来一场惊惶失措的shock（震惊）。而且，从“狼蛛”这个书名，就开始织入了严密的文学脉络，古今美外的历史文化氛围，以及表明迪伦的个人身份和声音的音乐生活情境，他的爱与痛，都已尽在网中。

我们以书名为例，探测这部作品中某一个词语可能达到的最大深度。

“狼蛛”（tarantula），在现代英语中常泛指各种毛绒绒的大蜘蛛，有些品种可以让时尚人士当另类宠物养着玩。究其原意，它是特指一种颇为神异的塔兰托狼蛛（*Lycosa tarantula*），源自意大利南部海滨古城塔兰托（Taranto）。它身体大如拇指，肢展长过巴掌，微毒，但对人体可忽略不计，当地的“熊孩子”早二百年前就爱捉了它养在玻璃瓶中玩耍。但实际上这东西却是“邪典”级的文化物种，交织着深厚的历史文脉。

鲍勃·迪伦从小就是个爱读书的好孩子，想必看过科普散文名著《昆虫记》。在“狼蛛”一章，博物学家

1　出自迪伦组诗《一些其他类型的歌……》（1964）。

法布尔做了细致的观察和历史思考：

> 意大利人给狼蛛安上了坏名声，据说被它螫伤的人会发生痉挛和狂舞。要对付这种“狼蛛病”（tarantism），你只能求助音乐，这是唯一的灵药，据说越急促的节奏越有效果。这些特殊的乐曲被记录下来，作为疗效舞蹈、疗效音乐。我们现在拥有的“狼蛛舞”（tarantella，塔兰泰拉），一种活泼敏捷的舞蹈，岂不是来自卡拉布里亚农民治疗术的传承？……但我们无从知晓被狼蛛螫伤，比如对虚弱或过敏的人，会不会导致一种可以用音乐来缓解的神经紊乱；也不知道通过热烈舞蹈而产生的大量排汗能不能减轻其伤痛造成的不适。[1]

所谓“狼蛛病”或某种狂舞症（choreomania），在文艺复兴以来的记载中言之凿凿，它像瘟疫一样在意大利以及欧洲其他一些地方传播。农忙时节下地干活的人最容易被感染，产生各种痉挛迷幻错乱，唯有奏乐舞蹈才能治愈。“疫区”聘请巡游歌舞班子前来为患者驱魔祛病，甚至举行盛大的“治疗舞会”，有时多达千百人参加，大家有病治病、无病强身，人们通宵达旦地疯狂跳舞，直到精疲力竭才罢休。历史记述者是认真的，但

1 参见《昆虫记 卷二》，梁守锵译，花城出版社，2001年，第139页。

科学研究者至今还不清楚这究竟是真正的传染病，还是一种社会心理学上的群体癔症，抑或假作真时真亦假的中古民俗游戏，但总之，极不准确的“舞蹈病”一词就这样流传了下来。如爱伦·坡的成名短篇小说《金甲虫》在开篇题词中便嚷嚷着：

> 哇呜！哇呜！这家伙手舞足蹈！他是被狼蛛咬到了。[1]

人人都以为主人公威廉少爷发了神经才相信“金甲虫”是一张藏宝图，但事实证明，唯有偏执狂才能在纷乱无序的世事中找出暗藏的严密逻辑，最终挖到宝藏。这与迪伦的创作何其相似，甚至在《狼蛛》中这位美国现代文学先驱还极具挑战性地试图在上帝面前争取权利：“埃德加爱伦坡从一个燃烧的树丛后面走出来……他看见埃德加＆他俯视下来＆说‘还没轮到你呢’＆将他击毙……”[2]

杰克·凯鲁亚克的偶像，美国现代小说家托马斯·沃尔夫对虫豸有一种顽强的怨念，他把狼蛛和毒蛇一并视为死亡的象征物、生命的敌对者、现代失乐园的

1　参见《爱伦·坡集：诗歌与故事》，曹明伦译，生活·读书·新知三联书店，1995 年，第 626 页。

2　Dylan 1971, p. 39.

两大轴心，并且在晚期作品中用浓墨重彩的抒情笔调反复强化着这种意象。比如：

狼蛛在烂橡树洞里爬行，蝰蛇对着乳房切齿，杯盏跌落：但大地会永世长存。爱的花朵在野地盛开，榆树根在相爱者的骸骨中伸延。

——《时间与河流》

在蕨叶层间和陌生植物的枝梢上，狼蛛、蝰蛇和角蝰吃饱了自己的毒液之后安睡，在茂密的丛林深处有金翠、艳红、亮蓝冠羽的华丽鸟儿们发出没头没脑的尖叫，月光沉静。

——《时间与河流》

有些东西从不会改变。有些东西永远都一样。[……] 狼蛛、蝰蛇和角蝰也从不会改变。痛苦和死亡永远都一样。但在人行道之下那脉搏般的震颤，在楼宇之下那哭泣般的震颤，在时间的废墟之下，在踩踏着城市的碎骨的兽蹄之下，那里会有某些东西像花朵一样生长，就像从大地再次萌发出来，永远不死的、确切的，就像四月正重新走进生活。

——《你不能再回家》

托马斯·沃尔夫的系列成长小说盛行于迪伦的中学时代，而且列入高中英文课读本篇目。迪伦对沃尔夫书中主人公的叛逆与向往应该心有同感，当他最终选择逃离闭塞的故乡、狭小的家庭，不顾一切奔向某种全新的人生体验的时候，这或许也是其中的一个促因。[1]

沃尔夫塑造的青春反叛、忠于理想、勇于体验、英年早逝的美式浪漫英雄悲剧，给狼蛛这种节肢动物赋予了浓重的黑暗象征主义色彩和阴郁的音乐性。但文学史上第一个上纲上线向狼蛛宣战的可能是哲人尼采。《查拉图斯特拉如是说》中也有“狼蛛”一章，他把那些口中宣扬平等和正义但心里暗藏宿怨和忌恨的“说教者”比作狼蛛：

> 注意，这是狼蛛的洞穴。你想看看它的样子吗？这里挂着它的网：碰一下，它就颤动！它果然出来了：欢迎你，狼蛛！……你的灵魂里盘踞着仇恨：只要被你咬中就会生出黑疮；你的毒液叫人的灵魂因复仇心而迷转。……你们这些宣扬“平等”、叫人灵魂迷转的说教者，你们就是心中暗藏仇恨的狼蛛！……因此我要撕开你们的网，让你们的愤怒把你们从谎言的洞穴里引出来，让

1 不过在所见资料中，迪伦本人未谈及托马斯·沃尔夫的影响，他更喜欢说到马克·吐温、约翰·斯坦贝克等人。

> 你们的复仇心从你们所谓的“正义”背后跳出来。因为对我来说，把人从复仇心中解放出来，才是通往最高希望的天桥，才是漫长雷雨之后的彩虹。……啊！此刻它要用复仇心令我的灵魂迷转！但朋友们，把我紧紧绑在这根柱子上吧，以免我迷转乱舞！我宁做柱顶苦修士，也不愿做复仇心驱使的迷转飞旋。实在地，查拉图斯特拉不是迷转的飓风或旋风；即使他舞蹈，也绝不跳狼蛛舞。查拉图斯特拉如是说。[1]

较早注意到迪伦和尼采之间关联的论者是克雷格·卡普尔，他从《悲剧的诞生》中看到“舞蹈狂”和酒神狂欢与1960年代美国青年运动之间的联系，并注意到音乐作为革命性传媒的沟通作用。[2]美学家戴维·戈德布拉特（David Goldblatt）将迪伦的《狼蛛》与尼采的《查拉图特拉如是说》进行了比较，他称之为“两本狼蛛”。他指出两者的共同点：文学与音乐的通感。

> 在《瞧，这个人》中，尼采解释了他写作《查拉图斯特拉如是说》的灵感缘起，他将理解这本

---

1 参见《查拉图斯特拉如是说》，钱春绮译，生活·读书·新知三联书店，2007年，第108—112页。

2 Craige Karpel, *The Tarantula In Me*, 原载于 *Village Voice*, 1972, 相关综述参见 Ledeen, pp. 42–48。

书比作理解音乐。他说，“作为朕兆，我发现我的审美发生了一个极为猛烈、深刻的决定性转变，尤其对于音乐。也许整部《查拉图特拉如是说》都可视同为音乐——无疑其先决条件是某种听觉艺术的重生。”[1]毫不意外，迪伦的《狼蛛》也同样是最适合大声诵读的，而且它从头到尾都交织着歌曲和舞蹈。[2]

但“狼蛛”进入音乐时，难免也会带着一种刺痛。在写作《狼蛛》的阶段（1965 年），迪伦心中应该惦记着他的青春偶像、美国现代民谣大师伍迪·格思里日益恶化的病情。格思里患有亨廷顿氏症，一种遗传性“舞蹈病”，晚景凄凉，在精神病院羁縻十年，直到去世。迪伦定期去探望、陪伴他，给他弹唱当年的老歌，而伍迪·格思里因严重的运动失调已多年无法操琴歌唱。迪伦对此种境况深有感触，他在晚年回忆道：

伍迪已经被关进灰石病院了。……这个地方没有人会赞美伍迪，对任何人来说这里都是个陌生的场所，尤其对这位美国精神的真正代言人来

1 参见《瞧，这个人：尼采自传》，黄敬甫等译，团结出版社，2006 年，第 113 页。

2 见 Vernezze, p. 158。

说。此地完全是一个没有任何精神希望的精神病收容所。哀嚎声响彻走廊。大多数患者都穿着不合身的病号服，在我弹唱伍迪歌曲的时候他们会一排排漫无目的地走来走去。……这情景很吓人，但伍迪·格思里对一切都茫然无知。通常会有个男护士带他出来见我，然后等我在这里待了一阵又来把他带走。这种经历真是发人深省又令人心碎。[1]

事情还有另外一面。狼蛛和“舞蹈病”虽然都很可怕，从中发展出来的塔兰泰拉舞却热烈奔放，充满拉丁式的情色魅惑。如易卜生戏剧《玩偶之家》，娜拉的丈夫就要求她打扮成一个那不勒斯渔女，拍着铃鼓(tambourine）跳塔兰泰拉舞，以满足他的欲望。当晚的舞会非常成功，丈夫看得心潮激荡，他对他的物化美人说：

你的血管里还在跳动着塔兰泰拉，所以你今晚真是美极了。……今晚我除了你什么都不想要。刚才看着你跳塔兰泰拉的诱人身段，我的血都在燃烧；我再也按捺不住了，所以我才那么急着带你下楼。[2]

---

1 Dylan 2004, pp. 98-99，参见中译本，第101—102页。

2 参见《易卜生戏剧集》第二卷，潘家洵译，人民文学出版社，2006年，第75页。

铃鼓，塔兰泰拉舞的标志性乐器和道具，在迪伦歌曲《铃鼓先生》（“Mr. Tambourine Man”，1965）中具有更迷幻的意味，他祈求铃鼓先生对他“施下舞蹈魔咒”，以获得超脱：

> 带我去远行吧，乘上你的飞旋魔法船，
> 我的感官已被剥夺，我双手抓不住东西，
> 我脚趾麻痹迈不开腿，只等皮靴后跟带我
> 四处去游荡。
> 我随时能去任何地方，我随时能消隐
> 在我独自的游行，对我施下你的舞蹈魔咒吧，
> 我保证一路跳到底。
> ……
> 带我消失吧，穿过我头脑里的烟圈，
> 进入时间的迷雾废墟，越过冰冻的枯叶，
> 和阴森闹鬼的树林，去到大风呼啸的海滨，
> 远离这悲催扭曲的苦境。
> 啊，在钻石星空下舞蹈吧，一只手自由地挥
> 动……[1]

1　Dylan 1985, pp. 172–173，参见《鲍勃 · 迪伦诗歌集：1961—2012·地下乡愁蓝调》，陈黎等译，广西师范大学出版社，2017 年，第 217—219 页。

就这样，通过“狼蛛”，我们又一步步进入神秘和迷幻的文学、音乐、舞蹈多维度交织集合的想象世界。我们可以看到西班牙现代诗人加西亚·洛尔卡那首弥漫着通感、通灵气氛的《六弦琴》（“Las seis cuerdas”）：

吉他，
令梦寐也哭泣。
那些迷失的灵魂的
呜咽，
从它圆圆的口中
逸出。
如同狼蛛
它编织一座巨星
以猎捕那些漂浮在
它漆黑的木头水箱里的
叹息。[1]

吉他，这种乐器，在诗中被人格化了，它已经取代乐手，而狼蛛仿佛出神入化的八臂琴魔，主宰着一个幽暗世界。二十四岁时，加西亚·洛尔卡陶醉于吉他、吉

1 参见《血的婚礼：加西亚·洛尔卡诗歌戏剧精选》，赵振江译，外国文学出版社，1994 年，第 69 页。

卜赛谣曲和弗拉明戈舞，激情地写下《深歌集》（*Poema del cante jondo*，1921，1931）；同样年纪的迪伦则在《狼蛛》中用西班牙文大写字母说道："SOLO SOY UN GUITARRISTA"（我只是一个吉他手），他要"走进猫头鹰和弗拉明戈吉他手们的狭窄巷道"，悼念"洛尔卡墓中那些死去的酋长和婴儿们"。[1]

在音乐圈，吉他高手的超凡控弦能力常被比作"蜘蛛"。如迪伦的《编年史：第1卷》这样描述他所推崇的老一代蓝调大师罗伯特·约翰逊，在一段仅有八秒钟时长的影片中：

> 他正用一双蜘蛛般的大手在弹奏，它们在吉他的琴弦上富有魔力地跳动着。一个架子支着口琴挂在他的脖子上。他的样子根本不像一个石头人，也没有高度紧绷的气质。他简直是孩子气的，一副天使般的模样，纯真得不得了。他穿着白色的亚麻套衫、工装裤，戴一顶很少见的小爵爷式金边帽。他根本不像一个被地狱之犬追猎的凡人。他似乎免除了人类的恐惧，而你眼看着他的形象却难以置信。[2]

---

1 Dylan 1971, p. 30, 56, 58.

2 Dylan 2004, p. 287，参见中译本，第 286 页。

显然迪伦和罗伯特·约翰逊从未谋面，但三十年后的不断慢放、定格、重复，这八秒钟的短片比八百秒还长，而且让他记住了一辈子，因此，它也成了迪伦的自我写照。但难免有点滥情味道的怀旧，带着亢奋、自恋和感伤，像杰克·凯鲁亚克《在路上》中的名段：

> 他们一同奔向大街，用他们早年的方式踅摸着各种各样的东西，在将来他们会变得更加忧伤、敏感和茫然。但那时，他们像叮咚仙童在满街上狂舞，而我踉跄跟随，我一生都这样跟着我感兴趣的人，因为对我来说只有这些人才是疯狂的家伙，他们疯着生活，疯着谈话，疯着得救，渴望一次性拥有一切，他们从不打哈欠，从不说老套废话，只会燃烧、燃烧、燃烧，像轰轰烈烈的黄色罗马烟花弹当空爆射，像蜘蛛在星海上纵横，当你看到那中天上蓝色的焰心炸响，人人都要大喊一声“哇！”在歌德时代的德国，这样的年轻人会叫作什么？[1]

在某些时代，这样的年轻人都叫作“诗人”。我是一个青年诗人，我要上路。

1　Kerouac, *On the Road*, Penguin, 2000，p. 7，参见《在路上》，王永年译，上海译文出版社，2006 年，第 8—9 页。

盘丝洞入门：

Plague the Kid, crusading in the blues dimension[1]

迪伦不是文学老炮，只是一个会长出皱纹和白发的老男孩，从前，他更加苍老。[2]在《狼蛛》中，他甚至已主持了他本人的葬礼。

鲍勃迪伦长眠于此
被身后
颤栗的肉体
谋杀而死
凶手遭到拉撒路拒绝之后
就扑上他
以求个清净独处
但惊讶地发现
他已经变成
一辆电车&
这样的结局正适合
鲍勃迪伦

他如今安息在现实太太的

1 Dylan 1971, p. 87.

2 参见迪伦歌曲《我的末版》（“My Back Pages”，1964）。

美容院
上帝抚慰他的灵魂
&他的鲁莽

两个兄弟
&一个赤裸的好妈宝
长得好像耶稣基督
现在可以分享他的病痛
的遗体
&他的电话号码

再也没有力量
可奉送——
现在每个人
都可以将它拿回

鲍勃迪伦长眠于此
毁于维也纳礼节——
他们现在可以声称发明了他
冷静人士现在
可以写有关他的赋格曲
&丘比特现在能踢翻他的煤油灯——
小鲍迪伦——丧命于被遗弃的俄狄浦斯
后者曾四处

转悠
调查一个幽灵
&发现
那幽灵同样
不仅只有一个人[1]

这首“墓志铭”就是《狼蛛》矿区出产的一大块老坑玻璃种，硬核的先锋派试金石。可以预见，在迪伦百年之后，它会射出洞穿时间的万磁力，横扫全球媒体文化版。而艺术家们“在同一时间生活，同一时间死去，在它的位置出现了某些时间，但那里从来未有过什么真正的某些时间”[2]。

我们可以认为，真正的作者——罗伯特·齐默曼先生在他的虚构实验装置中，把鲍勃·迪伦（这个人物）写成了一位被埋葬的死者/幽灵的合成体，他即死即生，因而得以在一个迷乱交错的时空中进行散漫的游历。老派的评论方式喜欢谈一个作者或作品所受的文脉影响，那么从这一点看去，《狼蛛》似乎可以联系到众多的文学经典。然而，与欧洲文艺复兴以来近现代诸位文豪不同，迪伦虽然也博闻广识，但他最精通的还是美国歌谣，它们已感染到他的每一个神经末梢，因此他能用注满乐

1 Dylan 1971, pp. 118-120. 斯科比对这首诗做了深刻分析，见 Scobie, pp. 57–61。

2 Dylan 1971, p. 136.

感的指尖在打字机上敲出魔咒和弦，把《地狱一季》的空间无限期开放，让《地下人》的队伍无限制扩招，激活了兰波的无数化身，凯鲁亚克的无数别名，迪伦的无数绰号，以及他在生活周遭和电波纸册中相识的各色人等，让他们“每个人都自带橡皮”[1]，热热闹闹地自行开动起来，打造一座异世浮生的迷幻之城——盘丝洞[2]。

我们会不断进入《狼蛛》，这个繁庶的盘丝洞时空。迪伦最初曾这样描述它：

> 我的小说没有什么目的
> 绝对毫无目的
> 比如说它根本不讲故事
> 但他有一百万场景那么长
> 要用大概一万亿张纸头来说完……当然我对他也不能看出什么。[3]

《狼蛛》全文共分四十七章，或不妨视之为该矿区的四十七个出入通道，多数章节由不分行的“散文诗”和分行的“书信诗”组成，它们风格一致，氛围一致，

---

1 Dylan 1971, p. 126.

2 参见吴承恩《西游记》，第七十二回《盘丝洞七情迷本 濯垢泉八戒忘形》。

3 Bob Dylan, “A Letter for Sis and Gordon”, *Broadside*, #38, Jan. 20, 1964, https://singout.org/downloads/broadside/b038.pdf.

合为一个整体，但相互之间没有情节线索的联系。甚至，它划分章节，安上名字，也许是出于好心的粗略导游图，或留在沙地上的脚印或字迹，也许有些部分只是蔫坏的误导。在这个世界发生了一些事情，但却不是故事，因为该蛛并不织造具体的网。但戈德布拉特认为，《狼蛛》在几个方面表明了它的全局的统一性。如同样的章节结构，尽管生活片段貌似各不相干，但实际上都可能牵涉到某个名为“迪伦”的叙述者，而那些署名千奇百怪的留言条或短信，从内容和文风的一致性足以指向同一个（福柯意义上的）作者，那层层叠叠的踪迹就仿佛该作者在行使他不断重置个人简历的艺术特权。[1]

《狼蛛》不是某些差评师所鄙夷的嗑药上脑痴人呓语胡乱堆积。迪伦的“饭圈老铁”史蒂芬·皮克林仔细地比较了官方版和一个早期流出版《狼蛛会见浆糊大王》（*Tarantula Meets Rex Paste*），从两者差异中可见出迪伦对书稿做过的细致修改和编辑。[2] 实际上，《狼蛛》的每一个词都经过精挑细选，铁板钉钉，这应该是细心读者最终都会发现的事实。唯一的问题只是，鲍勃·迪伦后来执意把这部书稿定性为一个“矿难”般的废墟，这给入坑淘金者带来很大疑惑。

1　见 Vernezze, pp. 157–158。

2　Stephen Pickering, “The *Two Tarantulas*: A Textual Comparison”, https://www.expectingrain.com/discussions/viewtopic.php?p=1576264. 另参见综述，Ledeen, pp. 80–85,104–109。

> 似乎什么事情也不曾发生。读者刚有点抓住线索的感觉，一切又改变了。在这些印象式的反叙述中，许多人物出现并活动，他们又随着语境时空的瞬间变换而突然消失，然后又重新出现，做着跟先前行动完全不相干的事情。这种写法造成的实际效果就是，让情节的推进或连续性成为不可能。你经常会感到自己是在观看那些文字，而不是阅读。[1]

因此，史密斯（Larry David Smith）认为，《狼蛛》是无法抽取片段来代表其整体的，如果想借用一些节选来谈论它，无异于背叛了这部作品，但如果把整本书全文都引用进来，那又太荒诞了。他在最新版的《写作迪伦》（*Writing Dylan*, 2018）中选择对《狼蛛》敬而远之，评论家没什么可说的，唯一的方法只能是让读者自己去探索各人的路径。

在评传《他是谁》（*Who is that Man?*, 2012）中，道尔顿（David Dalton）拉拉杂杂地给出了必须重视《狼蛛》的十三个半理由，大意如下：

> 1. 忘掉那些现代派大师名著吧，只需读《狼蛛》

1 Smith, p. 161.

即可完全体验。

2. 我们生活在一个破碎、重组的希腊化文化，一个痴迷于采样、截取、剪切、杂成、伪装（包括人格）的后现代社会,《狼蛛》预告了推特的时代。

3. 情节曲折、叙述巧妙的当代小说已经太多，我们想要点别的。

4. 安迪·沃霍尔的“小说”《a》更加语无伦次，却受到追捧。

5.《狼蛛》要配乐来读，要唱出来。

6. 要把英语作为外语或作为诗歌来看它。读者需要自备叙述线索。

7. 不一定要有意义，只要能让心灵进入颤栗、飞旋的迷离状态。

8. 迪伦把异质的碎片结合重生，“文案”开创了一种新的文学形式。

9.《狼蛛》可视为威廉·巴勒斯的剪切技法的应用。

10. 学术界已开始重新看待这本书。

11. 也许是外星人通过迪伦向我们发报。

12. 艺术史上神乎其神的超现实主义“自动写作”其实不如迪伦。

13.《狼蛛》为迪伦迷提供了食粮。

13½. 你正进入迪伦大脑内部。[1]

---

1 Dalton, pp. 242–246，参见中译本，第 283—288 页。

在笔者看来，《狼蛛》的时空位置还可以放到它产生的那个大现场去观察和体验，而非试图把它局限在玻璃瓶中。1966 年，就在迪伦撞车、《狼蛛》封笔的时候，与他同龄的法国文学研究生茱莉亚·克里斯蒂娃（Julia Kristeva）提出“互文性”或“文本间性”（intertextuality）的概念，成为后现代主义理论的重要部分，此外，在新先锋艺术领域，激浪派的迪克·希金斯（Dick Higgins）于早前发表“混合媒介”或“交互中介”（intermedia）宣言，在激进左翼政治领域，“处境国际”的居伊·德波（Guy Debord）在稍后出版了《奇境社会》（*La société du spectacle*），等等——《狼蛛》和那些佶屈聱牙、难以译解的新术语、新文本一起标志着一个后后后后主义时代的降临。1973 年，罗兰·巴特（Roland Barthes）在《文本的愉悦》（*Le plaisir du texte*）中更加佶聱地给蜘蛛们献上了及时的加冕：

> **文本** [*Texte*] 的原意为**织物** [*Tissu*]；但直至今日，我们仍把这织物当成一件制成品、一块业已完工的纱幕，在那背后似乎隐隐约约地藏着意义（真理）；我们现在要强调的是，在织物中，有一个**生成性** [générative] 的概念，文本通过一场永久的交错编织而生产自己，加工自己；在这织物——这文本——当中迷失，主体便解除了自身，就像

一只蜘蛛消融于它织网的建构性分泌。如果喜欢用新词，我们可以把关于文本的理论命名为**织造学** [*hyphology*]（*hyphos*，意即织物和蛛网。）[1]

我们可以进一步推论，语言或符号作为织物的组织单位或细胞，它们有各自的体块，有各自的全套的属性、特征，这样强行联合而成的织物 / 文本注定将是一块厚重的语符载体，甚至是一大摊异质共生的、不稳定的、叫人密恐的、团团簇簇的东西，它是活的，并且活动着。什么，你说一枚坚固而透明的单体结晶？那恐怕是神话学而不是文本学的范畴。因此，一个文本很难说是否具有某种单一而确定的大集体属性（意义 / 真理），毋宁说，那只是一个临时性的想象的共同体的临时性的共同想象，属于"念念不忘，必有回响"的通灵学概念。更严重的是，随着文本编织过程的永续进行，一部分甚至全部的文本又作为组织材料被动或自主地加入，这些活材料本身就有其完整的自足性、自主性，然后又不断地重组重织，成为互文本。巴特的意思似乎是，这些文本就像会交配生崽儿，générative，在无穷的编织生产过程中，主体渐渐耗尽、消散，此后，再也没有珀涅罗珀，她自我解散了。当奥德修斯历经艰险回到他那位于洋葱核心的美好家宅，只看到厚重无匹的文本积淀层中一个

1 Barthes, pp. 100–101.

纵横交错的多维盘丝洞，只看到一排排全自动的九张机，人工智能矩阵，狼蛛。这就是：作者死了，总之，他/她已经消失了，只留下一些隐约莫辨的疑踪，符号自由了！文本万岁！文本也死了，读者万岁！

另外，按照巴特的分类，《狼蛛》显然不属于"易读文本"(texte lisible)，而是"可写文本"(texte scriptible)，比如说是邀请读者一起来玩填字游戏的道具模板，它要带来玩耍的狂喜、高潮，而非传统的审美愉悦，更不是静观参悟。《狼蛛》就跟后现代文学教科书上的典型范例一样，暴露语言的生成性、文本的构建性和文学的修辞性，解构意识形态主导话语，在一个多维的空间里，各种各样的文本、互文本（它们都不是原文）搅合在一起，进行大面积、大尺度地文本戏仿、引征和策略性误读，异质共生（heteroglossia)，互相生成又互相颠覆，成为一个有待探索的动态的字符场域。蜘蛛精不需要被"解释"，而是要求互相的"解放"，它要释放出自由的词语或句群，在那背后或许并未预置着一个吁求权威解释的意义/真理，没有既定的秘诀可供破译和传授。它不是神秘朦胧的，同时也不是透彻明晰的，唯一的"鉴赏"方式只有参与进来一起"玩"，一起创造并经历这个交互促成的处境（situation)，每个不同读者留下各自的痕迹，留下新形而上学家们也说不清的各自殊异的此在（Dasein）和互相造就的共同此在(Mitdasein)，因为，"只有三样东西是持久的：生命——

死亡&伐木工来了”[1]。

而“此在”的体验可能会让专业读者联想到“身体”和“意义”，即生活着的某人对于在世之意义的身体性的追问以及具身认知之类，这又是《狼蛛》游乐场中有待开发的一大功能区。《狼蛛》是经过精心设计的停工废墟，是残缺美，它没有原经正典的无瑕本体（它不过是诸多盗印本中的一个合法知识版权，甚至不是原作者的签章完本），但书中每每标注出生理性的人类身体部位，又像一家大型综合医院门诊部的回廊上科别林立的示意图，却不曾看见一位连续、完整、独立的人格化对象。

罗宾·维廷（Robin Witting）是一位大胆的勘探者，早年他曾归纳：“《狼蛛》有六大主题：美国、越南、阿瑞莎、玛丽亚，以及——万灵仙丹——音乐。”[2] 后来随着更深的探索，维廷又拓展出身体器官、口腔、饥饿、干渴、病痛以及苦恼，音乐（声音之音），丰饶的象征（头发、血液等），水和雨的重生及毁灭的象征。[3] 在最新的文章中，他再次回到《狼蛛》开头的第一个小标题“Mouthbook”（口书），审视以“口腔之欲”为代表的

---

1 Dylan 1971, p. 137.

2 Robin Witting, *The Cracked Bells: A Guide to Tarantula, Revised Edition*, Exploding Rooster, 1995, p. 13.

3 Robin Witting, *A Crash Course on Reading Tarantula: 3rd. Edition*，Exploding Rooster, 2017.

身体迷恋症候群，他又增加了一些主题和中心：

> 美国（因越战而分裂）、阿瑞莎、玛丽亚、声响、音乐、食物、身份、永不满足的饥渴、嘴巴、眼睛、肉体以及死亡。……如嘴巴的品尝、吞咽、咀嚼、歌唱、嘟囔、舔舐、打嗝、啜饮、撕咬、结巴、呢喃、哈欠、啃吃、亲吻、窒息、窃笑……人体解剖学的每一部位，从肠道到子宫，从胸部到腺体，从骨骼到大脑，都像是一个角色。……更异想天开的是，书中不仅有大量的身体器官，还有一个医院——装满疾病和残障。[1]

有趣的是，维廷作为最热忱、最懂行的《狼蛛》专家之一，他的文章充满了彩画窗、万花筒以及淘金筛盆一般的洞见，他把《狼蛛》探索到了无人能及的深度，揭示出一场热烈、富丽、庞杂的多层次的大型狂欢盛典；但多年来，维廷却被文学教授们斥为“业余”，说他连论文格式都不懂，这对于号称要打破高雅 / 低俗文化壁垒的后现代派来说，真是一个绝妙的反例。尽管后现代理论还弥漫着太多虚空迷径和自说自话，但它们带来的时代潮流已在更改学院界和传媒界的知识地形图。通过

---

1 Robin Witting, “help those that cannot understand not to understand: Introduction” .

一些裂缝乃至决口，《狼蛛》终将脱出美国流行乐评的窠臼，一路如鱼得水，它也许会变成章鱼怪，八岐大蛇，哥斯拉。

地下人：

People goin' down to the ground[1]

“你们是世上的光。城立在山上，是不能被隐藏的。”[2]

但青年迪伦1961年初来到纽约的时候，却发现高楼在天上伸展，人们在地下穿行，这叫矿山子弟产生了一种既陌生又熟悉的蒸汽朋克错位感。当然，他肯定读过凯鲁亚克的小说《地下人》，这部小说1960年还拍成了电影，美国城中村的那一对白黑情侣形象可以说短暂而肤浅，而“地下人”这个概念却种进了迪伦的感知深处。

> 朱利恩·亚历山大是地下人中的天使，地下人这个名称是亚当·穆拉德发明的，他是一位诗人也是我的朋友，他说：“他们嬉皮但不圆滑，聪颖但不俗套，那些人满腹经纶，对庞德了如指掌，但又不装腔作势也不说个没完，他们其实都很安

1　出自迪伦歌曲《谈谈纽约》（“Talking New York”，1961）。

2　引自《新约·马太福音》5:14。

静，就像基督一样。”朱利恩的确就像基督一样。我那个时候正和雷利·奥哈拉从街上走过来他是我在旧金山一直形影不离的老酒友在我过去漫长的疯狂的生涯里我曾喝得烂醉而且事实上还常常“和蔼可亲”地向朋友们乞讨酒喝没有人真的注意到或者是正告我年纪轻轻的就已开始或正在染上这种吃白食的坏毛病但是就像我还有萨姆说的那样：“大家都过来加油吧，伙计，那是因为你这里有一个加油站。”或者是说些类似这样的话。[1]

迪伦的大部分歌曲，不言而喻，可以说都是在为地下人树碑立传，但他们不会有纪念碑，迪伦用另一种方式为他们修建。在歌曲《地下乡愁蓝调》中，迪伦自己的“地下人”概念正式挂牌，并得到艾伦·金斯堡的加持，随后在《狼蛛》中达到人口繁庶的鼎盛。

笔者没有统计过《狼蛛》一书中共出现多少人物，点了名的总有几百个吧。异世迷幻城的生活群像，显贵与盲流齐飞，贱民共富豪一色，真真假假、变幻不居，但他们不是，或不仅仅是一些畸零人。这些角色又不断切换着身份，按着盘丝洞世界的行为规范，继续出演奇人怪事，从空一格的先总统肯尼迪到打红叉的钦犯斯塔

1 Kerouac, *The Subterraneans,* Groove, 1994, p. 1，译文引自《地下人·皮克》，金衡山译，上海译文出版社，2015 年，第 1 页。

克韦瑟，在掘进面上并无区别。

显然，《狼蛛》从来不是超离的，它也许东鳞西爪，但一直扣着亚美利加合众国的神经弦。那些当权的政要高官、名流显贵已叫人耳熟能详，他们以真名实姓出没厅堂，并在拐弯抹角的井巷中登场入戏。但，没有批斗会，在《狼蛛》的周遭环境中，他们生活着，还原着。最日常的情形是这样的：

> 逃亡飞车一路上满载：布拉索斯河边闲躺的三个猎人——两个在窗前窥看的妈妈各自捧着些莉莉圣西尔的腐朽照片——小碟熏肉——几个失去特权的奖金宝贝满肚子右旋安非他命——脸上挂着图版的画家——杠铃一副——德古拉抽着烟&嚼着一个天使——猎豹之灵，琹夫人&布莱蒂墨菲全都裹在牙膏里——整箱的魔法杖&一个无辜的旁观者……不消说——车里根本没地方了——菲德拉绷着脸&她怒吼“爱是要疯狂透顶”&红酒瓶破碎——得克萨斯爆炸&海滨晚餐——仪表堂堂的船长们——他们被看见——他们被卡车司机看见——那些卡车司机控诉劫匪&眼看这些船长骑着种马进入咆哮的墨西哥湾&菲德拉驾到“爱是要彻底疯狂”……她身边是克拉普先生——笑眯眯的——他戴着一顶里朝外的帽子——他在吃好果子呢——他会一切顺利——克

拉普先生——他会一切顺利[1]

地下人的户口档案最有意思的部分不是人名，而是别名和绰号。迪伦说："我有个毛病就是经常记不住人的姓名，所以我就给他们另取一个，更能准确描述他们的那种。"[2]别名／绰号太多，随手即可翻阅，这里就不再引用罗列。另外，须知，"鲍勃·迪伦"也是罗伯特·齐默曼的别名。

命名即治理。这是现代政治对古典诗学的一大发展。外邦人进入盘丝洞，必先在移民局登记别名，此前的家系族裔作废，奉着圣徒而来的教名也不作数。他们一些人也许持有迪伦唱片友邦签证，但又不同，所有的别名都重新登记，并且不断重新更换、重新登记。狼蛛在看着你，这是邪典世界的运转机器，它唯一只怕或根本不怕某位乔装者掉落的假睫毛。这个兴盛发达的《狼蛛》地下城一页页揭示其面目，用某种异域情调在似曾相识的生活场景中挑逗我们的世界观，重估着我们对一个世界、一个人类聚居和交往方式的可能性的轻率想象。

"不，我的朋友，你的思维方式就叫做放弃"

"你爱怎样就怎样吧，你的方式叫做失败——

1 Dylan 1971, p. 103.

2 Dylan 2004, p. 169，参见中译本，第 170 页。

这甚至不是一种思维方式”[1]

数量是有意义的，两三个怪人经常就构成迪伦的一首歌，但是，当《狼蛛》中熙熙攘攘的地下人群如大面积的潮水在涌动的时候，构成的是一个世界，一个乌泱乌泱的世界。人太多，行动太快，若简单列举一批奇人怪事恐怕难有以管窥豹的效果，还不如读者随手去翻翻来得快当。若对书中多次出场的阿瑞莎、玛丽亚等女性形象或所谓“缪斯”进行不厌其烦地扒找，未必就能揭示出多少真相，而且太物化了，有点色眯眯。

那我就当上述这些人
实际上全部都是
同一个人……下次见。我得去
把戈黛娃夫人的画像拆下来因为那些
神经学生一个小时内就要来这儿
参观……[2]

地下人的生活方式与地上主流世界似是而非，甚至格格不入。比如，我们在译注中解释了几百个条目，亦真亦假的同名人、同名物，但它们就是它们吗，或只是

1 Dylan 1971, p. 116.
2 Dylan 1971, p. 51.

一些假定的影射（allusions）或投射（reflections）？阿瑞莎（aretha）当真是歌星阿瑞莎·富兰克林？抑或是用字母“a”开头出现在第一章第一个字的某种对象而已？当她一再复现的时候，她还是最初的那个她吗？就连“bob dylan”一语，当它在原文第118—120页出现的时候，是否有必要对这个词条加注：“鲍勃·迪伦（Bob Dylan，1941— ），美国著名歌手、唱作人，曾获得2016年诺贝尔文学奖，《狼蛛》是他最具争议的实验文学作品……”？严格来讲，有此必要，但是，更严格来讲，上述示例却是错误的，因为：《狼蛛》里的这位“bob dylan”早在1966年就已经入土为安，而同时，书中一切人等或许莫不是他的千万化身。

如果我们要为《狼蛛》写出哪怕一条真正的注释，那都将是一本小书，另一本有待更多注释的地下人之书。如果你不相信，可以看看1960年代的另一本诗文注释体混合“小说”，纳博科夫的《微暗的火》（*Pale Fire*，1962）。相对来说，纳博科夫只是在文士的职业区隔上更执着且更走运而已，他也非常出色，而且他喜欢捉蝴蝶，但是他不爱摇滚。

至于摇滚，恰恰是迪伦文学的弱点，他的阿喀琉斯之踵，而《狼蛛》却是他的一场惜败的翻身仗。他被限定、被禁锢，于唱片工业的浮华世界的一个类型区间，连笔者也总是情难自控地在文中频频引证这位流行歌手的代表曲目。就像只比迪伦大半岁的李小龙，他也有作为哲人、诗人的另一面，他想要“无形，无体，如水如流，注水入杯，它就是杯，注水入壶，它就是壶”，但永远被框定为一个咿呀怪叫的唐人街功夫小子 Bruce Lee。他们本身都在各自的浮华世界的表象上翻腾，他们都没有成为“地下人”，只是被地下小圈子奉为一个邪典符号，算是“地下人的天使”。

当年有不少左派人士恼火迪伦，因为他没能在《狼蛛》中对越战发出更公开的抗议，但我们在书中还是能找到对这场战争大量的指涉。加布丽埃·古德柴尔德（Gabrielle Goodchild）认为，迪伦的越战是一场超现实性质的“战争”，“它发生在我们的控制之外，同时又毒害着我们的生活”。[1]

> 他 & 大肉杰克——会同来自贝可斯的桑迪鲍勃——他们牵着白象去威奇托瀑布 & 国王大道之间的某处饮水——当时天色已晚 & 还是没有西贡的任何消息……趁着一片混乱，小棍儿偷走了白象……谁都没注意，包括布朗丹，他这一次是忙着用钢锯也要把大肉杰克活活揍死——总而言之，越南的局势非常乱[2]

“介入”（engagement，poésie engagée），这个词在

1 Shelton, p. 166，参见中译本，第 427 页。

2 Dylan 1971, p. 85–86.

日常生活中一般指订婚、雇佣、签约之类，又指交战、局部遭遇战，这是“自我&脊髓梦幻的联姻”。

> 脱衣舞娘来时戴着一枚
> 订婚戒指——她要柠檬水，
> 却说她也能接受三明治——
> 报童拽住她——大叫“求主
> 垂怜”[1]

而在那个紧张的冷战时代，紧张到全欧亚大陆青年都会修防空洞、演习核爆防护措施，而越南军民用步枪抵御降维打击的时代——

> 你也许会改变你通奸、吞剑的风格——你也许会改变你在钉床上睡觉的方式——涂涂你的鞋吧用幽灵骡子的颜色——纸老虎的利牙是铝制的——你有大把时间去巴比伦[2]

《狼蛛》因接地而通电。它的前辈们或多或少也曾面临乃至参与过铁血飞溅的战斗，但他们也许不曾那样抽象而又具体地面临过关于核子大战中确保互相毁灭的

---

1 Dylan 1971, p. 77.

2 Dylan 1971, p. 58.

媒体知识轰炸。上午打猎、下午捕鱼、晚饭后从事批判（马克思），抑或上午对俄宣战，下午游泳（卡夫卡），这些对迪伦来说也完全可以畅行无碍，他已经不差钱了。但作为“抗议歌手”起家的鲍勃·迪伦，他对时代悲剧性有着特殊体认，他在文学中还相信这些吗，他不相信吗？克里斯托弗·瑞克斯（Christopher Ricks）在《迪伦的七宗罪幻象》（*Dylan's Visions of Sin*，2003）中发现了一个伦理尺度：

> 《狼蛛》死亡之舞的表演者当中有着悲剧。毋宁说有一位特拉姬蒂 [Tragedy]。甚或是（令演员心荡神驰的）塔兰特拉姬蒂 [Taragedy]。但要注意，此处有个警告。**警告**：让他小心，至少要谨慎。因为尽管悲剧能够通过它对傲慢之罪的理解而变得深刻，然而一旦它本身也堕入傲慢，悲剧立刻就浅薄了。它不应自以为是地俯视喜剧，它们其实互为兄弟。《狼蛛》中有这样的沉思：“悲剧，破碎的骄傲，浅薄 & 不比喜剧更深刻”，而可悲的则是“厄运、屈服 & 结局美满的滑稽戏”。[1]

《狼蛛》是核能的，它通过点唱机接通了氢弹威慑的心理核聚变反应。

1　Ricks, p. 179.《狼蛛》引文见 Dylan 1971, p. 52。

你没那么厉害——的确，你对少年
违法行为立场强硬——你说过要
把所有阿飞都赶出城——哦你可真
威风——的确，你说你是爱国者——你
说你根本不怕扔一个什么氢弹&
让所有的人都知道你是说话算话的
但你却不肯说别的只会说你根本
不怕扔一个什么氢弹——你怎能说
我的孩子都必须跟着好榜样
学？他们跟着坏榜样学也
是可以的——他们可以跟你学也可以
跟我学——你再也不能把我按在你的大拇指
底下——不是因为我太难弄，而是因为
你的手是用水做的……[1]

鲍勃·迪伦毕竟主要是一位歌手，他对于大众情绪的敏感度可能比书斋作家要高一些，但我们不必过多纠缠于《狼蛛》和迪伦歌词的相通以及相似之处。在摇滚乐的星光大道辉映下进入《狼蛛》，是我们光临盘丝洞不能不走的一条宽阔歧途，然后探索者将各自分道扬镳。因为珍宝富集的老坑矿区并不在那里，“I’m not there”。

1 Dylan 1971, p. 121–122.

但反过来，同样，也有太多人试图从迪伦文学以及文辞，包括他的钦定版哥词集（*Lyrics*）系列经籍，打着头灯，提着金丝雀，想从暗道里摸进迪伦的音乐密室，也可能此路不通。这是多面人鲍勃·迪伦必然遭遇的多重误解，这个圈套恐怕是他当年精心制造的得意之作，如今连他本人也未必走得出去。

插电的语言：*Disillusioned words like bullets bark*[1]

《狼蛛》是一场快速、超速、高超声速的言语行动，因此，它在交叉跑动的紧急漫谈中飞掠着音讯或信号。它不是既定符码的制成品，它狠过火力全开的弹幕齐射，猛过泥沙俱下的洪荒塌陷，它是头脑的强磁暴，全域性的感官震荡。它是电，它是光，它歌唱那带电的肉体，它是唯一的神话……[2]

在鲍勃·迪伦作为摇滚天王的演唱会上，怎样语无伦次的废话都不为过。但如果转到文学场：文学是请客吃饭，是做文章，文学就是资本积累到一定程度而发

1　出自迪伦歌曲《没事的，妈妈（我只是在流血）》［“It’s Alright, Ma (I’m Only Bleeding)”，1965］。

2　混合改写自惠特曼诗《我歌唱那带电的肉体》（1855）、S.H.E 歌曲《Super Star》（2003，施人诚填词）。

展成的偶像。[1]在文学场，迪伦大概只勉强受得了金斯堡这个温良恭俭让的“老鸡婆”。包括笔者在内，已有太多的书斋评论家追溯过迪伦可能吸收或采纳的文学影响，从荷马、萨福，到兰波、乔伊斯，从《易经》、耶和华，到布莱希特、巴勒斯，但这些并不足以保证能够诞生一只狼蛛，没有任何一位产科神医能有足够的勇气来确保这种操作。说他嗑药的人请靠边练习键盘指法一百遍。因为《狼蛛》就是这样日以继夜敲出来的，无他，不过是别人聊天的时候迪伦还在一边码字而已。

《狼蛛》是一种文学推翻一种文学的话语权的暴烈行动。只因为这些情感没有在咖啡厅和大学课堂上宣讲，你就认为它们不存在吗？[2]它是美国文学的再次革命，是惠特曼的正义光复。迪伦明确地否决过娱记们提示的“意识流”（stream of consciousness）概念，凯鲁亚克的“自发性散文”（spontaneous prose）也不足以装载《狼蛛》，他的文学就是泥石流，是“flows of verbal lava”（口语熔岩流）[3]。

1　混合改写自毛泽东《湖南农民运动考察报告》（1927）、居伊·德波《奇境社会》（1967）。

2　混合改写自毛泽东《湖南农民运动考察报告》（1927）、惠特曼《我歌唱那带电的肉体》（1855）。

3　Mark Polizzotti, “On Bob Dylan’s Literary Influences: From William Blake to Jack Kerouac”, *Literary Hub*, Oct. 14, 2016, https://lithub.com/on-bob-dylans-literary-influences/.

迪伦用“泛滥”（flow）一词来替代“意识流”是恰当的。迪伦的语言和词句仿佛是直觉地、无过滤地冒出来。实际上，《狼蛛》的确是一系列的毫不拘束、漫无头绪、没头没尾的片段，而这些片段必须要互相配合起来才能起码成为一位独立作者的诗歌合集。不过，如果你期待在书中看到迪伦处处闪现的才华，那是不会失望的。它很独创又很古怪。但无可挑剔的是它的写作风格，从头到尾的连贯性，还有迪伦式的抖机灵，尖锐态度，是它最显著的特征。妙趣横生，但也充满智慧。[1]

《狼蛛》是灭世大文（瘟）疫中一场凶险的带病自救行动，因为，“language is a virus from outer space”（语言是一种来自外太空的病毒）[2]，而狼蛛的毒液就是以毒攻毒、活人无数的解药。[3] 它是对威廉·巴勒斯及其达达、未来、超现实等老先锋前辈技法元素的大规模冒用、篡改和存活性治疗，它是“L=A=N=G=U=A=G=E”的预先路演和未来重组，但它首先是一次罢课和占领。《狼

1　见 Vernezze, p. 158。

2　语出威廉·巴勒斯小说《爆炸的车票》(*The Ticket That Exploded*，1962，1967)。

3　John Olson, “Dylan Goes Magenta”, http://archive.emilydickinson.org/titanic/material/olsondylan.html.

蛛》是一场混乱或混沌（Chaos），迪伦说，“chaos is a friend of mine”（混乱是我的朋友）——

还有矛盾？

对，矛盾。

还有混乱？

混乱，西瓜，时钟，一切。

你在一张专辑背面写过，“我接受混乱但混乱接受我吗？”

混乱是我的一个朋友。就像我接受他一样，他会接受我吗？

你是把世界看作混乱？

真理就是混乱。恐怕美也是混乱。

像艾略特、叶芝这样的诗人——

我没读过叶芝。[1]

《狼蛛》是一首歌，民谣 / 蓝调 / 爵士 / 摇滚 / 灵歌 / 史诗的杂交混成曲，而且肯定是插电的、具身的演

1　1965 年 8 月访谈，Cott, p. 54。

奏，然而，它不会发生在三面墙的舞台。尝试从文学来谈论迪伦歌词会言不及物，但更甚者，试图用歌曲来收编迪伦的文学，这将是一条死胡同。而死胡同（cul-de-sac）就是一个麻袋，什么鸡零狗碎的都可以往里装。迪伦唱不了的长文字就叫小说，舞台装不下的大东西就是生活，正如莎翁所说，人生如戏，男女都是演员。迪伦无疑是世界剧场上最伟大的表演家之一，但他首先是自己的编剧和导演，他装备的三大法宝，是吉他、口琴和打字机。

鲍勃·迪伦的本体也许就是一个坐在打字机前的作家。迪伦的老班底，“乐队”（The Band）主音吉他手罗比·罗伯逊（Robbie Robertson）曾经感慨：

> 1966年他跟我一起到纳什维尔去录《美人复美人》，当时我才第一次看见居然有唱作人是用打字机来写歌的。我们都进了录音棚，而他还要写完几首准备排练的歌词。我能听见打字机的声音——咔嗒，咔嗒，咔嗒，叮，响得飞快。他就那样飞快地把东西敲出来；跟说话一样。[1]

从前，机械打字机比电脑键盘还要花样更多，那种

1 Robbie Robertson, “Bob Dylan”, *Rolling Stone*, Dec. 3, 2010, https://www.rollingstone.com/music/music-lists/100-greatest-artists-147446/bob-dylan-10-31068/.

山溪流水、转石跃坎、叮咚汩涌的操作感，指尖发出的命令以及回馈，每一根键条的往复运动都肉眼可见、骨节可感，甚至震动胸腹。哒哒哒，哒，哒哒，叮！提示字纸快到头了，请准备拨换行扳手。迪伦用过多种打字机，早先寄宿在纽约朋友家里，借他的 Remington 打字机写出了《暴雨将至》等杰作。那是在古巴导弹危机时刻的纽约深夜，打字机就像迪伦的武器：

> 我们整夜没睡——大家都想知道是否已经结束了，我也一样。明天的一点钟还会来临吗？……这是一首绝望的歌。我们能做什么呢？我们能够控制那些要把我们抹除人类边缘的人吗？词语飞快地涌出，非常快，这是一首恐惧之歌。一行接一行接一行，努力去捕捉那种虚无之感。[1]

在 1964 年以后的老照片上，迪伦的工作室和寓所的案头，是当年最时髦的便携机型 Olivetti Lettera 32、Royal Safari 等，此外他在 1965 年英国巡演的影片上也打过 Olympia SG1、Olivetti Lexikon 80 等标准中型机。直到 21 世纪，迪伦还是在一台老式 Remington 打字机上前前后后用了三年时间敲出《编年史：第 1 卷》的全部手稿。他根本停不下来，不然又要回头去重读修改这

---

1 Heylin, p. 102.

个部分。[1]

迪伦早期的字行简短，几乎每次打字著文都是分行的“诗”，看来他那时喜欢拨动回车扳子的呼啦啦的快感，或者是有点讨厌那台机的换行铃声。1965 年开始，迪伦不喜欢拉回车了，他对上档键产生了新的迷恋：咯噔，机头字盘全部应声抬起（换挡），然后迪伦快意地敲出一个&，以及满纸不绝的&！然后再放下，继续山溪流水或雨打林梢的叮咚嘀嗒。《狼蛛》中的句子或词群在急速流动，始终保持着简要、短促、跳跃，伴随着轻快而有力的呼吸节奏，以及应时合拍的一个个“&”，换气符。

The typewriter is holy! [2] 金斯堡在《嚎叫附录》中说，打字机是神圣的。我们可以肯定，在迪伦的指尖上，打字机就是一把有灵的乐器。迪伦没有选用当时最高科技的重达三四十磅 IBM Selectric 电动机，他自行给他的手提打字机通电了，生物电、感应电，用爱发电。而且，文学，或一个字码建构物，未必是由作者指尖的本能来主导，它也可能来自外部世界和他的相互观察、试探、摩擦、碰撞而形成的电力驱动。总之，我们应该深刻体认到，多年浸淫于乐器音声效果的鲍勃·迪伦，必然给

1 Edna Gundersen, “Dylan Chronicles His Journey”, *USA Today*, Oct. 4, 2004, https://usatoday30.usatoday.com/life/books/news/2004-10-04-dylan-main_x.htm.

2 Ginsberg, p. 142，参见中译本（上），第 198 页。

他的码字法宝通电了。这是古今其他作家和文书员都无法比拟的一种跨界生存的技术优势，李白和德·昆西已不可企及喧嚣轰鸣的工业时代，而未来也难以复现上世纪中期的巅峰全手动体感。

戈德布拉特似乎发现了《狼蛛》在超高速打字中的秘法和缺憾，他概括为“隐喻的滥用”（abuse of metaphor）：

> 在词组或语句的并置中，迪伦使用了某些类似乱喻（catachresis）的方法，当它们意义悬停的同时似乎不会发生相互联系，带来适当的审美冲击，推进到前景状态和氛围中。这就造成观察位置和透视法的切换太过快捷，思绪太过庞杂了。我们认为其中还有音乐的作用，就像从副歌进而成为合唱那样，它也具有变形力（transformative），把庸常生活化为新奇、异样的体验。音乐的变形力量是尼采的主题，而在《狼蛛》中我们也通过这样感人的句子看到对阿瑞莎的吁请：“唱着阿瑞莎……唱着主流上了轨道！唱着牛铃回家去！唱着迷雾……以后肯定有的是时间给你休息&学唱新歌……什么都不宽恕因为你什么都没干过&跟那高贵的女清洁工做爱”[1]艺术的变形力量在尼采

1 Dylan 1971, pp. 10–11.

> 和迪伦作品中都极为剧烈，因此伦理和审美的价值经常合为一体（conflated）。可以说，迪伦的《狼蛛》是一部肮脏现实语言的小型史诗。它纤弱地构筑在“阿瑞莎／水晶点唱机女王的圣歌&生哥儿”的王国，但它却是一个胆大妄为、到处割喉的世界。[1]

而在像克里斯蒂娃这样更奔放的设想中，各种文字游戏（paragramme，本义：超出的、旁侧的、异常的文字）才是语言的诗性之维，唯有它们的不安分和灵动跳跃才能让文学文本（织物）的多重互联网络的无限可能性得以成立。《狼蛛》是一座铿锵有声的不具形的体感交互装置，它不是那种雅致、从容不迫、文质彬彬的绘画绣花，因为，美学的改造就是解放。[2] 当懒惰的批评家从书架上抽取一摞摞现成的文艺读本，真真假假地要为这只宠物来打造一口饲养和观赏的玻璃生态缸，却眼睁睁地看不见《狼蛛》在星空上恣意纵横。没错，迪伦确实看过很多书，听过很多碟，他在这些方面非常谦逊，无论什么资源都乐意吸收或挪用为他本人的素材，他根本就是个饕餮鬼。

---

1 见 Vernezze, pp. 166–167。

2 混合改写自毛泽东《湖南农民运动考察报告》（1927）、马尔库塞《单向度的人》（1964）。

波德莱尔、洛特雷亚蒙、兰波的象征主义和通灵论、乔伊斯的意识流、布勒东的自动写作、艾略特的《荒原》、布拉克的拼贴、斯坦贝克和格思里的俚语、垮掉派老叟巴勒斯的剪切，金斯堡和旧金山诗派的呼吸节奏等等，所有旧版和新版现代派教科书的全部阅读材料，以及两千年前的各种经文，都可以拿来跟《狼蛛》扯上一腿。但是，太老了，太旧了，要么穿着别扭，要么就是生拉硬拽，太不像样，结果不免导致差评。因为，所有的话都被说过，每个人必须自带橡皮，《狼蛛》需要考生各自酌情改写。

当迪伦用“泛滥”一词取代“意识流”，弃绝了欧洲文化沙龙上沉积了二百年的脂粉气息，这“命名”本身就是一个革命。另外，他还消灭了拼贴和剪切；如果硬要比附当代艺术的语汇，笔者推荐这个词：撕贴(décollage)。就是把城市街头的广告墙上一层层一层层的黏着材料给扒开，暴露其累积性的、即生即死、错乱相覆而又稳定如山的话语规则和资本秩序。

> 我转头走进一家杂货铺……我要说的是一个不可言说的癫狂麦克风&盛大的鲜花庆典——那不是冒充的幻象而是温柔的黑暗——快看那黑暗——你的力量——那黑暗“自我&脊髓梦幻的联姻”瘟疫小子说&我们给他买一个车皮——歇斯底里——那歇斯底里的曲调——与之相反的是

音乐所呈现的每一个声响都令生命得以存在而非沉寂……胡迪尼 &其余的平民百姓在 61 国道把皱巴巴的耶稣招贴画全都撕掉——弥达斯又把它们贴回去——宝座上陷没着克丽奥——她之所以陷没是因为太胖了……这片土地是你的土地 & 这片土地是我的土地——那确实——但世界却由那些根本不听音乐的人来运转——“狂热病就是一种要打电筒才能听见的音乐”瘟疫如是说[1]

老现代派的拼贴或剪切，也许最多就三五六层材料，太浅，甚至遮不住它们背后作为艺术空间假设的那块厚板，而且，更重要的是，它们最终免不了要装饰起一个五颜六色的资产阶级生活的浮世表象。迪伦曾取笑说，绘画不应该藏在博物馆，博物馆是坟地，绘画应该挂在餐馆、一元店、男厕所的墙上，在大家活动的地方。你花了五十万买来挂在房子里，只有一个客人能看见它，那不叫艺术，那是耻辱，是犯罪。[2]说得太绝了！所以，现在的小便处已纷纷挂上美术作品。但那些都是不来电的形色体块线条，没有人会在小便时因观赏绘画而遭受电击，只会在你抖擞离开时，红灯亮，自动冲水。唯一会放电的，只有《狼蛛》，因为它要层层撕破、层层暴露，

---

1 Dyaln 1971, p. 88.

2 1965 年 8 月访谈，Cott, pp. 57–58。

以致其对象们霸气侧漏、狂舞不休。

小心狼蛛！

没有结束：*Life—Death & the lumberjacks are coming*[1]

1964 年春，迪伦拍过一组在书桌前打字的玉照，身后墙上挂了一幅汉字书法，（据说）是他亲手所写：

使 生 是 爱 谦 诚
现 命 基 情 逊 实

结果，传到在当代中国的网络上，大家都笑眯眯地看到两个字：基情。

这就是新老先锋派在工作室和车库、工具房里边都无法预见的原生态的拼贴剪切撕贴应用，以及某种弱电效应下的超摩登现象学实例。

我们也由此重新认识一位埋头书案的文学青年，他那幅字何止是“诚实”，根本就是“实诚”。他的一些镜头，发呆时，简直像个犯难的打字机修理工，专注时，跟试听的钢琴调音师毫无区别，实诚；而当他在键盘上轻舞

1 Dylan 1971, p. 137.

飞扬、纵横捭阖，仿佛胸有百万人生，也是那样的实诚。毫不奇怪，他是一个实诚的文学家。

如果就文学谈文学，面对鲍勃·迪伦，这位另具一格的诗人、作家，以及电影导演和画家，或者如他所说的杂耍艺人，如果我们能假装抛去摇滚天王巨星的一切盛名所累，来讨论真正的“Another Side of Bob Dylan”（鲍勃·迪伦的另一面），那会是文学史论上的大突破。这个课题的交叉太多，纷争太多，正亟待一场撕贴行动。

虽然现在市面上的迪伦相关书籍非常多，一批英国学者[1]对他的歌词进行了全面而深入的分析论述，如背景、细读和解构等。但就笔者所见，歌词之外的迪伦纯文学创作以及其他艺术尝试依然没有得到足够的关切，外国学者们大概还未做好充分的理论准备。

值得一提的是，罗伯特·谢尔顿在评传《归乡无路》中大量引用了迪伦诗文，并从文学角度对青年迪伦的写作（1963—1966）做了全盘梳理，包括主要歌词、“文案”组诗的每一首、《狼蛛》的先锋性以及摇滚诗的文学影

1　从文学角度进入迪伦研究，并取得公认成就者，如约翰·鲍迪（John Bauldie）、艾丹·戴（Aidan Day）、迈克尔·格雷（Michael Gray）、约翰·赫德曼（John Herdman）、威尔弗里德·梅勒斯（Wilfrid Mellers）、克里斯托弗·里克斯、斯蒂芬·斯科比、罗宾·维廷等，都是英国人，此外，重要的迪伦传记家伊恩·贝尔、克林顿·黑林、霍华德·桑恩斯（Howard Sounes）也是英国人，而罗伯特·谢尔顿则多年旅居于此，算半个英国人了。

响等等，其中，专章《翻滚吧，谷登堡》[1]的标题以西方活字印刷发明人的名义发出文学世代革新的召唤，令人印象深刻。但谢尔顿的这个尝试还略有薄弱，他主要是在一部资料详实、内容完备的“大传”中郑重提出了迪伦的文学评价问题，但可惜没能深入展开成一个专著；更可惜的是谢尔顿已作古，他错过了重估迪伦的高峰时期。像诺奖后最新出版的论著，如拉里·戴维·史密斯的《写作迪伦》就谈及了迪伦迄今的所有文学作品，只可恨他没真正说到《狼蛛》。评传《曾几何时》的作者伊恩·贝尔也怀着同样包揽迪伦文学的宏愿，他显得更有洞察力，也更小心翼翼，书中审慎地指出这个课题的学术难度：

> 如果说到文学方面，需要记住一点，这位美国诗人并未受过与该称号相配的高等教育。这种流派、那种流派以及各种各样的批评理论和元批评，对他成为一个作家并没有任何推动或影响。他会疯狂地阅读——这位诗人认识很多诗人，而且对其中一些有相当透彻的了解——但不是为了吸收智慧才去读他们。在本质上，他从一开始就是自修者，自己教自己听歌、读书并学习写作。迪伦创造了这个迪伦，并开辟了他自己的透视法。

1 Shelton, pp. 150–167，参见中译本，第 384—431 页。

这意味着，如果我们要试图去阐扬或驳斥他作为一个诗人的禀赋，就必须在我们的术语和假设上更多加努力。[1]

可以这么说，因为诺奖的激励，现在已经有了重估迪伦文学价值的最佳时机，但却仍缺乏一个足以评价迪伦的更强大的理论平台。

天上的神仙打架仍纷纭不息，到底什么才是“文学”，什么又不是“文学”，这样的初级问题居然还没有个硬核的定论。学界大腕们对迪伦文学的估价到目前基本上还是聊备一格的状态：确有书写到，yes，还有论文写到，也是；但在西方那种皮筋宽松的学术、出版和新闻环境下，在被传媒财阀收编了的流行文化潮汐中，迪伦的文学书（诗集、自传）虽然卖得很不错，而实际上却没有在主流文坛泛起多大的浪花。

这恐怕是一个有关科层区隔以及生涯规划的社会学复杂问题。迪伦从来就是一个标准的浪漫文艺青年，但他从来不肯为着一个著名码字人士的头衔而付出太多迎来送往的应酬。他在文坛上太懒，而他在歌坛上越是努力，就越被铆死于流行音乐工业的三六九之中。他曾不断想挣脱，但已不可能逃脱，甚至有些狂热歌迷组织了“解放迪伦阵线”要把他绑出来，但也改变不了他的个

1 Bell, p. 132，参见中译本，第 126—127 页。

人选择。

文学，以及其他一切艺术类型 / 类型艺术，在现代社会都需要有一个特指的鉴赏场所、沉浸空间或论述氛围，越宽敞越好。但迪伦的文学却处在夹缝之中，他在其他领域的一切尝试，他所有的跨界创作（文学、电影、绘画等）都是烙着“摇滚巨星”永久文身的玩票行为。如果不是“饭圈老铁”，如果没有课题费，这些尝试只会被绝大多数职业学者和职业论家视为“呵呵”，最多当成历史文化材料引用一下。

但太多人太严重地低估了一位自由者的创造力。实际上，当他放开吉他，去写一本书、画一幅画也同样是成立的；本来，他抱着打字机的时候，就根本不可能同时抱着吉他。我们完全可以就文学论文学，去观测作为诗人的迪伦另一面。

那么，欢迎光临盘丝洞！

我们分头探索，在不可捉摸的乱网纠缠中，各自寻找一个更接近正确的打开方式。

参考书目

迪伦作品：

Dylan, Bob. *Tarantula*. Macmillan, 1971.

——.*Tarantula*. tr. Andrea D'Anna, Alessandro Carrera & Santo Pettinoto. Feltrinelli, 2016.

——.*Tarántula*. tr. Alberto Manzano. Malpaso, 2017.

——. *Тарантул*. tr. Maxim Nemtsov. Eksmo, 2017.

——.*Tarantel*. tr. Carl Weissner & Heinrich Detering. Hoffmann und Campe, 2016.

——.*Tarantel*. tr. Carl Weissner. Hannibal, 1995.

——.*Lyrics, 1962–1985*. Knopf, 1985.（部分收入《鲍勃·迪伦诗歌集：1961—2012》[1—8 册]，奚密等译，广西师范大学出版社，2017。）

——.*Chronicles. Volume One*. Simon & Schuster, 2004.（《编年史》，徐振锋等译，河南大学出版社，2015。）

——.& Feinstein, Barry. *Hollywood Foto-Rhetoric: The Lost Manuscript*. Simon & Schuster, 2008.

传记和论著：

Bell, Ian. *Once Upon a Time: The Lives of Bob Dylan*. Pegasus, 2013.（《曾几何时：鲍勃·迪伦传》，修佳明等译，人民大学出版社，2017。）

Boucher, David & Browning, Gary. ed. *The Political Art of*

Bob Dylan. Palgrave Macmillan, 2004.

Corcoran, Neil. ed. *Do You, Mr Jones: Bob Dylan with the Poets & Professors*. Vintage, 2017.

Cott, Jonathan. ed. *Bob Dylan: The Essential Interviews*. Simon & Schuster, 2017.

Cran, Rona. *Collage in Twentieth-Century Art, Literature, and Culture: Joseph Cornell, William Burroughs, Frank O'Hara, and Bob Dylan*. Ashgate, 2014.

Dalton, David. *Who is that Man?: in Search of the Real Bob Dylan*. Hyperion, 2012.（《他是谁？：探寻真实的鲍勃·迪伦》，郝巍译，广西师范大学出版社，2015。）

Dettmar, Kevin. *ed. The Cambridge Companion to Bob Dylan*. Cambridge U., 2009.（《剑桥鲍勃·迪伦手册》，王宇光译，中信出版社，2019。）

Gray, Michael. *Song and Dame Man Ⅲ: The Art of Bob Dylan*. Continnum, 2004.

——. *The Bob Dylan Encyclopedia*. Continuum, 2006.

Hedin, Benjamin. ed. *Studio A: the Bob Dylan Reader*. Norton, 2004.

Heylin, Clinton. *Bob Dylan: Behind the Shades Revisited*. Dey St., 2003.

Ledeen, Jenny. *Prophecy in the Christian Era: A Study of Bob Dylan's Work from 1961 to 1967*. Peaceberry, 2005.

Pichaske, David. *Song of the North Country: A Midwest*

Framework to the Songs of Bob Dylan. Continuum, 2010.

Ricks, Christopher. *Dylan's Vision of Sin*. Ecco, 2005.

Scobie, Stephen. *Alias Bob Dylan Revisited*. Red Deer, 2004.

Shelton, Robert. *No Direction Home: the Life and Music of Bob Dylan*. Backbeat, 2011.（《迷途家园：鲍勃·迪伦的音乐与生活》[1、2 册],滕继萌译,重庆大学出版社,2017、2018。）

Smith, Larry David. *Writing Dylan: The Songs of a Lonesome Traveler, 2nd Edition*. Praeger, 2018.

Thomson, Elizabeth & Gutman, David. ed. *The Dylan Companion*. Da Capo, 2001.

Vernezze, Peter & Porter, Carl J. ed. *Bob Dylan and Philosophy: It's Alright Ma (I'm Only Thinking)*. Open Court, 2006.

Wilentz, Sean. *Bob Dylan in America*. Anchor, 2011.（《鲍勃·迪伦与美国时代》，刘怀昭译，中国政法大学出版社，2018。）

Williams, Paul. *Bob Dylan, Performing Artist, 1960-1973: The Early Years*. Omnibus, 1994.

Witting, Robin. *A Crash Course on Reading Tarantula, 3rd. Edition*. Exploding Rooster, 2017.

文化背景：

Barthes, Roland. *Le plaisir du texte*. Seuil, 1973.

Charters, Ann. ed. *The Portable Beat Reader*. Penguin, 1992.

Corso, Gregory. *Mindfield: New & Selected Poems*. Thunder's Mouth, 1998.（《格雷戈里·柯索诗选》[上、下册]，罗池译，河北教育出版社，2003。）

Dickstein, Morris. *Gates of Eden: American Culture in the Sixties*. Penguin, 1989.（《伊甸园之门：六十年代的美国文化》，方晓光译，上海外语教育出版社，1985。）

Ginsberg, Allen. *Collected Poems 1947-1997*. Penguin, 2009.（《金斯堡诗全集》[上、中、下册]，惠明译，人民文学出版社，2017。）

Guthrie, Woody. *Bound for Glory*. Penguin, 2004.（《荣光之路》，刘奕译，广西师范大学出版社，2014。）

Kaufman, Alan. ed. *The Outlaw Bible of American Poetry*. Thunder's Mouth, 1999.

Kerouac, Jack. *The Subterraneans*. Groove, 1994.（《地下人·皮克》，金衡山译，上海译文出版社，2015。）

Kerouac, Jack. *On the Road. Penguin*, 2000.（《在路上》，王永年译，上海译文出版社，2006。）

Kerouac, Jack. *Collected Poems*. Library of America, 2012.

Klein, Joe. *Woody Guthrie: A Life*. Ballantine, 1982.

Kristeva, Julia. *Desire in Language: A Semiotic Approach to Literature and Art*. ed. Leon S. Roudiez. tr. Thomas Gora, et al. Columbia U., 1980.

Warhol, Andy & Hackett, Part. *POPism: The Warhol Sixties*. Penguin, 2007.

附 录

“救救那些无法理解的人不要去理解”

罗宾·维廷

“不要再搞你那些观念——人人都有观念——让观念搞你吧 & 用旋律说话……”

——《满口子深情的窒息》

《狼蛛》写于 1965 至 1966 年间那狂热的十八个月，当时迪伦还做出了他最有里程碑意义的三张唱片：《统统带回家》(*Bringing It All Back Home*，1965)、《重访 61 国道》(*Highway 61 Revisited*，1965）和《美人复美人》(*Blonde on Blonde*，1966)。

在 1966 年环球巡演期间，他随身带着的就是《美人复美人》母盘以及《狼蛛》校样：一部三万词的非凡文本——一个青年艺术家的生动快照。

论者历来爱把《狼蛛》贬为纯属“意识流”的东西。其实，它无论如何都**不是**意识流。它用语整饬、精确：有着“节拍&心跳”。它是一部内容连贯的实验小说，有一以贯之的几个主题和中心：美国（因越战而分裂）、阿瑞莎、玛丽亚、声响、音乐、食物、身份、永不满足的饥渴、嘴巴、眼睛、肉体以及死亡。

跟他的唱片一样，《狼蛛》也是音声采录时代的产物。语言洪亮、铿锵、富有音乐性；它为人声而谱写，它是一场绕梁不散的演说，好比怀抱弦琴的荷马、炉边开讲的《贝奥武甫》、登台献艺的莎士比亚、麦克风前的狄兰·托马斯，还有现身歌舞厅的巴克利老爷。

亦如哈姆雷特的独白，它为现场**演出**而发。

经由摩登时代“不可言说的癫狂麦克风”，迪伦给文学送回了它久已丢失的声音；他为**在线视听**一代重新复活了一种古老的文学传统。在辽阔的神话口述传统中，在歌谣和蓝调中，语言生长着，呼吸着。在环环相扣的“自我&脊髓梦幻的联姻”中，有时，语言既谐音又不谐和，有时，它热情而流畅：

“口琴大军”；“打钉锤凄吟，在她的水槽上它们的声音像通奸的响尾蛇”；“我愿为你奉上一杯洗缸水——我们可以互相学习”；“午餐后，你听见一片轰隆的落石&车祸在扩音器传来”；“爱德华，他砍篱笆挣工钱”；“芭芭拉·艾伦——她每个月两次把摩洛哥煤渣偷运到布鲁克林&她穿一身床单——她打很多针青霉素”；“除了对我们黄油雕塑家说三道四”。

它根本就是**歌唱**!

《狼蛛》展示了一种独特的禅机——伊丽莎白朝（如莎士比亚）敏感性与现代失能症的接合。

禅可视为一种治疗“当代困境”的灵药；禅就是他的跳跳盒式句法以及整个儿不走寻常路的“他对于禅宗爆竹的就事论事的知识”背后的发条。

他用他独特的公案来迷惑我们：

“下雨了——雨声像一个卷笔刀”；“我也想去做些有价值的事情比如在海洋上种一棵树”；“我要感受我的蒸发”；“天空，正变成一种性感的意大利面条味儿，但仍颤颤不止”。

《狼蛛》所受的影响最主要来自 T.S. 艾略特的杰作《荒原》，这首长诗描绘了第一次世界大战过后的残破社会，在他的“一堆残破形象”里得以具象化。

（《荒原》第一行“四月是最残忍的月份”，在《满口子深情的窒息》中被改写成：“四月什么的是个残忍的月份。”）

《荒原》使用了一种简省的、碎片的风格，充满各种典故和依稀记识的名言。

如艾略特在《玄学派诗人》中所言：

> ……普通人的经验是混乱、不规则、碎片化的。他们坠入爱河或阅读斯宾诺莎，但这两种经验互相之间毫无关系，跟打字机的噪声或烧菜的气味也毫不相干；在诗人的心里这些经验总是在构成新的整体。

艾略特奋力去解析混乱，而迪伦却积极地迎接它、颂扬它，将它视为存在者的**阴**、**阳**本身。“她还老想／逼我去做一个管子工。／开头有点小混乱”；“世界并没有停止一秒——它只是爆掉了”；“诺曼梅勒家餐具室炸弹爆炸——导致他色盲”；“你听见一片轰隆的落石＆车祸在扩音器传来”；“一切都变得血腥”；“一千个愤怒的旅游者把他踩倒在地全都戴着棒球手套”。

所有的一切都转瞬即逝：

“朗格斯尥蹶子……费了好久＆好久时间在沙滩上刻他的名字。突然，一个浪头的震荡把他＆他的名字都冲到了海里（啃啃啃）”。

混乱之中有着不羁的雄性力：

“他用炒蛋擦身”；“没有——没有——只是我的腿有点发毛——就那么回事”；“你用帽子盛满朗姆酒＆把它砸到冰雹的脸上＆不期待有什么新东西会诞生”；“你成长中的／爆血伊万”；“你走在白雪地上哪怕一滴鼻血都会扰乱宇宙”。

血、雨、蛋以及毛发等等都是变化无常的生殖象征。

以其废品站式的散文，《狼蛛》捉住了我们这个时代喧嚣嘈杂的噪音，就像我们被每日川流不息的新闻快报、大标题、广播电流声、暴乱、战争以及传闻的战争、突发消息、广告、海啸、粒子加速器、超级病菌、股市崩盘、集束炸弹、高速公路连环追尾以及自杀炸弹所轰炸。

《狼蛛》是游击文学；是一本小说，没错，但不是我们熟知的那种；是一部长诗，没错，但不是我们熟知的那种。它是彻头彻尾的颠覆分子：“[他] 跟你的脑瓜玩耍＆他违背了你曾受教的有关为人的一切／他不在历史书上。”

此人就是《狼蛛》中的迪伦。

所有这些混乱都源自现代生活一团乱麻般的困惑，就像开了快进模式的传话游戏。书中人物经常是各说各的：

> “我明白你们目前正在／拼凑一本书来搜罗／那些上了黑名单或长了黑头粉刺的艺术家之类”；“啊罗密欧，罗密欧，为河洗泥？”；“冯伯斯大褶子……冯伯斯打褶子……嗡伯斯夯茬子……朗格斯尥蹶子”；“伍迪格思里不是古里古屁！”

正与力求“完整信息”的传口令游戏截然相反。

整部《狼蛛》都笼罩着一种无法平息的奇特食欲，而同时又有一大堆丰富过剩的食物象征。

如迪伦歌曲《我同情这可怜的移民》（“I Pity the Poor Immigrant”，1967）所唱：“他有吃但却没有满足。”

嘴巴占绝对主导地位，轰轰烈烈的开篇第一章的标题便是：“老枪，猎鹰之口书&逍遥法外的狗男女”。

> 我就走到天使那里，对他说：“请你把小书卷给我。”他对我说：“你拿着吃尽了，便叫你肚子发苦，然而在你口中要甜如蜜。”
>
> ——《新约·启示录》10:9

“口书”（mouthbook）这个词勾画出一种强烈的口腔迷恋，如嘴巴的品尝、吞咽、咀嚼、歌唱、嘟囔、舔舐、打嗝、啜饮、撕咬、结巴、吹哨、哈欠、啃吃、亲吻、窒息、窃笑……等等等等。后面的章节还说到：

"你会在灯泡上画一张嘴巴那样它就可以笑得更加自由";"永远闭嘴";"他们把他们的钱放进嘴巴的位置……&开始吃它";"没有太多地方能让她品味";"一嘴的塑料"。

如饥似渴的口交又被表现为阴森森的词句：

《满口子深情的窒息》;《霰弹枪的滋味》;"你也许会改变你通奸、吞剑的风格";"我饿坏了&把你的诡计吞进我的肚子"。

就连"味道"(taste)这样温顺的小词也有强大的内涵：

《霰弹枪的滋味》;"没有太多地方能让她品味";"我送给爱人一颗樱桃。你确实送了。她有没有告诉你味道怎么样?""杰克一整天都没吃东西了。他那嘴里的味道真够呛"。

"……面包的味道很寻常但谁又能&谁又有兴趣告诉别人它是什么味道——它的味道就是面包那样的味道呗……"

我实在告诉你们，站在这里的，有人在没尝死味以前，必看见人子降临在他的国里。

——《新约·马太福音》16:28

嘴巴集中体现了迪伦这部“口书”的深处那种永不满足的饥饿。

《……猎鹰之口书》；《……喝一杯怪怪酒》；《电影明星嘴里的沙子》；《满口子深情的窒息》；《吉他之吻……》；《霰弹枪的滋味》；《神圣破锣嗓……》。

“把你的头脑塞进你的嘴巴！”；“你会在灯泡上画一张嘴巴那样它就可以笑得更加自由”；“一嘴的塑料”；“她的嘴巴咧着——有个乞丐走出他的窝棚&挂着一根头发在她的嘴唇上”；“我唯一的遗憾就是我不能用嘴巴放屁”；“米奇·麦克米奇会从他嘴里抽出大拇指”；“她重新摆好她的嘴巴”；“嘴里含着海象一起埋葬”。

口书：为朗诵而谱写的书。

口书：充满了食物象征。

口书：开快进的口述传统。

人体解剖学的每一部位，从肠道到子宫，从胸部到腺体，从骨骼到大脑，都像是一个角色。

“穿过编结的长发”；“她迷上了你的前额”；“冰山脑袋”；“在满地骷髅上磕磕碰碰”；“抽你的脸”；“我的眼睛是两个旧车场”；“一根睫毛都没眨”；“我必须把耳朵贴在铁轨上”；“然后他擤擤鼻涕”；“她的鼻孔抽抽着”；“嘴巴像烤炉”；“他的一个指尖抵着下巴”；“探着她的舌头”；“必须去拔掉几颗牙”；“嘟着嘴唇”；“有些扁桃腺！”“垄断了我的声带”；“那个男的长得像一块

喉结”；”我的喉咙里有几颗绿子弹”；“她的脖子套进绞索”。

这还只是开了个头！

不过，这些东西总是有点道理的。

“他住在他的胳肢窝里”；“前进，开枪！你需要的只是／一张执照＆一颗软弱的心”；“我们谁都没有无穷的胆量”；“历史性的电话都打进你的肚子”；“她的肠道黑灵魂”；“自我＆脊髓梦幻的联姻”；“我的胸部感觉就像有／掘墓人在里面整夜整夜地／挖着”；“我就去找我的血液银行／＆提款”；“一个纯血的酒精中毒／天主教徒”；“你有大脚丫＆你会踩翻你自己”；“把它做成一月一日载着些饿肚皮”；“他的原子奶头理论”。

更异想天开的是，书中不仅有大量的身体器官，还有一所医院——装满了病人和瘸子。

“在山区有一种病”；“跛脚爱人”；“癌症批评家”；“在黑天使诞生时犯了心脏病”；“前进，开枪！你需要的只是／一张执照＆一颗软弱的心”；“泽尔达起了一脸疹子”；“关于这场世界游戏的／终局——如果你能为之发动细菌战／也许你可以卖上两倍那么贵”；“收买你的创伤”；“坎克夫人……她在世界博览会上卖冒牌水疱”；“他收藏的淤肿＆瓶塞”；“又及，阿道夫给你一块恶搞呕吐物／你往桌上一摆＆就看着那些／姑娘作呕吧”；“我真的好恶心那些圣经中人——他们就像蓖麻油——就像疯狗。”

疾病和道德沦丧常被联系在一起，就像麻风病人曾被视为贱民一样。

如迪伦歌曲《开开门，荷马》（“Open the Door, Homer”，1975）所唱：“要记住，当你到了那边／试图救治病人／你必须永远／先宽恕他们。”

《荒原》的核心主题是古代生殖典礼以那些渔人王式的角色得以重生。

这种象征主义也同样是《狼蛛》的中心。

在《荒原》中，腓尼基水手代表生殖之神，他的形象每年都被投入海中（如冥神的画像）以象征夏季的死亡。“腓尼基人弗勒巴斯，死去十四夜之后，／遗忘了鸥鸟的啼鸣、深海的巨浪”；“索索斯特里斯夫人……／有一副灵异纸牌……／……那个淹死的腓尼基水手，／我没找到／那个吊死鬼。恐怕死在水里。”还有：

你去年在园子里种下的尸体，
它发芽了吗？今年会开花吗？
还是被突降的霜冻扰乱了苗床？
把狗远远赶开吧，那是人类的朋友
不然他会用爪子又把它刨出来……

——《荒原·死者葬礼》

这部史诗取材于生殖神话和象征着重生的草木巫术。它是荣格精神分析的一个原型，穿梭在浩瀚的古代文化中，包括圣杯传奇、亚瑟王、前巴比伦时代的《吉尔伽美什》、冥神俄赛里斯传说、可能还有耶稣基督：一个王，但他必须牺牲性命才能将生殖力和秩序重新带回这个被诸神遗弃的精神荒芜的王国——昔日的“荒原”；旷野，现代都市丛林。

索瑟姆（B. C. Southam）在《T. S. 艾略特诗选学习指南》（*A Student's Guide to the Selected Poems of T. S. Eliot*）中说：“他特意使用了渔人王，在诸多生殖神话中反复出现的一个角色……他的国度遭到诅咒而荒废。渔人王因疾病或伤残而丧失生育能力，他的人民也同样无力繁衍……艾略特把这个神话联系到圣杯传奇……它丢失了，于是寻找圣杯成为一个强大的关于寻找精神真理的叙述意象……”

迪伦在歌曲《伊西丝》（“Isis”，1975）中回到这个主题。伊西丝原是古埃及月亮女神，也是冥神俄赛里斯的灵魂伴侣。《伊西丝》的效果如同神秘剧：

我们来到金字塔，在冰封雪冻里
他说“这里有具尸体，我一直在找
如果运出去，就能换一大笔奖金”
这时我才知道，他心里想的是什么

大风呼呼吹，大雪飘飘落
我们挖了一整夜，我们挖了一早上

他死的时候，我但愿不要传染到我
但我打定主意我必须坚持下去

我打进了墓室，但棺材空空
没有财宝，我想要的一切都没有
我才明白我的同伙只是说好话
我接受他的提议真是发了疯

我抬起他的尸体，把他拖进坟墓
把他扔进坑里，然后盖上盖子
我做个简单祈祷，我就觉得还清了……

不过，他自己的渔人王版本难免是有缺陷的。《我发现钢琴师是个斗鸡眼但非常结实》一章专门讲一个钢琴调音师他根本没法带来和谐："他来时在手腕上缠着胶布&他还扛着他自己的衣帽架"——是在戏仿基督的圣痕和十字架。

又如《满袋子恶棍》一章：

……刺杀受害人&死得顺顺当当……墓碑的另一面，业余反派耷拉着舌头沉睡&他的脑袋埋在枕套里边／没有什么能让他与众不同／总之他就是没人搭理。

在《咕咚咕咚听我吼声嗨嘀嘀》一章和这个传统的联系最为清晰：

> 他被撑在一棵橡树的枝杈上——往下看——唱着“有个人到处转悠点名”的确——我点头问好——他也点头问好“啊他点了我妈妈的名字——让我痛苦不堪”我一只手里端着一杯沙子&另一只手里是牛犊脑袋——我抬头看看&说“你饿了吗？”

“你饿了吗？”让人想到：

> 饥渴慕义的人有福了，因为他们必得饱足。
>
> ——《新约·马太福音》5:6

叙述者自相矛盾地对那人说：“如果你要人帮忙下来，你就进城&告诉我”，但是“他根本没听”。

然而：“他的声音在山谷里回荡——就像电话铃声——真是烦人”。

实际上，这些自诩的救世主都被证明是不中用的跛脚鸭。有一个“耷拉着舌头沉睡&他的脑袋埋在枕套里边”，钢琴调音师“在手腕上缠着胶布”只能让钢琴“听起来就像一路咣当的保龄球道”，爆米花男孩“两手空空”，还有一个被人撑起来的弥赛亚沦落到只会哼哼铅肚皮的老歌，连从树上爬下来都做不到。

这就是在《狼蛛》的核心处撕咬着的不可满足的饥渴。跟《荒原》一样，它最终是要寻求一个精神上的决断。

《狼蛛》对《圣经》符码的引用随处可见：饥、渴、饮、食、鱼、饼、酒、血、水、光、暗、烛、福音、羔羊、陌生人、朋友、服装、赤裸，等等等等。

反复出现的用语还有：理解、声响、干扰、信息、信仰和无信仰等，这些都是行话，同样，《狼蛛》还有大量饱含象征的符号，如：电影、电话、眼睛、高山。

这本书像个贮藏室塞满与食品有关的意象：饭店、食堂、餐车、酒吧、药店、厨房、食杂铺、超市、饭盒、冰箱、餐具室、菜谱、糕饼大会。

开篇第一章实际上就发生在餐车式路边店。

然后很多章节以吃食结束：

“没有太多地方让她品味”；“我所做的一切就是吃吃&喝喝”；“很快就去找你了——／先吃点东西”；“他在吃好果子呢——他会一切顺利——克拉普先生”；“边缘人认识了更多&更多人——他开始节食&后来他死了”；“超级市场从营养不良中爆发——上帝保佑营养不良”。

但这样的暴饮暴食并不能抚慰内在的饥饿。

“安拉大厨从他的地板上铲起饥饿”；“农民会说‘来吧。请你吃饥饿’”；“你已经变成了／一块饥饿”；“超级市场从营养不良中爆发——上帝保佑营养不良”；“你不知道在中国还有很多孩子忍饥受饿吗？”；“因为我饿坏了&把你的诡计吞进我的肚子”；“我永远不会饿疯了”；“把它做成一月一日载着些饿肚皮”；“正埋头于残羹冷炙”。

真是“他有吃但却没有满足”！

这种深深扎根的饥饿甚至发展到食人癖：

“在凤凰城，一男子在下午2点吃了他老婆”；“我是披头士食用者”；“我所饥渴的不是你老爸！但是我会带一个盒子给他玩玩。我不是食人族！”

以及政治的：

“红白&蓝汉堡／套餐”；“我们家人都讨厌意大利／风味”；“他端着一品脱法西斯酸奶”；“这些人把自己当成美食家因为没有出席查理斯塔克韦瑟的葬礼天哪呀香槟酒正般配异教徒”；“总统在宴会桌前放出尴尬臭屁”；“递送吃食杂货&拉斯维加斯寄出的爱心包裹”；“请不要／再给我寄老爷钟表——也不要／书籍或爱心包裹”。

胖墩芹菜、矮墩饼干之类的：

“坎克夫人……遇到紧急情况总是努力做出一副葡萄柚的模样”；“把自己想成一条熏肠”；“对。好。我猜你是个南瓜宝贝……你专有的，／炖肉王子”；“火腿骨，他要在牢里蹲一辈子了——帮小孩买啤酒&用一把小梳子谋杀食杂店主”。

《狼蛛》通篇响彻“黑夜撞车”的声音，咣当、轰隆、噗嗤，而“声响”则成为终极行话：

> 合众国**不是**隔音的——你能以为任何东西都无法触动那几万住在美元高墙背后的人——但你的惧怕却能够引出真相……
>
> ——《免责的黑夜撞击》

把华尔街崩盘等同于耶利哥之战：

> 于是百姓呼喊，祭司也吹角。百姓听见角声，便大声呼喊，城墙就塌陷……
>
> ——《旧约·约书亚记》6:20

> ……&那声音像约翰李胡克来了&哦老天爷老大声了像一趟火车……那个在鼻子下面有个伤疤的晕菜水手突然掌掴&脚踹小莎莉&叫她松开他工装裤的裆部&你知道他知道有些事情在发生&它不是那种司空见惯的声音让你看得清清楚楚&车嗡冲哧呜撞啊……
>
> ——《吉他之吻&当代困境》

> ……也许那是子宫的呼唤——你懂的——

也许在你还小的时候，你听见一棵树倒下&那声音响着唔姆&现在你长大了——每当你听到那个声音——当然是以这样或那样的形式——你就想——哦我们应该说——把它点燃？

——《牛仔天使蓝调》

在《冲破声障》中：

“声音才是女王”；“深情声波之残跛”；“他离开之后我试着弹我的钢琴——没用——听起来就像一路咣当的保龄球道”；“下雨了——雨声像一个卷笔刀”；“打钉锤凄吟，在她的水槽上它们的声音像通奸的响尾蛇”；“他的声音在山谷里回荡——就像电话铃声”；“声音的声音”；“声音是神圣的——进来吧&我们谈谈”。

“声响”（sound）是个含义丰富的词，包括探听、探口风等。而且声响还是非常禅机的东西，经典公案中有：“孤掌之声”、“叩天听声”、“请示钟声意”、“我是雨打声”——这个雨声**听来**正正“像一个卷笔刀”。

声响，念出来就是“**回响**”！

《狼蛛》的真意就在于它那种反动的禅机之乐，在《浮驳船上的玛丽亚》和精粹的《神圣破锣嗓&叮当咣当的早晨》这两章，他为性感女人们高唱赞歌。通过拉丁裔的玛丽亚、大地母亲般的阿瑞莎、异国情调的黛利拉和精明老道的乌鸦珍妮等等女性人物，她们强烈的、种族性的“血液意识”，以及那确证生命的“孩子的狂乱脉搏”，迪伦欢呼着不可遏止的生命之力。

你可以说，阿瑞莎之于《狼蛛》正如黑女士（Dark Lady）之于莎士比亚十四行诗。

试比较，睿智的就那谁，“回到了床上&开始读《一只橘子的意义》德文版”，而血统高贵的老太君奶奶则完全是在蹂躏一只橘子：

> ……老太君从兜里掏出一个橘子“在阿兹特克乡下得了这个——都瞧好了小子们”她抓着橘子&非常轻柔&缓慢地压挤它——然后她死命将它掰开&嗥叫着&它汁水横流&从她嘴里淌下来——滴满她的衬衫——继续滴着——滴着，她全身都被橘汁包裹了……
>
> ——《阿尔阿拉夫&军事委员会》

《狼蛛》尖刻抨击各种书呆、知识分子和临床理性，如“没用先生”和“就那谁”之类，还有教师、科学家、将军、商人以及政客们。

> ……下次见。我得去
> 把戈黛娃夫人的画像拆下来因为那些
> 神经学生要来这儿参观一个

小时……

就像《瘦人歌》（“Ballad of a Thin Man”，1965）中的琼斯先生，那些“神经”学生显然太难以接受戈黛娃夫人赤身裸体的场面。

他们的罪就是了无生趣。

而你现在拿到了这本《狼蛛》:“了不起的书 / 就是了不起的。”